25/6/19

Jenni‿ ‿nn Rake has been a primary school teacher for most of her ‿eer, specialising in music. Her life now revolves around writin‿ ‿nning her fair trade shop and looking after her three pamp‿ ‿d cats. She and her husband live in Dorset.

DECEPTION, LIES AND CHOCOLATE MUFFINS

...the guilty secrets of a wayward school teacher

Jennie Ann Rake

Book Guild Publishing
Sussex, England

First published in Great Britain in 2013 by
Book Guild Publishing
The Werks
45 Church Road
Hove, BN3 2BE

Typesetting in Baskerville by
Ellipsis Digital Ltd, Glasgow

Printed and bound in Great Britain by
4edge, Hockley, Essex

A catalogue record for this book is available from
The British Library.

ISBN 978 1 84624 919 8

For my daughter Helen, whose insightful comments have helped me tremendously and my furry friend Zola, who was the inspiration for Jezebel.

Acknowledgements

With grateful thanks to David, my husband, who has stood by me and supported me with his good humour while the fanciful ramblings of my brain have become a printed reality. Also thanks are due to friends and family who have cheered me on from the sidelines and to the wonderful team of editors at Book Guild whose wisdom and expertise have made all this possible.

Prologue

May

Hattie swerved into the first parking space she could find, beating a silver hatchback by a whisker. Judging by the furious expression and distorted mouthings behind the windscreen, she was grateful that the art of lip-reading wasn't her forte. She turned off the engine, silencing the relentless swish of the wipers, the last track of the Abba CD and Jezebel, mid-yowl. The fact that there *was* a parking space was a miracle in itself. Rain was still hammering on the roof, the sound bearing an uncanny resemblance to the furious pounding under her brand new teal jersey top. A few inches lower, the butterflies that had started their frantic fluttering half an hour earlier were now doing a lively conga in hobnail boots.

She swivelled round to be met by two angry, gleaming, green eyes and a pale pink button nose pressed up against the window of a smart new 'Kitty Kage'.

'Poor Jezebel,' she sighed, reaching out to tickle under the animal's chin. As usual, Jezebel had started her cacophony of indignant yowlings as soon as the key turned in the ignition and had kept it up non-stop for the entire journey. As far as Jezebel was concerned, being stuffed unceremoniously into the pet carrier meant a visit to the vet, which wasn't her activity of choice and was one she resisted with all ten claws and each one of her

1

razor-sharp teeth. If moving day wasn't already stressful enough, a moggy throwing a wobbly didn't help one bit. Hattie leaned closer to peer through the grill and sniffed. At least Jezebel hadn't sicked up seafood jelly chunks all over her fleecy blanket – that would have been a complete disaster, considering what was ahead.

'Take some deep breaths, relax,' Hattie told herself sternly, but her heart took no notice and continued pounding away furiously. She rooted around in her bag, crammed full of essentials – mostly of the edible variety of course – and her fingers closed around the crumpled foil wrapper of the coffee chocolate that she'd started earlier. This was no time for counting calories, not that she'd been much of a devotee of that sort of maths in recent months. More to the point, when faced with situations of serious stress, Hattie had found chocolate to be more reliable than husbands or the stock market.

'You'd better be there,' she muttered fervently to no one in particular, but with one man in mind, and reached for the phone in her pocket after gobbling one silky smooth square. Her thumb hovered for a few seconds over the buttons, tempted to make the call she should have made several days ago. The trouble was, it was now too late. Anyway, that had only been a rhetorical question on the note, hadn't it? He hadn't *really* intended an answer.

What would Fliss do, she wondered. Now there's a conundrum! She'd known Fliss for years; her friend, confidante, ally, but clearly there was much more to Fliss than met the eye. Fliss would not dither. Fliss had never been the dithering type, even if some of her decisions had been … hmm, well, better not dwell on that, thought Hattie angrily. Whatever her faults, Fliss's life seemed to be sorted, whereas Hattie's felt like the Nemesis ride at Alton Towers. She wolfed down the remaining chocolate and took another deep breath. Am I crazy? Am I gullible? Am I a total idiot? There were still no answers and the butterflies inside her were now looping the loop at twice the speed.

'Only one way to find out,' she told Jezebel, as she opened the car door, grabbed the carrier and stepped out into the rain that fell like stair-rods from a leaden sky.

1

Several Months Earlier

The significant change in Harriet Chesney's life started in early January, a day of red-raw, biting, north winds, the unwelcome arrival of a fresh crop of chilblains and the jollities of Christmas a fading memory. She craned her neck to scan the spring term playground duty list that deputy head Sonia Rowse was pinning on the staffroom notice board.

'Oh sh… sugarlumps!' she muttered despondently, seeing her name at the top, alongside the words 'lunchtime duty'.

'Well, someone's got to do it,' sneered Sonia unsympathetically, with just the suspicion of a smirk, 'and we *all* have to take a turn, you know.' She turned on her heel and strode out of the room, bristling with efficiency and triumph.

'I bet she's conveniently forgotten her own name,' commented Year 3 teacher Dave Sulecki sourly, as he fished out his diary. 'I see her poor TA, Patsy, is down for morning break.'

'Why does that not surprise me?' murmured Hattie sarcastically, spotting her name alongside at least three more lunchtime slots on the list. 'Teaching assistants are worth their weight in chocolate bars, but I don't think Sonia realises that yet.'

'Spring term,' muttered Dave gloomily. 'God only knows why it's called that. It's perishing outside and we won't be seeing spring for a good two months at least.'

'Thanks for the encouragement Dave,' sighed Hattie, and trudged off in the direction of the draughty terrapin huts that clustered on the far side of the playground.

After a challenging morning with the sparky Year 1s, Hattie bolted down her sandwiches and then dragged on her coat, hat, scarf and gloves over her saggy-kneed tracksuit to withstand the unrelenting buffeting of a near gale-force wind. It did nothing for her image, but at least it kept her teeth and anything else from chattering. While the rest of the staff were cosied up together in the staffroom, she was dealing with mud, mayhem and half the school kicking lumps out of the other half. In fact, the only comfort in the completely dismal day had been the appearance of a swanky box of chocs that Sophie, the recently recruited, tall and leggy Year 6 teacher, had brought back from her Christmas skiing trip. The glistening, jewel-coloured wrappers winked enticingly from their gold tissue nest, but by the time Hattie came within grabbing distance, all that remained were the plain chocolate squares, with not a whiff of whipped fondant brandy cream or caramel mousse.

At precisely half past three, as she settled herself in Angus Neill's stuffy inner sanctum, awaiting his arrival, her fingers closed protectively around the purple foil wrapper that nestled in her pocket. It was a treat worth saving for the end of a tiring day at Hazelton Primary. She had been puzzled by the Head's sudden summons. Although she had worked at the school for several years, their paths seldom crossed. He rarely indulged in small-talk with part-timers and supply teachers, hence Hattie had never gone beyond addressing him as 'sir', although some of the more career-minded staff had been on first name terms from the start. Addressing him as Angus was more than she dared.

He was on the wrong side of fifty and was generally kitted out in ageing tweed which reeked of mothballs, obvious to those who were unfortunately close enough to notice. His bushy beard was abundantly speckled with grey and his matching eyebrows resembled two fat, furry caterpillars, which caused endless fascination for the youngest pupils. It was reliably reported that most of his waking hours were taken up with school league tables, budget shortfall and Scottish dancing, which he had failed to introduce into the school curriculum, much to his chagrin. A feature of his character was his ill-disguised appreciation of the more endowed members of the female sex. This gave an added dimension to his recruiting strategy. Some of the staff made no secret of their opinion on this matter; namely, that certain members of the team were appointed because of their hourglass figures and plummeting necklines rather than their teaching skills. Secretly, Hattie thought that Sophie's success with the interviewing panel was one such example.

The summons to his office had arrived towards the end of the afternoon via Gail, one of the school's admin staff. Hattie had taken Sally Burfitt's Year 2 class for outdoor games and was thawing her hands on a dismally ineffective radiator while the children were supposed to be changing out of their PE kit. Suddenly, World War Three broke out. Flavia Bradwell and Poppy Figg, two of Sally's more noxious little horrors, were squabbling over an orange plastic kitten. With a creditable amount of quick thinking, Hattie deftly prised the girls apart and with an airy smile, grabbed Gail's proffered memo.

'Now children,' she called, trying to sound calm and authoritative, 'it's nearly home time, so could you please finish changing and get lined up super quick.'

'Mine!' shrieked Poppy, who had managed to slip past Hattie while her attention was diverted. She lunged at Flavia with teeth bared and succeeded in leaving a neat imprint in her arm. Fortunately, Gail was well out of earshot by the time the teeth had met their target, but what Mrs Bradwell might say about the matter was anybody's guess. Flavia emitted a piercing screech, promptly dropped the plastic kitten and inspected the punctured limb, willing it to ooze blood to win sympathy from the rest of the class. As her screams resounded off the plasterboard walls, the entire class ceased their usual end-of-day bickering and gazed with greedy anticipation of a full-scale pitched battle.

'Mine!' she yelled, grabbing one of Poppy's plaits and tugging with ghoulish pleasure.

'Stop that at once!' commanded Hattie, pulling the girls apart and receiving a painful kick in the ankle from Flavia's boots. 'Into the naughty corner, both of you!' she rapped fiercely.

'Need reinforcements Mrs Chesney?' came a friendly voice. It was Trina French, the Year 2 teaching assistant who had been tidying bookshelves in the adjoining room. She bustled in and, between the two of them, order was quickly restored.

'You're a life saver Trina,' breathed Hattie in her ear. 'Rearrange the following words into a well-known phrase or saying… No, just rearrange them… I, about, was, to, them, just, throttle!'

'Absolutely,' giggled Trina, 'and I'd back you all the way if this was 1812 and not 2012!'

Ten minutes later, the riot act read, war wounds washed and tears dried, class 2B were speedily despatched into the arms of waiting mums, dads and carers. Hattie breathed a sigh of relief and quickly retreated to the staff loo. With any luck, Sally Burfitt would pick up the pieces the following day while she was snugly closeted at home in her kitchen, turning out batches of scones and listening to Vale FM. Or maybe she'd get Fliss over for coffee and a good old chin-wag. Fliss always seemed to be operating on flexi-time and apparently had Tom, the practice manager, wrapped around her perfectly manicured little finger. She also had a high-earning husband, a dedicated little treasure called Myscha who pushed the Hoover round twice a week and three orderly offspring who had mastered A-stars as naturally as breathing. Hattie couldn't help coveting her friend's situation, especially the high-earning husband bit; not that she fancied Mark himself – just his pay packet.

As she had made her way from the terrapin hut, across the war-torn playground and into the comforting fug of the main building, she wondered if the unexpected summons might hold some promise of more hours. Perhaps Mr Neill had found a little pocket of money in the budget and wanted to invest it in some extra supply cover for staff training. Sonia Rowse seemed to have claimed more than her share and every week was off on some course or other, mostly including posh buffet lunches in conference centres in the leafier parts of Bucks. Or maybe he was going to offer Hattie another half day to release Greta, the frazzled special needs teacher, who always seemed to be struggling to find enough hours to get her paperwork licked into shape. There was also the possible prospect of landing a full-time contract. Rumour had it that one of the Year 5 teachers was considering handing in their notice.

Hattie didn't have long to wait. Angus Neill arrived with an armful of dog-eared folders and dumped them in a pile beside his desk. They slithered untidily into a heap, which reminded Hattie of her teenage son's own method of filing in the disorganised tip he used as a bedroom. Angus eyed the undisciplined folders and sighed heavily. On a grimness scale of one to ten, he looked around nine plus. The possibility of a tasty offer of extra hours looked as likely as the lollypop lady swapping her white coat for a G-string and stilettos to entertain the local motorists. If ever there was a moment for a much-needed chocolate fix it was now. However, Hattie suspected that a bulging cheek and surreptitious chomping probably wouldn't be advisable. Perhaps he'd discovered the budget shortfall was even worse than he'd calculated and her job was being axed?

'That business with the, er, school review,' he began gruffly, 'was most unfortunate, if I might say. Whatever possessed you to cancel it?' The fingers of one hand drummed on the desk as he clicked his biro with the other, in what Hattie found a most irritating fashion. Clearly, this was a man who had mastered multitasking.

'Well, to be perfectly frank,' she retorted in a spirited fashion, aware of her heart speeding up in response to the shock, 'I was losing helpers faster than rats deserting a sinking ship.'

8

'There's no need for flippancy, Mrs Chesney,' he snapped. 'It's not a very attractive quality to my mind and certainly not very professional.'

Hattie felt herself starting to fume. This was so unfair. Here was a man who had not *once* enquired about how the review was progressing during the previous term. Nor had he bothered to make a single comment when news of the cancellation had hit the staffroom in early December. After all, he apparently had much more important matters to consider, such as the school's SATs results compared with local rivals St Oswald's and the plans for the hall extension.

'I gather you took it upon yourself to email the rest of the committee, telling them you'd decided to cancel, without even consulting them. What are committees for if not for consultation and joint decision-making? I call that very high-handed indeed.'

High-handed, thought Hattie mutinously, and *this* from a man who, up to now, hadn't shown the slightest flicker of interest.

'And why should I have consulted them?' she snapped back bravely, because her reputation as an organiser was now on the line. 'Hardly anyone was committed to helping me. It was all very well in the beginning. Oh yes, they *said* they'd help out, but when it came to the crunch – the real hard slog of rehearsals, making and painting the stage set, writing out music parts and taking the practices – there was barely a handful of dedicated souls who were prepared to put in the hours. It was a very lonely task I can tell you. Either *it* was going under or *I* was. Given that choice, the decision to cancel was quite clear.'

'Oh, come now, Mrs Chesney. That's a bit melodramatic. Some of you ladies are all too ready to get your... er...'

'Knickers in a twist, were you going to say?'

Angus Neill blushed deep crimson and abruptly dropped his biro. 'Certainly not,' he spluttered adamantly. 'Er... get yourself in a stew, was what I was about to say. I don't see the need to descend to vulgarity.'

Hmm, thought Hattie. According to Gail in the office, he was known to have a fund of rather risqué jokes, mostly on the subject of kilts, sporrans and haggis – and not the sort you'd tell to your shy maiden aunt.

There was a pregnant pause while Hattie dredged her brain for a suitable riposte. If she was about to lose her job – indeed, any chance of a secure future with Hazelton Primary School looked as if it was speedily disappearing down the plughole – she'd prefer to go down fighting. This was surreal! She'd hardly exchanged two sentences with the man in the last ten years and here they were, embroiled in a heated exchange that was in danger of deteriorating into a full-scale slanging match. She frowned and glanced down at her ankles, where there was a hole the size of a cherry tomato, courtesy of Flavia's boots. All she needed now was a tailback on the ring road, one of Jezebel's sicked-up rodent offerings on the doormat and her day would be complete. The option of an evening in a darkened room with the gin bottle was beckoning seductively to her. The trouble was, they'd probably guzzled the last of that on Sunday evening. Life could be so unfair!

Then it occurred to her that Gloria Preston, prima donna of the PTA, had something to do with this unexpected lecture. She'd been very cynical about Hattie's idea of putting on a New Year Review, favouring coffee mornings and sponsored pancake races when it came to fundraising. However, Hattie found coffee mornings and sponsored events utterly boring and predictable. With a good team behind her and oodles of talent from staff, parents and pupils-past and present-Hattie had been convinced that they could raise plenty of cash. The job of convincing Gloria, however, had failed miserably. Nevertheless, with others pledging their support, a date had been set, brainstorming meetings had generated plenty of ideas and the review had started to become a reality.

Belinda, the committee secretary and her aspiring husband, Fraser, had been keen to push two of their brood into starring roles. They still held fond memories of Hayley (aged eight) wowing the audiences of past talent shows with sweet renditions of 'The Good Ship Lollypop'. However, Hayley was now chock full of hormones and was more set on wowing lanky youths behind the cricket pavilion. They were also convinced that little Justin would be perfect as a performing poodle with his cousin Tara. Justin had other ideas.

'Gross!' he yelled, when the costume was produced, which signalled the end of his short-lived acting career.

Caretaker Kenny's rock band suddenly found they were double-booked and Barry the compère was head-hunted as panto dame by a nearby drama group. It was like a cascading row of dominoes. Hattie had been in despair until she'd taken the brave decision to cancel the whole thing, just four weeks short of the planned date.

The silence in the office was deafening. Hattie was hard pressed to think of a suitable reply. It was obvious that Gloria had been bending Angus's ear. She had also organised a fund-raising drinks party as a replacement for the cancelled review, but had quite forgotten to invite Hattie, who happened to hear about it in the post office queue the following morning.

'It's very easy to be wise after the event, especially if you haven't been involved in all the hard work,' asserted Hattie, with as much dignity as she could scrape together. 'In fact, if more people on the committee had bothered to help, there would have been no need to cancel.'

'Gloria Preston is a very accomplished and innovative lady,' remarked Mr Neill with a sneer. 'I'm sure she could have rescued your show if you'd had the presence of mind to consult her.' He bent to pick up his biro and resumed the mindless clicking.

There it was, thought Hattie: proof that Gloria Preston was responsible for this dressing-down. She gulped in disbelief. It needed a great stretch of the imagination to picture Gloria donning a leotard and filling Mary's place in the chorus line. Or maybe Gloria would have had a hotline to all the local rock bands. Hardly likely. Or was she an expert at recorder parts or painting scenery? No, Hattie could only picture Gloria with a clipboard in one hand and a Campari and soda in the other, but she didn't dare mention it. After all, she currently taught two of Gloria's precocious offspring and her sense of self-preservation was winning the battle over rubbishing one of the more influential and outspoken members of the school community.

However, she was by no means naïve, and had already guessed why Gloria Preston's star was in the ascendancy and hers wasn't. Gloria had the looks, the cash, the connections and the vanity to match. 'If you've got it, flaunt it!' seemed to be her slogan and Gloria never did anything half-heartedly when it came to her own interests. Gloria's necklines plunged and her hemlines rose, until there was very little left in between. By contrast, Hattie felt decidedly frumpish. Besides which she had nothing much to flaunt. 'Two aspirins on an ironing board, that's me!' she used to quip, and refused to be a slave to the fickle winds of fashion. She dressed for comfort and practicality in low heels and mid-calf length skirts that could withstand the battering of school life

Angus's roving eye had obviously roved as far as Gloria and concluded that, in his opinion, she could do no wrong, whereas Hattie, it seemed, could do no right. What could she possibly say? She doubted whether anything would make the slightest difference. She also suspected that Sonia Rowse shared his opinion, judging by the way she offloaded her least favourite lessons and duties in her direction. If it hadn't been for Gail in the office, who allocated supply slots, she probably wouldn't have had such a lucrative relationship with the school over the past few years.

'Gloria Preston had plenty of opportunity to get involved when I first mentioned the review,' stated Hattie defensively, 'but she was very dismissive of my idea from the start.'

'Is that so?' replied Mr Neill, scornfully. 'Perhaps next time you'll have the foresight to involve her before you start dreaming up any more unrealistic projects. It'll save a lot of people wasting valuable time and effort.'

'I'm not sure there'll be a next time,' replied Hattie boldly, retrieving the chocolate from her pocket and ripping off the purple foil wrapper. 'Now, if that's all, I'd like to go home now and consider the rest of my life.' With that, she popped the chocolate in her mouth, strode to the door and lobbed the balled-up foil neatly into a waiting bin.

Home at last! The recent damp weather had played havoc with the front door yet again. Hattie gave it a hearty shove and fell into the hall, aware that she'd be nursing a new bruise on her shoulder before long. There was a happy, feline cry and Jezebel came trotting to greet her, all bushy tail and quivering whiskers. She proceeded to wrap herself round Hattie's legs, the glossy coat gently caressing her calves and leaving a trail of white hairs. Hattie carefully scanned the hall floor, looking for signs of anything nasty loitering on the carpet, ready to glue itself to unwary footwear. So far, so good, until a whiff of something male and sweaty reached her nostrils. It was Josh's gym kit festering in an unruly heap at the foot of the stairs. A relentless, rhythmic thud from upstairs, that rippled the dangling lampshade fringe, confirmed that the kit's owner was in residence, listening to what might loosely be described as music. The kit itself, however, was undecided whether it had given up the will to live or was hoping to hitch a lift to the nearest washing machine. Hattie felt sorry for the abandoned mess and wearily dragged it through to the utility room, Jezebel following her with delighted chirrups at the prospect of supper.

She found it hard to understand how two siblings could be so different. Laura, now in her second term teaching in an outer London borough infants school, had mastered school, homework, bedroom organisational skills and exams in that order. Josh, on other hand, seemed to be the offspring from an alien galaxy where timetables and the twenty-four-hour day were undiscovered phenomena. Maybe, however, he was simply repeating the inherited behaviour of Nick, whose teenage years were, to her, a closed book. Or maybe it was a male/female thing.

Once she had spooned out Jezebel's tuna and pilchard chunks and made a cup of her favourite brew, Hattie was feeling much calmer and less likely to throttle the accomplished and innovative Gloria Preston when next they met. Innovative? Where did he get that? She was still organising coffee mornings as if they were the best thing since panty liners. Still, the innovative Mrs P probably thought that putting on live entertainment was only for fools who had too much spare time on their hands. She sighed. It was going to take ages to recover from this. However, the light bulb moment in the car on the way home might change all that. It was brilliant! The trouble was, Nick might not agree. In fact, he might think it was definitely OTT, and merely her feeble attempt to escape from the harsh realities of Hazelton Primary's top dog stakes, in which she was failing miserably.

Some while later, the gentle thud of the front door announced Nick's arrival. He huffed and puffed wearily as he struggled out of his coat and Hattie sensed, even at a short distance, that his day had been not much better than her own.

'Bad day in the office, Nick?' she enquired sympathetically, dunking a fresh teabag in his new Arsenal mug.

'Well, not really, I suppose,' he sighed. 'It was the traffic around the college entrance that was the trouble. Some pillock had taken the corner much too tight and smashed a bollard right across the carriageway. It was a right mess! Then I was stuck behind the Oxford bus all the way home. Traffic was tailed back in both directions. I hate that journey.'

He slumped into the only chair that was not occupied by Jezebel, a pile of marking or bags of supermarket shopping and swallowed down his tea in two or three gulps. This was just the opening Hattie needed. Perfect!

'Well, what about moving?' she suggested casually, pausing in her table-laying to make quite sure that Nick could hear her brilliant idea.

'Moving? What, shelling out a few thousand on a house move just to get away from jams on the ring road? That's just a little extreme isn't it? What did you have in mind? One of those new townhouses they've squeezed in just along from the shopping centre, where that garage used to be? Bijoux, I think they've been described as, apparently. In other words, they're ridiculously small, have virtually no back garden and the only parking is round the corner in a block, if you're lucky. I'd be able to walk to work but it would be much further for you.'

'No, I didn't mean anything like that,' Hattie replied, setting the timer on the microwave and giving the sausage casserole a quick stir. 'Actually, it can wait till later. It's been a pig of a day.'

'G and T?' suggested Nick, dumping his mug and looking for glasses.

'Thanks, sounds like we both deserve one. You'll find a new bottle in one of those carriers next to you. The thought of gin was the only thing that kept me sane on the way home, but don't worry, it's only a supermarket own brand. *And* I bought some chocolate muffins while I was about it, and not just because of some special offer.'

'Whoa!' chuckled Nick, fetching two tumblers and then rootling around in the bottom of the fridge for a lemon. 'It must have been pretty bad if you've resorted to gin *and* muffins!'

In Hattie's opinion, there was something about a chocolate muffin that sliced bread couldn't beat, even when toasted and smothered in strawberry jam.

'So what's all this about moving, Hat?' Nick zapped off the TV and drained his coffee mug. They'd endured Josh's monosyllabic grunts during supper as he shovelled down huge quantities of casserole and then quickly slunk away to try out the decibel level of some new piece of high-tech music kit.

'Well, to put it bluntly, I've just about had enough of Hazelton Primary, Nick, I really have. In fact, I've had *more* than enough. The kids were abysmal today. Then old misery guts had a go at me because I cancelled the review and as for the odious Gloria Preston rubbishing me...'

'Ah, I see,' he chuckled. 'Handbags at dawn again, is it? Miss

Whiplash has rattled your cage again, has she? It's a mystery to me why you're still on that PTA committee. Actually I'd rather assumed that you two had buried the hatchet or, should it be the staple gun!'

'And all behind my back!' continued Hattie, furiously, choosing to ignore Nick's glib remarks. 'I pretty much told him where he could stick his rotten job – well, inferred it anyway.'

'Right, so you didn't actually…' Nick was struggling to keep up, but he'd heard enough about the mounting review problems in the previous two months to realise that it was still quite a sore point.

'No, not quite, but I was *so* close. Of course, it was all about money; it always is with *him*. He'd not shown the slightest glimmer of interest in all my efforts, but I bet he'd been busy counting his chickens and hoping for enough to pay for some pet project of his. You know, he might even have spent it already, which would account for why he was so loathsome. And of course the talented – no, *accomplished* – and innovative Mrs Preston is the rising star in his firmament because of her cosy little drinks party.'

'Her *what* party?'

'Forget it, Nick. We weren't invited and I'm not really bothered anyway. You wouldn't catch me paying £2 a glass for supermarket plonk and standing around being bored senseless by her dreary husband and his town council buddies – oh, and of course most of her precious committee.' Hattie paused for breath and the brief silence was punctuated by reverberations from above. 'After all that biting and hair pulling too.'

'Biting and hair pulling?' Nick gasped, picturing his wife and the famous Gloria grappling in an undignified brawl on the staffroom floor.

'Oh yes,' sighed Hattie wearily. 'Flavia Bradwell and Poppy Figg were locked in mortal combat *again*. No blood spilt this time, thank goodness! For a few minutes, it was pandemonium though, until Trina started throwing her weight around – bless her. Fortunately, I managed to get them all lined up and out of the door, spot on time. Sally can deal with it tomorrow.' She gave a huge sigh for the sheer relief of not having to battle with anyone younger than her resident testosterone-charged teenager until nine o'clock on Friday morning. Ah yes, remembered Hattie with a sinking heart, Friday morning that term meant supply cover for Sonia Rowse, high-flying deputy head and Year 4 teacher, with the infamous Jacob Pocock on roll. She'd previously taught him as a sweet little Year 1, but in the intervening years he'd acquired a reputation for a colourful vocabulary, trendy gear, a devoted following of Year 3 and 4 girls and dumb insolence. Hattie hadn't relished the prospect of taking 4R every Friday, but it was only one session of PE and she couldn't say no to the extra money.

'You know what you need, Hat,' began Nick, thoughtfully. 'You need to get away from it all.'

'Exactly,' agreed Hattie, nodding. 'As I said earlier, I want to move.'

'Well, I didn't actually mean that. How about going away this weekend? Just a short break – somewhere really nice.'

'And we can talk about the house move then?' suggested Hattie, eagerly.

'Well, okay, if you like,' agreed Nick. 'I know Christmas wasn't much of a break for either of us, what with my folks here. You were great pandering to Mum's every need, on top of all that stress over the... er... well, you know. So how about booking a couple of nights at that nice little coaching inn we stayed at for our anniversary? We could go for some bracing walks, nose around the market stalls and those crafty type shops you love and enjoy supper in front of a roaring log fire. How does that sound?' He was secretly hoping that a weekend away would deflect Hattie from thoughts of moving house. The cost of two nights away was a whole lot cheaper than solicitors' and agents' fees.

'Nick, that sounds like heaven,' she sighed gratefully, making a mental note of adding in at least two cream teas and exchanging bracing walks for leisurely strolls. 'I guess Josh might possibly manage to look after himself for a weekend, now that he's a grown-up college student. Or we could ask his devoted godparents to put him up, I suppose.'

'Put up with him you mean,' chuckled Nick. 'No, I don't really want to lose the friendship of Toby and Celia. On the other hand, Josh *could* always stay with a mate.'

'Then who would feed Jezebel?'

'Okay, Josh stays here on cat-feeding duty and I whisk you away for two days of total relaxation. I'll go and book it right away.'

They'd hardly been on the road ten minutes when Hattie was frantically texting Celia Halverson. The idea was that she would call on Josh at ten the following morning, under the pretence of returning one of Hattie's books. In reality, her call was to check that he was awake, sober, not in police custody for possession of banned substances and had fed Jezebel. To save Celia's feelings, Hattie had mentioned only the first and last reasons on her list. Hopefully Celia's call wouldn't lead to the discovery of a houseful of drunken partygoers and a mountain of discarded bottles, cans and fast-food wrappers littering the floor. On hearing this plan, Nick had pointed out that Jezebel was well able to feed herself.

'What, and vomit vermin all over the floor?' Hattie had protested. 'Who'd clean up all the mess? Can't quite picture Josh with mop and bucket.'

She'd also been plagued with lurid visions of puking teenagers slumped over her recently cleaned, three-piece suite or her lovely new, Ikea duvet covers.

'Are you sure you want this weekend away?' asked Nick, just a tad irritated by her fixation with vomit. To emphasise his feelings on the matter, he reduced speed, ready to execute a nifty three-point turn. 'Because if you don't, I'd rather go home now.'

'Okay! Okay!' she'd agreed, promising she'd trust Celia to make the early morning call and Josh to restrict his social life to merely running up a record phone bill.

'Knowing our son and his struggle to sort himself out for college, I doubt he'd be capable of organising anything resembling a party,' remarked Nick dismissively.

'Oh don't you believe it,' warned Hattie. 'Beneath the surface of every lethargic, half-baked adolescent lurks a fun-loving, gregarious "life and soul of the party" type just waiting to burst upon the scene. All they need is the sound of their parents' car disappearing down the road to jolt them into action. I reckon they have this sort of herding instinct, like wildebeest at a watering hole. I'm convinced that a sniff of booze or the pop of a ring-pull can is enough, and next thing you know, there's a whole bunch of them at the door –'

'Hat!' warned Nick sternly.

'Okay,' she sighed. 'You win.' And she'd snapped her phone shut.

'Anyway, how come you're such an expert on the secret lives and herding instincts of lethargic, party-planning adolescents, seeing as we haven't yet managed to rear one that fits your description? Nor has Fliss apparently.'

'For goodness' sake, Nick. You *do* read the papers don't you? Any of that stuff could happen in *our* back yard any day now. Trina French has some horrendous stories to tell about *her* two. She's had to have the locks changed *twice* in the last six months and been woken by the police ringing her doorbell in the middle of the night to haul one of them away in handcuffs.'

'Oh God!'

'It was all a case of mistaken identity as it turned out, but you can guess what a shock it was. Confronting a police officer in her skimpy nightwear was bad enough, let alone seeing one of her lads taken off in a police car at three in the morning. She's wondering if details of her sleeping attire have been bandied about the station rest room and she'll never dare to look an officer in the eye again, just in case he's goggling over the thought of her dressed in a teddy and G-string. Anyway, her kids have calmed down a bit since that little episode, but it *could* mean that they're doing it somewhere else instead. Trina never actually told me what they're supposed to have done, although it starts you imagining all sorts of unsavoury possibilities.'

The thought of the not insubstantial Trina French in a teddy and G-string was exercising Nick's imagination too.

That was forty or so minutes earlier. As they were negotiating their way down twisty country lanes and around sharp bends within just a few minutes of their destination, Hattie suddenly remembered a call she should have made.

'It's just a message to Laura, Nick. I realised I hadn't told her we were going away this evening, just in case she'd been planning on phoning for a bit of a chat.'

'Now promise me, Hat,' ordered Nick, decelerating as they passed the speed limit sign that marked the leafy suburbs of the small market town, 'that you'll switch off from school, the kids and anything else that might prevent us from enjoying this weekend.'

'I promise,' replied Hattie dutifully, with a giggle, pocketing her mobile and relishing the prospect of a meal she hadn't had to plan or sweat over.

Street lamps loomed out of the pitch-black darkness and occasional porch lights could be seen twinkling through chunky privet hedges and frosted boughs, as the car slowed to a gentler pace through the narrowing streets. Then, before them, there opened up a wider space. They were reaching the heart of the little town, passing neat rows of shops on either side of a square, which was dominated by a war memorial, set on a stone plinth and surrounded by squat, chain-linked pillars. Most of the shopkeepers had packed away their Christmas decorations, but across the square, rows of fairy lights criss-crossed the space giving a magical effect. The window of Savill and Daughter, Nick's favourite antique shop, was lit subtly enough to give tantalising glimpses of pine dressers, cane-backed chairs, hat stands and various stone and brass pots stuffed full of winter greenery. Then there was Robin's Nest, the gorgeous art and homeware shop that was a showcase for local artists and craft workers. On they drove, past the general stores, Edwin's Book Emporium, the hospice shop, butcher and bakery until eagle-eyed Hattie spotted an unfamiliar name – Pins and Needles. Six months earlier, when they'd come for an anniversary treat, the premises – formerly trading in pet supplies – was empty. The couple who'd run it for many years had finally closed up when they decided retirement was long overdue. She made a mental note to explore Pins and Needles in the morning. Hattie was a creative soul who could easily be tempted to start a new cross-stitch project or splash out on some exotic yarn to turn into a designer cardi or stylish pair of gloves.

Before long, they were hauling their overnight bags into the oak-floored entrance of The Six Bells, a well-appointed three star coaching inn that boasted fine dining with locally sourced ingredients. Once the preliminaries were over, they made their way to the first floor, passing rural landscapes and hunting scenes attractively displayed on every available wall space. Shelves, nooks and crannies were crammed with enough farming implements and memorabilia to stock a modest museum.

'Ta-da! The Orchid Suite!' announced Nick, flinging open the door to reveal a four-poster bed draped with acres of cream and gold fabric. There were exquisite matching curtains and soft furnishings, soft thick-pile rugs and well-chosen vases and prints that gave an air of honeymoon suite meets country manor drawing room. It looked like a page out of *House Beautiful*. Hattie's eyes were on stalks.

'This weekend must be costing a fortune, Nick,' she gasped in amazement.

'No, no. Not at all. It's off season so it's cheap as chips – relatively speaking,' he assured her nonchalantly, with a twinkle in his eye.

'You certainly know how to make a girl feel special don't you?' she chuckled.

'Hey, come and check out the bathroom,' he called.

Hattie pushed past Nick who was hogging the doorway. 'Wow, a sunken tub, and big enough for two,' she breathed, eyeing up the his and hers bathrobes, satin-edged fluffy towels and hamper of oils and lotions.

'No time like the present,' announced Nick, flicking on the taps and emptying a sachet of something with the heady scent of roses into the swirling water. 'Last one in's a sissy!' he chortled gleefully, unzipping his jeans and kicking off his loafers. It was the perfect start to a weekend, set to blow away the cobwebs for a jaded supply teacher and weary accounts executive.

Hattie's diet sprouted wings and flew out of the window that evening, when sticky toffee pudding was ordered, to swiftly follow broccoli and stilton soup and venison hot pot. Several glasses of house red, followed by brandy with the coffee, ensured neither were sober enough to discuss anything more brain-stretching than the taxing behaviour of Madge, Nick's office co-habitee. Madge was short, efficient, single and hovering around fifty. She favoured severe haircuts and sensible lace-ups and had the knack of precision storage and filing down to a fine art. Nick, who was several grades her senior, was responsible for a fistful of lucrative accounts, but lacked the time or inclination for paperclip and petty cash slip regimentation. By rights, he should have had his own space, but some internal reorganisation the previous year had meant he had to rub along with his least favourite choice of work companion. Over coffee, he regaled Hattie with Madge's latest waspish remarks.

'She wasted at least half an hour harrumphing around the office, muttering to herself, then proceeded to clear and sort out an entire cupboard because the stationery organisation wasn't up to her exacting standards. The poor old girl is just a frustrated spinster,' Nick moaned. 'If she can't get a husband to boss around, she takes it out on the staples and rubber bands – and me!'

'Don't be too harsh on her,' sympathised Hattie. 'Okay, so she's a spinster and has been with the company since the year dot, but I'm sure she's got a heart of gold beating under her tweed and twinset exterior.'

'Hmm! Not sure about the heart bit, Hat, but she's certainly got plenty of something less solid beaten into submission under her knitted workwear,' he chuckled.

'Well, of course, if we move house, you won't have to suffer Madge's cutting remarks or harrumphing anymore,' remarked Hattie, seizing the heaven-sent window of opportunity to press her case about major relocation.

'Er... right... um, now where is it?' he fussed, searching his pockets busily and ignoring Hattie's change of subject. 'Ah yes, chocolate... your favourite brand.'

The mention of chocolate did the trick and reminded Nick of Pavlov's dog, because Hattie's carefully prepared speech suddenly seemed to have been forgotten. The first two squares disappeared in record time.

'Hmm, dark mint chocolate,' she sighed, as the rich flavours caressed her taste buds.

'And now, sexy lady,' he murmured, nibbling the nearest plump, pink earlobe, 'let's get up to the Orchid Suite, where I'm hoping you'll hop into something disgustingly skimpy and provocative and I'll have my wicked way with you.'

As he quickly ushered her to their waiting four-poster, he congratulated himself on his skilfully-executed diversion tactics. With any luck they'd hold out, even if the chocolate didn't.

A bright and frosty morning greeted them. After enjoying the delights of the breakfast buffet – fresh fruit, yoghurt, croissants, ham, cereals, toast and not forgetting the cooked Full English – they were set up for the day and ready to hit the Saturday market and as many shops as they could fit in before a coffee stop. Pins and Needles turned out to be a quilter's paradise and so, while Nick was nosing around Edwin's books, Hattie acquainted herself with fat quarters, cutting wheels and sumptuously illustrated books

23

with every bedcover design imaginable. Before she knew it, she was hooked. The quilts on display were breathtaking and although she had never tried anything like it before, she was keen to learn the basics. There was all sorts of information about courses and websites, so she picked up a few leaflets to help her track down a local course.

Nick picked up some back copies of *The Economist* and Hattie splashed out on a quirky 'Do Not Disturb - Genius Recharging His Brain Cells' door sign that she thought Josh would appreciate. In Savill and Daughter, Nick spotted some pretty Victorian ceramic doorknobs being appraised by a formidable female. They were blue and white and just what Hattie would love for her little stripped pine sewing cupboard. Nick held his breath as the woman replaced the knobs then strode off in search of her husband who had slipped his leash and was enjoying some relative peace behind a set of folding screens. Seizing the opportunity, Nick quickly snatched the abandoned knobs and paid for them.

'Gorgeous, aren't they?' said the assistant, as she wrapped them in layers of cream tissue and popped them in a neat Savill and Daughter carrier bag. 'We don't get many of these and when we do, they're snapped up very quickly.'

'They're for my wife's birthday,' Nick told her. 'It's not till the summer, so I'll have to hide them until then. Thanks a lot.' As he was pocketing his change, the woman he'd just seen admiring the knobs bustled up to the counter, with her husband now in tow.

'Miss,' she interrupted, ignoring Nick, 'there were some dear little ceramic drawer handles over there a minute ago. You haven't sold them, have you?' The question sounded more like a threat.

'Oh, yes; to this gentleman,' the assistant replied breezily.

Hard cheese, Nick thought, and gleefully carried off his prize. Outside the shop, he spotted Hattie wrestling with two carrier bags.

'A bit of shopping, Hat? Thought you were just getting something for Josh.'

She showed him the door sign then pulled out a handful of assorted garments.

'I couldn't resist these bargains in the hospice shop,' she giggled. 'Look, designer labels, hardly worn and just right for school. And what's in that dinky little bag Nick?'

'Ah, you'll have to wait to find out,' he told her enigmatically. 'In fact, wait until your birthday. Now it's time for coffee I think.' He made a mental note to hide the bag at the bottom of his chest of drawers.

Over cappuccinos and muffins at The Rendezvous, Hattie indulged in some people-watching while Nick caught up on the previous night's football results, thanks to the piles of newspapers provided. She gazed at the little row of cottages clustered around a green on the far side of the square, dreaming of life in such desirable dwellings. It would certainly make a change from the dull, mid-sixties semi that they currently called home. For Hattie, cottages suggested inglenook fireplaces, stone-flagged floors, rustic beams as well as neat little gardens, vegetable patches, sheds and coalholes. Unfortunately, old cottages also meant dry rot, wet rot, rising damp, leaking roofs and rotten window frames. They also boasted ancient rights of way that allowed the world and his dog to trample through your property whenever they pleased. Nevertheless, a cottage was what Hattie now lusted after, and as far away from Hazelton Primary as possible. But, how to go about it? New locations meant new jobs and as Nick's job was crucial to her scheme, it was important to convince him if they were going to achieve the complete break Hattie was planning.

'What now?' she asked eagerly, as Nick wearily folded the sports section he'd been studying.

'Nil-nil draw... They'll have to do better in the next match or they won't get into Europe. The ref awarded a penalty and then they went and wasted it.' He shook his head sadly. Nick took his footie very seriously. Not a good time to broach house moves, decided Hattie, realising that timing was everything.

After lunch, they went to explore the vast grounds of an impressive stately home. Hattie loved beautiful lawns and well-tended gardens, but the huge expanse that greeted them suggested more than a leisurely stroll if they were going to see a quarter of the grounds. Suddenly, Nick's idea was not such an appealing one.

'Home to the eleventh Duke and Duchess of Marlborough and birthplace of Sir Winston Churchill,' read Nick with his nose in the guidebook.

'Oh really,' commented Hattie, wondering how much history she'd have to endure until she could make a dash for the tearooms.

It was a beautiful afternoon when they arrived, with a clear blue sky and just a dusting of fluffy white clouds. However, after a few minutes the sun disappeared behind a huge bank of grey cloud and the temperature plummeted dramatically.

'There are two thousand acres of parkland landscaped by Capability Brown,' continued Nick cheerfully, as he strode towards the lake that was edged with clumps of snowdrops. Hattie hurried on behind, wishing she'd suggested an afternoon in their room watching romantic comedies from the comfort of their four-poster. She wrapped her scarf tighter around her neck and wished she'd remembered to bring her woollen beanie.

'Two thousand acres?' she echoed, hoping Nick wouldn't expect to cover every single one.

'The formal gardens were planned in the twenties with the help of the French landscape architect Achille Duchene. Your day out would not be complete without a visit to the Water Terraces, Rose Garden, Arboretum and the Secret Garden,' read Nick, as they rounded the lake and set off towards a cluster of trees. 'Sounds great, doesn't it, Hat?'

'Wonderful,' she replied dutifully, her ears now more like blocks of ice, 'but I'm freezing. We could always finish this off another time, couldn't we?'

'Okay,' Nick agreed, pocketing the guidebook.

'Right, time for a pot of Earl Grey and a plate of scones I think.' They set off in the direction of the tearooms. As they did so, Hattie's mobile sprang to life. It was a brief message from Josh whose godmother had clearly plummeted in his estimation. At least it meant that Celia had kept her promise, much to Hattie's relief.

A cream tea and three course supper later, Hattie seized her long-awaited opportunity, before Nick knew what was happening. The liquid gold streams of an excellent single malt had, by then, induced in him a sense of wellbeing and a satisfied glow. He was like putty in her hands.

'About the house move, Nick,' she murmured, stroking his thigh. 'It's not just about getting away from Gloria Preston you know. It's more like having a fresh start and getting out of the rut we're in.'

'I hadn't really thought our life was in a rut,' he protested. 'More like a nice regular routine.'

'Oh, Nick, don't be so boring. You'll be getting yourself a pipe and rocking chair next by the sound of it.' Before he could protest, she produced one of her watertight reasons that she knew would appeal to him. 'And I also thought it would be good to be nearer the parents, just to sort of keep an eye on them.'

'What? But your mum and dad are down in Highcliffe-on-Sea now and my folks are in Romsey. That's a bit of a hike to and from work each day.'

Hattie despaired. He could be so dense at times. However, she could see the whole picture, including the quaint little cottage – roses round the door optional – and its garden, and wondered when the penny would drop in Nick's befuddled brain.

'Oh, for goodness' sake, Nick. I'm hardly expecting you to drive between the New Forest and Aylesbury Vale every day. Credit me with more than one brain cell. You'll have a different job of course. How else did you expect it all to happen?'

Nick threw his head back and chuckled, squeezing her knee

playfully. 'Oh, of course, a new job! Fancy missing that tiny little detail. Harriet, my cherub –'

'Are you suggesting I've put on weight?' she demanded, indignantly.

'Pax, pax!' he laughed, holding up his hands in mock surrender. 'No, not at all, Hat. There's not a love handle in sight,' he chuckled. 'Okay, new job… absolutely… spot on… Now Hat, tell me where this job is supposed to be. I mean, it's all very well suggesting it, but in these difficult economic times, with the government announcing cost-cutting measures and all the knock-on effects, new jobs for blokes like me aren't exactly as plentiful as cobwebs in the downstairs loo.'

'What exactly are you inferring there, Nicholas Chesney?'

'Oh nothing old girl,' he chuckled, 'I was just trying to make a point about the current job market. I mean I'm lucky to have the one I've got.'

'But, Nick, you've worked for Padgett and Bicton for ages. You've got a responsible position and they're bound to give you a glowing reference. It's a shame they don't have another branch near Romsey.'

Then Nick had *his* light bulb moment. 'Of course, the Group Bulletin! Remember when we amalgamated with that group from the Southampton area last year, well now we get a monthly newsletter with sits vac and other stuff. There's always jobs in that and anyone can apply. Basically, they're treated as internal appointments, so the chances of getting them are quite good. I'll bring the latest one home and we'll see what's what.'

Hattie couldn't believe how easily Nick was warming to her idea.

'When we get back, I'll call a couple of estate agents for a valuation, so we can get the ball rolling,' she enthused gleefully, 'and before you know it, you'll be waving a fond farewell to dear old Madge and I'll have great pleasure in telling old fungus face where he can stick his precious job. Whoopee!'

Three locals perched on barstools rubbernecked quizzically

in their direction, beer mugs frozen in mid-air.

'Can't take her anywhere,' Nick sniggered, jerking his thumb towards a beaming Hattie. However, she didn't care; her plan was coming together very nicely indeed.

2

'Good morning, Mrs…er… Chesney. Brian Samways of Samways and Partners at your service. You phoned for a valuation, I believe.' Smiling broadly, he offered a podgy hand, a clipboard tucked under his arm. He was the first of two agents Hattie had picked at random from the telephone directory on their return from the weekend away.

'Do come in, Mr Samways.'

'Call me Brian, please,' he replied, pumping her hand energetically. 'Nice houses these,' he observed, marching in without a moment's hesitation and digging out his pen to make notes. 'Been here long?'

'Oh yes, about ten years,' replied Hattie, hastily removing her pinny and stuffing it in the umbrella stand.

'Yes, good, solid, family homes these are,' he commented, more to himself than Hattie. 'And of course you've got a splendid view from the back. We had number eleven on our books back along and it flew, Mrs Chesney. People are always after three-bed semis; they're the bread and butter of our trade.'

Hattie thought that 'boring' was a better description, but bread and butter was boring, after all. She also knew for certain that number eleven had been on the market for ages, with several agents' boards festooning the garden. But maybe that was down to a pampas bathroom suite and Artex ceiling? Hattie and Nick had got rid of theirs years ago.

30

After a quick tour around most of the house, Hattie scooted back to the kitchen to put the kettle on, leaving Brian to complete his measuring and note-taking. Now, would she splash out on rich roast filter coffee or just stick to cheap old instant? In the end she opted for freshly made coffee, hoping it might impress him enough to give a good valuation. She heaped generous spoonfuls of the rich aromatic powder into a cafetière and then opened a packet of shortbread left over from Christmas.

'My, that's an appetising aroma, Mrs Chesney,' Brian chuckled, spotting the cafetière on the worktop beside two stripy mugs and a dish of shortbread fingers.

Goodness, she mused, he sounds like someone on a TV ad.

'I'll have milk and just one sugar. Have to watch the waistline, what with all the indulgences of the festive season,' he confided, patting his ample stomach and leaning towards the dish. 'Well, perhaps I'll just try these, seeing as you've gone to the trouble of putting them out,' he added, reaching in and scooping up a couple of fingers. Without a pause, he polished off one in double-quick time. As he munched contentedly, he scribbled a few notes then settled himself in Jezebel's favourite chair before Hattie could stop him. She knew there'd be a generous layer of white fur on his rear end when he got up, but decided it wouldn't be prudent to mention it now.

Two mugs of coffee and several shortbread fingers later, Brian had revealed his considered market value, set out company policy and outlined fees and commission rates.

'Will you want to go on the market straight away?' he enquired, adding a few more scribbled notes to his clipboard.

'Well, not quite yet,' hesitated Hattie. 'You see, I'm getting Mia Casa to do a valuation tomorrow and then there's my husband's job to sort out, but I'll keep in touch.'

'If you don't mind me saying, Mrs Chesney,' he declared, with alarming directness, 'you need to be very wary of some of the local firms, especially the new ones. They'll give you a much higher valuation than your house is actually worth, just to get the business, and then wonder why they can't shift it. It pays to be realistic – trust me. I've been in the business long enough to know what I'm talking about. There're a lot of cowboys out there.'

After he'd gone, displaying a white furry covering on the seat of his otherwise immaculate trousers, Hattie wandered back to the kitchen and found, to her dismay, that only one shortbread finger remained.

'The greedy man must have snaffled another one while my back was turned,' she told Jezebel, who had strolled back, hoping to regain possession of her chair. 'Ah well, his waistline, not mine!'

Their decision about moving had not gone down well with Josh, even though plans to fix up local digs or even a change of college had been discussed. In fact, if truth be told, Hattie and Nick had discussed it while Josh had sat sullenly and grunted. Still, it was early days and they hoped that the benefits of independence might soon infiltrate Josh's consciousness and he'd become wildly excited about the whole idea. Then they re-entered the real world. Josh didn't do excitement, wild or otherwise, or at least not when his parents were around.

Over coffee, Nick dug out the 'situations vacant' bulletin and circled two possibilities at Lydford Cross that looked very promising. One was a grade higher than his current post and the location was ideally placed. He would send for application forms the following day. Lydford Cross was not far from Nick's parents, yet far enough away to prevent them making too many impromptu visits. The thought of Bryony Chesney popping in whenever she fancied it filled Hattie with dread.

'Did you sort out a valuation with another agent?' Nick asked, draining his mug. 'The Samways one is okay, but it makes sense to see what someone else thinks we're worth.'

'Oh yes, didn't I say? I have someone from Mia Casa coming. It's a new firm I believe.'

'Mia what?' spluttered Nick, in derision. 'Pretentious – moi?' he mimicked, remembering a line from a favourite sitcom scene.

'Mia Casa,' answered Hattie, feeling slightly affronted, 'I think it means "my home".'

'Yes okay, Hat, my vague grasp of Italian just about stretches to that, but who in their right mind calls their firm Mia Casa, unless they're selling villas in Italy?'

'Well, *I* like it. It's sort of romantic, even if Brian Samways implied that they were just a bunch of cowboys.'

By ten o'clock the following morning, the house was all spruced up ready for another appraisal – basins and taps gleaming, stray cobwebs removed from the downstairs loo, carpets immaculate, cushions plumped, coffee and biscuits ready and Jezebel safely curled up in her chair – *and* Hattie had remembered to slick on some lippy and a touch of blusher. However, when she answered the ring at the door, nothing could have prepared her for the sight that greeted her. In the few seconds before realisation dawned, the agent smiled and made a slight bow. It was that little detail that brought the memories flooding back. Open-mouthed and incredulous, she gazed in disbelief at the piercing brown eyes, aquiline features and crinkly black hair of a man she hadn't seen for over twenty years – well, twenty-six to be absolutely precise.

'Oh my God... Leo!' she gasped. Despite the passage of time, he'd hardly changed, except for a mere sprinkling of grey hairs and some slackness around the mouth. There was certainly no sign of a paunch. Keeping fit had always been important to him, she recalled. He stared back at her quizzically, the bright smile that had first greeted her now fading with alarming speed. Whatever his opening gambit was supposed to be, it had clearly been erased from his mind.

'I can't believe it... Is it really you? And what on earth are you doing here?' she demanded. Tumbled emotions all jostled for first place within her and a struggle for composure was being lost by the second. Mixed with the shocked surprise at seeing him after so long was the growing anger at the way he'd so mysteriously and suddenly disappeared from her life. Not a call, not a letter... Zilch!

'Mia Casa at your service... er... madam,' he announced after several moments of confusion.

It was clear to Hattie that either his memory was not as good as hers or she had changed beyond recognition. Back then, she'd worn her hair in cascading waves over her shoulders, but now it was cut in a neat bob with the occasional grey hair making an unwelcome appearance. No longer was she a size 10 – more a 14 on a good day – but her figure was still firm and in good shape. However, there didn't seem to be an inch of spare fat on him.

'I wondered for a moment if I was in the wrong place,' he continued, hardly making sense of the situation.

'Wrong place?' echoed Hattie. 'You mean like the last time? Does Victoria Station or the name Hattie Morrish mean anything to you by any chance?'

After what seemed minutes, but was probably only seconds, light appeared to dawn in Leo's eyes and his expression became more guarded as memories of that distant July overtook him. He had been left in confusion after that day. Was it totally his fault or partly hers? Or Alex's fault, or just circumstances out of their control?

'Hattie, my dear Hattie, is it really you?'

'*Your* dear Hattie? No, Leo, I don't think so. I'm Nick Chesney's dear Hattie now and have been for over twenty years.'

'Permit me... May I come in?' he asked hesitantly, after checking to see if a clutch of neighbours were witnessing their conversation. He was working hard at a smile, but was aware that he also had to work hard at something else, like a plausible explanation for past events, before he could carry out the purpose of his visit.

'Oh, of course... Yes, you'd better come in, Leo. I'd prefer the neighbours not to know about our unfortunate history.'

He followed her meekly as she strode through to the kitchen and busied herself with making coffee. The more she thought about that awful day, the more the anger grew inside her, anger that had melted away over the years.

Leo shuffled his feet nervously. He glanced around Hattie's kitchen, trying to look business-like as he took out a pen and began to make notes in a folder.

'So… er… how are things with you, Hattie?' he began, trying to make conversation, his confidence now a few notches lower since his arrival at her front door.

Hattie wheeled round sharply, trying to decide which choice phrase she could fire at him. No, I must get him sitting down, she decided, remembering her own humiliating session in the Head's study.

'Oh, do sit down, Leo. You're making the kitchen somewhat cluttered,' she declared icily, plunging the coffee grounds with more force than usual. Scalding black liquid shot out, spattering the work surface and her hands.

'Are you okay? Have you burned yourself? May I help?' he offered, leaping out of his chair and attempting to mop the puddle with a crumpled tissue.

Hattie spun round, waving away his offer, her eyes flashing with anger. 'Am I okay? What a stupid question! Spilt coffee is nothing compared with your track record, Leo.' Inside her, the floodgates opened. 'You stand me up at Victoria Station, leave me looking like a proper fool waiting there and not one word do I get from you. Not *one* phone call or letter or anything… And you have the nerve, the gall, the cheek…' Hattie was really warming to this now and was searching for a few more suitable synonyms to throw at him. '…the sheer audacity to ask me if I'm okay! What do you take me for? I know it's a long time ago, but you don't forget these things in a hurry I can tell you. Just because you obviously didn't care enough to go through with all those plans you made – *we* made – don't think that *I* didn't!' Furiously, she snatched a dishcloth and swabbed the mess with more than necessary vigour. Remembering the red rose that he'd left on her doorstep, with that note, added more fuel to her fury. Leo, however, just stood in silence like a startled rabbit.

'All those things you said to me were obviously part of your chat-up routine, just to get a girl to drop her knickers.'

'No, Hattie,' he protested. 'It was never like that!'

'So *you* say,' she snapped. 'God, I was blind to your shallowness, because anyone who tells a girl what *you* told me *has* to be shallow. Well, it's a good thing I found out what you were really like, even if you didn't have the guts to admit you'd made a huge mistake or had just changed your mind about us. I know for sure that *I* made a mistake. I let myself be sweet-talked into...' Hattie was close to tears, but the last thing she wanted was to let him see. She turned back to the waiting coffee mugs and took a deep breath. 'Oh God, what a fool I was to believe you! Well, thank you for that, because I ended up *much* better off!'

The silence that followed could have been sliced up neatly, cling-wrapped and sold on a bring-and-buy stall.

'How do you take your coffee Leo?' she asked him curtly. 'It's a long time since I made you any. And I want to make it quite clear that as soon as you've finished it, you're to exit my life just as quickly as you've entered it. I never want to see or hear from you again, but that shouldn't be too difficult, should it? I mean, you're quite an expert at that. We shall be instructing Samways and Partners just as quickly as we can and hopefully soon be miles away – for good!'

Leo's restraint was commendable, but also just that bit irritating for Hattie. She'd known him well enough to have experienced his flashes of anger and passion – oh, that passion – but all she was seeing were sorrowful eyes and a guilty hangdog expression.

'Black, no sugar, thank you.' He waited while she poured the coffee, which gave him time to muster his defence. 'But, Hattie, you've got it all wrong,' he implored. 'Please let me explain. I didn't stand you up, although I can see that's what it looked like. If you let me tell you what happened that morning, you'll understand. Maybe, in time, you'll find it possible to forgive me.'

Hattie placed a mug in front of him on the table, but decided against the custard creams. Even a rich tea would be more than he was worth as far as she was concerned. She took a deep gulp from her mug, leaning against the worktop and maintaining a good distance from her opponent. Leo sipped his coffee, his brows furrowed in thought. Hattie suspected he was concocting a convincing sob story. In fact, if it had been any quieter she was sure she'd have been able to hear the sound of cogs whirring feverishly in his brain. Gullible she may have been then, but the hard knocks of life had edited out that particular weakness by now.

'That morning when we planned to meet,' began Leo.

'When *you* asked me to be there,' corrected Hattie primly, remembering again the red ribbon-tied rose. How corny, she now thought.

'Please, Hattie, allow me to explain.'

She sighed impatiently and took another gulp to avoid meeting his eyes.

'That morning I had a meeting at the Pimlico Wine Company that my father had asked me to attend.'

Ah yes, remembered Hattie, Signor Marcello Senior was owner of a huge flourishing vineyard in Tuscany and Leo had supposedly been lined up to take over one day. That's why his appearance as an estate agent was so puzzling. Perhaps it wasn't exactly flourishing or maybe it didn't even exist.

'The wine company wasn't far from Victoria Station, so I was sure my ten o'clock meeting would be over in less than an hour, giving me plenty of time to get to the station before midday. The offices were just off Belgrave Road, so I knew I could walk it easily.'

So, what's coming now, Hattie wondered: tripped over a manhole cover and twisted his ankle or bitten by a runaway rabid dog or was he the sole witness of a smash and grab raid? Come on now, Leo. Come up with something interesting. However, on this occasion, she kept her thoughts to herself.

'Well, I got there well before ten and the PA told me that Jack

– what was his name? – Jack... er... Jack Edlin. Well, anyway, the chief buyer was delayed – some emergency dentist appointment I seem to remember. Eventually he turned up and it was almost ten thirty by then.'

Hattie found Leo's ability to remember such inconsequential details as a dentist appointment quite incredible. On the day in question, remembering to contact her had evidently completely bypassed his brain. This interesting comparison had her suspicions marshalled and ready for action. To Hattie, this story of Leo's was sounding exactly that – a piece of fiction, just make-believe. Before he could continue or Hattie could give her candid opinion of his story-telling ability, her mobile kicked into action. Grabbing it, she saw her best friend Fliss's number on the caller display.

'Fliss?' she said, moving into the hallway. 'Yes... Oh, Fliss, what's up? No! Oh, I'm so sorry,' she gasped, listening to a tearful outpouring. 'Do you want me to come over? Okay. Yes, of course... No, I'm not teaching this afternoon. Look, there's someone here,' she told her, lowering her voice, 'but I'll get rid of them... No, I mean it... Right, see you soon. Bye.' Perfect timing, thought Hattie, although not good for Fliss.

Leo had evidently heard enough to know that his time was up. As Hattie quickly gathered the mugs, dumped them on the drainer and then snatched up her shoulder bag and keys, Leo followed mutely.

'My friend needs me,' Hattie told him, although she couldn't think why she'd bothered to elaborate.

'I heard,' he replied, searching for his car keys. 'I hope it's not bad news... er... well, of course it's not my business.'

'Quite correct, Leo,' she snapped, reaching for her jacket.

'But if it's possible, may I sometime finish what I was telling you?'

'Leo, what part of "I never want to see or hear from you again" do you not understand?' she shrieked, her eyes blazing with fury.

'I hoped –'

'So did *I* once!'

Within seconds he had left, and she stood shaking with pent-up anger and frustration while the sound of his car disappeared. Her breath came in short gasps and tears started to prickle her eyes. She wouldn't tell Nick about this incident, she decided. In fact, she'd tell him the agent hadn't shown up. There was no need to go over the painful Victoria Station business that she'd never shared with him in all their years of marriage. Nor would she tell Fliss – that would be a big mistake. No, she thought, I'll keep this to myself. It's not deception; it's simply consigning it all to the recycle bin and clicking delete. The trouble was, it might not be as easy as that. What if she bumped into Leo in the supermarket or dentist's waiting room? The fact that their paths hadn't crossed already was a miracle in itself.

Meanwhile, Nick was learning about Mia Casa from a very surprising quarter...

'Has anyone seen the new bulletin?' demanded Madge, adding a bulging folder to the stack balanced precariously on Nick's in-tray. He glanced up from his calculations and checked around the room. No, it was just the two of them, but based on Madge's question he'd wondered if there'd been a sudden influx of extraneous bodies that had slipped his attention.

'Anyone?' he queried, po-faced, then leaned down to look under his desk.

'You lost something too?'

'No, just looking to see if anyone was hiding under here,' he replied innocently. 'It sounded to me as if you were addressing a room full of people.'

Madge huffed in irritation and jerked open several drawers fiercely. 'The bulletin – have you seen it?' she repeated. 'I'm sure it was beside the photocopier with the other staff notices yesterday afternoon and *I* haven't moved it. It's not in the restroom either. Everyone knows it's supposed to stay by the photocopier.'

Nick jabbed at his calculator and continued with his report

while Madge bemoaned the state of the world and the habits of the rest of the Padgett and Bicton workforce in particular. 'It's all become very slipshod these days,' she ranted, 'compared with when I first joined the company. In those days people showed proper respect *and* there was loyalty. Now they come and go just as they please. I don't know what it's all coming to.' Madge now attacked the filing cabinet, preparing to give it the third degree, but after an apparently fruitless search and much muttering, she collapsed in her chair and broke into a virgin pack of mint imperials.

'Oh… is this what you were looking for?' Nick asked, feigning innocence, having surreptitiously fished the newsletter out of his briefcase while she was locked in mortal combat with the filing cabinet.

She sprang out of her chair, seized the bulletin and muttered, 'I might have known it!' If looks could kill, Nick would have been in the hands of the crash team. Everything went quiet for a few minutes as Madge sat and leafed through the pages and Nick tried to make an impression on his in-tray. Suddenly, there was an outburst of tutting.

'Who's been defacing the staff bulletin?' Madge demanded, fixing Nick with an accusatory stare.

'What's that you said, Madge? Someone's really rattled your cage this morning, haven't they.'

Madge ignored his remark. 'I said,' she repeated in a long-suffering tone, 'who's been defacing the staff bulletin?'

'What?' he replied in mock horror. 'Has someone drawn a beard and moustache on madam chairman's picture?'

'No, of course not!' she snapped. 'Someone's been scrawling all over the vacancies page. It really isn't necessary.'

'Mea culpa!' chuckled Nick, hands held in surrender.

'Mea what?'

'Mea culpa. It means "I'm to blame". Sorry, Madge, I'm guilty as charged. What's the punishment? Lose five minutes' coffee break for a week or write out two hundred times "Thou shalt not deface the staff bulletin"?' he sniggered, tipping back on his chair – one of the seven deadly sins in Madge's book.

'I'll thank you to stop messing around with staff documents. *I'm* responsible for these, as you well know,' she huffed. 'And while I remember, you can kindly keep your hands off the stationery. I always know when you've been touching it. You're to fill in a chitty like everybody else.' Madge obviously had X-ray vision or some sort of sixth sense.

'Keep my hands off your documents? Certainly, Madge. I wouldn't want to get my hands on your stationery, documents or anything belonging to you. Heaven forbid! It'd be more than my life was worth! Mind you,' he rambled on, 'Denise in human resources is a different matter. I wouldn't mind getting my hands on... um...' he chuckled.

'Disgusting, that's what you are!' sniffed Madge. 'Men are all the same. It's sex, sex, sex all the time!'

'Not quite all the time, Madge,' he protested, his eyes twinkling in amusement. 'We like to have a bit of time to eat, sleep and recharge our batteries ready for the next onslaught. Oh, and of course we have to fit in a few hours of work. Ah, it's a hard life!'

Madge shuddered. 'Nicholas Chesney, you are the limit!' she snapped, leafing through the bulletin in a distracted fashion.

'Ah, but you'd miss me if I weren't here, wouldn't you?'

'Like missing a toothache you mean?'

'Touché!' laughed Nick. 'Come on, Madge, can't we have a truce? So, I'm interested in a couple of jobs at Lydford Cross. What's the problem? I took the bulletin home to show Hattie and as a result I've phoned for application forms.'

Madge calmed down, so Nick filled her in with a few details, telling her *she* was the first to know, but to keep it to herself for the time being. The knowledge of a shared secret worked wonders.

'You'll be putting your house on the market then,' she commented, brightening up considerably.

'Well, not quite yet, but Samways did a valuation yesterday and someone from that Mia Casa place is coming today.'

41

'Mia Casa?' twittered Madge excitedly. 'My friend Sandra's nephew is one of the partners you know.'

'Oh really?'

'Hmm, Greg Allanby's his name – such a nice young man. He's set up the business with some Italian chap he was at school with. It was all Greg's idea, so Sandra told me. Greg used to work for some agent over High Wycombe way – nasty piece of work he was, by all accounts – so then he decided to branch out on his own.' Madge had come over all proud mother hen as if the enterprising Greg was her own lad. 'Sandra wangled me an invitation to the official opening back in September. Ooh, it was such a swish do! Don't remember what Greg's partner is called, but he was very charming and friendly. They have a girl working for them too – very pretty, got legs up to her armpits and wears great dangling earrings that would give you a black eye if you weren't careful, and as for her hemlines, well downright indecent I call them! Still, Greg appointed her, so she must be all right I suppose.'

'It sounds like Greg knows how to run a business,' twinkled Nick.

'He does indeed,' replied Madge, totally missing Nick's innuendo, 'and they're doing very well indeed. Go with Mia Casa and you'll not regret it.'

Madge in defrost mode was quite a refreshing change, reflected Nick. As he opened up a new spreadsheet folder, he wondered which of the acclaimed Mia Casa partners was now taking the particulars of the house. It would be interesting to know how their valuation compared with Samways's and if Greg was all he was supposed to be, they'd have no difficulty selling.

Hattie slammed the Clio into reverse and shot out of the drive, narrowly missing the wheelie bin. There was an ominous crunch. On inspection, one of their neighbour's gnomes had sustained a fatal injury. 'Bilge water!' she cursed, quickly bundling it into her boot and hoping Wilf wasn't peering out of the window. Most of the time he was stuck in front of the telly with the sound whacked up full blast. With any luck, she'd be able to mend and replace the gnome before its absence had been noticed. The four remaining gnomes were still clustered around the pond, their rods poised. Hattie engaged first gear, took a deep breath and set off steadily, cursing Leo for the gnome's temporary demise and her shredded nerves.

It was only twenty minutes to Fliss's house but as soon as she emerged onto the main road, edited highlights of her student days flickered through her mind's eye. She had first met Leo at the fresher's ball in their first term at Birmingham. Tall, dark and very dishy, he was soon attracting plenty of attention and was considered to be sex on legs by most of the girls. Before long, it was rumoured that his dad was the millionaire owner of several vineyards. So now, Leo was rich as well as dishy. Rumours of his exploits became well-documented facts, although some of the racier details, Hattie decided, were pure fabrication from cynically minded females who'd failed to catch his eye. Being in the same tutor group as Leo put her at a distinct advantage, but it wasn't until the final year that their friendship developed into something more intimate. Eventually, they became an item. The rest of Hattie's group were wildly jealous and bitchy remarks about sluttish gold-diggers were bandied about. However, Hattie didn't care; she had the delectable Leo all to herself and she wasn't going to let him go in a hurry. More importantly, Leo told her he loved her, just as she loved him. What more could a girl want?

The end of the final term was in sight and with it, Leo's plans to return to Italy. The TEFL course Hattie had planned for the holidays then promptly lost its appeal. Packing a bikini and joining Leo in a villa on his family's sprawling estate in Tuscany was a much tastier prospect. The trouble was, Leo had been a smidgen on the vague side when it came to travelling arrangements. Moving out of student digs and then having various errands for his father also complicated matters. However, he promised to get in touch and then they'd definitely be heading out to Italy for the summer. Hattie sighed as she remembered the mounting excitement she'd felt at the time. However, life was so different back in 1984 – pre-mobile phones, pre-iPads, pre-anything instant, apart from coffee. The only blackberries around grew on bushes and mobiles were decorations you hung from nursery ceilings. Keeping in touch was tricky. All she knew was that he'd be dossing down on some friend's floor while he got a few things sorted.

On the morning she was quitting her digs, with her summer plans still up in the air, she'd heaved a sack of rubbish to the door, ready for the bin men. Had all his talk of taking her to Italy been deception, she wondered yet again? Was it just a ruse to get her into bed? But on opening the door, she saw a rose with the ribbon-tied label and with it, her doorway to the future.

Cara Hattie,

Meet me by the main departure board at Victoria Station on Friday July 13th at 12 noon. Tickets for the 12.25 to Dover ready and waiting.

Ever yours,

Leo xxx

Friday the thirteenth! Hattie had never been superstitious by nature but even so, that choice of date was unfortunate. Still, he'd bought the tickets and had changed from vague student to highly organised man about town, so why worry?

In the weeks leading up to the end of term, Hattie had secretly dreamed of becoming Signora Marcello, wife of the heir to a flourishing wine business. It had all been mapped out in her mind: the romantic proposal while sipping chilled white wine in their holiday villa; the diamond solitaire ring set in white gold or platinum; a short engagement, wedding in Hampshire, possibly in Winchester Cathedral; the hot and wildly expensive honeymoon before settling in a villa in Montelugia in a secluded corner of the estate; regular shopping trips to Florence to top up her wardrobe with designer outfits; a year later, baby number one followed at regular intervals by babies two and three.

With the arrival of the rose came a dilemma. How much should she tell her parents? Almost at once, she knew a safe alternative was needed. So she decided to tell them she was going to Italy with Lottie, a friend from uni – a friend they knew very little about but who Hattie had described as sober and sensible. Lottie would have a relation, an aunt maybe, who lived near Florence and who had invited her and a friend over for the summer. She was sure this would be the only way she could keep her parents happy about the proposed trip. As it happened, her story was even more convincing than she expected. How she would explain the Leo connection, once he'd proposed to her, was something that still needed some work. Surely her parents wouldn't object when they learned their daughter was marrying a millionaire's son?

With just a week to go, Hattie flew into frenzied preparations. To start with, her underwear and swimming gear needed a radical overhaul. Saggy, greying and otherwise frumpy undies were ditched in favour of the more skimpy and lace-trimmed styles on offer in the Dotty Perkins sale. Naturally, this put a strain on her rapidly shrinking bank account, until her parents quite unexpectedly stumped up some cash 'to help with travel expenses'. Bless them! Although this all happened years ago, Hattie could remember some of the details with amazing clarity.

She slowed down to turn onto the Bledlow Ridge road, catching sight of a train on the embankment, on its way to High Wycombe Station and then eventually to Marylebone. With a jolt, it reminded her of her own journey on that fateful day. The leaden clouds and relentless drizzle could do nothing to spoil her anticipation as she had waved goodbye to her father at Winchester station. Won't they be amazed, she had thought, when I phone them from Italy and tell them I'm engaged. Avidly, she swotted up on Tuscany and some useful Italian phrases in her new student travel guide as the train sped on towards Waterloo. As mile after mile of sodden railway sidings and dripping trees flashed by, Hattie had imagined the warm Italian sunshine that she'd be enjoying in just a few hours. She had a dinky, red, polka-dot bikini that she was dying to wear and had stocked up on every sort of sun cream imaginable. She had pictured walking hand in hand with Leo across flower-strewn hills, exploring fascinating street markets and then relaxing over a few bottles of the local vintage in the evenings and getting hopelessly drunk.

Before long, she arrived on the station concourse at Victoria, full of excited anticipation, with just a quarter of an hour to spare. The whole place was heaving with passengers and so it had taken a while to work out exactly where she was supposed to wait. When at last she spotted the main departure board, she was disappointed that Leo wasn't already there, waving a pair of tickets in the air. She remembered how her heart had pounded as she stood watching the hands of a huge clock moving ever closer to midday. With a minute to go, she extracted the message card and re-read the instructions, wondering if she had muddled the date, time or place. Yet Friday the thirteenth had been so etched on her mind she knew there was no mistake on her part.

Where was he? All sorts of feasible explanations filled her mind: a delayed appointment with his father's contacts, or maybe he'd missed a train, missed a bus, or was stuck on the tube. Or what? Surely he hadn't changed his mind. Surely he hadn't ditched her. By quarter past twelve, Hattie was close to tears. She had paced back and forth, scanning the crowds for that familiar face, but there was no Leo at twenty past or half past or quarter to. The 12.25 to Dover had long since departed. She'd heard it pulling away from the platform, packed with cheerful holidaymakers all bound for the ferry terminal for the afternoon crossing. By one o'clock she was in despair, until it occurred to her that he could have had some horrible accident and might be lying injured or unconscious in hospital. But which one? She'd vaguely remembered him mentioning that his meeting was not far from the station and racked her brain trying to recall what he'd told her.

Unfortunately, she'd not paid much attention at the time. Was it Chelsea or Pimlico?

As Hattie drove up to the top of Bledlow Ridge, she was reminded of the interesting little story Leo had been telling her just half an hour before, about *his* version of that day. Whatever had happened certainly didn't include him ending up in hospital, because her next move was to phone every single one in the area. She'd found a phone box and used all her loose change calling the accident and emergency departments. But no one by the name of Leo Marcello could be traced. Defeated and dismayed, she bought a ticket home and concocted a story for her parents' benefit about Lottie's sudden change of plan, all the while hoping that Leo would get in touch. She'd remembered giving him her parents' address and phone number, so it would just be a matter of time. So, exercising more patience than ever before, she'd decided to sit tight and wait for him to call her. But he never did. It seemed to Hattie that Leo had quite simply vanished into thin air, with no call, letter or postcard from him then or since.

In the days that followed, the first feelings of disappointment and humiliation were closely followed by anger and then misery. Over time, as she gradually put the anguish of that day behind her, she started to rebuild her life. Leo's sudden appearance though now revealed that under her efficient and well-ordered exterior was a seething mass of fury that had never had a chance to escape – until today. As she approached Fliss's driveway, she reminded herself that there was a lot more Leo baggage in her brain's recycle bin that needed to be deleted. The trouble was, there seemed to be no end of it swirling around, making her feel wretched. However, this wasn't the time for self-pity, she reminded herself. Fliss was the one who needed sympathy now.

Hattie and Fliss, short for Felicity, had met at antenatal classes, proudly displaying neat bumps and glowing with the excitement of impending motherhood. Fliss and Mark had successfully started to climb the property ladder, while Hattie and Nick were on the point of outgrowing their period, two-bed terrace in everything but budget. Daughters Laura and Katherine erupted noisily into the world within days of each other and firmly cemented their mothers' friendship. Within two years, Hattie gave birth to Josh while Fliss was still in shock from a miscarriage – the only unplanned catastrophe in her otherwise well-ordered life. However, producing Thomas and then Dominic in quick succession helped her cope with her grief over the lost baby. Then, with a great sense of achievement, she promptly ditched her shapeless maternity gear to emerge the trend-setting yummy mummy. A house move or two later, the two friends were now experiencing the demands of burgeoning manhood in the guise of spotty adolescents. Their daughters, to their great relief, had embarked upon careers and no longer needed the frequent cash injections upon which their sons relied. Those challenges for Fliss, however, had now been trumped by something of a far more sinister nature.

'Oh, Fliss,' sighed Hattie sadly, giving her a hug. She hadn't seen Fliss as despondent since the last pair of Jimmy Choo, size 5, scarlet pumps had been snatched from under her nose in a Harvey Nics' sale. A suspicion of smudged mascara showed the morning's news had already taken its toll on her usually immaculate appearance. Fliss, she noticed, had yet another new hairstyle, all black, spiky and elfin-like with burgundy-reddish tips.

'Coffee?' Fliss suggested, after releasing herself from Hattie's reassuring hug.

'Absolutely. Make it strong and black,' Hattie said, silently adding, 'looks like we *both* need it.'

Fliss filled in the details of her father's early phone call as the kettle boiled. Meanwhile, Hattie carried out a fruitless search for something more appetising than slimmers' wholewheat crackers or arrowroot biscuits.

'Mum's only just admitted that she knew something was wrong. The trouble was, she was too scared to go to the doctor,' explained Fliss. 'But then she started losing blood.' She paused to fill the cafetière while Hattie predicted where all this was leading.

'The tests came back positive. The cancer's quite advanced.' Fliss's shoulders started to shake uncontrollably as she dissolved into tears. 'Oh, if only she'd done something about it sooner.'

'Come and sit down, Fliss,' said Hattie, passing her a handful of tissues. 'I'll see to the coffee.'

'I feel so helpless,' sobbed Fliss, dabbing at her eyes and then giving her nose a good blow. 'They're down there in Cornwall and we're up here in Bledlow and... Oh, stupid, stupid woman!' She angrily beat her fists on the sofa.

'Don't be too hard on her, Fliss,' soothed Hattie, shocked by her outburst.

'No, not *her*,' wailed Fliss. '*I'm* the stupid woman and a poor apology for a daughter as well. I should have made more time to visit and keep an eye on them, but it's too easy to make excuses.' She paused to gulp down some coffee then mopped her panda eyes. It was at moments like this, pondered Hattie, that a couple of milk chocolate digestives would go down a treat. She eyed the arrowroot morsels with distaste and wondered briefly if an offer to rustle up a plate of toast and jam might be appreciated.

'And now Mark's about to leave for some trade fair in Germany,' Fliss continued, 'and the boys are up to their eyes in coursework revision and everything.'

Hattie was just about managing to keep up with her friend's line of thought. 'Look, Fliss,' she suggested with a sympathetic smile, 'if you want to nip down to St Austell for a few days, the boys can come and stay with us. They can bunk down in Laura's old room. I know Josh would be pleased to have the company.'

Fliss's look of appreciation was briefly replaced by one of apprehension as she considered the threat to her sons' grades posed by the proximity of Joshua Chesney. It was a win-some, lose-some situation.

'Thanks Hat,' she sighed gratefully, realising that the boys' travelling arrangements to school would be much simpler from the

Chesney home. 'We'll sort out the timing later and I'll get in touch.'

Hattie bit into a biscuit thoughtfully. So far, her own and Nick's parents were amazingly fit for their age, but the unwelcome onset of serious illness could just as easily affect them. The decision to move south now made even more sense. The trouble was, exciting though the prospect of moving might be, there was also the stark reality of leaving behind close friends like Fliss, who needed friends more than ever now. Hattie started to feel guilty, realising she'd have to tell her what was being planned. Little did she realise, however, that her guilt was obvious and Fliss's finely tuned radar had already detected that something was amiss.

'What's up, Hat? You're very pale. Something's wrong, I can tell. I was so churned up with Mum's news, I hadn't even thought about you. I mean, you just dropped everything and came over, even though you were obviously busy with something else. Did whoever it was mind you rushing off?'

'Oh… er… no, it was just a JW,' Hattie flustered. She realised with a sinking heart that she'd omitted to invent a cover story.

'What, you mean you actually invited a Jehovah's Witness into your home?' Fliss was aghast. 'That was brave of you, or did they shove a foot in the door? Personally, I don't give them the time of day. They get short shrift from me I can tell you.'

'So you've said before.'

'Anyway,' asserted Fliss, 'I thought JWs only went out in twos, you know, like in the proverbial ark. How on earth did you manage to pick up a stray one?'

Hattie gulped in panic. The gaps in her story were rapidly becoming a huge black hole.

'No, that was yesterday… and of course there were two of them. No, it was a double-glazing salesman.' She hoped her attempt at temporary memory loss would be convincing.

'Oh, I see.'

But Fliss wasn't convinced, especially as Hattie's ghostly pallor had now been replaced by a crimson blush.

'Actually, Fliss, there's something I ought to tell you,' she admitted awkwardly. Deserting her friend seemed tantamount to betrayal. Eagle-eyed Fliss studied Hattie's face intently, wondering what sort of development could produce such a ruddy glow. At moments like this, her wicked sense of humour frequently came into its own.

'It's not a secret lover, is it?' she joked, waiting to see Hattie collapse into helpless giggles. But she didn't. In fact, as Fliss waited, she sensed something in Hattie's expression that filled her with dismay. Surely, clean-living, faithful Hattie wasn't straying into an illicit liaison? Or perhaps it was Nick?

Hattie froze; in an instant, her little speech about the house move deserted her and she was back in her kitchen doing several rounds with Leo. His handsome features seemed to be taking over her consciousness. Could it be, she wondered, that some of the deep desire of her youth had not trickled away completely, but had simply been jolted out of dormancy? In fact, had the fury she'd felt been but a whisker away from wild, unbridled passion? This stark possibility came as quite a shock, but one she had no intention of sharing. Meanwhile, she had to deliver some unwelcome news.

'Secret lover? No, of course not,' she insisted, managing a half-hearted smile. If she'd managed a little chuckle, her reply would have been more convincing, but her capacity for laughter currently seemed to be running on empty. 'Actually, we're thinking of moving away.'

'Oh, I see.' Fliss, however, was still puzzled by the varying hues that had passed across her friend's face. 'So how did this happen? Does Nick have a new job? Has he been head-hunted?' If she had to be honest, Fliss doubted if someone like Nick Chesney was an obvious target for head-hunters.

'Well, nothing like that,' Hattie explained, 'but he's applying for a couple of posts at Lydford Cross.'

'Lydford Cross?' repeated Fliss. 'Where on earth's Lydford Cross?'

'Hampshire. Sort of between Winchester and Southampton.'

'But why there?' Maybe if Hattie had mentioned somewhere smart and aspiring, Fliss would have been more impressed.

'Why not?' replied Hattie airily, relieved that the swirling cesspool of emotions in her brain had been successfully reduced to a mild and containable simmer. 'It's not far from Nick's parents. They're becoming more dependent on help from the rest of the family, you see.'

'Ah, I understand,' Fliss said sympathetically, assessing the geographical implications of her own situation.

'Then there's Mum and Dad down on the coast. And of course my brother and his tribe down in Dorchester, who we scarcely see. The move will help us keep in touch.' As Hattie trotted out her watertight reasons, she reminded herself that absolutely no mention of slanging matches with Angus Neill should be revealed. Fliss would immediately sniff out the real reason and tell her how stupid she'd been to embark on dramatic productions when any sane person was busily writing Christmas cards and planning their festive partywear. Meanwhile, Fliss poured the last of the coffee into their mugs and struggled to connect the planned house sale with a visit from a double-glazing salesman.

'So, why are you bothering about new double-glazing?'

'Double-glazing?' echoed Hattie, completely forgetting her cover story.

'Yes, you said you'd had someone call this morning.'

'Oh, well, it was a mistake. He turned up at the wrong house when the estate agent arrived.'

'And?'

'I had to get rid of him as well.'

'Goodness, you had quite a gathering then? I'm sorry my timing wasn't very helpful. So, you've got as far as appointing an agent then? What about the one you had to get rid of?'

'Not at all suitable,' replied Hattie dismissively.

'You mean too expensive? Too pushy?' suggested Fliss,

wondering how an estate agent could be unsuitable. It seemed an odd reason.

'Definitely,' said Hattie abruptly, signalling an end to the estate agent and double-glazing salesman subject. 'Anyway, we've had a really encouraging valuation from Samways and Partners, so I expect we'll be instructing *them* when the time comes. Then, when we've moved to our dream cottage, complete with veg patch, chicken run and room for special guests like you and Mark, you'll have to come and stay.'

'And Josh?' asked Fliss. 'What will you be doing with him?'

'Not sure yet, but basically it'll come down to the lure of independent living over Mum's cooking. He'll have to decide which is more important.'

'So what's your secret plan to help him with his decision?' Fliss's frequently aired goal was for empty nest status at the earliest possible date.

'Soft pedal on the comfort food in favour of plenty of healthy rabbit fodder,' asserted Hattie, 'and ignore the mutinous mutters around the dinner table.'

'My sentiments entirely. Although, if my family had to endure my culinary skills, without the help of M&S microwaveable ready meals, they'd be stashing away their apartment deposits or suing for divorce. It's a good thing I have Myscha to wield the vac occasionally, or they'd be knee-deep in dust balls,' she giggled, back to her usual good humour.

As Hattie drove home later, she congratulated herself for her quick thinking. Mentioning a Jehovah's Witness in the singular, however, was a serious slip. Never, in all her years, had a solitary JW turned up at her door, and they certainly never used sneaky tactics to gain entrance. In the state that Fliss was in, though, details about her own domestic trivia were of very little importance. She rehearsed her version of the morning for Nick. Recalling his sarcasm over Mia Casa, she was sure he wouldn't be bothered about their involvement, or rather lack of it.

Fliss, however, was left with an uneasy feeling about her friend.

In fact, she was convinced that there was something Hattie wasn't telling her and she would have wagered her dress allowance that it wasn't just about the house move. Maybe she had a thing going with the double-glazing salesman or even the Jehovah's Witness. No, she decided, that really was too far-fetched for words.

'That traffic!' groaned Nick, slamming the door shut. 'It gets worse every day. If it's not smashed bollards, it's road repairs or the Gas Board digging up half the road and then waiting a week before deciding what to do next. I tell you, Hat, when we're looking for our next home, I'm going to check the travelling *very* carefully.' He dumped his briefcase and then Hattie heard the TV emitting sounds of cheering crowds. No matter what time of day or night, there seemed to be a sporting fixture of some sort that had first call on Nick's attention, to the exclusion of anything resembling DIY or gardening. Spotting him with a tool of any description was indeed a red-letter day in the Chesney household. Witnessing him using it was even rarer.

Half an hour passed while Hattie chopped, mixed, stirred, boiled and simmered while mentally rehearsing her account of the day's events.

'You'll not believe it,' chuckled Nick, now that the need to refuel had overcome the hypnotic lure of the sporting channels, 'Madge has been smitten by a toy-boy estate agent.'

Every word that preceded Nick's last two completely bypassed Hattie's brain. The words 'estate agent' triggered a sinking effect in her stomach, a quickened pulse rate and a deep, pink flush to the cheeks. In the circumstances, it was proving impossible to join in with Nick's light-hearted banter, so she turned her attention to the bubbling stew pan. Nick hadn't noticed and continued his tale of office intrigue.

'You should have seen her simpering over him. It was Greg this and Greg that and I could tell she was smitten, because she went very pink – a bit like you as a matter of fact.'

'That's just the cooking, Nick,' Hattie replied matter-of-factly, stirring vigorously and wondering what an estate agent was doing in Nick's office.

'Anyway,' continued Nick, with a chuckle, 'it seems Greg heads up that new agency in town – you know, the one you had booked for this morning. She kept on about him, singing his praises and going all coy and giggly. It turns out her bosom pal Sandra is Greg's aunt. I never thought I'd ever see Madge getting so worked up about a mere bloke.'

'Well I never,' was all that Hattie could manage, while feigning some concern for the state of the dumplings. Her addled brain had at least managed to establish now that the office hadn't been inundated by extraneous estate agents.

'So, old girl,' Nick enquired, planting a delicate kiss on her cheek, 'how did old Greg shape up with the valuation?'

'It wasn't him... I mean, he didn't come... I mean, whoever was supposed to come, didn't.' She was intending her reply to sound dismissive with just a touch of irritation.

'Sorry, Hat, I missed some of that.'

'Nobody came!' she snapped sourly.

'Really? So, did you call and give them an earful about wasting your time?'

'Well, no. As a matter of fact, Fliss phoned. She'd just had some awful news about her mum, so I went over to see her. She was in such a state.'

'Poor Fliss. Not the big C?'

'Yeah, I think the whole situation's much worse with her parents being so far away.'

'Ah yes, which makes moving closer to my folks a very sensible decision.' He mooched around the kitchen as he spoke, ignoring the pile on the drainer awaiting its turn in the dishwasher, and cogitated on Hattie's news. 'Of course, you could have dashed off before poor old Greg had a chance to get here. Surely, Fliss wouldn't have minded if you'd told her you were expecting someone.'

'No, I didn't dash off before... er... I know I didn't!' she flustered, wondering if any of this was making sense. She was finding the art of lying more difficult that she'd thought.

'Are you sure, Hat?'

Hattie threw her oven mitt down in frustration, bopping the sleeping Jezebel on the nose.

'Look, Nick, I left here well after ten. In fact, more like half past. The appointment was for ten. End of story!'

'Okay, Okay, Hat! No need for a strop! Well, well, poor old Greg's not such a whizz-kid after all.'

'Actually, Nick,' she remarked determinedly, 'we don't need another agent. I'm sure Samways know the market well enough. I'd be more than happy to leave it in the safe hands of biscuit-loving Brian.'

'Okay, if you think so.' Nick couldn't help feeling disappointed. During the day, he'd imagined future chats with Madge about how her idol was faring in the house-selling stakes. It would have certainly made a change from sniping over the stationery.

As Hattie dolloped out the stew, she assessed her fibbing perform-ance and awarded it a B-minus.

'I told Fliss we'd have her boys so she can visit her mum.'

'That's big-hearted of you,' replied Nick.

'Cool,' grunted Josh.

'How soon are they coming?'

'Well, probably early next week,' Hattie told him. 'It all depends on the timing of Mark's flight to Munich. He could drop Fliss at Reading to catch the train and then carry on to Heathrow. Fliss isn't keen about driving all the way down to St Austell. I can easily go and meet her when she comes back. As for the boys, they can pack an overnight bag, take it to school with them and then come straight here by bus. I think Mark's due to be away a week.'

'The Tarrier boys on a bus?' hooted Nick. 'Well, that'll be a novelty. How will they cope without their mum's taxi service? I hope they won't expect the same from us. Ah well, it's good to help out though. I'm sure they've done plenty for us over the years – Fliss especially.'

'Great stew, Mum,' volunteered Josh, as he tucked in greedily.

'Hmm!' agreed Nick. 'Great dumplings too.' He winked mischievously. Pleasant as the compliments were, Hattie realised she'd not made a suitable choice of menu if she was aiming to push Josh towards independence. Big mistake!

While they were drinking coffee Hattie remembered the close encounter with Wilf's gnome, which still languished in her boot, forgotten, abandoned and in need of some quick surgery.

'Oh Nick,' she gasped guiltily, 'I've got a terrible confession.'

'Not put your red tracksuit in the wash and turned my Y-fronts pink again have you?'

'What do you mean *again?*' she countered frostily.

'Just recalling a particularly embarrassing moment at the gym after one of your lapses of washday concentration, that's all.'

Hattie sniffed. What did he want? A working wife, sex kitten *and* domestic goddess all rolled into one? She could manage the first, but was a bit iffy when it came to the other two.

'So, what have you been up to? As a matter of fact,' he admitted, 'I thought you seemed a bit distracted earlier on.'

'It's one of Wilf's gnomes.'

'Not sold it on eBay have you?'

'Nick,' she replied, glaring, 'be serious... please!'

'I am. You can get loads of cash for those little beauties,' he quipped.

Hattie ignored his frivolity. 'I've knocked off its head. It's hidden in the boot at the moment, but I need to mend it before Wilf notices.'

'Hang on, Hat. How did you manage that? Did you go out and attack it with a broom? Was it making lewd remarks? I've always thought those gnomes had lecherous tendencies – judging by their expressions,' he sniggered.

'Oh stop it!' she snapped. 'No, of course I didn't. I sort of reversed into it.'

'Blimey, Hat, you must have been all over the place. I'm surprised you didn't clock the wheelie bin.'

Hattie glared mutinously in Nick's direction, but he was still chuckling to himself.

'Well, I bet he deserved it. Losing his head I mean,' he continued. 'A decapitated gnome, eh? Actually, if it's that ugly one with the pipe, I don't blame you.'

'It's not funny, Nick. I need to mend it and I need your help.'

'Don't look at me, Hat. You know I've got two left thumbs when it comes to DIY, but I can point you in the right direction for the wherewithal.'

'Really? That's a surprise.'

'Ooh! We *are* feisty today, aren't we, old girl! Utility room, second drawer down. And you can do your own dirty work. I'm off to do some urgent online investigation.'

'Oh yeah,' muttered Hattie sarcastically. 'More football stuff I suppose.'

However, Nick was well out of earshot, leaving Hattie to carry out emergency surgery. The paint was chipped, but a dab of nail varnish seemed to do the trick. Meanwhile, Nick was determined to find out about Mia Casa. He'd been reflecting on what Madge had told him and was puzzled about the missed appointment. Surely, a new company would be keen to take every opportunity offered, especially just into the new year when the housing market was still waiting to kick into action. It didn't seem to make sense. Or maybe they were concentrating on the top end of the market and properties like theirs weren't good enough. He hoped not. Of course, it could be that the company wasn't half as good as Madge implied. They could be a pair of cocky amateurs with limited business skills and sloppy organisation. Well, he decided, he was going to find out, even if Hattie wasn't prepared to give them a second chance. She could be very impatient at times.

He typed in Mia Casa and quickly navigated to the website, which answered all his niggles most satisfactorily. It turned out that Greg was a fully qualified estate agent whereas his partner had a business degree. So far, so good. The third member of staff was Rebecca Vaudin, who was studying for her estate agency qualification. And very attractive she was too, if they hadn't airbrushed the picture. The two blokes looked, to Nick's eyes, quite presentable. Clicking back to the home page, he noted the address and decided he'd go and find out for himself exactly what had happened. Nick had plenty of respect for anyone setting up a new company when the world's money markets were in turmoil. Besides which, he'd come across Brian Samways in the past and didn't rate him highly. In fact, he was about as dynamic as cold rice pudding. Perhaps it would be good to let Mia Casa handle the sale after all. Hattie would be proud of him, he was sure.

3

'Good afternoon. Can I help you?' the young woman asked brightly. Rebecca Vaudin, with piercing blue eyes, ash blonde curls and bold clusters of assorted beads hanging from her ear lobes, was even more striking in the flesh. She was probably also very high maintenance.

'Is it possible to see Mr Allanby?' Nick enquired, enjoying – in his opinion – the sight of Mia Casa's best asset. Then, spotting the huge diamond that sparkled from her left hand, he realised that some other lucky bloke had already staked his claim. She was perfect eye-candy.

'No, I'm sorry. Mr Allanby's busy with a viewing at the moment. Would you like to see Signor Marcello instead?'

'Yes, if that's possible.' It was then that Nick noticed the interview area at the far end of the office, where Signor Marcello was seated, busy with paperwork. As Nick approached, he got up from his desk, smiling warmly.

'Do take a seat... Mr... er?' Leo hesitated.

'Chesney. Nick Chesney,' he answered, reaching into his inside pocket for his diary and thereby missing the alarmed expression that flitted across Leo's face. Meeting Hattie's husband so soon felt about as welcome as having teeth pulled. By the time Nick looked up, Leo had regained his former composure.

'I decided to come in, rather than phone. I wanted to sort things out,' began Nick, matter-of-factly. Leo experienced a sudden sinking in the pit of his stomach. 'It's to do with yesterday's missed appointment. I was hoping to schedule a new time?'

'Missed appointment?' Leo was wondering exactly what Hattie had told her husband. As of yesterday, she'd made it quite clear she wanted no further dealings with Mia Casa.

'Yes, missed appointment,' replied Nick, seeing the confusion on Leo's face and then concluding that maybe it *was* Greg who was supposed to have called. By this time, Rebecca had moved up to the row of filing cabinets adjacent to the interview area. She was busily rooting around for house details and as she did so, wafts of her perfume reached Nick's appreciative nostrils.

'My wife, Mrs Chesney,' he explained in a patient tone, 'phoned earlier this week to arrange a valuation for ten yesterday morning. I guess Mr Allanby must have been down to do it but —'

'Oh no,' interrupted Rebecca, 'I'm sure it wasn't Mr Allanby's appointment.'

'So who *was* supposed to come? You see, my wife had a distress call from a girlfriend and had to rush off to help. She said that, up to then, nobody had called. It was well after ten when she left the house.'

Leo began to think quickly. Perhaps he should admit there'd been a mix-up and keep up Hattie's version of the morning. But no, that wouldn't work, he realised. Rebecca, the epitome of efficiency, would have the evidence in the office diary that he'd been booked to carry out the Chesney valuation. He was desperate to see Hattie again so he could finish his explanation and clear the air. Of course, that was only possible if he could engineer some time alone with her. However, it was not hard to imagine how she might react if he turned up at her door again, even at the invitation of her husband.

'Well, yes I *did* try to call,' explained Leo carefully, hoping his excuse would be convincing enough, 'but your wife must have left by then.'

'But didn't you think to leave a card that might have jogged her memory when she returned?' Nick was beginning to have doubts about the man. He either seemed to be in some other world or was suffering from something: a hangover? Migraine? Flu?

'Er… I may have done. Now you want another appointment, you say?' replied Leo, quickly changing the subject. He reached for his desk diary and turned to the following day's page, which was only sparsely filled in. He peered at it hopefully as if wishing for a clutch of appointments to appear. Trade was evidently not too brisk, Nick noted with interest, which made the sloppy time-keeping of the previous day even more surprising.

'But of course, Mr Allanby could possibly do the valuation if you'd prefer,' Leo added.

'Mr Allanby's booked all morning and then he's got a personal appointment for most of the afternoon.' This was Rebecca, bright as a button, still battling with the filing cabinets, but with every appointment efficiently logged in her brain, as well as in her diary.

Nick gazed at Leo, concluding that the poor chap was definitely having a bad day or was dead wood as far as the business was concerned. If this was how he usually was with clients, it was a wonder they did much business at all. Greg, on the other hand, must be absolute dynamite, unless everything that Madge had passed on from Sandra was a gross exaggeration. If he were to be perfectly frank, he might have admitted that there was an ulterior motive in his pursuit of what might have been a comparatively minor mix-up. Secretly, with all the flack he'd had from Madge over the past year, he was hoping to prove that Mia Casa was not all it was cracked up to be and watch her deflate.

'So, shall we say mid-morning?' he suggested, seeing the only other morning entry was for eleven forty-five.

'Er… ten thirty?' faltered Leo, feeling hot under his pristine, white collar at the thought of Hattie's reaction. Yet, with her husband close at hand, she'd hardly have a chance to scratch his eyes out. 'Will that suit you?'

'Absolutely fine, thank you,' Nick agreed, checking his diary. 'Yes, as far as I know it'll be okay with both of us.'

Leo made a diary entry and managed a wintry smile.

'Do you have a card so we can call you if there are any problems with the time?' Nick asked as casually as possible. Was he imagining it, or was the man actually reluctant to do business?

'Of course.' Leo passed a card across the desk, closed his diary and then rose to shake hands. By some effort of self-discipline, Leo regained his composure and seemed to grow in stature as he escorted Nick to the door. Rebecca, now back at her desk, glanced up and gave her sunniest smile and just the suspicion of a wink.

'Right, well, see you again,' said Nick with a twinkle in his eye, directing his remark towards her. It was good to know that he could still attract the attention of girls as young as Miss Vaudin.

'Till tomorrow then,' Leo murmured, opening the door. As Nick left, he paused briefly on the pavement to check the properties displayed in the window. He was pleased to see there were plenty of three-bed semis featured in their range.

Back at his desk later on, in a lull between phone calls and various interruptions, Nick was aware of Madge returning to her desk after, he assumed, a comfort break. Because he'd spent most of the day with the company auditor and had taken his lunch at a different time, he'd hardly exchanged a dozen words with her all day. He couldn't decide whose company was least nauseating: the geriatric auditor or busybody Madge. It was a close call.

'Did Greg give you a good valuation yesterday?' she enquired, remembering their conversation.

'Well no, actually.'

'You mean you think you're worth more?' she snapped back, her hackles rising. 'I'm sure Greg knows better than you what properties are worth. He's been in the business long enough you know.'

'No, Madge. It's not that,' Nick insisted. 'Nobody called. I went down there in my lunch break to sort it out.'

'Oh,' she replied, slightly mortified. 'Well, Greg's not the sort of chap to ignore his clients. He's very conscientious you know.'

'Actually, Madge, it was his partner who was supposed to call.'

'Oooh, the handsome signor!' trilled Madge, with a sigh.

'And he made a right hash of it. In fact, it seems he was either very late or missed the appointment completely and didn't have the guts to admit it.'

'Well, I'm sure there's a perfectly reasonable explanation,' she asserted with a sniff, ready to uphold the good name of Mia Casa.

'Hmm,' he agreed, 'one answer could be that Hattie rushed off to see her friend and completely forgot the appointment.'

'Bad manners, I call that. Fancy going off without a by your leave when someone's taking the trouble to come.'

'Well, Hattie insists she didn't leave the house until half an hour after the man was due. Mind you, she was in a bit of a state about her friend. She even managed to mow down one of the neighbour's gnomes.'

Madge had come to her own conclusion on the matter. That Mrs Chesney had struck her as a bit on the impulsive side when they'd met at the Padgett and Bicton Christmas do. She'd been knocking back the wine and making a right exhibition of herself on the dance floor. And a teacher too!

'So is Greg going to do the valuation for you after all?'

'No, we've got that Marcello chap booked for ten thirty tomorrow morning. Who knows, Madge; if all goes to plan, it might not be long before you have the office all to yourself.'

The look of smug triumph on her face, as she bustled over to the photocopier, was certainly a rare sight and one that Nick hoped he'd not have to endure much longer.

Reviewing the more interesting moments of the day on the drive home through the rush hour, Nick felt more perky than usual. Cheeky Miss Vaudin – or, as Stan Burke in sales would say, that 'tasty bit of skirt' – had certainly put a spring in his step. He was also preening himself about re-booking the Mia Casa valuation. Hat had often moaned about his lack of get up and go, so he reckoned that the day's bit of action should certainly impress her.

For Hattie, Friday was her least favourite day – well, not the whole day. The Year 5 classes after lunch were fine. The Year 4s were the problem, with more than the average quota of naughty boys, whom she taught either side of morning break. She had a sneaky feeling that Sonia Rowse had deliberately swapped the timetable around so she'd have to take the PE lesson – not exactly a bundle of fun for any supply teacher on a cold Friday morning in January. On that particular Friday, bats and skipping ropes became weapons in the hands of the more unruly children, and a record number of balls ended up on the terrapin hut roofs, much to Hattie's despair. Throughout the lesson, her whistle was put to good use as she sounded shrill blasts in a desperate attempt to keep the children in order. Then caretaker Kenny, who loathed the junior of the species, was frequently summoned to retrieve the stray missiles with his long-handled broom. Kenny, with an evil glint in his eye, was a force to be reckoned with and even had Hattie quaking in her shoes. Why he didn't get a nice, quiet, child-free job as a road sweeper was beyond her and obviously one of life's mysteries. It may have been something to do with the job title being changed to site manager, a name that obviously appealed to Kenny's inflated ego. The bell that signalled the end of the morning session couldn't come soon enough. Consequently, it was with great relief that she was able to slope off to the comfort of the staffroom for her well-earned lunch break.

'That Jacob Pocock!' she moaned to Trina, as they munched their sandwiches. 'I'll swing for him one day, I really will!'

'Jacob Pocock – say no more,' said Trina gloomily. 'Some of the worst moments of his time in Year 2 are forever etched on my memory in full Technicolor and I swear the boys' toilets down there will never be the same again. He and his gang used to pee up the walls as if there was a target painted there, visible only to little boys of six and seven. It drove Kenny crazy. He kept threatening to resign until old Haggis-bag hauled the parents in and regaled them about their son's toilet activities.'

Hattie listened in fascinated horror, realising that she'd been fortunate not to have encountered Master Pocock as a Year 2.

'Pocock Senior is to blame, if you ask me,' confided Trina. 'I've seen him – all nose studs and tattoos – throwing his weight around at the school gate. It wouldn't surprise me if he'd instigated the target practice himself.' She paused to tip sweet Thai chilli crisps into her palm. 'Anyway, he and Jacob's mum forked out for a job lot of disinfectant and said they'd stop his pocket money for a month to pay for it.'

'And did they?'

'Seen any flying pigs in the past two years?'

'Not so you'd notice,' replied Hattie, chuckling.

'A clip round the ear is probably more like it.'

'After this morning's debacle, I think I'll be keeping well away from Kenny,' vowed Hattie. '4R and outside PE are not my top choice for a trouble-free Friday morning.'

'Ball on the roof you mean?' ventured Trina.

'In the plural, I'm afraid. I wondered if *I* was going to get the business end of his broom when the third one went up. He'll be mighty relieved when that boy moves on to–'

'A secure institution, you mean?' joked Trina cynically, having survived the trauma of her own son's brush with the law.

'The trouble is,' put in Sally, who'd just joined them, 'Jacob's here for another two years. I bet some of the Year 5 and 6 staff are already turning grey at the thought, except Tony of course. If he and Mr P met in a dark alley after a few beers, I'm not sure who'd come off worse.'

'I can't imagine Sophie being too worried,' said Hattie. 'She's not easily fazed.'

'Don't be sure,' remarked Dave wryly. 'He'll have moved on to pinching bottoms by then if he takes after his dad.'

'Oh well, with luck I won't have to put up with him much

longer,' announced Hattie with a grin. This seemed the moment to announce her plans.

'How's that then? Not won the lottery have you?' Sally ventured.

'I wouldn't have bothered coming in this morning if I had.'

'What, not even to crow about it and bring boxes of cream cakes for your cash-strapped colleagues?' asked Trina. 'Remember how I bailed you out when those two little madams had their sparring match?'

'Okay, Trina, I owe you one,' promised Hattie. 'Anyway, I'd better warn you now that we're planning to move to Hampshire.'

'Really? So I'll be losing my favourite supply teacher will I?' sighed Sally.

'Well, not quite yet,' explained Hattie. 'Nick's applying for a couple of jobs near Romsey but we'll only put our house on the market if he's successful. I've got high hopes for him.' How she was managing to put on her bright exterior, she didn't know. There was no certainty that Nick would even get shortlisted, let alone an interview.

Warm-hearted Norma from Early Years sank heavily on one of the last available chairs and took a long swig from her mug. She'd long ago lost the battle over calorie control and had embraced her middle-age spread with resignation. After *her* morning, a session with 4R would have been like a stroll in the park.

'Sorry to say, folks, but there's a whole lot worse to come. You try having Lorretta Bailey in your class,' she warned them.

'But I thought your little lot were really sweet,' put in Hattie, making a mental note to try and avoid that particular class from now on.

'Little?' repeated Norma. 'Since when has twenty-two been a little class? There's ten more due in the summer intake too.' She pulled the wrapper from a chocolate bar and crunched content-edly, as her colleagues waited for more of the Lorretta Bailey saga.

'Last term was okay,' agreed Norma at last, 'like a time bomb's harmless enough to start with. Lorretta was a quiet little mite when she first started – butter wouldn't melt in her mouth and all that. Fooled me. Fooled Val as well.'

Sally exchanged horrified glances with Trina. Both knew that Val was one of the most experienced teaching assistants in the school. If she could be caught off guard they knew they'd be in for a tough time when it was their turn.

'Since Christmas, the child has found her feet and has a penchant for scissors – bless her! A proper little kleptomaniac she is too. When Lorretta's on the loose with scissors, nothing's safe, I can tell you – registers, clothes, books… even hair!' Norma wasn't holding back on the grisly details.

'Got a career in hairdressing in mind has she?' quipped Trina.

'Who knows?' sighed Norma, rolling her eyes. 'I found three pairs in her tray this morning and a whole wodge of hair – not hers either.' Norma swallowed the rest of her coffee as several more staff members awaited the next instalment with morbid interest.

'You can't take your eye off her for a second, and in a class of twenty-two five-year-olds that's no mean feat. Don't quote me girls,' she murmured confidentially, leaning towards Hattie and company, 'but in a weak moment yesterday I even considered handcuffs, until I remembered my pension.'

'You must have been desperate,' gasped Sally with a giggle.

'I lost sight of her when we had a sandpit emergency – an everyday occurrence in my neck of the woods as it happens – and I was busy sweeping up sand while Val was trying to clean up a couple of boys who'd been pouring it down each other's necks. When I caught up with Miss Bailey, she was under my desk with my bag open, having snipped her way through a twenty-pound note, several pages of my diary and two whole books of first-class stamps. I just managed to grab the scissors from her as she was making a start on my passport.'

On hearing this cheery news, Dave turned strangely pale, grabbed the latest *Times Educational Supplement* and started scouring the jobs section.

'Poor you,' Hattie sympathised. 'I expect it's just attention-seeking.'

Hattie's afternoon passed without incident. The Year 5s were a particularly keen and compliant bunch, so her well-practised crowd-control skills were not needed on that occasion. Golden Time, with its choice of activities, was their favourite time of the week and a small army of mums had been drafted in to help with cupcakes, stencilling and chess. By the time the end of afternoon bell rang, Hattie's confidence had returned. Should she do her weekly supermarket shop on the way home rather than let it eat into her weekend? Crowds of frazzled mums pushing laden trolleys, with screaming tots in tow, was not really her choice of company for a late Friday afternoon. However, when you're down to half a bag of frozen peas and a loaf of sliced white in the freezer, you really don't have an option. Even Delia Smith would be hard-pressed to come up with something nutritious and satisfying with *those* ingredients.

By the time Nick arrived home, the shopping had been packed away and their usual Friday supper of pizza and chips was turning golden brown in the oven – not quite up to Delia's standard, but Nick had never complained. Some mixed leaves with a drizzle of dressing were ready in a stripy salad bowl and some cheap Hungarian white was chilling in the fridge. Hattie was ready for the weekend.

'How's my gorgeous wife after a day with the little terrors?' Nick asked, giving her a hug and nuzzling her cheek with his five o'clock shadow.

'Well, I survived, but no thanks to some of the rougher elements of 4R.'

'But, Hat, they're only eight or nine aren't they?'

'More like nine going on nineteen as far as I'm concerned. *You* try it; you wouldn't last five minutes with some of them.'

'Ah, well, it's not a teaching job I'm after. See what I've brought home!' He flourished the handful of forms that had arrived that morning. 'I'll be filling in these tonight, so you won't need to worry about your streetwise Year 4s for much longer.'

'Here's hoping,' agreed Hattie.

'Okay, so have you got anything in your diary for tomorrow morning, my sweet?' he asked brightly, ready to amaze her with his alpha-male action. He could tell she had been impressed by the way he'd suggested the weekend away, so this would show her that Nick Chesney could be spontaneous if he wanted.

'Nope.' She extracted the pizza and then went in search of her kitchen scissors.

'Sure about that, are you?' he prodded. 'No church flowers, pulpit dusting or door-to-door jumble collecting with Hilda Makepeace?'

Hattie giggled, intrigued that Nick was so concerned about her Saturday morning plans. 'Definitely not. Why do you need to know?' she asked, starting to snip the pizza into neat wedges. Nick's air of mystery had started to raise her hopes.

'Ah, well, as it happens I've got something organised.'

Was he planning to treat her to coffee at the newly refurbished garden centre on the edge of the village? It was rumoured to sell the best chocolate muffins for miles around. Or maybe his perennial, half-hearted, new year fitness resolution was actually going to happen this time and he was going to suggest a session in the gym and pool at the leisure centre? If so, maybe the leisure centre first and then the coffee and muffins, so she wouldn't feel so guilty about the calories.

'Well, as long as it's a change from boring old housework, I'm up for anything,' she told him brightly.

'Actually, some housework *is* involved, but only a little, I promise. In fact, I'll lend you a hand.'

'Sorry, I think I missed that,' she giggled. Nick and Josh tended to suffer from the same allergy to cleaning. However, the coffee/muffin/swim treat was vanishing fast.

'You'll be very impressed, Hat. Well, I know you were upset for Fliss yesterday and things didn't work out in the morning and everything, so I went to Mia Casa in my lunch break and fixed up a valuation for tomorrow morning.'

'What?' she gasped. A scattering of chips landed at her feet. 'Oh fish-hooks!' she exclaimed irritably and went to retrieve them. 'So, Madge's toy boy is paying us a visit is he?' Her voice was suddenly out of control. It had sounded more like a nervous squeak and her stomach had started to churn. Please, God, she prayed silently, don't let it be Leo. I'll do anything if you'll make it anyone but Leo. I'll put a fiver in the collection on Sunday, I'll go on the cleaning rota, even though I can't stand most of the people on it, and I'll even learn to smile at Hilda Makepeace when she bullies me into doing the Christian Aid collection.

'Greg? Oh no, whizz-kid Greg is fully booked. No, the other bloke's coming: the Italian one,' continued Nick, oblivious to Hattie's agitation.

Oh thanks, God! Thanks a bunch! So much for all my promises.

'You see, Greg wasn't there when I called in, but this other bloke, Marcello – who I gather was supposed to turn up yesterday – has agreed to come. Mind you, he didn't look very keen. Claimed he'd arrived here and found no one in, but I'm not sure. Personally, I think he was having a bad day and didn't want to admit it. Here, shall I put these on the table?' he offered, taking the plate of chips from her trembling hands. Hattie felt the blood drain from her face. 'Hey, Hat, you've not been knocking back the wine already have you?' he joked. 'You looked a bit wobbly just then.'

'I suppose you're implying that I'm drunk – as if I've had the chance!' she snapped. 'And what do you mean by messing up my Saturday? I thought we were going to do something nice!' She marched to the fridge, fetched the chilled Hungarian white, poured herself a generous glassful and swallowed it in one gulp.

'But, Hat, I asked if you were busy.'

'So, what if I'd planned to do something? Would you have expected me to cancel it for this... this... man?' she spat. There were plenty more colourful words she could have used, but not if her secret was going to remain just that.

'Of course not. That's why I asked. I'd have phoned and changed the time. Don't be too harsh on the poor bloke; he got the time wrong yesterday or something. I think we ought to give him another chance,' he protested.

'Well, I think it's very high-handed of you to arrange this behind my back.' Angus Neill's accusation of her own supposed high-handedness had been totally unjustifiable compared with what Nick had done, she decided. 'Very sneaky too. In fact, you and Sonia Rowse would make quite a pair!'

'Oh, so that's what all this is about, is it? I wondered what had rattled your cage. What's she done to make you so tetchy?'

This heaven-sent red herring about Sonia was just what Hattie needed to divert Nick's attention away from Italian estate agents with a bad track record.

'I think she deliberately dumped her PE lesson on me and then went off on some cushy deputy head's course leaving me to deal with her little thugs.'

'But I thought you said it wasn't too bad.'

'If you remember,' she snapped, 'I said I *survived*. I bet they did something peaceful like handwriting or circle time last term and she decided to swap things around to suit herself. The snooty cow!'

'Come on now, Hat,' he soothed. If her arms had not been flailing around so much he could have attempted a cuddle. 'I'll call Josh – we need to eat – and I promise you, we can go out straight after that bloke goes tomorrow. Okay? You can choose where we go. I mean it.' He took her gently by the shoulders and watched as she relaxed just enough to suggest that her outburst had passed out of the danger zone.

'Okay,' she murmured, sighing. The thought of coping with Leo in the house the next morning was beyond her. Maybe she could phone Fliss and engineer something that would conveniently take her away from the house. It would be worth trying.

*

Hattie blearily opened one eye. It was ten past eight. She groaned and pulled the duvet over her head. She'd had the perfect plan, which effortlessly dropped into her mind as she was scraping the last of the black cherry yoghurt from the pot. She'd drive over to Fliss's the next morning and collect the bulkier of Tom and Dom's belongings to save them carting them into school the following week. No one could argue with that. It was the most practical solution. It would have been perfect if she'd been able to get hold of Fliss, or even Mark. It wasn't to be.

During the night, she'd woken up in a sweat, imagining all the worse-case scenarios: Leo forgetting his cover story, Leo knowing his way around the house and – God forbid – Leo knowing her name and using it. For a few crazy moments, she'd even wondered about pretending to recognise him: 'Well I never! Leo Marcello? Thought that name was familiar. Fancy meeting up after all this time.' No, that wouldn't work. She'd not made a single comment about Leo's name when Nick had mentioned him and, more to the point, she'd never told Nick about him in all the years they'd been together. When Nick walked into her life twelve months after Leo walked out of it, she'd let him to believe he was the only serious boyfriend she'd ever had. 'Least said, soonest mended,' her gran used to say, and so the name Leo Marcello never passed her lips. Nick might not have the charisma and sex appeal of Leo, but he was steady and reliable. After Hattie's past experience, 'steady' and 'reliable' were assets worth treasuring.

Feeling utterly miserable, she dragged herself out of bed to make the tea, leaving Nick snoring gently. At the bottom of the stairs, a trail of sicked-up rodents lay in wait for her unwary slippers.

'Hell!' she cursed, as the slimy, congealing mess spread itself over the freshly vacuumed pile. In the kitchen, Jezebel sat by her empty bowl looking sorry for herself.

'Indigestion, is it? Well, I've no sympathy whatsoever!' she scolded. 'Now listen up, pussy cat, it costs me 30p a pouch to keep you bright-eyed and bushy-tailed, but if you'd prefer to catch your own then it's the garage for you, young lady, and no more kipping down in a nice cosy kitchen.'

Jezebel, well-versed in cute-kitty poses, blinked and then lazily washed behind an ear while Hattie set to with assorted cleaning equipment. In the battle between humans and felines, Jezebel won paws down every time. It was not an auspicious start to the day. Scrubbing smelly cat sick in your nightie, Hattie decided, was not exactly therapeutic, but it gave her time to plan a positive strategy for the morning. Top priorities would be: 1. Stay cool. 2. Keep a low profile. 3. Avoid unnecessary conversation (i.e. let Nick do all the talking; it was all his idea anyway). 4. Focus on chocolate muffins and coffee at the garden centre.

'Tea,' she announced some ten minutes later, placing a steaming mug beside her slumbering husband. 'The Hoover awaits,' she added, giving his shoulder a shove, 'and your visitor's due in less than two hours.'

'Blimey! What time is it?' Nick's eyes snapped wide open.

'Time to get up. I've been up ages, cleaning cat sick to stop you and Josh treading it around the rest of the house. Just be grateful I didn't leave you that little task.'

'Dratted animal,' he muttered, heaving himself upright to enjoy his early morning cuppa. 'Shut her in the utility room. We don't want any more mess on the carpets this morning.'

'Good idea,' agreed Hattie, thinking perhaps she'd stay and keep Jezebel company.

Nick did as he'd promised – a miracle in itself. When the children were tiny, he'd quite excelled at housework, but over the years, his relationship with the cleaning equipment had become estranged. Meanwhile, Hattie enjoyed a long, hot soak, using up the last of the Christmas bubble bath, while Nick blitzed the house with the Hoover – except Josh's room. In fact, Josh was completely forgotten until ten o'clock.

'Oh, leave him where he is,' suggested Hattie. 'He'll only be in the way.'

'No, I'm booting him out of bed. The bloke's expecting to see the whole house.'

Hattie heaved her bag of marking onto the kitchen table and had barely made an impression on 4G's maths books when Josh appeared at the door with an expectant grin. Surveying the scene, however, his grin promptly vanished.

'Dad said you were cooking me some breakfast,' he protested.

'He said *what?*' Hattie exploded. Leo was expected in less than twenty minutes. Josh's droop resembled that of Jezebel's two hours earlier.

'Oh, all right,' Hattie sighed, reluctantly, 'but there's only time for scrambled eggs.'

'Everything under control in here?' Nick asked, finally making an appearance.

'The cheek of it!' glowered Hattie. 'Next time you hand out breakfast bribes, you can jolly well take care of them yourself.'

'But I thought you seemed bright-eyed and bushy-tailed this morning,' Nick protested.

'That's Jezebel's prerogative, as I was reminding her earlier.'

'Talking to the cat again? I dunno!' he muttered with eyes to heaven.

'Well, I get a lot more sense out of her than I do from you two some days.'

'Ouch! That PMT's got a lot to answer for.'

'Who said anything about PMT?' she snapped back, but recognised that if anything was to blame for the current tension in the kitchen, it might as well be PMT.

'Just assumed,' Nick muttered nonchalantly, deciding that the subject should be put to bed. He opened the door to the utility room and was pleased to see that Jezebel was curled up asleep in her basket. 'Now Josh,' he said, deciding to retreat from the battle zone, 'the computer's free, so I suggest you crack on with whatever you need to do. Mum and I are expecting a visitor.' He made it sound as if Leo was an honoured guest.

'Nothing to do with me!' commented Hattie airily, and then the doorbell rang and her stomach performed several somersaults in quick succession.

'Hat,' Nick called, 'come and do the meet and greet with me, then I'll do the rest.'

Take a deep breath, she told herself, keep calm, stay cool and remember the muffins.

'Ah, good morning, do come in,' Nick greeted Leo affably. 'Spot on time too.'

Was he trying to make some point? thought Hattie.

'Good morning, Mr Chesney,' replied Leo. He had achieved an air of confident professionalism with just a touch of aloofness. Hattie hung back, trying to distance herself from the situation.

'And may I introduce my wife,' began Nick, wondering why Hattie was still hovering by the kitchen door. 'This is Mr Marcello from Mia Casa – or perhaps it should be Signor?'

Leo peered beyond Nick's shoulder and caught sight of Hattie's guarded expression. If she was playing a game, so would he.

'Good morning, Mrs Chesney. So pleased to meet you at last.'

'Good morning, Signor Marcello. So sorry I wasn't here when you called. My best friend phoned up in a terrible state; I had to go and see her. Sorry you had a wasted journey,' replied Hattie, straight-faced, confident and finding the lie so convincing that she started believing it herself.

'I'll lead the way,' announced Nick, setting off in the direction of the study and sitting room. Hattie loitered in the hall, mentally tossing up between marking 4G's mental maths tests and keeping an ear open for any incriminating remarks from Leo. Loitering came a close first. She peeped into the sitting room and watched him making notes and then crossing to the window that looked out onto the back garden.

'You have a good location here, Mr Chesney,' he commented as Nick went to join him.

'Yes, it's great in the summer, but at this time of year it can be a bit bleak, especially when it's blowing a gale across those fields. We planted all that over there,' he explained, indicating the shrubs that grew to a moderate height at the bottom of the garden. They formed a windbreak that still allowed views of the farmer's land and the Chiltern Hills in the distance. 'But the best view is from the conservatory. It gets the late afternoon sun too.'

To Hattie's ears, it was all going well. Another fifteen minutes and it should be all over, she calculated, deciding she might as well go and mark another few books.

'Dad,' called Josh grumpily as Hattie passed on her way to the kitchen, 'This programme won't download.'

'Not now, Josh!' Hattie hissed from the door. All she wanted was for the ordeal to be over, but Josh took no notice.

'Er… Signor Marcello, excuse me for a moment. The lad needs a bit of help. I'm sure it'll only take a minute,' said Nick, leading Leo from the sitting room. 'My wife will show you the rest of the ground floor and after we've done upstairs and the garden, perhaps you'd like to stay for coffee?' Nick turned to Josh and grabbed the mouse. 'I thought kids knew everything there is to know about this sort of stuff. Nice to know we oldies can still teach them a thing or two.'

Leo and Hattie exchanged looks of panic.

'I'll just show you the kitchen and utility room if you like,' Hattie announced stiffly, heading off to the kitchen, 'and then I'll put the kettle on. We'll have coffee in the conservatory when you're finished.'

'Thank you, Hattie. I mean, Mrs Chesney.' Leo had corrected himself, but it was too late. She spun round with eyes blazing furiously, made a throat-cutting gesture and stomped through to the utility area.

'Idiot!' she muttered. This was the faux pas she had really dreaded. Nick certainly hadn't used her first name that morning and it was highly unlikely that he'd used it when making the appointment. Up to that unfortunate remark, every exchange had been formal and business-like. So, why use her name? Was it deliberate? Hattie stood at the back door, blindly staring into the garden, waiting for her fury to subside. Had Nick heard or was he too wrapped up with Josh? It was true that Leo had quickly corrected himself, although that could easily have been all part of his plan. Was he so goody-goody that her little bit of deception rankled with him?

Leo slowly made his way into the kitchen. Judging from Hattie's expression, he could see that he was – as the English so quaintly put it – in the doghouse. Being in her home again was difficult enough, especially when Nick had taken him into the sitting room where so many family photos were on show: Nick and Hattie's wedding, the children as babies, then in school uniforms and a young woman in cap and gown – so like Hattie – proudly holding her graduation certificate. Back in Montelugia, of course, there were similar photos in sleek, steel frames displayed on the villa's pale walls – so different from the homely style in the Chesney house.

Leo cursed his lapse in concentration; calling her Hattie was stupid. He had no alternative but to follow her and make his apologies. This was becoming a habit.

'Hattie, I'm sorry. Please forgive me,' he begged, hoping they were out of earshot of the study. Hattie turned around, glared at him and then firmly closed the door that led to the kitchen, to make quite sure that no stray words should reach Nick.

'It was a mistake. I didn't mean to say your name, I promise you,' he implored.

'Promise? It's too late for that now! What if Nick heard you? One minute it was "Good morning, Mrs Chesney. How good to meet you at last" and the next minute it's "Thank you, Hattie". He's going to wonder how we managed to become so chummy so quickly. Nick's no fool, you know.' Hattie huffed and folded her arms across her chest angrily. 'You should have heard him going on and on about Thursday's non-event; thought you'd have left a calling card at least, if my story about leaving the house before you arrived was true. I really couldn't understand why he was so fussed about one silly valuation, except that the woman he works with knows your partner's mum or aunt or someone.'

'Listen, Hattie,' Leo told her firmly, 'it's not my fault you decided to lie to your husband. To be quite frank, I was put in a very embarrassing situation. When he turned up yesterday and I realised who he was, I was quite prepared to tell him that a phone call had interrupted my visit, which was the truth. But he was obviously under the impression that I hadn't even kept the appointment and probably thought I was some lazy, laid-back, incompetent foreigner who couldn't be bothered to put in a proper day's work.'

'That's not fair! Nick's not like that,' protested Hattie, knowing that was exactly what Nick was like, but ready to defend him in the circumstances. 'And anyway, I had no idea he would go to your office, especially after his first comments about Mia Casa. I mean, he was quite sarcastic about the name – said it was pretentious. I told him I thought the other valuation was okay and there wasn't any need for another one, and then he takes it upon himself to organise *this*!'

'Sounds like you two don't talk to each other,' Leo observed.

'Oh really,' she retaliated scornfully. 'Like you not talking to me about changing your mind when we supposed to be going off to Italy together?'

'Who said I changed my mind? If you recall, on Thursday morning, you'll remember I started to explain what *actually* happened, you silly girl. If you think I'm some heartless Casanova, then you're completely wrong –'

'How dare you call me a silly girl!' Hattie shrieked before she could stop herself. Footsteps could be heard on the other side of the door. Much to Leo's relief, Nick's reappearance had saved him from another verbal lambasting. By some superwoman effort, Hattie changed from screaming harpy to charming householder in a matter of seconds.

'We find this utility area perfect for drying the washing on wet days,' she explained enthusiastically, indicating the retro clothes airer that dangled from the ceiling. Nick popped his head round the door, clearly concerned.

'Hmm, very useful,' agreed Leo, adding a note to his folder and promptly adapting a professional demeanour.

'Everything okay in here?' Nick asked. 'I thought I heard shouting.'

'Oh... er... yes... it was Jezebel up to her usual tricks,' flustered Hattie, gathering her wits for a plausible story. 'She tried to bring some little furry creature through the cat-flap, so I screamed at her.

'Looks like she took notice too,' commented Nick, noting Jezebel curled tightly in her basket with not a whisker out of place, exactly as she'd appeared a few minutes earlier.

'So she should. You think she'd have learned her lesson by now.'

Leo shuffled his feet awkwardly, not sure whether to be impressed by Hattie's gift for quick-fire improvisation.

'Well,' Nick began, baffled by the slightly bizarre nature of the situation and sensing an atmosphere as tense as an FA Cup draw, 'perhaps I'll go and flick the switch on the kettle. Sorry it took me so long with Josh. Problem sorted.'

He set the kettle to boil and took Leo upstairs, leaving Hattie with the rest of the preparations and her shredded nerves. As he plodded upstairs, he found himself puzzling over several aspects of the utility room scenario:

1. Why was the door closed?
2. He'd definitely heard a rather loud male voice as well as a female one.
3. Hattie was acting strangely.
4. Signor Marcello seemed embarrassed.
5. Hattie had been very snappy since dropping chips over the floor the night before.

6. Jezebel didn't look as if she'd been hauling anything small and furry anywhere!
7. And most puzzling; he could have sworn he'd heard Signor Marcello address Hattie by her first name just outside the sitting room, although they'd only just met. How strange was that?

After showing Marcello the three bedrooms, master en-suite, family bathroom and airing cupboard and pointing out the double-glazing, phone extension and TV points, he took him to inspect the garage, garden, greenhouse, tiny potting shed and excellent countryside views. While on the way back for coffee, he came to the following logical conclusions:

1. The door was closed to stop the cat escaping into the rest of the house with its prey.
2. Signor Marcello must be squeamish about cats with half-dead rodents in their mouths and had shouted out in fright.
3. Hattie was still angry that he'd arranged the viewing without consulting her.
4. Signor Marcello was embarrassed about appearing a bit of a wimp.
5. Hattie was in the grips of PMT – again!
6. Cats are funny creatures anyway, as he'd learned over the years.
7. Hattie must have told him her first name, but he couldn't think when she'd had the opportunity.
8. His memory wasn't as good as it used to be.

By the time they returned, Hattie had calmed down and had coffee ready in the conservatory. Leo had made comprehensive notes, to prove to anyone who was interested just how thorough and business-like he could be. The predicted current market value, when he announced it, was ten thousand more than Brian Samways's figure, but was still in line with similar properties in

Mia Casa's window. Over coffee, Nick quizzed him about their fees but made it clear that they weren't yet in a position to appoint an agent. All the while, Hattie kept to one of her golden rules about keeping conversation to a minimum. Everything was conducted in a very professional manner and Nick concluded that the man knew his business, as well as having excellent taste in suits.

'Goodbye then and thanks. We'll be in touch,' Nick said, shaking his visitor's hand ten minutes later, as he left.

'Over my dead body,' muttered Hattie, under her breath.

Leo managed a faint smile as he left, but still looked as if he'd just had a few rounds with a heavyweight opponent. Hattie, on the other hand, was quietly congratulating herself on her brilliant acting ability and was now considering the promised outing to be her due reward. Minutes later, they were in the car.

Nick glanced across at his wife as he waited for the traffic to clear before pulling out from their close. 'A penny for them?' he asked cautiously, noting her clouded expression.

'Oh, nothing, Nick,' she replied, horrified to think that her A-star performance in the utility room might not have done its work, 'except, of course, not consulting me on a couple of little decisions recently.'

'Ah, right. Point taken. Sorry, Hat.'

'Anyway, it's all forgiven now. Or rather it will be once the coffee and muffins are sitting in front of me.'

He breathed a sigh of relief. Hattie was easily pleased: a quality that he'd been gratefully aware of ever since they'd met some twenty-five years ago.

When Nick had met Hattie, a year after her graduation, she'd just returned from working as an au pair in Holland for an English family. At the time, he was house-sitting for his parents while they were cruising around the Bahamas. He was a hard-up trainee accountant and grateful for a free holiday with a freezer full of his mum's home cooking. He and Hattie met at a rather wild party thrown by one of her old school friends. Nick knew the girl's brother through football, which they had played and watched together in their teens. Hattie hadn't told him much about her time at uni, except that she'd had a few boyfriends, but no serious relationships. She'd taken the au pair job on finishing her degree, she told him, because she hadn't been sure what to do next. However, during her year in Holland, she'd decided to do a B.Ed course, because primary teaching appealed to her. Fortunately, the college at Winchester offered her a place, meaning she would be able to live at home while she studied.

As far as Nick was concerned, it was love at first sight. Hattie was so bubbly, outgoing and attractive, as well as having a great sense of humour. As their friendship grew, he found they shared similar views and although she wasn't particularly interested in football, she would occasionally go to a match with him. This was more than many of his former girlfriends were prepared to do. Despite the miles that separated them, they met as often as they could, but when cash was short they'd talk for ages on the phone instead. Within three months, they were engaged, with a wedding planned for the following summer, after Hattie had completed her course. To their delight, she secured a teaching post near Amersham, not far from where Nick worked. It was here that they bought their first home – a compact, two-bed semi. A few years and two children later, Nick decided it was time to move. The new job in the accounts department of Padgett and Bicton – a decking and fencepost company – on the outskirts of Aylesbury, gave him more variety, a better salary and the means to move to a larger property. But now it was time to move once more.

Rosehill Garden Centre was surprisingly busy for a chilly Saturday in January. Customers were stocking up on pet food, which the manager had recently added to his expanding range, as well as browsing through the extensive seed collection, ready for spring planting.

'I don't think Jezebel deserves any pussy treats today,' commented Hattie as she made a beeline for the gingham-themed coffee shop.

'Oh, I don't know,' put in Nick. 'I think it was an impressive show of obedience on her part, the way she hunkered back down in her basket. I think pussy treats are most definitely in order.'

'Priorities, Nick! We're here for coffee and muffins.'

Hilda Makepeace's daughter, Melanie, was busy intimidating a teenage helper behind the serving counter when Hattie took her place in the coffee queue. Melanie was bearing all the hallmarks of her mother's character, with a suitably sharp tongue and a lack of discretion.

'No! No! No!' she admonished, loud enough for everyone in the café area to hear, 'You clear out the old coffee grounds first!' Melanie wrenched the dispenser from the machine while the girl cowered behind a display of teacakes and muffins. The queue promptly broke into animated conversation to hide the general embarrassment. A few minutes later, the comforting hiss and bubble of the coffee-maker restored calm, and soon froth-topped mugs were being born away to the few remaining tables.

'Yoo-hoo! Mrs Chesney!'

Hattie, stood dithering with her loaded tray, and scanned the seating area.

'Yoo-hoo! Over here!' The waving hand belonged to a smiling, buxom female with short, greying hair and a huge grin. It was Madge. Seated beside her was a woman of an uncertain age, with peroxide blonde hair, and a pair of plump pouting lips. Her horn-rimmed specs gave her a hawkish appearance, which was accentuated by well-pencilled brows. Madge, by comparison, was as fresh-faced as a girl guide, apart from a clumping of eyelashes, which hinted at a hasty, heavy-handed application of mascara. She would have looked better without it, thought Hattie. With no more vacant tables, she had little choice but to take the two seats Madge was indicating with her flapping hand.

'So kind,' said Hattie, with a cautious smile, suspecting that Nick wouldn't be delirious about her choice of company.

'This is Sandra,' Madge giggled. 'She's been my best friend since junior school. Sandra, this is Mrs Chesney, my work colleague's wife.'

Sandra proffered an impressive set of cherry red nails. 'Charmed,' she murmured with a delicate chuckle that set her chins quivering.

'Actually, you can call me Hattie.'

'And where is Mr Chesney this morning? In front of the telly, is he?' asked Madge, smearing her scone with a thick layer of jam.

'Oh no, he's here somewhere. I'm not having all this myself.' Hattie nodded towards the two double choc-chip muffins and mugs of frothy cappuccinos, wondering why Nick was taking so long. 'Ah, here he is.'

'We were about to send out a search party,' Madge informed Nick, in between mouthfuls of cream and jam. Nick grimaced unenthusiastically and sat down.

'This is Madge's friend Sandra,' said Hattie. She gave his ankle a sharp knock with her foot and pushed his plate towards him. 'Behave yourself!' she hissed in his ear.

'Greg's auntie,' Madge added conspiratorially. 'Greg of Mia Casa.'

Sandra simpered proudly as she cut her cranberry and raisin flapjack into tiny squares and popped one into her mouth.

'Aha! Mia Casa, eh?' chuckled Nick, having decided to make the best of the situation. 'We had our valuation this morning as a matter of fact. Signor Marcello did the honours.'

'Ooh,' sniggered Sandra coyly, 'the lovely Leo!'

'Well, that's as may be,' remarked Nick, 'but as a mere male I can't comment on another of the sex.'

'Not my type at all,' muttered Hattie, dismissively.

'No, you like your men a bit frayed around the edges, don't you, Hat?' he chuckled, and gave her knee a playful squeeze.

'Anyway, it was the lovely Leo, as you said, Sandra; not to be confused with the gorgeous Greg, eh Madge?' Nick teased with a twinkle. Madge blushed, her cheeks resembling the hue of a ripening loganberry.

'Beeehave!' warned Hattie, *sotto voce.*

'Mia Casa are doing well, are they?' Nick asked. He stirred the froth and tried a spoonful topped with chocolatey sprinkles.

'They certainly are, Mr Chesney,' Sandra told him, beaming with family pride. 'Those two have a wealth of business experience, you know. Of course, they both had a good start – went to the same private boarding school,' she boasted.

Madge then spotted the packet of Seafood Snax that Nick had bought for Jezebel. 'Well, is that what took you so long?' she enquired in between mouthfuls.

'Hmm? Oh yeah... queue a mile long. But our little puss-cat certainly deserves a treat today, doesn't she, Hat?'

Hattie ignored his banter and concentrated on the glorious sensation of melting chocolate chips on her tongue.

'Blasted cat nearly scuppered our valuation with a dead rodent. It really put the wind up Signor Marcello I suspect, until Hattie here gave the cat her marching orders. Quick as a flash, she leapt in her basket and was in the land of nod before you could say tuna chunks in jelly! I reckon it was a miracle. Last time anything like this happened, three wise men and a heavenly host turned up,' he said, lowering his voice for effect.

'Old joke,' sighed Hattie, her voice heavy with sarcasm, but Sandra and Madge fell about laughing. 'And a gross exaggeration!'

'Anyway,' continued Nick, 'no harm was done and the signor wrapped up the business very efficiently. It's now a case of wait and see on the job front.'

'Did you see the lovely textiles, Madge, just over in the corner?' asked Hattie, longing to steer the conversation away from estate agents.

'Indeed we did, didn't we, Sandra?'

'When I see what some people make, I think to myself, I'd love to have a go,' she continued. 'Last weekend, up in Oxfordshire, I saw some lovely patchwork and even thought about a course. My good intentions seem to have been crowded out by work and this house business, though. It's probably too late to join a course now.'

'Not at all, Hattie,' Madge told her, slicing another scone. 'Aylesbury College doesn't start its evening classes until next week.'

'That's right,' agreed Sandra. 'I know quite a few people who are trying out new courses this term.' She glanced towards Madge and raised her perfectly defined brows. The eye contact between the two friends was heavy with meaning, but other than shy giggles from Madge, Hattie was none the wiser.

'Oh, I'm so glad we've had this conversation,' said Hattie eagerly. 'I'll phone the college on Monday.'

4

'Come in, number four; your time's up!' quipped Hattie.

'What's that?' mumbled Josh. He continued typing at high speed, choosing to ignoring his mother's humour.

'Look, sunshine, you'll have square eyes at this rate. You must have been glued to this machine for three hours at least.'

Josh clicked 'send' and sighed. 'Dunno why I can't have my own machine. *All* my mates have,' he whinged.

'All?' repeated Hattie sceptically. 'Then they must have saved up their pennies and bought one,' she suggested, knowing her optimism on the subject of self-financing teenagers was being stretched to the nth degree.

'Well, I dunno, but all my tutors talk like we've got our own PC, like it's sort of expected, like it's part of the course. And you want me to do well, don't you, Mum?'

'Oh, emotional blackmail is it now? Don't try that one on me. Remember what we told you when you started college? It's time you found yourself a little part-time job? Dad and I had to when we were your age,' she reminded him curtly.

'Yeah… well…' he mumbled resentfully, 'but can't you and Dad buy me a laptop in the sales – you can well afford it – and I'll pay you back when I'm earning?'

'No, Josh. *You* get yourself a Saturday job first and *then* we'll discuss some kind of easy repayment plan. I don't know why you don't go down to Tarrant's Garage and find out if they need any extra help. After all, you *are* doing a car mechanics course.'

'Hmm, right,' he sighed and slouched off to raid the fridge.

Hattie's Internet search proved very fruitful. Sandra was correct in saying that the college evening classes were due to start the following week and – even better – Beginner's Patchwork was down for Wednesday evenings. She noted the college contact details, ready to phone the administrator on Monday. Meanwhile, Nick beavered away at his applications for the two Lydford Cross jobs and then knocked up a pithy letter, tweaked according to the slightly different job specs. Full of justified self-satisfaction, he nipped out to post them before the afternoon's football was due to reach the most interesting final score stage.

Later, while Hattie was making a cup of tea and thinking about supper, Josh sauntered in with a smug grin plastered over his spotty face. One glance at his trainers told her that he'd not been holed up in his bedroom all afternoon. There was a disturbing excess of mud clinging to them, which he'd failed to remove, and a surprisingly ruddy glow to his normally pallid complexion.

'Guess what, Mum?' he announced with a rare twinkle in his eye.

Goodness, thought Hattie, not a girlfriend, surely!

'Can't imagine, Josh. Unless it's a case of *cherchez la femme*,' she teased, finding his unusually high spirits quite infectious.

'*Cher*-what? You know I was rubbish at French.'

'But not at the art of conversation,' Hattie replied brightly.

Josh eyed her suspiciously, unsure whether the last remark had been subtly laced with sarcasm. He was a lad of few words. On the girlfriend front, however, Hattie realised that when there *was* a breakthrough, she'd probably be the last to know.

'Okay, I'll guess,' she ventured playfully. 'I know! You were dragged into the Rovers team and clinched the match for them with a last minute goal.'

'No way,' snarled Josh, idly kicking at the table leg and detaching another clod of mud from his trainers. 'Anyway, *that* team's all old geezers.'

'I hardly think so, Josh. Kevin Taylor's only thirty.'

'Yeah – old geezers. Anyway, it's not anything like that. It's about earning cash – loads of it,' he boasted with a swagger. 'Cos skills like mine are in demand.'

'Oh yes?' Hattie suspended a teabag over her waiting mug in disbelief. Josh had evidently undergone some sort of miraculous metamorphosis in the last two hours and the transformation was jaw-dropping. 'Someone's offered you a job?' she gasped. 'I thought I saw a pig fly past the window earlier.'

Josh affected an air of indifference, but the little lunchtime chat had obviously paid dividends. Hitting the male of the species in the wallet, Hattie had found, tended to give speedy results.

'Yeah, well I need cash don't I?' Josh had somehow passed through the aggrieved student phase and emerged into aspiring independence. 'So I thought I'd offer my brilliant skills to the local businesses – well, old man Tarrant actually.' Josh was evidently taking all the credit and seemed at least two inches taller with all the strutting and preening. Hattie found it quite endearing, even though this change in Josh's circumstances was due to *her* suggestion in the first place. She chuckled to herself, dunked her teabag in the mug and gave a few prods before adding a splash of milk.

'Modest as ever Josh!'

'Yeah, well, what with you and Dad clearing off and taking the PC with you…' he commented peevishly.

'*Our* PC, actually. Paid for with *our* hard-earned pay packets.' Hattie leafed through a new Delia collection, trying to decide which tempting dish she could knock up for supper.

'Thought I could start earning and get myself a nice little notebook,' Josh continued, enjoying his moment of glory.

'Notebook?' echoed Hattie, totally confused by Josh's line of thought. 'What's a notebook got to do with all this? You can get notebooks for 50p down at the post office.'

Josh sighed in a superior way. 'A notebook is a neat sort of laptop, Mum. Don't you know *anything*? Anyway, I don't want any old-fashioned stuff like you've got; mine's gonna be real sweet. Got any tea going?'

Before Hattie could blink, he'd removed a fistful of ginger cookies from the open tin and had breezed out to the study, managing to tread on Jezebel's tail in the process. Had she just witnessed a complete change in her son, or was it a sneak preview of the young adult who was struggling to break out of the spotty youth chrysalis? Whatever the answer, she estimated that he'd used up his conversation allowance for the week.

Closeted away, well clear of the whistle-blowing tension of the football scores, Hattie selected her recipe, assembled and weighed out the ingredients and had reached the stickiest stage with her pastry when the phone rang. It was Laura, ready for her weekly chat and update. When they reached the subject of moving and, more to the point, where Josh might lay his weary head, her daughter made the perfect suggestion.

'Have you thought about asking Celia and Toby?'

Hattie and Nick had met the Halversons in church shortly after moving to the village when Josh was a few months old. Celia had been a real godsend, with offers of meals and the odd spot of ironing. Once they had settled in, and their thoughts had moved beyond packing cases and redecorating, Josh's christening was planned and the Halversons, together with Hattie's brother, Charles, made the perfect choice as godparents.

'I must admit I hadn't actually given the subject that much thought,' she admitted, 'knowing the drawbacks of living with someone whose standards of personal hygiene and bedroom organisation are well-matched by his appreciation of decibel levels in the parental home.'

'Oh, so no improvement on those then?' chuckled Laura.

'Zilch. However,' Hattie added, in a more positive vein, 'if this afternoon is anything to go by, we might be seeing a light at the end of the proverbial tunnel. But your suggestion about the Halversons is brilliant.'

'Thanks, Mum. I'll put my bill in the post,' Laura teased. 'It does make perfect sense though. Celia and Toby must be rattling around in that mansion of theirs, now both daughters are married, *and* they think the world of Josh, judging by their generous cash hand-outs each birthday.'

'Handing out cash is easy, living with the beast is another matter entirely. So, how's school?' Hattie asked.

'Oh, fine really. Apart from little Noah stuffing loo rolls down the pan, an impending Ofsted and one of the TAs embroiled in an affair with the chairman of governors.'

'Whoops!' gasped Hattie. 'Ah, well, it all adds to the rich tapestry of life.'

As Leo left his flat the following Wednesday evening, he was having serious second thoughts. In the quiet winter months, with the house market virtually dormant, there wasn't as much commission, but tutoring wasn't his obvious choice for extra income. A spot of business consultancy was more in his line, more high profile *and* was better paid. The trouble was that the area seemed to have reached saturation point with business consultants – casualties of companies who'd pared down their workforce or early retirees hoping to subsidise their pensions.

Greg had spotted the ad in the *Bucks Herald* back in November. It read: *Temporary Course Tutor required for the spring term for Conversational Italian.*

'If they suddenly need a temporary tutor, it sounds as if someone has just pulled out. Wouldn't it have been easier to cancel the course?' remarked Leo disdainfully. 'After all, the English assume everyone speaks their language when they go on holiday.'

'Not me Leo, if you remember when I used to stay with you,' protested Greg.

'Yes, I know, my friend,' replied Leo patiently, recalling those times. 'But people like you are in the minority. Anyway, I always looked on you as one of the family.'

Leo and Greg had first met when Leo had been sent to a prestigious boarding school in Somerset at the age of ten. His family had been living in London for a couple of years while his father had been setting up a wine importing company in Pimlico. Back in Montelugia, the family vineyard was entrusted to the care of several uncles. Leo and his sister Sophia had been sent to a prep school in Kensington, where they learned perfect English and made good progress in their general education. Twins Bianca and Maria created a stir at their nearby kindergarten, while two year-old Francesca had her mother's undivided attention and became thoroughly spoilt. When the new business was well established and could be left in the reliable hands of George Leask, the Marcellos planned their return to Italy. Leo, however, was destined to complete his schooling in England. An excellent public school was selected; one with an impressive list of academics and statesmen amongst their alumni and a note-worthy pedigree of examination results. Signora Marcello was satisfied that Leo's school would give her plenty to boast about in the upwardly mobile circles of Montelugia's small population and would make her the envy of her sisters. Consequently, Leo was despatched to Somerset to complete his studies, where he met Greg, whose mother was one the housekeepers and his father a groundsman. Naturally Greg went to one of the local primary schools. However, because his family lived on the premises, he was always around in the evenings and at weekends, sometimes helping his dad white-line the football pitches or prepare cricket wickets. Despite their different backgrounds, he and Greg struck up a friendship that lasted right through school and into adulthood.

Unlike Leo, Greg wasn't academic and so, on leaving school at sixteen with a modest clutch of grades, he needed to find a job where he could gain a qualification and earn a reasonable wage at the same time. A national chain of estate agents had a vacancy in their Bristol office, where he worked his way up over several years then applied for a transfer to their High Wycombe branch. Throughout this time, the friendship with Leo continued, with the occasional invitation to Montelugia for holidays, where plenty of sun and free booze were the main attractions. Unfortunately, he wasn't quite the hit with the local girls that he'd hoped. Compared with Leo, he'd always felt inadequate. Leo had an air of confident assurance that came with the security of family wealth, as well as his obvious good looks and charm. Leo was never short of female attention.

Back in England, Greg eventually met and married Hazel who, in due course, produced daughters Emily and Hannah. By now, Greg's contact with Leo had almost petered out, along with the chance of cheap holidays in Tuscany. Contact between the two friends seemed to have come to a natural end until, after a long period of silence, an email from Leo landed quite unexpectedly in Greg's inbox. He wanted to know if Greg knew of any interesting investment possibilities.

The timing couldn't have been better for Greg, who wanted to start his own agency. He'd discovered the ideal vacant premises in nearby Aylesbury, but was short on cash and a suitable business partner. Leo's email was the solution to his problems. Although, why Leo, heir to a Tuscan wine estate, would want anything to do with estate agency was a mystery. Whenever Greg tried to find out exactly what had happened back in Montelugia, a shadow passed over Leo's face.

'So sad... I did my best...' Leo would murmur with a shake of his head. After that, Greg gave up trying. If Leo wanted to confide in him, he'd surely do so when he was ready.

In a relatively short time, the premises were secured and Mia Casa was launched. Enlisting Rebecca Vaudin had been a stroke of luck. She'd been working in Wendover, but was fed up with the bitching in the staffroom and the lack of prospects. When she learned about Greg's new enterprise, she was on the phone straight away offering her services. By then, she'd notched up two years of experience, was studying for her estate agency qualification and was stunningly attractive as well. What more could Greg hope for? However, the new team knew life in the property business would be tough, so chances of extra earnings would always be welcome. Greg and Leo weren't absolutely sure what Rebecca did to improve her personal cashflow, but there were rumours she'd been seen dancing in one of the not-so-local nightclubs.

Leo strolled down the corridor with his folder of notes and sets of hand-outs that he'd assembled with help from the college staff, still unsure about the new venture. He'd learned that there were about twenty students, which at least made the course viable. On opening the door and meeting the eager faces of the early arrivals, however, Leo felt that maybe this Wednesday evening activity might not be such a bad idea after all.

In another part of the college, Hattie found the room allocated for the Beginner's Patchwork Workshop. Back at home, she'd left Thomas and Dominic happily settled in and busy with home-work. Fliss was with her parents down in St Austell and Mark had flown off to a trade fair in Germany. Apart from the extra helpings of food needed, not much had changed at home. Hattie found the Tarrier boys relatively undemanding, no doubt still in shock over their grandmother's rapidly declining health. She'd phoned the college during mid-morning break two days before and was relieved to learn that it wasn't too late to join the course. Some essential pieces of equipment would be required, she was told, but these could be bought from the course tutors on the first evening. That sounded expensive, recalling what she'd seen on sale in Pins and Needles, but *essential equipment* was exactly that. Her chequebook was braced for a battering.

It was just a few minutes before seven thirty when she pushed the classroom door open, feeling like the new girl on the first day of term. There were large worktables arranged in an open rectangle, with two or three ladies seated at each. At the front, with piles of folders and boxes of equipment beside them on a long desk, were two ladies in their middle years. From their air of authority there was no doubt that they were the course tutors. Hattie quickly found a space and glanced around at her fellow students with interest. None were known to her and their ages ranged from thirty upwards, nor were any as splendidly dressed as the two who stood poised for action.

'Good evening ladies. Welcome to our first session of Beginner's Patchwork. My name is Zena Gossage and this is my friend and colleague, Marigold Hellaby-Yule,' announced the diminutive Zena in shrill tones. One of the ladies on Hattie's table giggled quietly to herself. Zena was petite in figure with short, bright orange, spiky hair. She wore heavy-rimmed specs, slung by a chain around her neck, a glorious patchwork waistcoat and slim-fitting, chocolate, velvet trousers. Marigold, by contrast, was tall and tending towards plumpness. Her height was accentuated by a silvery bun that was starting to escape from a curious metal clip shaped like a treble clef. Her long purple skirt had an embroidered hem, with tiny pieces of mirrored glass that reflected the light, and she sported a fluffy, cerise sweater, tightly stretched across her ample bosom. The juxtaposition of the cerise bosom and orange spikes was a remarkable sight, and all sixteen pairs of eyes were riveted on the duo as they set out their expectations for the weeks ahead. When it was Marigold's turn to address the class, her voice had a soft, gushing quality, with a tendency to rise and fall in a rather singsong way and in stark contrast with Zena's shrill delivery. They were quite a double act!

Introductions over, the students were shown the various pieces of equipment that were part of the patch-worker's armoury, including the fiendishly sharp cutting wheels with sliding safety covers.

'Now, ladies,' trilled Zena ominously. 'Make sure you all remember to click the blade cover back in place after each cut. This is the first rule of patchwork. Any blades left open will incur a 50p fine.'

A few mutters could be heard around the room.

'Goodness,' murmured Hattie to the next lady, 'it's like being back at school.' She started to wonder what the 50ps might be used for: a first aid kit for sliced fingers, or maybe Zena and Marigold were planning to nip off to the pub afterwards? However, once in use, the potential hazards of exposed blades were understood by all.

The evening passed agreeably from then onwards, with stunning patchwork cushions, throws and quilts being shown to the enraptured class. Ideas for their first project were suggested and a simple design for a patchwork square was cut and assembled. Everyone was then encouraged to have a go with oddments of fabric supplied for the purpose. Zena and Marigold quickly circled the room, handing out templates and instructions to the students. Hattie wondered how she'd cope with the first simple square, but selected two contrasting pieces of blue fabric and made a start.

'Simple?' she heard someone despair. 'It may be simple for the experts, but not for me. I'm bound to make a mess of it!' The lady in question then introduced herself as Cynthia Dacey. It was she who had giggled during the introductions.

'Don't worry, Cynthia,' said Hattie sympathetically. 'We're all beginners. Why don't we work together? I'm sure it'll be fine if we go slowly.'

They chatted together as they took turns with the sewing machine, and with plenty of determined concentration, started to produce results that closely resembled the ones that had been efficiently stitched by their tutors. Much to Hattie's amusement, Cynthia turned out to be quite a mine of information.

'Of course, you know about the Hellaby-Yules don't you?' she whispered as they worked. Hattie had never heard of such a family and suspected that Cynthia had guessed that too.

'No,' replied Hattie, intrigued by a sniff of gossip.

'Filthy rich,' she confided knowingly. 'They own most of Quaintly. My cousin Dotty keeps house for the old boy – that's

Marigold's father. She'll inherit the lot when he pops his clogs – worth millions.'

'Really?' gasped Hattie, as she pressed yet another seam flat before pinning another section. 'And what about Zena's family?' There was a good chance that Cynthia knew about them as well.

'Quite the opposite, as it happens,' commented Cynthia wryly. 'Common as muck, from what I recall. Well, her mum was, but the old girl's passed away now. Her dad was in and out of Grendon prison when Zena was in her teens. We were at the same school, but not in the same year. But she's done very well for herself, I must say; especially now she's latched on to Marigold – if you know what I mean…' She raised her eyebrows in a display of disapproval.

'You don't mean that they're… er…'

'In a relationship?' murmured Cynthia. 'Oh yes… Dotty's seen enough to know they're *very* close friends!' Fortunately the whirr and hum of the machines covered their conversation as Marigold drew closer to examine their work.

'Simply splendid!' she gushed, selecting Hattie's square and turning it over to check the seams. 'Well done!'

By nine fifteen it was time to pack up and everyone was given an envelope containing fabric samples for their homework. Hattie then queued up to buy a cutting wheel, guide and mat, and made a mental note to bring a large holdall with her next time for all her paraphernalia.

'Now, ladies, don't forget to bring your homework next time,' Zena reminded them as they left clutching their newly purchased equipment and sheaths of notes. Hattie and Cynthia made their way down the corridor chatting together. She learned that Cynthia lived in the next village to Fliss and knew her by sight. No doubt, if there was anything murky in Fliss's past, Cynthia would be sure to know it, but she said nothing. The old rumour about a fling with a jobbing gardener might have been fiction after all.

Arriving at the main entrance hall, still chatting amicably, Hattie glanced towards one of the other corridors that fed into the central area, only to scc Leo coming towards them. Leo? What was *he* doing there? He hadn't seen them, engrossed as he was in listening to a couple of pensioners enthusing about their time-share in Sorrento. Hattie increased her pace, quickly dodged to Cynthia's right and hoisted her cutting mat, hoping Leo wouldn't see her.

'Oh good, Donald's here to meet me,' announced Cynthia. 'See you next week, Hattie, and thank you for your kind help.' She turned and trotted off excitedly.

Unfortunately for Hattie, Cynthia's ringing tones had reached Leo's ears.

'Hattie!' he called. 'Ah, scusi,' he apologised to the Sorrento pair. 'Ciao!'

'Ciao!' they replied, chuckling.

Hattie tried to pretend she hadn't heard him and beetled towards the main door, head down and determined to shake him off in the pitch black of the car park.

'Watch out!' a voice bellowed in her ear, as Hattie collided full-pelt with a thickset, overall-clad body. It was the caretaker with a huge bunch of keys and a discontented scowl.

'Blast!' she cursed, as she lost her grip on the cutting mat and handful of notes, which slithered onto the floor. 'Oh no!' she wailed, as her shoulder bag slid off her arm.

The caretaker strode off muttering irritably, 'Look where you're going next time!'

'Please, let me help,' came a familiar voice. Leo had managed to catch her up and there was no escape.

'Leo?' gasped Hattie, feigning innocence. 'Didn't see you there. I'm fine, thank you very much.' She set off briskly, still struggling to control her unwieldy armful.

'Please, Hattie. Wait a moment,' he begged. 'We should talk.'

Hattie stopped, feeling the anger rising within her.

'No, Leo. There's no *should*. I've already made it quite clear; I've no time for any more excuses,' she hissed, trying to keep her voice down.

'Hattie, please!' he implored

'Stop it, Leo!' she snapped, feeling acute embarrassment. Several ladies from her class were passing by and were craning their necks. She felt a hot flush on her cheeks and paused, muttering furiously to herself, while they trooped on towards the door, giggling.

'I'm sorry Hattie, please forgive me. I didn't mean to upset you,' he murmured gently. 'I really wanted a chance to explain about… well, what happened… so many unfortunate events out of my control. I just wanted a chance to clear the air.'

She glared at him suspiciously. He looked like a drowning man going under for the third time. Don't expect *me* to throw you a rubber ring, she thought.

'Maybe next week, after classes, you'll let me buy you a coffee so we can talk? Just a few minutes?' he pleaded.

She'd really had enough of his pitiful wittering by now. However, if she agreed to meet him, she could easily change her mind later.

'Maybe,' she conceded tartly.

Leo brightened visibly and sighed. 'Thank you! Thank you! Until next week then.'

Hattie said nothing, but plodded on her way, weighed down with all the gear.

'Permit me,' he offered, rushing ahead to open the door.

'Thank you,' she muttered and with that she was out in the gloom of the damp January night, leaving Leo alone.

During her drive home, Hattie reflected on the puzzling encounter. What was Leo doing at the college? Was he doing a course? If so, which one? He was too smartly dressed for anything vaguely messy, so maybe some sort of business course? Then she considered the possibility of him being one of the tutors, but dismissed that. Surely he'd need some teaching qualification. She remembered hearing him say 'ciao' – not the sort of word he'd use with strangers. Definitely very odd, she thought. Then she re-ran his claim about 'unfortunate events' being 'out of his control' and started to wonder if he really *did* have a good reason for what happened. Or maybe he was just a persistent liar? If she could keep her nerve, it might be interesting to hear his version of 13th July – anything to get him out of her life for good.

The second slam of the front door announced that the male contingent of the house had now left – bliss, a whole day stretched out before her. It was the perfect opportunity to catch up on her patchwork. After two cups of Earl Grey and a bowl of muesli, she set up her sewing machine and unpacked her patchwork bag. Selecting some fabric, she laid it on the cutting mat and lined up the cutting guide carefully. With her cutting wheel poised she remembered the importance of precision. Just a fraction this way, she thought, moving the guide carefully. Perfect! A moment later there was a strident blast from the doorbell.

'Oh faggots!' she cursed, wondering if Leo Marcello would have the nerve to land up on her doorstep and trot out his tale of woe. He'd better not, she thought mutinously. After a few moments of wimpish deliberation, she finally plucked up courage. It wasn't Leo, but Wilf, her next-door neighbour, bristling with indignation. Hattie's guilty gnome secret reared its ugly head.

'I've had vandals!' he growled. 'It's Stanley. 'E's lost 'is 'ead!' said Wilf, pointing to one of his collection, his finger shaking and his face growing more puce by the second. The superglue evidently hadn't been quite as super after all.

'I want the blighters rounded up and punished!' ranted Wilf, vengeance written all over his weathered face.

Hattie squirmed with secret guilt. 'I don't think it's a capital offence,' she murmured, but Wilf was not in the mood for humour. 'And it might just be frost damage. But tell you what, I'll see if I can fix it.'

Well done Hattie, she told herself, that was inspired, but when she set to work back in her kitchen, the damage was worse than she thought. A visit to Rosehill Garden Centre beckoned and Hattie's wayward driving sliced a neat £15 from her patchwork fund.

'And all Leo Marcello's fault,' she muttered, as she heaved Stanley's replacement out to the car and sped off home.

All was quiet at number five when Hattie returned, with not a glimpse of twitching curtains. She scuttled inside with her booty and slammed the door shut, her heart set at a spirited gallop. Her few moments of triumph, however, were short lived. Even without his head in place, she could see that old Stanley was several inches taller than his replacement.

'Sugar lumps!' she cursed, but decided to brazen it out and counter any comments from Wilf with a few reflections on the recent sub-zero temperatures, a theme she was warming to with increasing enthusiasm. By the time she had placed Stanley Number Two beside his new companions and returned to her cutting mat, it was after eleven. Her precious sewing time was disappearing like suds down the plughole.

Hattie set to work with the cutting wheel and considered her likely patchwork project. A modest cushion cover would be quick and easy, but would hardly justify the cost of the course and equipment. Hattie needed a challenge. She completed her cutting and then pinned and stitched a green version of the square she'd made the night before. The design was quite straightforward and produced a pleasing chequerboard effect. If all the designs were as easy as that, perhaps she might aim for a throw or even a bed cover. Full of newfound confidence, she sketched out a diagram and made some calculations. It would be an expensive project, but one of which she could be proud.

Just then, the phone rang. It was Fliss, sounding brave and calm and Hattie guessed at once that the news was not good.

'They've suggested chemo, but Mum's said no,' Fliss told her.

'But if there's hope of an improvement...'

'Well no, there isn't, realistically. The cancer's reached secondaries you see. It'll only give a little more time.'

'Ah, I think I understand. She's scared of losing her hair; is that it?' asked Hattie sympathetically.

'Hmm, she wants to keep her dignity and doesn't see the

point of prolonging the situation. Telling the boys will be the worst part,' she continued, bravely. 'And working out when I can take them. We're never going to know when the last visit will be.' There was a brief pause while Fliss collected herself. 'I'm coming back on Saturday, but Mark's still in Germany and I just wondered...'

'Meet you at the station? Yes, of course I will,' said Hattie. 'Reading?'

'Yeah, that's the obvious place. I'll text you when I know the arrival time, but it won't be earlier than two. Thanks, Hat. I'm really grateful.'

Fliss emerged from the platform a few days later, eager to catch sight of her friend.

'Yoo hoo! Fliss! Over here!' called Hattie. 'Here, let me help,' she offered, rushing up to take Fliss's holdall and throwing her spare arm around her shoulder in a warm hug.

'Oh Hat it's so sweet of you to come *and* to have had the boys too. Can't think what I've done to deserve such a wonderful friend,' Fliss said wistfully, aware that if Nick and Hattie's plans worked out she'd see a lot less of her. The same thought occurred to Hattie, but some things were best left unsaid.

'Anything for you, Fliss. You know that.'

As they were stowing the luggage in the boot, Fliss noticed Hattie's shopping.

'I say, Hat,' she exclaimed in surprise. 'Had a little retail therapy already I see!'

'Ooh, yes,' Hattie chuckled. 'It's all my patchwork stuff. I hope Nick doesn't blow a gasket when he finds out how much I've spent.'

'Hmm, well it's not every day you have a splurge. Anyway, tell me more!'

'Well, the course tutors told us to choose a project to work on over the eight weeks, which is especially good for me, what with all the waiting over Nick's application and all that. So, guess what

I'm going to make?' Hattie giggled, as she selected first gear and pulled out of the parking space.

'Judging by the amount of stuff you've bought, it's obviously not a pair of cushion covers.'

'Well, I *was* tempted to make some as Christmas presents, but that seemed a bit boring, so then I made a rash decision. I'm making a quilted cover for our bed.'

'Always suspected you had a screw loose, Hat.'

'Screw loose? If you think I'm a bit wacky, you should see the two old girls who run the course – talk about little and large. And their outfits! Cynthia, a lady I met on Wednesday has some interesting info on the pair too. I gather she lives near you.'

'Cynthia? Would that be Cynthia Dacey by any chance, or Sin-Bin Dacey, as she's sometimes known?' asked Fliss, whose level of interest had suddenly cranked up a couple of gears.

'Sin-Bin? Has she got a bit of a reputation then? She seemed sort of mousey to me. Said she knew you.'

'Well, it's not surprising in such a small community. Cynthia knows everyone and everything worth knowing,' Fliss told her. 'She's not exactly a naughty girl – not with a husband like hers – but she seems to have a hotline on who's been up to what.'

'A husband like hers?'

'Oh yes, Donald Dacey wears the trousers in that household, a bit of a straight-laced so-and-so, if you know what I mean. He and Mark play in the same cricket team; that's how I know.'

'Ah, I see.'

'Anyway, it's just as well we've got nothing to hide, isn't it,' remarked Fliss coyly, 'because Sin-Bin Dacey would be sure to sniff it out.'

Ah yes, Hattie recalled again, the jobbing gardener rumour. If it *had* been true, Cynthia would have dished the dirt on that tasty bit of scandal. But what would happen if Cynthia spotted *her* in conversation with Leo one night? The details would probably be round Saunderton and Bledlow at the speed of light.

Fliss listened open-mouthed as Hattie elaborated on the more interesting aspects of Zena and Marigold's partnership. As they ploughed on through the busy town centre and out into the suburbs, she also entertained her with her other observations on the college and her encounter with the grouchy caretaker. Then, before she could stop herself, she found herself referring to her meeting with Leo, who seemed to be popping into her head with surprising regularity.

'So, who is he?' Fliss asked a little too keenly for Hattie's liking. She was going to have to do some speedy improvising.

'Oh, he was just someone in my year at uni, but I don't think he'd have recognised me if I hadn't said anything. I had long hair back then and my figure's filled out, more's the pity,' sighed Hattie.

'You can't turn back the clock, Hat,' Fliss remarked wistfully.

'I know, but I must admit I wish I was ten again.'

'What? With all that lumpy puppy fat and scary talk of periods and so on!'

'No, you clot; I wish I was *size* ten again. The trouble is, I find it so hard to say no to chocolate!'

They both convulsed in laughter.

'Anyway, Hat, are you going to meet up again or was he just passing through?'

Hattie realised, with a sinking feeling, that trying to explain this seemingly innocent meeting was fraught with danger. Her talent for improvisation was being tested to the limit and there were so many gaps in Leo's life. Was he married, divorced, separated, single? Where was he living? Well, whatever the answers were, it didn't actually matter, because she hadn't intended to tell Fliss in the first place.

'I'm not exactly sure,' she began, 'but I got the impression that he wasn't going to be around for long. He said something about making a business call... Yes, that's it... I remember now... It was just a flying visit.'

'So who *was* he?' Fliss urged.

Hattie paused to think of the right answer.

'Golly, Hat, your memory's not up to tricks.'

Hattie bit her lip and stared at the traffic ahead before saying, 'It was Len something. Um... Len Marshall. That's it.'

'Len Marshall? That's quite an old sort of name for someone our age.'

'Hmm, it is,' agreed Hattie, silently cursing herself for such a poor choice. Thankfully, the welcome sight of the house appearing before them offered the perfect escape from the conversation. As she steered carefully onto the drive, she vowed to keep a tight rein on her tongue in future. If Fliss had suspicions about the encounter, she didn't say anything, but she was probably too distracted by the thought of confronting her sons with the facts of Granny Wardill's illness, a task she wasn't relishing one bit.

5

The cutting mat, cutting wheel, cutting guide, fabric, folder of worksheets and of course the homework square, just about fitted into the large art folder that Hattie had unearthed from the glory hole under the stairs. It hadn't been used since Laura had discarded it after finishing her A levels and it still had a pink flower key-fob dangling from the handle. As Hattie prepared to leave for the second patchwork session, she felt a sense of foreboding that had been building all day. She'd woken that morning, the first day of February, regretting that she'd ever agreed to meet Leo. Half an hour, she decided, is all he's having. If he couldn't explain in that time, then tough!

Naturally she'd had to concoct a suitable cover story to account for being home later than usual and that's where Cynthia fitted quite conveniently into her plan. She'd already told Nick about striking up a friendship with someone from the class, so at nine thirty she'd text him and tell him they were going for a coffee together in town. Perfect! To make her story watertight, she was planning to find out as much as she could about Cynthia during the evening, on top of the gossip from Fliss. Nick would be sure to ask about her and Hattie had learned her lesson about incomplete cover stories.

Arriving at the classroom, she was pleased to see Cynthia already seated at the worktable they'd shared the previous week. With five minutes before the class was due to begin, there was plenty of time to glean a few useful facts (as casually as she could, of course). Much to Hattie's delight, Cynthia loved talking about herself. It was rather like winding up a clockwork toy and letting it run. By the time Zena and Marigold had taken up their starting positions in front of the class, Hattie had squirrelled away plenty of background information to scatter in her account of the evening.

'Welcome, ladies,' began Zena crisply. 'It's so good to see everyone here again. Marigold and I can't *wait* to see what you've all been up to since last we met.'

Marigold nodded and beamed, her chins wobbling in perfect co-ordination.

'I've spotted some of the homework pieces already, but I'd like *everyone* to take out and display their work,' Zena instructed in a no-nonsense tone. Everyone did as they were told, some with nervous giggles. 'Now ladies, let's all circulate and admire everyone's efforts,' she added.

'And don't let's be coy about our work,' gushed Marigold, smartly attired in a grey version of last week's embroidered skirt and a burgundy mohair jumper that accentuated her ample bosom. This week, Zena was cutting a dash in skin-tight, knee-high boots over rust trousers, teamed up with a lime-green overshirt. Compared with her stunning ensemble, Hattie felt as dowdy as a discarded teabag.

She and Cynthia joined their fellow students, drifting round the worktables, peering intently at the array of homework squares. Nobody dared say a word, but instead made polite murmuring noises. Zena and Marigold, on the other hand, felt quite at liberty to say exactly what they thought, but were somehow tactful enough not to wound anyone's pride.

'What a perfectly unusual juxtaposition of colours,' commented Zena with a slightly puzzled air as she held up a square that mixed clashing shades of pink and orange. 'So adventurous!'

'A bit like Zena and Marigold's colour schemes last week,' whispered Hattie in Cynthia's ear. Cynthia sniggered into her hand.

Marigold swooped on another effort, where no two sides were

equal, and gazed at it wide-eyed, struggling for the best choice of words. 'Such individuality!' she exclaimed warmly. 'Now let's see if your next one can be a *teensy* bit straighter. Well tried though.'

Hattie nervously awaited the pronouncement on her own effort, but when the moment came, all the pair could manage was the usual 'super' and 'well done'. It was almost as bad as enduring a dreaded Ofsted inspection.

During the rest of the evening, a more relaxed atmosphere settled on the class as Zena and Marigold demonstrated two new designs. However, a few worried looks were exchanged by the less accomplished students. The designs were more complicated than the previous week – a sign of things to come, no doubt.

'Now, it's over to you, girls,' announced Zena.

'And let's have some really precise cutting,' Marigold added encouragingly, with a meaningful glance towards the creator of the wonky square.

'*And* remember your blade safety at all times!' Zena reminded the class in her well-honed schoolteacher delivery.

Hattie and Cynthia rummaged through their fabrics and then set to with their cutting guides and wheels, carefully checking the dimensions on the worksheets. Around the room there was an air of feverish activity and excited chatter. As Hattie worked, Leo suddenly popped into her mind unbidden, a reminder of her rash promise to meet him in less than an hour and a half. Anger and apprehension gripped her and for a brief moment, there was an odd fluttery feeling in her stomach. She was finding it very difficult to concentrate.

'Aha! I spy a blade!' came a voice uncomfortably close.

Hattie jumped guiltily and turned to see Zena brandishing the naked blade.

'50p my dear!' she demanded smugly, deftly clicking the blade cover back into place with one hand and brandishing her collecting pot with the other. Hattie sensed a hot blush spreading over her face as she rummaged in her purse for some small change.

'Oops! So sorry, Miss – I mean Zena.' Hers was the first 50p to go into the pot and was clearly heard as the entire class went into silent, suspended animation.

As the minutes ticked away, the tension inside Hattie grew: her heartbeat stepped up a gear, her stomach seemed to turn several somersaults in quick succession and then her bladder decided it was time for some attention. On returning to the room, Zena's strident tones could be heard again.

'Naughty, naughty!' she shrilled, grabbing another abandoned wheel. '50p please!'

Although she now felt a nervous wreck, it was comforting to know she wasn't the only student with too much on her mind.

By twenty-five minutes past nine, an aura of self-satisfaction had settled over the assembled company and many of the novice patch workers were giggling like boisterous first-formers ready for the holidays. Without exception, everybody's cutting and stitching had passed muster and even Marigold was heard to comment that they were certainly the most promising class they'd had for a long time.

'Now, don't forget to finish your squares for next week,' Zena reminded them as they left the room.

Now for it, thought Hattie, with a mixture of terror and impatience. Timing was crucial if she was to avoid any compromising encounters. If Leo was already waiting, she'd have to be ready with Plan B, although there was precious little time to concoct one. As they walked down the corridor, Cynthia relaying cousin Dotty's latest gossip from Quaintly, Hattie's Plan B became clear. It would have to be another quick loo dash. While Cynthia prattled on, Hattie nodded and smiled, hopefully in all the right places.

As they approached the foyer, she feverishly scanned the area for a tall, dark, handsome, Italian presence.

'Till next week then, and happy stitching!' Cynthia called as she sped off to her waiting husband. Hattie nervously glanced round the foyer, now heaving with a motley assortment of students on their way home. For a moment, she was tempted to leave, convincing herself that *she'd* turned up on time, but Leo hadn't. The pounding and churning inside her seemed to reach a climax and she was amazed people weren't turning round wondering who or what was responsible for all the noise. Just one more minute, she decided, and not a second longer. It would be meagre punishment for the anguish he'd caused her at Victoria Station. Pulling back her cuff, she watched the second hand ticking slowly around the watch face and prepared for a quick exit.

'Hattie,' breathed a familiar, deep voice from somewhere behind her. She leapt several inches in the air, emitting a startled shriek. Her stomach went from somersaults to free-fall while her heart rate accelerated into top gear. Then everything went black.

'Here, have some water.' It was the same voice, but even closer this time. Hattie opened her eyes to see a glass of water in front of her. The hand holding it was definitely masculine and another arm was wrapped firmly round her shoulders. But why was she on the floor? She took a few tentative sips.

'What...? Where...?' she muttered, her head swimming.

'It's okay, Hattie. You fainted, but I caught you. It's a good thing I was here,' came the voice again. It was Leo sounding extraordinarily pleased with himself.

How dare he, she thought. How dare he sneak up and scare the living daylights out of me and then smugly congratulate himself for being the knight in shining armour. However, try as she might, she couldn't summon enough energy to tell him. She was still feeling woozy, but even so, she was aware of a hubbub of voices and a sea of anxious faces peering at her. Were her knickers on show? She hoped not. Was she wearing the tights with the gaping hole around the crotch? From her undignified sprawl on the floor, it was difficult to know how much of her underwear was attracting unwelcome attention. She was mortified.

'Some more water?' Leo murmured, kneeling beside her.

'No, I'm fine now. I am, really,' she insisted, struggling to her feet. 'And, Leo, please remove your arm.' The crowd of gawpers that had homed in at the promise of some excitement now drifted away, seeing it to be very short-lived. Two elderly grannies from the spinning and weaving group gazed in admiration at Leo's chivalrous efforts and then ambled towards the door.

'It was touching the way that chap went to the rescue of that poor woman, wasn't it?' said one to her friend.

'Hmm, she came over all peculiar,' replied the other. 'Properly flushed wasn't she? Menopause… Bound to be.'

'Nasty hole in her tights though,' sniggered the first one, mercifully for Hattie, now well out of earshot.

'What you need is good strong coffee,' suggested Leo, taking command of the situation. He snatched up her folder and started to steer her towards the door After a few steps, though, she remembered her plan to text Nick about her coffee date with Cynthia. She had to do it straight away. She'd no idea how long she'd been unconscious, but it must now have been several minutes after nine thirty.

'Wait, Leo. I need to send a text.' As she typed out the message she started to feel distinctly uncomfortable about her subterfuge. Ironically, she really *did* need that cup of coffee and it was too complicated to change her plans now, despite the nagging voice of her conscience. To add to her guilt, Nick texted back almost immediately:

Enjoy yr coffee, c u soon, Nick.

'I know a wine bar where we can get coffee,' Leo told her. Hattie tucked her mobile away and they made their way through the car park and along the canal walkway into town.

The Four Seasons was an attractively lit establishment with gleaming chrome and dark wood fittings. The seating was arranged in low-level groupings at the front, with tables in alcoves towards the rear.

'I'd rather sit over there. You never know who might come in,' said Hattie, pointing to the back and implying that her choice of seating was more to do with avoiding noisy drinkers than the prying eyes of friends, colleagues or acquaintances. In the relative shadow of the doorway she quickly scanned the assembled clientele, satisfied that it didn't include anyone she'd rather avoid. Then Leo went to the bar while Hattie tried to decide exactly where to sit. The last thing she wanted was Nick to hear that she'd been seen having a cosy tête-à-tête with a handsome stranger in the secluded corner of an Aylesbury wine bar.

They had found a table in an alcove where the subdued lighting and luxuriant foliage of some potted palms conspired to create a shady and private hideaway.

'We need to be quick,' she hissed. 'Sorry, but I can't be too late. I'm supposed to be having coffee with Cynthia.'

'What? Now? But where? When did you arrange that?'

'No, Leo,' she replied irritably. 'I don't mean I'm having coffee with Cynthia as well. *This* is having coffee with Cynthia,' she explained.

'Oh, I get it,' said Leo. 'Still not talking to your husband then?'

'No, not when it comes to mentioning your name, Leo.'

A waiter arrived at their table with their drinks.

'Right, Leo, let's have your story shall we?' she suggested, glancing at her watch, alarmed to see that it was close to ten o'clock.

'Story?' He frowned at her glibness. 'Hattie, please don't assume I'm just making up something, even if that's what you seem to be doing.' His remark, true as it was, roused her irritation, but she didn't comment, leaving him free to continue.

'On that day, that Friday, I had a meeting at the wine importers in Pimlico,' he began.

'Yes, you already told me that,' broke in Hattie, frustrated by his backtracking.

Leo carried on undaunted. 'Jack Edlin, the chief buyer, was delayed. It was some emergency appointment – doctor, dentist, something like that…'

'Leo, please stick to the point,' Hattie growled, glancing at her watch.

'Well, eventually he arrived and I told him I was due to meet someone at noon at Victoria Station and had a train to catch. He assured me that we'd be finished in good time and that he'd organise a taxi to get me to the station.'

She was amazed by how well he had remembered each detail, unless they were merely part of his own fabrication.

'Hattie, believe me when I tell you that all I wanted was to get that meeting over so I could be with you. Everything I had to do that morning was a necessary chore, but I kept in mind the prize at the end – a lovely girl whom I dearly loved.'

As he spoke those last words he looked at her wistfully. The words melted her heart and she gulped in amazement. He looked and sounded sincere. So why, she wondered for the umpteenth time, did he not show up? Was he about to tell her he'd had last minute doubts about their relationship? Did he have some drop-dead gorgeous village girl waiting for him back in Montelugia? Or was there some other student who had caught his eye?

'So, what happened?' asked Hattie, as patiently as she could. 'I've been waiting twenty-six years to discover the answer.' In reality, she'd never expected to learn what had happened, but it seemed to be taking a long time to be revealed and time was in short supply. She took a few more sips from her mug as Leo paused to swig another mouthful of the bitter, black brew that he preferred. Her gaze drifted towards the door as she heard some laughter.

'So, we finished the meeting around eleven thirty and –'

'Oh no! I don't believe it!' Hattie spluttered, aghast at what, or rather *who*, she'd seen arrive.

'What do you mean? I assure you the meeting –'

'No, I don't mean *that*. I'm sorry Leo, I've got to get out of here somehow – without being seen,' she whispered tensely, ducking down behind a handy menu card.

'But why?' Leo demanded, the colour draining from his face.

'Fliss and Mark have just come in. They mustn't see me!'

'Who? Where?' asked Leo, skewing round in his seat.

'Leopard-print jacket and bottle-green anorak,' she hissed. 'Quick, Leo, could you sort of turn your chair a bit so they can't see me?' He did so and then leaned towards her, staring into her eyes with tenderness and concern.

'So much deception, dear Hattie,' he murmured sadly, shaking his head.

'And all *your* fault, Leo,' she hissed back.

Hattie lifted her mug higher and with the help of the carefully positioned menu, checked on Fliss and Mark by peeping to one side. They were at the bar ordering drinks, their backs turned towards the alcove. If they stayed exactly where they were, this would give her a chance to make a speedy exit.

'Sorry, Leo. Must dash.'

'Again?' Leo sighed, trying to hide his exasperation. 'Very well, but can we please exchange phone numbers?'

'Okay, but quick!' Why was she agreeing to this? she wondered. Was it that Leo charm?

Numbers were quickly scrawled on serviettes, Hattie keeping a check on her friends who were chatting together just a few feet away. Fliss was perched on a bar stool facing away from the door and another couple had very conveniently stationed themselves in the way, forming an extra barrier. Hattie worked out that if she kept to the darker side of the bar and walked straight out, she should have a good chance of leaving undetected. Fortunately, she was wearing her nondescript, grey coat, but her cherry red beanie would be too easily spotted, so she stuffed it down in her pocket.

'Must go,' she muttered, pulling her collar up round her ears. She set off at a pace that was brisk but not obviously hurrying. What she *didn't* spot as she made her way to the door was a stray foot carelessly dangling in the way. It belonged to a thirty-something male engaged in chatting up a girl who was alternately giggling and texting her mates. The unfortunate position of his long limbs was an accident waiting to happen for the unwary wine bar customer – in this case, the fleeing Hattie.

115

'Sugar!' she yelped, making contact with the well-padded, designer footwear. Her fairy godmother must have been at hand because, miraculously, she did not fall. Her folder, however, went flying across the floor and landed with a clatter.

'Sorry love,' drawled the trainers' owner, reluctantly rearranging his limbs. 'You okay?'

'Idiot!' cursed Hattie, tight-lipped with fear and trying to ignore her throbbing ankle. Snatching up her folder, she quickly reached the door, not daring to look around. The chill night air was a welcome relief and she fervently hoped that the noise in the bar might have masked any of the thumps and clatters of her undignified exit.

As Hattie was failing miserably at a quiet escape from The Four Seasons, Fliss and Mark were catching up on the evening. It was a nuisance to be without her car while the brakes were being fixed, but Fliss was flexibility personified. Dropping Mark at the college much earlier had fitted perfectly with her plan to top up her tan at the solarium in a new health and fitness club on the other side of town.

'So how was it? Any progress with organising the course?' she asked, sipping her iced tonic water. Mark had been on a fact-finding mission for his company. They were regularly exhibiting their greetings cards at trade fairs all over Europe now that they were printed in several languages. To maximise sales potential, Mark was pushing for additional language training for some of his team. Although most of their European contacts were fluent in English, the company's policy was to make an effort to speak their customer's language whenever possible. Mark had been tipped off about a new 'Italian conversation for holidaymakers' course at the college and that led him to explore the possibility of a business version. It had been arranged for him to sit in on the session that evening to meet the tutor and then discuss how the college might accommodate such a course the following term.

'Well, it's looking quite likely. The tutor happens to be Italian too,' Mark explained.

'Really? Is he on the regular college staff?'

'No, he's just filling in while the usual tutor's off sick,' Mark continued. 'Although he doesn't have a teaching qualification, the fact that he's Italian and had a lot of his education in English schools means he's basically bilingual.'

A clatter, dull thud and startled cry cut through the chatter at the bar and several heads turned automatically to see what had happened.

'Oh, poor thing,' sympathised Mark, spotting a female just about managing to stay upright after colliding with something or someone.

'What?' Fliss twisted round and caught a glimpse of the unfortunate woman in question, who seemed unsteady on her feet. 'Looks like someone's been knocking back too many cocktails or something!' she chuckled. 'I bet she'll have a sore head in the morning.'

'No, I think some berk had his feet in the way,' Mark told her, craning his neck to get a better view.

The woman, who had dropped a large folder in the collision, now snatched it up and made for the door. A small pink key-fob was the only bright note on the uniform grey of the retreating figure. It dangled from the handle with a jaunty air. Fliss did a double-take.

'D'you know, Mark, for a moment that tottery lady looked a bit like Hattie, from the rear,' she giggled. 'But I hardly think that our Hat's the sort of girl who frequents wine bars on her ownsome.'

'Not unless she's leading a double life,' Mark agreed. 'I think the tottering lady may have been sitting over there somewhere.' He nodded in the direction of the low-lit alcoves.

Leo, meanwhile, was trying to work out if the 'sugar' he'd just heard had come from Hattie's lips. The sound had made his heart sink and he'd had to stop himself from leaping up in another chivalrous act. It would be bound to turn into another complicated drama for which he wouldn't be thanked. On top of that, he knew that Mark was the visitor in his class just an hour earlier. It was the sort of business contact he liked to make, but wondered if he really wanted to spend his free time teaching sales reps. However, with the current state of the housing market, he realised a little extra income wouldn't go amiss. He even wondered about setting up and marketing his own course.

For the time being, he stayed in his seat and a phrase popped into his mind. What was that quotation? 'Oh, what a tangled web we weave… when we…' something about deceive. That was Hattie for sure and now she had dragged *him* into the deception. After he'd drained his mug and convinced himself that all the deceit was definitely *not* his problem, he decided he'd just get up and leave. If Mark happened to spot him, then he'd be genial and, for Hattie's sake, try to give the impression that he was there by himself.

The crowd at the bar had thinned out a little and Leo could see Fliss perched on her stool while Mark leaned nonchalantly against the bar. However, fate decreed that Leo's decision to leave coincided exactly with Mark turning his head. Leo had decided to keep his head down and eyes averted so he was unaware of the flicker of recognition in Mark's face.

'Oh… hi, Signor Marcello!' called Mark, recognising the same aquiline features and crinkly dark hair of the Italian tutor.

Leo froze in his tracks then turned with a quickly assumed look of surprise.

'Ah, Mr Tarrier,' he said with a smile, intending to keep the exchange brief, but somehow failing miserably in the first few words. 'Good to meet you again. And this is…?' he added, turning to Fliss.

'Oh yes, may I introduce my wife, Felicity – Fliss to her friends. Fliss, this is the Signor Marcello I was telling you about.'

'Well, there'd hardly be several Signor Marcellos would there?' giggled Fliss, amused by the way he'd taken her hand and made a slight bow.

'The rest are back in Italy,' Leo replied politely, 'which is a lot warmer than England, most of the time.'

'Oh, and what part of Italy would that be?' asked Fliss, feasting her eyes on his handsome features.

'Tuscany, quite near Florence actually. I was brought up in a very small village perched on a hillside,' Leo told her. 'Pardon me, but I must go. I just dropped in for a quick coffee before going home. So good to meet you again.'

'I'll be in touch through the college office, as I said earlier, and thank you for allowing me to sit in on your session. It was most stimulating.'

When Leo moved out of earshot Fliss rolled her eyes and gave a little shudder of pleasure. 'I bet the female students sit and drool all evening,' she sighed.

'Hmm, there were definitely some who were hanging on his every word,' Mark agreed. 'Strange thing though, Fliss; I could have sworn that tottery lady came from the same alcove as Signor Marcello.'

'The tottering totty?' sniggered Fliss, collapsing in giggles at her witticism. 'You think the dishy Signor Marcello might have had a lady friend with him? Maybe she's a secret girlfriend or mistress and he's got a little wife at home waiting for him.'

'And maybe you've got too vivid an imagination my sweet,' teased Mark.

Fliss ignored this remark. 'Hmm, well, whoever it was it can't have been Hat, even though the back view seemed familiar. Our Hat's never shown the slightest inclination for extra-marital indulgences. In fact, she and Nick are the most devoted couple I know,' she continued. 'Besides which she's always been boringly unadventurous in my opinion.' However, even as Fliss spoke with confidence, she recalled, with a sinking feeling, that time when she'd joked with Hat about a secret lover. Instead of chuckling a 'you must be joking!' she'd gone strangely quiet, with an odd look on her face. Where was she meant to be this evening? Fliss remembered about her friend's patchwork course, but not when it was, with her mum's cancer concerns buzzing around her head.

Hattie pondered over her cover story as she negotiated the round-about at the end of the ring road. Well, she'd been attending a patchwork class, had a dizzy turn – the time of the month, of course – a stranger had helped her then she'd gone for a reviving cup of coffee with one of her classmates. That was all perfectly respectable. But then came the niggling thought that Fliss or Mark might have spotted her at The Four Seasons. What would she say if challenged? How could she explain away her so-called patchworking companion whose presence was strangely absent? She'd say Cynthia had to leave early and she'd just stayed to finish her drink. Did that sound plausible? She hoped it did.

As she came close to the village, her mind went back to Leo's story and especially the bit about loving her dearly. He sounded sincere. He looked sincere, but there always seemed to be a 'but' with Leo. She couldn't decide if she despised him, was furious with him or was just a bit intrigued to know exactly what *did* happen on that fateful July day. Well, now that they had exchanged mobile numbers, he knew how to get in touch. Hattie had to admit to herself that that was, in itself, quite unnerving.

Fliss's brain had been working overtime. Something about Hattie wasn't quite right – in fact, several things – and the only solu-tion was to invite her over for coffee. She was only a few minutes' drive away and they'd even organised their part-time jobs so that neither worked on a Thursday – ideal for an occasional get-together.

'Hi, Hat. Fancy popping over for coffee? I'm dying to hear how your patchwork is coming along?'

Hattie's stomach tightened and her heart started racing. This was the call she dreaded, coming so soon after her close encounter the night before. Maybe she *had* been spotted, but short of an outright challenge, she was determined to play the innocent. She took a deep breath. 'Coffee?' she asked brightly. 'Sounds lovely, Fliss, but I was about to cut out the pieces for a new patchwork square and get it stitched this morning. It's my homework from last night.'

'Oh, I see.' Fliss sounded more than a tad disappointed.

'Tell you what, Fliss; why don't you come over here instead? I can get some cutting done while you're driving over, if that's okay.'

'That's fine, Hat,' agreed Fliss. 'See you soon.' The conversation confirmed that her friend had been at her evening class the night before, which wasn't a million miles from The Four Seasons. She was intrigued to find out more.

Hattie hurried back into the sitting room after the call and surveyed the mess. The contents of the old art folder were strewn over the floor and sofa and the rest of the room was in desperate need of some TLC. Resignedly, she hauled out the vacuum cleaner to remove the worst of the mess: debris from Josh's trainers, Jezebel's fur and strands and snippets of fabric left over from her previous cutting session. Fliss might be her best friend, but it pained Hat to admit to her own slovenly ways, considering Fliss's show-home standards, even if they *were* the result of paid help. Next, she filled the kettle, remembering that they'd used the last of the filter coffee after Sunday lunch. They'd have to make do with plain old instant and a few BOGOF supermarket ginger nuts. Sylph-like as ever, Fliss was usually on some unnecessary diet, and only indulged in boring but top-brand arrowroot biscuits.

Back in the sitting room, Hattie found her cutting wheel and prepared to slice up a jade- and navy-spotted fat quarter into triangles. She was planning to team this with a pale grey background; quite subtle, she thought. Among her selection of fabric, there was a length of navy with a swirly leaf design that would provide an interesting contrast. It was just the sort of design she'd seen in the home section of *Country Living* magazine. This she would use for the larger triangles, but just as she got her cutting guide lined up, the doorbell chimed out.

'Lovely to see you,' she said, greeting her friend with a sunny smile that she hoped would disguise any uncharitable or guilty thoughts. 'Just go on through to the sitting room. I'll bring the coffee in a couple of shakes.'

Fliss found a smug-looking Jezebel stretched out on the sofa, claiming as much of it as she could. As she made herself comfortable in an armchair, Hattie's mobile leapt into life. Of course, Hattie was too far away to hear, until Fliss realised it was a text coming through. Out of sheer nosiness, she glanced at the upside-down screen and briefly saw the name of the texter on the display, just as Hattie made her entrance with a laden tray. Len? Was he a secret lover? After all, it seemed that they had, in fact, exchanged phone numbers.

'Hat, your phone just rang.'

'Oh, really?' She picked it up and Fliss watched intently for any tell-tale reaction. A mixture of surprise and annoyance briefly flickered across her face, but she quickly put the phone down without reading the message.

'Anything important?' Fliss asked casually.

'No, it's just the library. I expect they're reminding me there's a book due back soon,' Hattie remarked casually. She certainly didn't intend explaining the Leo saga. Fliss, however, was intrigued, knowing the text was nothing of the sort and that Hattie obviously had something to hide.

'So how's your course going then?' she asked, keen to diffuse the situation. She picked up a steaming mug and sipped it tentatively. There was a distinct lack of aroma – obviously some cheap brand.

'Oh, it's going well actually; except being fined 50p for breaching Zena and Marigold's health and safety rules.'

'What?' giggled Fliss.

Hattie demonstrated with a deft click how the blade could be opened for cutting and then covered when not in use. 'Zena and Marigold are very strict, you know.'

Fliss found this highly amusing. 'Goodness, it sounds like being back at school again!' She took another sip. No, it wasn't any better, she decided. If this was all Hat could afford it wasn't surprising that Nick was trying for a better job. 'It's Aylesbury College you're going to, isn't it?' she asked.

'Yes, that's right.' Hattie shoved Jezebel off the sofa and started picking off cat hairs distractedly, dreading the way the conversation might be heading.

'What an amazing coincidence. You'll never guess!'

Oh yes I will, thought Hattie with a sense of foreboding. Determined not to give any clue, she assumed a quizzical expression. 'What won't I guess?'

'Mark was at Aylesbury College last night.'

'Really? Was he doing a course? I wouldn't have thought Mark had any time for evening classes with all that jet-setting.'

'No, he was fixing up a language course for his sales team. They go all over Europe, you know, and there are quite a few customers in Italy now. He thinks it's disgraceful how lazy we Brits are about learning other languages. Then he heard about a new course at the college – "Conversational Italian for Holidaymakers", or something like that.'

Hattie gulped and realised with a horrible sense of inevitability that Leo Marcello might be about to figure in the scenario that Fliss was unfolding. 'Oh really?' was all she could manage, hoping her tone was tending towards ever-so-slightly-bored. She reached for another ginger nut and dunked it carefully in her mug.

'Yes, and he sat in on part of the class to get an idea how it might possibly adapt to a business language course. The tutor is a real dreamboat, Hat. I met him afterwards,' Fliss sighed with a smile.

Hattie was in despair now, knowing that Leo was a weekly obstacle to be avoided and also exactly where Fliss had met him. She thought herself lucky to have made a speedy exit, even if Leo hadn't.

'Oh really?' She seemed to be running out of other replies, but it was difficult to know how to react to this little snippet. If she was being true to character, she should really show a bit more interest; after all, she and Fliss had a long record of giggling over the more delectable examples of the male gender, and Leo – despite his obvious failings – definitely fitted into that category.

'So, you went to the class too did you, or are you planning to enrol for next term if he's such a dish?'

'No, as a matter of fact, I tried out a new health and fitness centre last night – hence my healthy glow – but with my car's brakes being fixed, we had to combine forces as it were. All okay now though; Ted's Motors had it ready for me first thing. Anyway, where was I? Ah yes, well Mark and I went to have a nightcap later at The Four Seasons and that's where I met the gorgeous Signor Marcello.'

'Hmm, I see… And?' Hattie was wondering what might be coming next. Inside, her stomach was churning nervously, so she picked up her coffee and took a few more sips.

'He was charming, Hat, in an old fashioned and genteel sort of way, as well as oozing sex appeal,' Fliss gushed. 'You won't believe it, but he actually took my hand and made a sort of bow. Talk about the tingle factor!'

'I know.'

'You know?' asked Fliss quizzically.

'Um… I know the sort of chap you mean, like in the old movies,' Hattie added hurriedly.

'Yes, well Mark was very impressed with him, so hopefully something might get fixed up for next term.' Fliss needed to introduce the next topic very carefully, so she paused and took a final sip from her mug. 'Something odd happened while we were at The Four Seasons. Well, not odd exactly, but I saw someone who looked like you, from the back.'

'If it was from the back, how can you say they looked like me?'

'Oh, I just wondered if you'd been there. I mean it's not *that* far from the college after all. You'd have loved Signor Marcello!' Fliss remarked.

'Marcello?' said Hattie, realising that she had a perfectly good reason to admit she'd seen him. 'That name's familiar, now I think about it. Nick decided to get another valuation after all. I think the chap from Mia Casa who came had that name but I only glimpsed him briefly. I was out in the garden, with the secateurs, you know me Fliss!'

'Oh yes, that must be the same chap. Mark said he was an estate agent.'

She glanced across to where Hattie's patchwork gear had been tidied and saw a large art folder, identical to the one the tottering totty had been carrying. In fact, it was the very same, with a pink daisy key-fob dangling from the handle. Out of the corner of her eye, Hattie saw Fliss's interested stare. Fliss's words were still echoing in her head as she held her breath, wondering how she should react. Then, in a frantic bid to clear her reputation, she remembered the perfectly good cover story she had fabricated for Nick's benefit.

'Er... The Four Seasons did you say? Which one is that?' she asked frowning as she fished in the bottom of the biscuit caddy and found a stray and slightly stale chocolate digestive – bliss!

'The one just round the corner from Canal Walk, between the snazzy florist and the mobile phone store. It's all chrome and dark wood. You must have passed it dozens of times.' Fliss remembered the sprawling woman and glanced down at Hattie's ankles. Yes, there was a small bluish bruise on the right one. Game, set and match, she thought with some satisfaction.

'Of course!' laughed Hattie, as if a great logjam in her memory had just shifted. 'The Four Seasons! Do you know, I keep getting that one muddled up with The Three Wishes in Goose Street. Yes, of course I was there. That's where Cynthia and I went for coffee after the class.'

Fliss couldn't help feeling just a bit disappointed with such a boring reason. At least that accounted for her being there, not some clandestine meeting with the mysterious Len after all. Poor old Hat; even a coffee with an old uni chum sounded more tempting than another half hour with Sin Bin Dacey – unless it was to catch up on some fresh Zena and Marigold gossip.

'So it *was* you I saw!' exclaimed Fliss. 'I couldn't be sure at the time. But I didn't see your friend.'

'Oh, she had to leave early. Her husband was picking her up and he doesn't like to be kept waiting, apparently,' explained Hattie, adding more embroidery to her story.

'Oh yes; Donald Dacey's definitely the possessive type. Remember what I told you about him wearing the trousers?' affirmed Fliss. 'So, how's the ankle?'

'Not bad, thanks,' she said, giving it a rub. 'Some stupid man stuck his foot out just as I was passing. One moment I was upright and dignified, the next moment I was in free-fall!' They both chuckled and Hattie awarded herself an A-star for pure inventiveness.

An hour later, they'd exhausted their news updates and, to Hattie's relief, Fliss remembered a few urgent chores on her to-do list that she couldn't put off a moment longer.

'It's a shame we didn't spot each other last night, Hat,' she commented as she zipped up her jacket in the hallway, 'I'd have introduced you properly to that gorgeous Italian hunk.'

'Hmm, Leo…' Hattie agreed, quite forgetting what she was supposed to know.

'What did you say?' asked Fliss, quick as a flash.

'Leo Marcello, of course. You said that earlier. Don't you remember?' blustered Hattie, cursing herself for another stupid foot-in-mouth. Fliss hadn't even mentioned his first name.

'Did I? I don't remember. Or perhaps I did.' Now she was having doubts herself.

'Yes, Fliss; you said you and Mark went to The Four Seasons for a nightcap and that's where you met the gorgeous Leo Marcello. I remember it most distinctly.'

'Hmm, right, maybe I did,' pondered Fliss. 'Anyway, as you're at college on the same night, you might even spot him around the campus.' She then went on to describe Leo with amazing accuracy from one brief meeting. Hattie could have added some more intimate details. However, she assumed an interested expression, while guiltily recalling Leo's warning about deception and lies.

'Well, I'll keep an eye open for him,' she said casually as Fliss left. 'And give my love to Mark and the boys.'

Quickly, she returned to the sitting room where Jezebel had successfully knocked her mobile off the coffee table and was batting it around the floor.

'Bad girl!' she scolded, retrieving the phone and reading the message that had been sent an hour or more earlier:

Can call @ 12, plse txt if not OK, Leo

'Oh no,' she groaned, checking her watch. It was close to midday. Sod's law seemed to be getting the upper hand yet again. There was every chance that Leo and Fliss might have passed each other in the road. In a panic she flicked to 'compose' and texted back:

Not a gd time, sorry 4 dlay, Hat

Just down the road, Fliss had reached the junction where the cul-de-sac met the main village road. Because of the bend there, drivers had to stop completely before emerging, unless they were downright stupid. As Fliss was checking for approaching traffic, a neat little Italian car came from her left, indicating a right turn. Fliss gazed with admiration as it slowed down – she just loved those sexy little cars – and realised there was something familiar about the driver. At the same time, Leo saw the waiting Fiesta and thought he'd seen the woman driver somewhere before. Almost subconsciously, they exchanged a glance of recognition, but it wasn't until a few moments had passed and they were on their separate ways that both realised where they'd met.

'The Italian hunk!' murmured Fliss with a smile.

'Hattie's friend, Fliss,' murmured Leo with approval, at the same time hearing the text signal from his mobile. He drew up at the side of the road.

'Now you tell me!' he muttered in frustration, as he read her message. With an impatient grating of gears, he turned and set off back into town, wondering if he'd ever get a chance to tell *his* side of what happened.

'Called in on Hat today,' Fliss told Mark, as they were enjoying mugs of coffee after supper.

'Oh yes? And was she the mysterious tottering totty?' Mark sniggered.

'She was,' confirmed Fliss, 'but it took ages to get a confession out of her. In fact, she was acting particularly furtively, and Hat's always been a straightforward sort of girl. Someone sent her a text while she was in the kitchen and I couldn't help noticing…'

'Couldn't help?' spluttered Mark. 'Didn't know your eyes were that good!'

'Well, all right, I took a sneaky peep if you must know, and I'm sure it was a message from her old uni chum Len, but our Hat tried to shrug it off as something quite different.' Fliss nodded her head sagely. 'She's got a guilty secret, mark my words.'

'Not the only one I suppose.' They exchanged meaningful looks.

'Hmm, well, as I was saying, she was acting quite oddly; sort of edgy and nervous. I'm sure if I'd shouted "Boo!" she'd have jumped out of her skin.'

'So did you manage to steer your cosy little interrogation round to last night?'

'Well, I started telling her about the dishy signor.'

'Thought he'd get a look in somehow. Got the hots for him, my sweet?'

Fliss glared at him and then continued. 'Mentioned where we met him and your plans for the course, but she just sat there listening,' continued Fliss undaunted. 'Then she suddenly tells me that the signor had been round in his official capacity, as if she'd just recovered from a spot of amnesia.'

'Poor girl's probably got a lot on her mind, stress at work or whatever. It affects the memory, you know.'

'Then she eventually comes to and tells me, yes, she was at The Four Seasons – always gets it confused with The Three Wishes, for some reason…'

'Three … four … I suppose if you're not so good at maths you might get confused,' reflected Mark. 'So did she confess to being a secret drinker?'

'No, she was there with Cynthia Dacey, having a chummy coffee together after the rigours of patchwork.'

'Oh-ho, Sin-Bin Dacey! I'm surprised Donald lets that woman off the leash. Didn't spot her though.'

'No, apparently she'd already gone running off to hubby, leaving Hat to finish her nightcap on her own.'

'Ah well, mystery solved,' yawned Mark, putting aside his empty mug.

'No, there's more!' breathed Fliss, with a grin. 'About the dishy signor and something Hat said.'

'Quite the hot topic, eh?'

'Well, it was something that just sort of slipped out. She said "Leo", just as if he was more than some chap who'd turned up to do his estate agent's stuff. Although she told me only minutes before that she was down the garden when he came.'

'Hmm, not quite the scandal of the century.'

Fliss snorted with frustration. 'Up to then, it had been signor this and signor that and I'm sure I hadn't even mentioned his first name. In fact I don't remember you mentioning it last night.'

'Sounds as if your memory's playing tricks.'

'Not a senior moment, is it? I'm too young for one of those, surely.'

'Ah, comes to us all. Any more revelations my love, or can I get to bed? I've a long drive to Harrogate tomorrow.'

'Well, amazingly, I saw the dishy signor turn into Nick and

Hattie's road not five minutes after we were talking about him. How weird is that?'

'Ah, so you thought you'd sort of willed him there?' Mark mocked. 'The powers of persuasion; they're wonderful to be sure. Doesn't quite work like that, Fliss, sorry to say, even with all the drooling the two of you were doing. I mean, think of all the times Nick has bored me senseless about his team over a pint and not once did the Arsenal team bus pull up outside.'

'Stop it Mark, I didn't mean that, I just thought it was a coincidence.'

'He was probably on his way to measure up some lucky householder.'

'Ooh, he could measure me up any day,' giggled Fliss, rolling her eyes.

'And on that interesting note, I'm off to bed. Got to leave by six.'

'And they say romance isn't dead,' sighed Fliss reaching for her new copy of *House Beautiful*.

6

Friday 3rd February – closing date for the Lydford Cross vacancies – passed uneventfully for Nick. Nevertheless, he couldn't help wondering how many late applications might have turned up that morning and how stiff the competition might be. According to Madge, who was always tuned into the general grapevine, someone else from Padgett and Bicton had also applied, but as she didn't mention any name, he assumed she could be deliberately winding him up.

For Hattie, however, 3rd February was as demanding as any Friday could be, with relentless rain and gusty winds most of the morning, and the children roaring around like caged animals. They'd been confined to their classrooms without a chance to let off steam and even the more timid ones were pushing the boundaries. She was due to take Sonia Rowse's class for PE straight after break – a task she did not relish at all. On days like this, a job at the checkout of the local supermarket seemed bliss by comparison. She decided that letting class 4R loose in the hall with the climbing apparatus seemed marginally less risky than dodging the showers in the playground where opportunities for mayhem had rather more scope. How wrong could she be? She spent half the lesson being given the run-around by the little blighters and the other half trying to persuade Jacob Pocock to come down from the apparatus after he unleashed the climbing rope on his class members from a great height, knocking them down like bar skittles. By comparison, the rest of the day was like a quiet stroll down a country lane with only the sound of blackbirds and crickets to disturb the heady silence. The Year 5s were using Golden Time to run a café in the hall for parents and governors and had been busily baking biscuits and cakes and decorating menu cards all morning. Several took on the roles of waiters and waitresses, while the recorder group tooted their way through 'Frère Jacques', 'London's Burning' and 'Au clair de la lune' several times.

'Splendid, splendid,' murmured Angus Neill, making one of his rare appearances. He sauntered across the hall, smiling amiably, narrowly missing wobbling waitresses with piles of fairy cakes, until he reached a table of mums who were being dominated by Gloria Preston, PTA chairperson extraordinaire. She was sporting one of her more dramatically plunging necklines and, even at a distance of several yards, Hattie could tell that Angus Neill's careful positioning had secured him a grandstand view.

'Dirty old man,' she muttered, under her breath, as she scurried away with a tray of empties to supervise the clearing up. She hoped that if her next head was a man he'd be ruled by his head rather than any other part of his anatomy.

By the time the end of day bell rang, the Year 5 staff were congratulating themselves and their weary charges on the successful conclusion to an otherwise dismally wet day. To Hattie, the brief showdown with Jacob Pocock seemed light years away.

The phone was ringing as Hattie arrived home at Monday lunch time.

'Hello,' she gasped, managing to grab the receiver before the call minder cut in.

'Hi, Hat. It's me!' It was Nick. 'Guess what, I've got an interview!'

'That's great, Nick. When?' Images of country cottages floated into her mind.

'Friday. *This* Friday at eleven, but I need to be there at ten so they can do the usual conducted tour stuff before the interview itself,' he explained, sounding suitably smug.

'I just *knew* you'd have an interview,' Hattie told him. 'I mean, who could resist you, what with all your experience and qualifications.' Although, if she were to be honest, she'd half expected that Nick might have been passed over for a twenty-something whizz-kid.

'Well, I hope the selection panel can see my valuable potential, that's all I can say,' boasted Nick, his initial confidence evaporating as he wondered about the calibre of the competition.

'Valuable potential? Hey, bighead, is old Madge eavesdropping?'

'No, it's okay. Madge is on a late lunch with Sandra, so I can flick paperclips to my heart's content,' he joked. 'Anyway, how were the little darlings this morning?'

'Oh, fine. The Year 3s are actually quite a decent bunch – *any* class is better than 4R. I heard that Daisy Brewster's mum has been on the warpath about Jacob Pocock's anti-social behaviour in PE. I'm keeping my head down as far as that woman is concerned.'

'Well, you might not have to cope with grotty kids and their bolshie parents much longer.'

'Oh, bring it on,' sighed Hattie. Just then, her mobile started singing to her from inside the shopping bag that she'd dumped on the floor. 'Must go, Nick; someone's calling me on my mobile and I'm gasping for a cuppa. See you later.'

Hattie rooted around in her bag, which was stuffed full of class 3M's handwriting books and accumulated rubbish, as her mobile continued its cheery tune. All at once, she heard an almighty clatter from the kitchen, followed by flapping and scuffling noises. It had to be Jezebel returning from yet another attempt to decimate the local bird population. Having heaved out the schoolbooks, balled up tissues, pens and now silent phone, Hattie cursed and went to inspect the battleground of her kitchen. The caller would have to wait. The sound effects were ominous, but she had no doubt of what awaited her.

'Jezebel, you wicked girl!' she yelled, flinging open the door and rushing to find out what had been hauled in through the cat-flap. Apart from a trail of wet paw prints leading from the utility room, there was no obvious sign, at first glance, of cat or prey.

'Jezebel,' she coaxed, in gentler tones, stooping to peer under the overhanging tablecloth that made an ideal hiding place. That cat had about half a brain cell and absolutely no imagination when it came to concealment.

There was a muffled cheep and a frantic flap as Jezebel adjusted her grip on a bedraggled starling.

'Wicked cat!' scolded Hattie. 'Aren't tuna chunks in jelly good enough for you?' Jezebel eyed her mistress warily. Tuna chunks in jelly were all very well, but what she lusted after was nice fresh meat – preferably the sort she'd caught herself. However, Hattie's renown at rescuing the feathered victims of Jezebel's hunting forays was impressive, so she wasn't fazed by the sight before her. Experience told her it was just a matter of careful positioning and precision timing when it came to prising open the jaws just long enough to allow the prey to escape; that and putting up with the odd slashed finger – a mere inconvenience when it came to saving the local bird life. This she managed to do, but not before another interruption from her phone which sent Jezebel scuttling back to the utility room. Once freed, however, the startled starling quickly regained its senses and with a whoosh and squawk, it took off in the direction of the old apple tree. The RSPB would have been proud of Hattie's quick action. But Jezebel was not impressed and indulged in what might have been a phrase or two of feline swearing and much grinding of teeth.

'Detention for you, young lady,' announced Hattie as she removed the cat to the confines of the kitchen. It was time for a reviving cuppa and a nice tuna salad sandwich, but as Hattie was taking the first bite, her mobile sprang to life, abandoned as it was on the hall carpet. The caller was very persistent. Fliss? No, she worked at her local health centre all day on Mondays and the Supervisor, who had banned staff from using mobile phones while on duty, could sniff one out with unnerving accuracy. Even Fliss knew not to overstep the mark.

She retrieved her phone and checked the display – Leo!

'Hello Leo,' she sighed, with a sinking heart.

'Hattie, at last! I've been trying to get hold of you,' he told her.

'Really? Oh, I wondered who it was. Bad timing, Leo; the cat chose that very moment to drag a bird in, so it was Hattie to the rescue.'

'And did you? Rescue it, I mean?'

'Oh yes. The lucky old starling lives to see a few more sunrises, peck up a few more crumbs and sing a few more drunken choruses with its mates in the apple tree.' She wandered back towards her lunch, amazed at her ability to discuss mundane domestic affairs with a man who still had a lot of explaining to do.

'You agreed we could meet,' Leo reminded her, 'so please tell me when I can come.'

'You can't come *here*, Leo! What if someone saw you? The local gossips would have a field day. I wouldn't trust Jean at number four as far as I could throw her.'

'But what's so wrong about an estate agent paying a visit? Really, Hattie, I don't... Ah, you mean your neighbours might think we were having some passionate love affair?'

'Absolutely, and we both know it's impossible, but I'm not prepared to give anyone the chance to spread rumours.'

'It wasn't impossible once,' Leo reminded her.

'Oh, so it was only an *affair* was it? Is that why you thought it was fine just to toss me aside?'

'No, Hattie, please. At least give me the chance to finish explaining,' he insisted, trying to keep cool. 'Now, perhaps you can suggest where we can meet?'

Hattie thought for a moment, but was hard-pressed to come

up with a suitable place. It needed to be on neutral ground – somewhere public, but not a café after what happened last time. Perhaps the swimming pool? If things got tricky she could always make for the rapids. No, the thought of stripping down to her cossie was not appealing and there were a few lumpy and saggy bits that she wouldn't like him to see, even though *his* opinion wasn't *that* important any more. 'What about the library?' she suggested. The library was just the place: easy enough to hide in but also easy enough to make a quick exit from if there were to be a sudden influx of nosy-parkers.

'Very well,' Leo agreed with some resignation. The library was not far from his office, but the chance of having a satisfactory conversation in its forbiddingly silent atmosphere seemed unlikely. 'It's certainly somewhere we can visit without fear of suspicion. Of course, if you'd not be so secretive…'

'Stop it!' Hattie snapped. 'I'm not bothered about seeing you again. It's *you* who insists on meeting, so you'll just have to put up with my suggestion. Just stop judging me!'

'Judging *you*?' Leo retorted, becoming rattled. 'From where I'm standing, Hattie, it feels as if I'm the one who has already been judged; judged, pronounced guilty and given a life sentence.'

There was a brief silence. Leo wondered if he'd gone too far. He hoped not. It was incredible that their paths should cross again after so many years, and here was a chance to talk about what had gone so terribly wrong.

'Hattie?' he asked, much calmer now. 'Are you still there?'

'Yes,' she answered in a small voice.

'So when shall we meet?' he asked gently, not wishing to make matters worse.

'Well… I can't do anything until Wednesday. Is that any good for you?'

'Right, I'll just check my diary. How about midday?'

'Okay, you'll find me in the kiddies' section, checking out the fiction.'

'Till Wednesday then.'

'Till Wednesday.' She snapped her phone shut and sighed heavily. She wouldn't relish that meeting, but if it meant that Leo would be out of her hair for good, it would be worth it. Meanwhile, Leo was glumly reflecting on the limited suitability of a library as a rendezvous and wondering if he could organise a change of location.

Goodness! What shall I wear, wondered Hattie, rummaging through her drawers for some inspiration. It was a bitterly cold Wednesday and the weather girl on breakfast TV had cheerfully predicted the likelihood of snow before the end of the day. The clouds were indeed heavy with gloomy foreboding and there was a sinister stillness in the air as she set off for the lunchtime meeting. In the end, she plumped for several layers from her wardrobe that hadn't quite been relegated to the 'suitable for gardening' category: a chunky polo-neck, zip-up cardi, padded anorak, well-worn corduroy trousers, and fleecy lined ankle boots; not forgetting her knitted beanie and long, striped scarf. No one could suggest that she'd dressed for a date. In fact, with so many layers, she hoped there wouldn't be enough of her showing for positive identification. However, for some reason she *had* put on make-up and added a pair of dangly earrings for a change.

Leo arrived at the library in good time and was mooching around a section that gave him a good view of the entrance. At a minute or two after midday, Hattie, adopting a casual and yet business-like demeanour, pushed open the door. Before she'd taken half a dozen or so steps, she spotted Leo and an Ordnance Survey map locked in fierce combat. Either the map was winning or Leo was deliberately hiding behind it. Hattie chose to ignore him and made straight for the children's section. The local library service must have had a recent cash injection, she concluded, noting several large, dice-shaped seats, pristine in their startling primary colours. It was also stiflingly hot, so she unzipped her anorak and removed her hat and scarf. Next, she lowered herself carefully onto a red velour dice, hoping she wouldn't be unceremoniously tipped onto the floor and give the unsuspecting browsers unexpected lunchtime entertainment. Choosing a book at random, she sat and leafed through casually until a pair of trousered legs appeared beside her.

'Oh, hi, Leo. Care to join me?' she proposed with a grin, patting a nearby dice, motivated more by sarcasm than by good humour. Leo taking up her suggestion was as likely as the chief librarian leaping up and performing a striptease.

'I'd rather not, if you don't mind,' he replied with dignified reserve.

'Oh well,' she sighed, struggling to her feet. 'Maybe we'll go and check out the kiddies' DVDs.'

'I've a better idea,' he murmured, selecting a *Thomas the Tank Engine* case and studying the blurb on the reverse.

'What sort of better idea, Leo?'

He replaced the case and took a step closer. 'Do you think you could manage some lunch?'

'Why? Could it be that you've brought a couple of cheese sandwiches in your pocket?' Hattie joked.

'No, I've booked a table at The Three Wishes, for a bowl of soup or whatever you like.'

'You've what?' she hissed, moving around the end of the shelves. 'I thought the deal was that we meet *here*. You agreed! How dare you move the goalposts.'

Leo looked perplexed. 'Move the what?' What he knew about football could be written on a cotton bud.

'Oh forget it. What I mean is, *you* changed the rules. We agreed *here*. Have you forgotten what happened last week at The Four Seasons?' she snapped irritably. 'What if someone came in and saw us having a cosy tête-à-tête in a back street café?' It was just the sort of place Gloria Preston might go for. 'What would they think?'

An officious-looking librarian at the main desk looked up and glowered in Hattie's direction.

Leo sighed audibly and shook his head. 'I'm sorry. All right, so I agreed to meet you here, but then afterwards, I thought as it would be lunch time, it would be more pleasant to have something to eat.' He paused, hoping Hattie would soften. 'Look, we don't have to walk there together. You'd obviously prefer not to be seen in my company. So I'll go first and you can come in your own time.'

At this, Hattie folded her arms angrily across her chest and pouted, but Leo chose to ignore her irritation. 'And I'll have a drink ready for you – a fruit juice and tonic if you like?'

She nodded resignedly, aware that the growing emptiness in her stomach might welcome something warm and sustaining. Leo strode off purposefully without a backward glance, leaving her with a battle between refusing to agree to his sneakily arranged plan or just giving in and letting it all happen. It felt like a dreaded dentist appointment – a painful prospect, but sheer relief when it was all over. She zipped up her jacket, wound her scarf around her neck, pulled her beanie well down over her ears and set off slowly in the direction of Goose Street. The most obvious route took her past Mia Casa, where she couldn't help but pause. Beyond the window display of properties for sale, she noted well-chosen modern fittings and comfortable seating in what was probably the interview area. The only person in the office was a strikingly attractive blonde girl in her twenties, sitting at the reception desk, chewing a biro and staring into space. When God had dished out the top-drawer female attributes, she must have elbowed her way to the front of the queue. Hattie scanned the property details, feigning interest in a smart pied-à-terre in a nearby street – all part of her ruse to keep Leo waiting. After two or three minutes, she decided it was time to be on her way. A spot of lunch was actually quite a good idea, especially as he was paying. Perhaps they might have chocolate fudge cake on the menu.

As she approached the turning into Goose Street, a familiar figure came lumbering towards her – Daisy Brewster's mum – a woman she'd hoped to give a wide berth for a while yet. Hattie quickly pulled up her collar and gazed intently into the nearest shop window, which featured the latest in Zimmer frames as well as commodes and incontinence pads. As Ms Brewster approached, Hattie could hear her wheezing and coughing. How could she ensure she wouldn't be spotted and harangued? With a well-timed flash of inspiration, she dived into her bag and ferreted around for a pen as if to note details of the shop's current bargains:

This month's offer: Incontinence pads – Buy one pack get one pack free!

For what seemed an eternity, she continued to rummage as Ms Brewster waddled past then Hattie nipped round into Goose Street. Just a few yards on the right was the hanging sign and quaint bow window of The Three Wishes. Hattie's pace slackened as she started to wonder about the chances of bumping into someone she knew. It was well into lunchtime by now, although there weren't many people in town: put off, no doubt, by the weather. She glanced up at the small patch of sky that was visible between the overhanging roofs and noticed that the solid cloud cover was even darker and more forbidding than when she had set out. At least it wasn't snowing. Feeling furtive, she pushed open the door, setting a little bell jangling, which guaranteed her arrival would not go unnoticed. Quickly looking around, she saw only a handful of diners, all complete strangers – so far, so good. But where was Leo? Surely he hadn't given up and gone off in a huff?

Rather like The Four Seasons, this cafe featured high-sided alcoves, this time with old church pews, as well as an open dining area with small, round tables and Windsor-style chairs. Leo had evidently heard the jangling because he suddenly popped up from behind one of the pew seats halfway down on the right-hand side and smiled as Hattie went to join him. The little alcove was private enough for their meeting, but the layout meant that Hattie would not be able to keep a check on who else might come in.

'Here, a drink for you, Hattie. I hope it's okay.' He glanced towards the door as another customer arrived and for a moment, could have sworn he saw a few white flakes drifting down, but he said nothing.

Hattie frowned at the ice cube bobbing in the tumbler of tonic and regretted that she hadn't suggested a steaming mug of hot chocolate instead.

'Thanks,' she murmured, pulling off her thick outer layers and sinking into the deep seat cushion. They chose soup of the day with French bread and as they waited, Hattie sipped at her drink.

'Well, you'd better make a start,' she urged, preparing herself for Leo's last instalment. So far he'd made two attempts at explaining why he had abandoned her, but perhaps those interruptions had helped buy him some time. After all, he'd had a whole week to come up with a suitably plausible conclusion.

'I seem to remember I got as far as telling you about the delayed meeting,' Leo began, a serious expression replacing the more relaxed one that he'd had before. It was as if he was mentally re-living the events of that day. He took a mouthful from his glass and paused to organise his thoughts. Hattie recalled, with an involuntary shiver, the frisson of excitement she'd felt when he'd told her that everything he'd had to do that morning seemed like a necessary chore. Then he'd described her as... No, she shouldn't dwell on it.

'Although the meeting didn't finish until eleven thirty, there was still enough time to get to the station. So I said my good-byes and assured Jack that I could easily sprint down to Victoria in ten minutes, although he'd offered to call a taxi. Being on the fourth floor, I naturally chose to take the lift down to the ground floor.' He paused briefly as a waitress brought their order. Meanwhile, Hattie was bemused by the incredible amount of detail as she concentrated on buttering her hunk of bread. Leo drank a spoonful of soup before continuing.

'The lift came after a matter of moments and I joined a secretary who was on her way down to another floor. We set off, but after a few seconds there was a sudden jolt and a shuddering and then the lift stopped.'

'Oh God!' exclaimed Hattie, her spoon poised midway to her lips.

'According to the panel of signs on the wall,' continued Leo, 'we hadn't even reached the third floor. I tried pressing the button that opened the door, but nothing happened. Then in desperation I tried the third-floor button, hoping the lift would start moving again, but still nothing.'

'That's one of my worst nightmares,' Hattie told him earnestly.

'The secretary – her name, as I learned later, was Angela – started panicking. She told me she usually avoided the lift because she hated confined spaces.'

'Claustrophobia.'

'That's right, but she'd been asked to take some folders of notes to reception for a lunch-time meeting and was running late.'

'That's ironic,' mused Hattie, engrossed in the unfolding drama. 'She should have kept to the stairs.' Looking across at Leo, she realised that sort of comment was pointless now.

He paused to dunk a chunk of bread in his soup while Hattie was considering this new revelation. Could Angela and Leo have suddenly fallen madly in love as they were randomly thrown together in a malfunctioning lift?

'Of course, we'd already tried to raise the alarm by hitting the emergency button and then Angela started hammering on the door and shouting. I joined in for a while, but I was doubtful that anyone could hear us. Oh, Hattie, I was desperate to get out of that place, especially with that hysterical woman shrieking her head off.' He shook his head, remembering how he'd felt. 'After what seemed ages, we heard some knocking sounds, so we knew help was on its way, but by then it was getting close to midday and I kept picturing you arriving at the station with your rucksack.'

Hattie looked up and nodded. 'I *was* there, Leo. I was waiting by the departure board.'

He shook his head and sighed regretfully. 'I couldn't stop thinking

142

of the plans I'd made for us and there I was, stuck in a stupid lift with a stupid female with time running out. Why hadn't I just used the stairs? Laziness, I suppose, but that one decision was the difference between arriving at Victoria on time and... well... it's history now.' He petered out and gloomily stirred his soup before continuing. Hattie was transfixed. This had to be true, surely.

'How did you escape? How long did it take?'

'Well, for several minutes we heard all sorts of noises and then there was an awful moment when the lift did a sort of downward lurch. Angela started screaming again and I can't pretend that I was feeling very brave. You imagine the worst, like the cables snapping and plummeting down three floors to —'

'Oblivion?' Hattie shuddered.

'I guess so. The fire brigade eventually managed to cut through the top of the lift and Angela was hysterical, even though they'd been calling out to warn us. The noise was awful; they were cutting through metal after all. Then she started vomiting.'

'Yuck!' Hattie's soup had suddenly lost its appeal.

'It turned out she was pregnant and was still at the sickness stage. I was trying to comfort her at the time and my jeans... well...'

'Oh no!' Hattie grimaced at the thought of the hysterical vomiting Angela. 'Poor Angela! Poor you!'

'Then the firemen lowered a ladder and helped us climb out, but Angela was shaking all over and had to be carried. Once we were out of the lift, we had to climb another ladder up to the fourth floor. By that time, there was a whole crowd waiting for us and they'd even called an ambulance. Everyone seemed to be talking at once, offering to get glasses of water or make cups of tea, like you English people do, but all I wanted was to get to the station.'

'And there was I, thinking you'd stood me up, pacing up and down, watching the minutes tick by, hearing the trains leaving...' The anger and resentment that Hattie had been carrying around for two weeks or more seemed to melt away and she reached across the table to squeeze Leo's hand. He looked up and smiled wistfully. Hattie was gripped by the story as it unfolded; it was the stuff that films were made of.

'Well, Jack was all for sitting us down, handing out the brandy and having the paramedics check us over, but I reminded him I had a train to catch.'

'If that happened now, the health and safety bods would have a field day. People weren't so clued up in those days, were they?' Hattie commented. It was, indeed, a different world back in the eighties.

'But that wouldn't have stopped Jack worrying about the consequences,' he added, ready to defend the man's reputation, 'even though the landlord would ultimately have been held responsible.'

'Hmm, I guess you're right.'

'Anyway, he called a taxi and I did my best to clean my jeans. It was too late for the Dover train by then, but I held onto the hope that you'd still be waiting for me. The traffic was dreadful. Every light was against us.'

'How frustrating,' Hattie sighed.

'I kept urging the driver to go faster, but he took no notice or deliberately chose to ignore me.'

'One of those jobsworth types by the sound of it.'

'It was just after one by the time I reached the departure board…'

'And I wasn't there.'

Their eyes met and it was as if they were, once again, twenty-one year olds. They'd had so many dreams and hopes, all reduced to nothing by fate and a faulty lift cable.

Leo reached inside his jacket pocket for his wallet and withdrew a dog-eared newspaper clipping. With great care, he unfolded it and passed it to Hattie. The account was titled, *Two rescued in Friday 13th lift drama*. She fished out her specs and started to read, her heart racing as she wondered how she could make up for all the vitriol she'd lashed out at him.

Emergency services were called to Tuscan Wine Importers of Pimlico at midday yesterday – Friday 13th July – when a faulty lift cable caused two employees to be stranded between the third and fourth floors for over an hour.

'I didn't know you were working for them,' began Hattie, puzzled.

'I wasn't. They got that bit wrong.'

'Hmm, some of our local reporters are experts at that!'

She continued to read:

Twenty-six year old secretary, Angela Selmes, who is twelve weeks' pregnant with her first child, praised the emergency services and twenty-one-year-old Leo Marcello, who was trapped with her. 'I owe my baby's life to the bravery of those wonderful men,' she said after spending a cautionary night at her local maternity unit.

A spokesman for the landlord was unable to issue a formal statement, but indicated that stringent safety checks would be implemented as soon as possible. Jack Edlin of Tuscan Wine Importers said, 'It was a miracle that no one was injured or worse. The safety and well-being of my staff is of great importance and so I shall be keeping in close contact with the landlord to ensure nothing like this happens again.'

Hattie re-folded the clipping and passed it back with the slightest of sighs. What could she say? 'I'm sorry,' seemed like a possible candidate. Picking up her spoon she set about finishing her lunch while trying to convince herself she'd every right to feel aggrieved. How was she to know? Flooded with embarrassment, she recalled one or two of the choice phrases she'd lobbed in Leo's direction recently – and all the time he was innocent.

'I waited at Victoria for a whole hour,' she told him, determined that he should know exactly how frantic she'd been.

Leo gazed back at her with the same doleful expression, as if a great heaviness rested upon him.

'Then I imagined the worst scenario – perhaps you'd been run over or something – so I spent ages in a station phone box dialling all the local hospitals I could find, until I ran out of change. I had visions of you lying injured in some A & E department.'

'Oh, Hattie,' Leo groaned. 'So when I arrived hopelessly late, you were –'

'A matter of yards away, phoning hospitals.'

'And I thought you'd given up on me.'

There was a moment of silence, except for the genteel chink and clatter from the rest of the café, while Hattie and Leo contemplated the fiendish idiosyncrasies of fate.

'What did you do next?' Hattie wanted to know, still recalling those distressing phone box minutes. But before he could reply, she remembered the worst part of that awful experience – he'd never phoned her. She'd made a point of giving him her parents' address and phone number, just in case, because life isn't always predictable and sometimes emergencies *do* happen. Remembering that glaring omission on Leo's part, Hattie's anger came flooding back. She narrowed her eyes, feeling justified in pointing out certain inconsistencies that needed explanation.

'Apart from not phoning me,' she began, but stopped as the familiar sound of coughing and wheezing approached from behind. 'Oh no!' she moaned, looking up and meeting the disgruntled gaze of Ms Brewster, who was liberally sprinkled with snow. What was *she* doing there?

'Hello, Mrs Chesney,' said Ms Brewster, with the suspicion of a scowl.

'Hello,' replied Hattie, not sure if she was more panicked by the arrival of snow or of someone whose stray comments might jeopardise her reputation.

Ms Brewster stared at Leo with interest. 'Hello Mr Chesney,' she said.

'I'm not –' Leo began, but was prevented from making matters worse by a sharp tap on the shins and a furious warning glance.

'Whatever,' muttered Ms Brewster indifferently, as she lumbered past, her generous bulk brushing a pile of serviettes onto the carpet as she went.

'That's all I need,' hissed Hattie angrily, 'and *you* didn't help, Leo!' She craned her neck around the side of her pew seat and stared in horror at the café window. Thick flurries of snow filled the air and, by the evidence on the carpet, it was laying very quickly. Any thought of grilling Leo about the rest of his actions – or lack of them – deserted her in the panic over the state of the roads and her chances of driving home safely.

'Look at that snow!' she gasped. 'There's a blizzard outside. Didn't you notice it, Leo?' she added accusingly. 'I must go. Goodness knows what the roads are like.' With that, she grabbed her belongings and was soon rushing out of the door, muffled up against the storm.

Leo shook his head in disbelief, knowing it was useless to try to stop her. He was painfully aware of some details he needed to get off his chest – he owed it to her – but circumstances were definitely conspiring against him. Life had certainly treated him harshly when it came to relationships. There was Hattie, for whom he'd had so many hopes, snatched away by a series of misfortunes; then there was Gina and the whole Montelugia episode of his life... But that was another story.

The promised snow had started shortly after Hattie's arrival at The Three Wishes and now lay at least 2 inches thick. Hattie pulled her beanie well down against the swirling, white onslaught and headed in the direction of the multi-storey.

'Oops! Sorry!' she spluttered, feeling the weight of another pedestrian as she all but skidded around the corner into the main street and collided with a well-wrapped female.

'No harm done,' replied the woman frostily. Her face seemed familiar as well as the tone of her voice. The woman evidently had a similar thought. She frowned in concentration while trying to work out Hattie's identity from the miniscule amount of face peering out from layers of woolly muffling.

'It's Mrs Chesney, isn't it?' she probed pointedly.

'Er, yes,' replied Hattie, having eliminated the possibility of the woman being another pupil's mum, although a granny might be more likely. 'And you are…?'

'Madge Wilson,' she replied.

'Oh yes, Madge… Well, well.' Meeting Madge was rather unfortunate. It was bad enough running into Ms Brewster, but to be bust-to-bust with Nick's work colleague was even worse. 'Not very nice weather is it?' remarked Hattie brightly, in what was one of the understatements of the year.

'Diabolical!' fumed Madge. 'I hate this time of year. Plays havoc with my feet, it does. If you suffered with a circulation like mine, you'd not be so perky about it.'

'Well, must dash before the roads get too blocked. Just on my way to the library,' she said, and beetled off as fast as conditions allowed.

'You're in the wrong part of town!' called Madge to Hattie's disappearing back, but Hattie chose to be deaf to Madge's parting remark. She hadn't intended another library visit, but realised that a couple of books would add credence to the little nugget of news that Madge would no doubt pass on to Nick about their meeting. A quick U-turn in a side street would take her there as soon as she was out of Madge's sightlines.

As she reached the multi-storey, the snow flurries were easing off, but already the town had been transformed into a winter wonderland. Grit lorries were out in force around the ring-road and the verges were edged with banks of muddy slush. Crawling home at snail's pace, she wondered at the chances of driving back for patchwork later. Another snowfall and plummeting temperatures would certainly curtail that possibility, unless Nick could be persuaded… Well, it was worth a try.

'Just bumped into your wife,' Madge announced. 'Or rather, *she* bumped into me – literally!' It was one thirty and she had returned to the office, regretting she'd ever set foot outside. Nick,

148

on the other hand, had enjoyed a cosy hour in the staff canteen, talking football and in particular, Arsenal's chances in the cup run.

'Oh really?' chuckled Nick, picturing the scene.

'Oh yes,' continued Madge in an accusatory fashion. 'She came hurtling out of Goose Street at top speed and almost had me sprawling in the gutter – in these conditions too!' She rubbed her hands together in a vain attempt to revive her circulation.

'Is that so?' replied Nick. 'I didn't know she was planning to come into town today.'

'Something to do with going to the library I think, but she went rushing off in the opposite direction. I called after her, but she *completely* ignored me, *and...*' Madge paused for emphasis, 'there was definitely something odd about her.' She settled herself in front of her terminal, pulled a bulging folder out of her in-tray and started leafing through it in a distracted fashion.

'Odd?' asked Nick, already treating Madge's remarks with scepticism.

'And shifty,' she added, tapping away at her keyboard.

'Shifty?' chuckled Nick. 'Oh come on, Madge. She was probably just winded by the... er... impact!'

'What was that?' snapped Madge, glaring at him fiercely.

'Oh, nothing, Madge,' he replied in mock innocence. 'I expect Hattie was on some undercover mission or maybe Wednesday's the day she meets her secret lover.' He chuckled at the improbability of both suggestions as he fished around for his calculator.

'You'd be laughing on the other side of your face if she *was*,' answered Madge primly. 'I know about that sort of thing,' she added enigmatically.

'Oh really?' asked Nick, looking up from his spreadsheet. 'So you've your own lover hidden away somewhere have you, Madge?'

'How dare you!' she snapped. 'Your mind's like a sewer, and that's typical of the male species!' She snatched up her folder and sniffed to show her unqualified disgust. 'I'm going down to Janice and Rhoda's office, if anyone wants to know.' She marched to the door in high dudgeon. 'Where there's *civilised* company and no smut!'

'And not a single lover in sight,' sniggered Nick under his breath.

'What's that Nicholas?' barked Madge.

'I just said, where I'll be out of sight. Bye, Madge!'

7

By the time Nick and Josh arrived home, the roads were well gritted and no further snowfall meant the evening rush hour kept moving, as opposed to being held in mind-numbing gridlock. Josh arrived with a liberal sprinkling of snow and soggy trainers. No prizes for guessing what he'd been up to on the way home. With glowing red cheeks, he was like a little boy once again. Nick, though, hated anything that disturbed the normal balance of life – extreme cold, extreme heat, gales, torrential rain – and made sure everyone heard about it. He and Jezebel, Hattie concluded, not for the first time, must be twin souls. No amount of coaxing or shoving had succeeded in ejecting her through her flap, although it was obvious that she couldn't keep her paws crossed indefinitely. One cautious glance at the blanket of thick snow was enough and she sunk her teeth into Hattie's hands to make the point. Wearily, Hattie conceded defeat, hauled out a sack of cat litter – used only on rare occasions – and poured a modest amount in a tray. As she did so, Jezebel rubbed around Hattie's legs and purred loudly as if to say, 'Whoopee! Indoor loos!' then leapt in for an enthusiastic digging session, spraying litter in all directions.

'Blasted weather,' moaned Nick, as he tucked into his favourite comfort food: casserole. 'Just what we *don't* need for the match tonight.'

'You're not going out to watch football, surely?' asked Hattie, her brain momentarily numbed by the arrival of the white stuff outside.

'Course not,' Nick replied dismissively, 'it's on TV. I just wondered how bad the snow was in London.'

'No probs, Dad,' put in Josh, pausing between mouthfuls, 'they've got under-soil heating and anyway, Sky pays mega-dosh, so no way will they call it off.'

'That's a shame, I don't usually ask for a lift…' sighed Hattie, who had been hoping against navigating another treacherous journey.

'Well, you seemed to manage it earlier,' commented Nick. 'Madge said she'd literally bumped into you in town at lunchtime. I must say that was brave of you, considering the forecast.'

'But it was fine when I set off,' protested Hattie. 'Anyway, I wanted to get some quilting books from the library.' No surprises about Madge's report, she thought.

'Didn't they have any in the village library?'

'No, of course they didn't. Why else would I drive into town?'

'Oh, right.'

'Zena and Marigold have said it's important to study different designs, but most quilting books cost a fortune.'

'Ah, I see,' agreed Nick. 'Got to save the pennies for the house move.'

'Tell you what,' he offered, after Hattie had dolloped out seconds. 'I could run you into college and then nip off and watch the match in The Pig and Partridge. They always have the football on.'

'You mean that?' asked Hattie.

'Of course I mean it. Great dumplings again, Hat – as always.'

'What time does the match finish?' Hattie wanted to know. Since meeting Leo at lunchtime her mind had been going over the subject of his sudden silence after the Victoria Station business. Just one last question needed an answer and she was determined to prise it out of him.

'Well, if there's no extra time and penalties, it should finish around ten, then there's the –'

'Yeah, Nick.' Hattie knew the score, in a manner of speaking. There was always that endless waffle from studio summarisers: usually ex-players who liked to air their opinions on the box now that their playing careers were over. 'So *you* just sit tight and I'll join you when my class finishes.'

'Are you sure? It's a bit of a trek from the college, and bars full of yelling footie fans aren't usually your scene.'

'No, it's fine, Nick,' she said firmly. 'I was intending to have a chat with Zena and Marigold about my quilting project at the end of the session, so you stay put. You don't want to miss any of the action, do you?' Hattie's lies were slipping smoothly off her tongue and were now as familiar as old friends.

Two hours later Nick dropped her off at the college.

'See you later!' she called as she set off across the tarmac, a distance behind Cynthia who she'd just spotted at the entrance.

'I'll have a ginger wine ready and waiting,' Nick promised, then drove off, welcoming the prospect of a great cup tie and an evening by a roaring log fire. Meanwhile, Hattie went straight to admin to find out where Leo's class met.

'Room E17 – that's in East Corridor, just past the refectory,' the assistant informed her. 'But we're not taking any more students this term; the class is full, I'm afraid.'

'No, no,' replied Hattie. 'I'm just meeting a friend there later.'

Retracing her steps, she saw that East Corridor led off the central foyer and judging by a steady stream of students in all directions, classes were due to start any minute.

'The design we'll be demonstrating this evening is…' Zena's strident tones could be heard as Hattie pushed open the door.

'Sorry!' she apologised, smiling and quietly slipping into a chair beside Cynthia. Tonight Zena was dressed in black and white to match the current weather conditions, accessorised with jet earrings and matching beads. Marigold was still favouring the mohair theme and tonight's fashion accent was a tan, fluffy scarf that resembled a ginger moggy draped around her shoulders. She wore it over a wide, corduroy dress, fringed with bells and tassels that would have made a perfect Red Indian tepee. The duo had certainly learnt the knack of commanding their students' attention, if only to gaze in awe at their bizarre attire.

The class watched as the two friends demonstrated 'log cabin' then set to work cutting rectangles to assemble their own versions. Cynthia kept up a relentless stream of chatter as they measured, sliced, pinned and stitched, boasting about the progress she'd made with her granddaughter's quilt. With a sinking heart, Hattie realised she'd need to set aside more time if she was to finish her quilt sooner rather than later. If Nick landed one of the Lydford Cross jobs, they'd have to leap into house-selling mode in the next week or so. That would mean extra cleaning and tidying for the benefit of would-be buyers. Jezebel would *definitely* have to take up temporary residence in the utility room to reduce fur fall-out and the threat of sicked-up rodent on the carpets, both of which would severely reduce their chances of a quick sale. Now, all Hattie had to deal with was the Leo enigma. A straightforward, honest answer was all she needed.

With five minutes to the end of the session, Hattie started to pack away her tools and fabric, ready for a speedy exit.

'You're keen to be off,' observed Cynthia, as she carefully tied and snipped the strands on yet another rectangle of her growing design.

'Yes, I've arranged to meet Nick at The Pig and Partridge. He's such a sweetie, offering to drive me in because of the awful weather. I'm surprised you made it yourself, Cynthia. Bledlow Ridge must be almost cut off.'

'Oh no, it's not so bad where we live. So has your hubby been in the pub all evening?' probed Cynthia, raising her eyebrows.

'Oh, goodness, that sounds bad doesn't it,' chuckled Hattie. 'He's only watching football and knows how to make a Diet Coke last ages.'

In the bustle of tidying up and leave-taking, Hattie quickly grabbed her folder and said her goodbyes. She was determined to be outside room E17 before the last of Leo's students left.

Down in the town square, a bar full of gloomy football fanatics groaned into their pints as the referee blew his whistle and walked off the pitch, followed by twenty-two disgruntled players. He'd already consulted the two linesmen on more than one occasion as the light snow shower accelerated into a full-blown blizzard. Visibility had reduced to a few yards and the players had blundered around the pitch in a fruitless effort to pass to each other, let alone find the goal. Whoever decided their team should wear an all-white kit had definitely made an odd decision; even the home side's red and white kit was difficult to see. The game was abandoned less than halfway through the second half. Resignedly, Nick drained his glass and decided he might as well head on down to the college to meet Hattie. It was pointless sitting around listening to all the whingeing and loudly-voiced opinions on the stupid ref, dozy linesmen and state of English football as a whole. As he set off for the multi-storey, he felt the crunch of freezing snow underfoot and realised the conditions were becoming treacherous – even more reason for meeting Hat.

Having parked at the college, he arrived at the entrance just after the classes had finished, and students were now streaming out on their way home. Where was Hattie's workshop? He had no idea, but a helpful young woman in admin soon pointed him in the right direction. On his way to the patchwork room, he passed groups of women clutching an assortment of workbags and, noticing some with the same kit as Hattie, guessed they must be in her class. They were chatting away excitedly and seemed in good form. Other groups passed him, glowing from something more energetic, by the look of their flushed faces. For a moment, he thought one of them looked a bit like Madge, but decided she was just a look-alike. Madge hadn't mentioned anything about evening classes, and certainly wasn't likely to be playing badminton. Madge and sport were poles apart.

Reaching the room in question and hearing voices, Nick peered in, remembering that Hattie had made a point of wanting to consult with the tutors about her project, but clearly she had already left. However, of the few that remained, one seemed to be in fancy dress: probably either the famous Zena or Marigold that he'd heard so much about. Another one had bright orange spiky hair, a lot of black jewellery and plenty of attitude. Nick lurked hesitantly at the door.

'Can I help you?' she demanded in a shrill, commanding tone.

'Oh, er… um… I was looking for my wife,' he mumbled, glancing at the handful of remaining students and feeling intimidated by the woman's head prefect manner, 'but I seem to have lost her.'

'Lost her?' quizzed the woman. She tossed her head playfully, which set her earrings twinkling in the light of the overhead fluorescent tube. 'Well, that's very careless of you. And your wife's name is…?'

'Hattie. Hattie Chesney.'

'Hattie? Oh she was the first to leave tonight,' answered one of the dowdier women who was struggling with a huge bag. 'In fact, she dashed out in a proper hurry.'

'Really? Oh, I thought she'd still be here. I must have missed her then.' Poor old Hat, he thought, wondering if she was even now arriving at The Pig and Partridge or slipping and sliding her way along Canal Walk.

At that precise moment in East Corridor, Hattie loitered at the door of room E17, where she watched Leo trying to disentangle himself from an effusive elderly couple. The woman kept pawing him flirtatiously, while Leo was turning on the charm in bucket-loads. Eventually the husband, weary or embarrassed by his wife's behaviour, grasped her spare hand and moved towards the door.

'Come on, Pam,' he urged with a tight smile.

'Ciao!' the woman called with a girlish giggle, despite her senior years. Leo watched them go then noticed Hattie, who took a couple of steps into the room.

'You got home safely then,' he said smiling, their curtailed conversation temporarily forgotten.

'Obviously,' replied Hattie stiffly, 'and Nick kindly dropped me off this evening. Now, Leo, some unfinished business...' She was in no mood for pleasantries or time-wasting preamble.

'But I *told* you what happened, Hattie,' he protested as calmly as he could.

'About the lift, the screaming, the vomiting and arriving late... But what then?' she demanded, glaring at him. 'Leo, you *never* phoned me. I gave you my parents' number, so why didn't you call me? It's all very well telling me how upset you were about missing me at the station, but was that the end as far as you were concerned?' Feelings were one thing, Hattie had decided, but facts made a deeper impression.

Leo's smile vanished abruptly, his usual calm and poise abandoned him and he assumed the appearance of a frightened rabbit caught in car headlights.

'It wasn't my fault,' he protested, gesticulating wildly. 'There was a muddle over the bags. It was Alex's fault.' Hattie watched, transfixed, as Leo's Italian genes took over; he really did look convincingly angry. She wavered a moment, wondering if she might have misjudged him, until the name Alex was mentioned. Who was this Alex? Was *she* the reason for his silence?

'Alex?' she snapped furiously. 'Who was Alex and *what* bags?'

'But then I got confused by your name,' he gabbled, ignoring Hattie's question.

'My name?' Hattie exclaimed. 'What's *that* got to do with it?'

'It was how it ended that was so confusing,' he protested.

'Well, I agree with you for once, Leo,' she retorted, her eyes blazing. 'I found how it ended even more than confusing. I mean, you just left me dangling in mid-air.'

'No, no, I don't mean that,' he moaned. 'It was the "h" that

157

confused me. I didn't know if your name had an "h" or not.'

'What do you mean?' she snarled. 'I had the same name all the time I knew you. Or maybe you'd had so many girls by then that you forgot which one you were supposed to be meeting?' By now, her heart was pounding furiously and she felt a burning hot flush spread over her cheeks. There was a wild, hunted look in Leo's eyes, no longer like a dazzled rabbit, but more like one of the bedraggled specimens that Jezebel proudly dragged through her cat-flap from time to time.

'No, Hattie,' he complained. 'That's not fair.'

In truth, Hattie realised her last salvo had been well under the belt. However, she was past caring, especially as he had now admitted that someone else was involved.

'Well, Leo, if that's the best you can do,' she fumed, 'I think it's time to go! Do you know what, Leo, I think you've lost it!' It seemed to Hattie that this Alex, who was a key player in the drama, was the reason for his silence. Who was she, she wondered, trying to remember anyone by that name in her year at uni. The only one she could recall was a short, plump girl with an unfortunate complexion, who had been planning a future in something horsy. No, *this* Alex must have been some local girl. No wonder he'd told her he couldn't be contacted at the end of term – it was all part of a clever smokescreen. The story about the lift drama was obviously true, but as for the rest...?

'But, Hattie, it's the truth!' he moaned, but Hattie's patience had finally evaporated.

'The truth?' she snapped. 'I'm not sure what's true anymore! Back in that cafe I was believing you for a while, but now none of it makes sense. Let's forget it, Leo, and please don't bother to contact me again,' she snapped and stormed out, regretting that she'd ever bothered finding out his reasons or excuses. All that soft soap about being his 'dearly loved girl' didn't mean a thing. He'd obviously been intending to tell her he was finishing with her, but didn't have the nerve to admit it to her face. All she wanted was closure, but Leo seemed incapable of giving straight-forward answers.

She hurried, head-down, along the corridor, remembering that Nick was still waiting for her in the pub. East Corridor was L-shaped and, on rounding the corner, she collided full-pelt with a tall, solid body in a brown jacket. This was getting to be a habit.

'Oh… Sorry… Sorry!' she gasped, trying to sidestep the bulk that blocked her way.

'Hattie! Hey, I've been looking for you everywhere.'

She looked up, confused and startled. 'Nick? What are you doing *here*?'

'That's just what I was wondering about you,' he replied, full of concern. 'I tried texting, but my battery ran out. I was down in the foyer, wondering if you were in the ladies' loo, but I wasn't sure which way it was. Then I heard shouting. I thought it sounded like your voice, so I came to find out. Hat, you look terrible. What's up?'

'I… I… er… was sure there was a short cut this way,' she stammered, trembling and glancing nervously towards the way she'd come. 'Nick, can we go please?' Her knees had turned to jelly, but worst of all was the need for a quick, convincing reason to explain why she was in such a state. Blaming the time of the month again was out – even Nick had an idea where she was in her cycle. But why was he *there*? Could she really have taken so long with Leo that the match had already finished?

'I heard shouting. Are you okay?' he murmured sympatheti-cally. Judging by the expression on her face, she was anything but okay.

'Oh, it was just a bolshie caretaker. He accused me of being out of bounds – the cheek!' Hattie snapped, conjuring up a good show of justifiable irritation. Her collision with him on a previous occasion reminded her that he could be surly when crossed. 'He refused to unlock the door for me and said they only used *that* door during the day. How was *I* to know?'

'Well, maybe he was tired – end of a long day and all that,'

Nick suggested with a sigh. 'He's probably fed up with people trampling snow and slush all over his nice clean floors.'

'But he was horrid to me,' she complained. 'Oh, no!' One end of the folder's webbing handle had come adrift. It slipped from her grasp and spewed paper across the floor. Nick grabbed clumsily at the worksheets, dislodging paperclips in his attempt to help.

'No need to get het up, old thing.'

'Why didn't you wait for me in the pub?' Hattie demanded, once the folder was firmly tucked under Nick's arm. 'I said I'd meet you there.'

'The match had to be abandoned,' he told her. 'You should have seen it. It was a real blizzard. I don't know who was more upset: the teams on the pitch or the landlord who was hoping to sell more beer. Anyway, I thought I'd come and meet you, to save you walking into town. It's really treacherous out there.'

'That's kind of you.'

'But when I found your room —'

'You went there? Why?' Hattie flustered, realising she quickly needed to re-jig her version of the evening's events.

'To meet you of course. I thought you were staying behind to chat with the tutors, but someone told me you'd left straight away.' Sensing some awkward vibes, he scrutinised her expression. 'Didn't realise you were quite so keen on football,' he joked, aiming at some light relief.

'Hardly! I managed to have a word with Zena and Marigold during the class after all. Sometimes they're too busy with everything, but for once, I managed to corner them. Don't make an issue of it.'

'Okay, Hat.' Her teeth and fists were clenched and her brows were furrowed. Clearly, the fracas with the caretaker had really upset her. 'Sorry. I was just concerned for you, that's all.'

Footsteps further up the corridor attracted Nick's attention. Perhaps it was the bolshie caretaker on the warpath for stray students. But no, it was only a smartly dressed chap carrying a folder under his arm. With collar up and head down, Nick didn't recognise him to start with and turned back to Hattie, who was marching determinedly ahead.

'Come on, Nick,' she called back to him. 'I've had enough of this place for one night.'

Then Nick remembered: of course, this was Signor Marcello from Mia Casa. Seeing the man out of context had momentarily thrown him. Car maintenance, Chinese cookery or badminton? he wondered. Hardly – not in *that* suit, anyway.

'Ah, Mr Chesney,' said Leo, smiling. He had learned enough about Hattie's desire for secrecy over the past few weeks, to guarantee his name wouldn't have figured in any conversation between the Chesneys in the last few minutes. 'Any more snow on the way, do you think?' He'd also learned enough about the English and their fanatical fixation about the weather.

'Hope not,' Nick replied, with a weary grimace. 'Well, must be off. The wife's back at the car by now I should think.' As he reached the foyer, the place was almost deserted, with just a dribble of students making their way home. Over by a free-standing display board, Nick noticed a jovial, thickset man leaning on a broom with a steaming mug in his hand. He was engaged in an animated conversation with the young woman from admin, who was giggling at something he'd just said. Not the bolshie caretaker, thought Nick, as he pushed the door open. Certainly not bolshie, nor anywhere near the scene of Hattie's unfortunate encounter. Poor old Hat probably only had a run-in with one of the cleaners.

Hattie was shivering sulkily by the car door when Nick eventually joined her.

'At last!' she muttered disagreeably. 'What kept you? It's freezing!'

'Sorry, Hat,' Nick apologised, after he'd finished scraping ice from the windscreen.

'Just saw that bloke from Mia Casa... Martello... er... Mar-something-or-other.'

'Who?' asked Hattie, feigning a temporary memory block.

'Marcello... *you* know, the bloke from Mia Casa,' said Nick as he carefully reversed out of the parking bay. 'Did that valuation for us.'

'Oh him,' muttered Hattie, in a convincingly bored tone. 'So what?'

'Nothing. Just happened to see him, that's all.'

'Funny place to see an estate agent. So what were you chatting about?' Hattie ventured, trying to keep the same lack of interest.

'We just talked about the weather,' replied Nick. 'Funny that: didn't think Italians talked about the weather like we do,' he chuckled. Hattie breathed the tiniest sigh of relief.

Except for the swish of the windscreen wipers and the splash and squish of roadside slush, their journey home was silent until they reached the edge of the village.

'Hope there's no more snow before Friday,' Nick commented anxiously. 'I really need to get to that interview.'

'I'm banking on it,' stated Hattie, still a long way off lukewarm.

'No pressure then,' joked Nick. However, his concern for his wife was really no joking matter. Wasn't Hattie rather young for the menopause? Perhaps not, he thought gloomily, hoping it wouldn't signal a sharp decline in their sex life, which tended to be rather intermittent even at the best of times.

Leo drove back to his flat from college with a heavy heart. He knew he'd messed up, allowing himself to become so rattled. The trouble was, Hattie turning up like that, unannounced, had turned him into a gibbering idiot. Why hadn't he simply given her the facts without all that gabbling and arm waving? It really was quite simple and straightforward. Naturally, he felt guilty, especially as Alex's actions and decisions had managed to overrule everything he'd planned. That's when he decided to write a letter. Yes, he'd set it out clearly and post it to her. Even the usually laid-back Leo Marcello was becoming increasingly frustrated by the interruptions. A letter would deal with the unfortunate business for good. Carefully, he considered his plan, making sure there were no weaknesses in it. He'd organise an official valuation letter then fold up his own and tuck it inside. By addressing it to Mrs H. Chesney, Hattie would be guaranteed to open it. Being a teacher, she'd be home first, so she'd be sure to deal with the post herself. Leo congratulated himself on his excellent course of action.

Dearest Hattie, he began the next morning. No, *Dear Hattie.* Yes, keep it simple. However, despite his intention to convey facts, Leo couldn't help reminding his reader of the feelings he'd had for her. His feelings had been genuine, even though the facts evidently painted a different picture. Where was that sweet, fun-loving girl, he mused, as he wrote and rewrote his letter. The memory of Hattie's recent venom and vitriol lingered in his mind, but he was sure that would be swept aside once she had his explanation in her hand. Perhaps then, they'd be able to have the occasional pleasant exchange when their paths crossed, maybe even become friends again. He remembered the pretty diamond cluster engagement ring he'd bought. It was such a shame it had never been worn by the girl he'd intended.

Hattie was full of good intentions the following day, but the shadow of the previous night felt like an impending cloudburst and Leo's words gnawed away like an irritating earworm. Frittering away two hours of coffee and chat with Fliss might have once been her favourite rest-day occupation, but Hattie had now reordered her priorities: finishing her quilt was at the top of the list.

She set up her sewing machine and ironing board, shut Jezebel in the kitchen and soon the log cabin square, started in class the night before, was completed and packed away with the rest. After a reviving cup of coffee and chocolate digestive, she decided to cut another set of pieces in different fabrics and then beavered away with Vale FM for company. Easy-peasy, she thought proudly as she ironed the last seam flat and admired her handiwork.

'Fish hooks!' she exclaimed angrily, when she realised that she'd used the wrong sheet of measurements and made this square bigger than the first. The project was going to take much longer than she'd imagined. Once the quilt was completed, with its riot of spots, stripes, florals and plains, all she needed was a cosy bedroom in a characterful cottage to set it off – roses around the door an optional extra. If only she could get Leo Marcello and the mysterious Alex out of her mind. Just the thought of his guilty blabbering made her grind her teeth in anger. It was all very well when Leo told his chilling account of the lift drama, but caught off-guard, he fell apart like a choc-ice in a heat wave.

'He's history!' she snapped to a bemused-looking Jezebel, as she thumped the fridge door shut and set the jars of chutneys and sauces rattling. 'Just history, and don't give me that "I've-not-been-fed-today" look, pussy cat. Just be grateful you had the snip years ago. Tomcats aren't all they're cracked up to be!'

Come on now Hattie, she reminded herself, Nick's really the top of your priorities, followed by that dream cottage. It was time to do a little Internet surfing in the Lydford Cross area.

'Ah,' she gasped, gazing longingly at picture perfect village cottages, until she saw the price tags. 'Hmm,' she sighed, impressed by Lydford Cross's period semis, until she noted their miserly dimensions. The search for her dream cottage would not be easy.

The following morning, Nick was up as soon as the seven o'clock alarm sounded, and he was showered, suited and booted in time for a sustaining cooked breakfast before his journey. There wasn't much in the way of preparation for the interview and he knew the journey to Romsey almost blindfold. With the postcode of the Lydford Cross company in his sat-nav, there'd be no problem at all. It was a relief to see that there had been no more snow, and the Five Live weather reports told him that the only overnight snowfalls had been in the north of the country.

'Good luck, Dad,' Josh muttered into his cornflakes as Nick dumped his empty plate on the drainer and went to fetch his coat.

'Thanks, Josh. I'll certainly try my best.'

'I know you will,' added Hattie, hugging him fondly. 'When do you think you'll be back?'

'Er... well, mid to late afternoon I should think. Let's see: company tour at ten, interview at eleven, lunch about half twelve... I don't suppose I need to hang around much longer. They'll be contacting the successful candidates by email then sending a follow-up letter I gather. If there's time, I might even drop in at a couple of estate agents, just in case...' He stopped short, not wanting to tempt fate.

'Oh well, if you're home first, you might like to have a pot brewing. I shall certainly need it after the likes of Jacob Pocock and co. today.'

'Cheer up, Hat,' chuckled Nick. 'My aim in life is to whisk you away from all those little horrors ASAP – promise!' He pecked her on the cheek and was out of the door just as the eight o'clock news pips beeped on the kitchen radio.

An hour later, as Hattie was registering class 4N, the post arrived at 7 Witchert Close. Together with flyers and buff envelopes lying on the doormat, was one white, hand-written one, awaiting her attention.

As Nick cheerfully tucked into a plate of quiche and salad, he reviewed the morning, feeling confident about his performance in front of the selection panel. Fortunately, the journey had been trouble-free with well-gritted roads and no hold-ups. There were four other candidates, none of whom worked at Padgett and Bicton, so Madge was wrong about that. Two of them were a good ten years younger and judging by their appearance, considered that the 'dress-down Friday' style extended to interviews. Nick thought that was a risky assumption. Both rivals had the same arrogant air of high-flying whizz-kid, which had given him a few moments' doubt about his own suitability. Nevertheless, he had emerged from the boardroom feeling relieved and yet satisfied that he'd handled the questions well. He'd made sure he'd emphasised how much he relished the prospect of more responsibility, and his experience and excellent references surely made him a strong contender. Now all he had to do was wait for a decision.

Shortly after two, he set off from Lydford Cross, having collected his travelling expenses and, by avoiding the rush hour, was home before most commuters were on the road. Jezebel met him with her tail held high as he opened the door, and mewed loudly, brushing against his trousers. A scattering of mail lay on the carpet, which he scooped up and dumped on the hall table. First things first, he decided and filled the kettle for a cup of tea. It was just after three thirty, so Hattie wouldn't be due home for another half an hour or so. However, Jezebel's internal clock ignored real time. She wound around Nick's legs insisting on being fed, so to keep her quiet, he forked out a dishful, topped up her water and added a handful of Seafood Snax for good measure.

While his tea was brewing, he collected the post from the hall and sifted through it: a couple of bills, a supermarket flyer, a bank statement and a handwritten, white envelope with a Mia Casa crest in the bottom left-hand corner. It was addressed to Mrs H. Chesney. He dumped his teabag, added milk and sugar and then sat down at the kitchen table, puzzling over the omission of his name on the envelope – obviously some mistake. They'd already received a letter from Samways and Partners, setting out their valuation, so Nick guessed that this one from Mia Casa contained similar information. He gulped down half of his tea, quickly dealt with the mundane items and then tore open the white envelope. Sure enough, inside was a typed letter with the valuation figure and terms of business as well as the hope that Mr and Mrs Chesney might be instructing them in the near future. Just as Nick was setting the letter aside, a smaller folded piece of paper fluttered to the floor. Assuming it was a compliments slip, he bent to pick it up. However, on unfolding it and seeing the handwritten greeting, he saw at once that this was a letter.

Dear Hattie… Who was writing a personal note to Hattie? he wondered. Before reading any more, he turned the sheet over and saw the name 'Leo' written with a stylish flourish. How odd, he thought, yet something told him that this was more than odd. His hand began to shake as he started to read:

Dear Hattie,
    Because of the deep love I have had for you, I have been so sorry that the recent chain of events has prevented me from telling you what you wanted to hear.

'Oh my God!' spluttered Nick. The words on the page started to swim before his eyes and he flung the sheet down in disgust. Sickened and shocked, he gulped the rest of his tea – although something stronger might have been more appropriate – and shook his head in despair. What was going on? Something, obviously, but he didn't have the stomach to read any more. Hattie was involved with another man. That's why the letter was only addressed to Hattie. It was a *love* letter.

His breath was coming in short gasps as he slowly leaned down to retrieve the sheet. What should he do? Should he throw it away? Should he hold on to it and confront Hattie with the contents? The shock of the discovery had left him reeling. No, he couldn't confront Hattie just yet. He needed time to think about this. He quickly went up to their bedroom and hid the letter at the back of his underwear drawer, under the boxed bow tie that he seldom wore. The valuation letter was left on the kitchen table; that was all Hattie would see.

He returned to the kitchen and slumped in a chair, aware that she'd soon be back from school, all excited about his interview. Or would she? The letter had changed everything. He'd arrived home feeling confident about the interview, but now he was struggling to retain any sense of purpose about his life. Was Hattie having a wild fling? Was she planning to leave him? *Deep love?* Just how long do you spend in someone's company to fall deeply in love? Marcello had paid *one* visit to the house after all. Or had he? Then there was that business at the college. He recalled chatting to him at the door and finding him quite formal, even a bit on the stiff and starchy side; perhaps that had been a cover for a guilty conscience. He'd come from the same part of the college where Hattie had been and she'd been in a right state when he'd found her.

'Oh God,' he moaned, his head in his hands. 'What do I say to her?' But it seemed to Nick that the Almighty was holding back on quick-fire solutions for the time being.

Several minutes ticked by while he sat slumped at the table, paralysed with fear and at a loss to know what to do or say. In fact, he was so far away from his comfort zone he might as well be pitched up at the South Pole with only a bin bag between survival and oblivion. He knew how to cope with Arsenal losing at home: a few well-chosen expletives, a can of lager and half an hour or so rubbishing the ref and opposition, then it was on to the anticipation of the next match. He'd coped in the past when missing promotion and he'd cope today if the Bennington's job wasn't to be his. However, he was out of touch with his feminine side and all the attendant vocabulary. Perhaps he'd been taking Hattie for granted. Maybe he'd lost his touch in bed...

He stared at the floor with its mock tile design in tasteful beige and brown vinyl and studied its pleasing regimented lines. If only life could be so consistent. He could deal with spreadsheets and reconcile balances to three decimal places, but it now felt as if someone had dumped a sack of miscellaneous figures on his desk and caused every calculator on earth to malfunction. Suddenly life was unpredictable and no university degrees or letters after his name would be of any use. Jezebel leapt up and sat purring beside him, pleased with herself for wangling an early tea. Nick looked up and watched her fastidious washing of each ear.

'It's all right for you,' he sighed, stroking her silky coat.

Where had he failed, he wondered, and what was so special about that man? From the little bit he'd read, it was obvious their relationship was more than householder and estate agent. Was she passionately in love with him? If so, why was she so keen on the move? Perhaps he ought to read the rest of the letter, he decided, but by the time he'd reached the hall he could hear Hattie slamming her car door and the moment passed.

He hurried back to the kitchen and flicked the switch on the kettle, hoping that mundane domesticity would help him find his equilibrium. Going at her, all guns blazing, would not be helpful. Just stay cool, he ordered himself, stay cool and see what happens. It wasn't exactly that he was emulating the ostrich, but it was about all he could manage for the time being.

'Hi Nick!' called Hattie, with a slam of the door. 'Got that cuppa brewing? I'm whacked! God, those kids were really pushing their luck this afternoon but I kept their noses to the grindstone, the little perishers!'

She bustled into the kitchen with a look of triumph, despite her weariness. 'So how did my brilliant husband get on today?' she asked eagerly as he placed her mug on the table. 'I hope they thought you were the best thing since Sky Sports Extra.'

'Well, I'm not sure about that,' Nick replied, with the merest suggestion of a smile. He could have coped with a gloomy or snappy wife, but up beat enthusiasm was hard to take.

'Oh, didn't it go well?' she asked sympathetically before taking a sip. 'Did the so-and-sos put you through the third degree? Oh, I just remembered...' She broke off to root around in her bag. 'Chocolate muffins! Talk about a life-saver.' She tore off the cellophane wrap and pushed one across to Nick.

'Well... I think it went quite well,' Nick told her, focussing on the painstakingly slow removal of the paper case.

'That's good,' mumbled Hattie, between mouthfuls. 'Are you okay, Nick? You seem a bit down. Bad journey?'

'Yeah, traffic was awful,' he improvised. 'Actually, I need to log onto my email soon to find out if there's a job offer waiting for me.'

'Well, finish the muffin first, Nick,' Hattie suggested, as she popped in the last piece and folded the case into a neat dart. 'Did you have a chance to recce the Lydford estate agents?'

The words 'estate agents' plunged Nick back into the black hole, out of which he'd just managed to crawl.

'Sorry, no,' he told her, keeping his attention on a particularly chunky piece of chocolate that protruded from the muffin's well-rounded contours.

'Oh well, there'll be plenty of time for that, *if* you get the job.'

'I'll just go and get the PC warmed up,' he said quickly, abandoning his half-consumed muffin. 'And don't let Jezebel con you into feeding her. She's already had plenty.'

It was a relief to escape to the seclusion of the study, where the PC was already simmering nicely after a lengthy trawl through the estate agency websites of mid-Hants. To one side of the desk, Nick noticed Hattie's list of scribbled notes about some of the Lydford Cross agents, including the addresses and prices of two properties highlighted with asterisks and exclamation marks. It was all so baffling. Nothing seemed to make sense. Currently, two and two seemed to make three point nine five.

Logging onto his email screen, he was disappointed not to be greeted by the voice telling him, 'You've got mail.' Even a glimpse in the spam folder revealed only a clutch of dubious offers for body enhancement and inheritance windfalls. He logged off and decided to try later.

'Just going to lie down!' he called on his way through the hall.

'Okay, love. You deserve to chill out,' sympathised Hattie, poking her head round the kitchen door. 'I see we've had a valuation letter from Mia Casa. Talk about syrupy sales talk! Did you read all that waffle assuring us of their promised efforts to sell our home? They sound really desperate for business.'

It seemed to Nick that for a woman with a secret lover, Hattie came over as strangely dismissive of her beloved's company. He grunted a nondescript reply on his way upstairs, where he flung himself on the bed and tried to clear his mind of unanswered questions. But every time he closed his eyes, Signor Mar-something-or-other would appear, smiling that smarmy smile and bowing and scraping in that period drama style. After twenty-three years of marriage he thought he had Hattie sussed. He'd convinced himself that her recent mood swings were all down to women's problems, but it was obvious now they were the result of living a double life. God, she was clever!

Half an hour dragged by miserably while Hattie hummed and clattered her way through supper preparations below. At a quarter to five he returned to the study and logged on again, reckoning some decisions must have been made by now. A job offer would certainly test Hattie's sense of loyalty.

'You've got mail,' announced the sexy voice, but there wasn't anything more exciting than a supermarket promotion, an update from his old school website and a brief thank you from sister Helena in Oz. However, eight messages lurked in the spam folder, one of which had been sent by admin@benningtonltd.co.uk. Bingo!

Dear Mr Chesney,
   Thank you for attending the interview earlier today. We are pleased to be able to offer you... etc... etc.

'Yes!' whooped Nick, punching the air, all thoughts of his wife's duplicity temporarily driven from his mind. Jezebel, who had not long taken up residence in the armchair, shot from her cosy nest, tail bushed up and hackles hoisted at ninety degrees.

'Did I hear something like a cheer?' Hattie called, rushing from the kitchen with dripping hands and a vegetable peeler trailing a loop of carrot. 'Well?'

'Yes, they've offered me a job!' announced Nick proudly.

'Oh wow!' shrieked Hattie, flinging her arms round his neck and smothering him with kisses. 'Clever, brilliant husband!' she crowed, once she had surfaced.

'Don't you want to know which one they offered me?' he teased, feeling the immense weight of Hattie-stress roll from his shoulders.

Perhaps the fling-thing with the Italian was more one-sided that he'd first feared.

'I guess so,' she replied, clearly thrilled that the waiting was now over.

'Only the post of senior accounts manager,' he boasted.

'Oh double wow! Which you're going to accept, naturally.'

'I expect so, if you think I should,' he continued, in a more serious vein.

'If *I* think you should?' she exclaimed, incredulously. 'Is the pope Catholic?'

'I take it that's a yes?'

'A one-hundred-per-cent-you'd-be-crazy-not-to-accept-it yes, you silly man! Email back straight away and accept it,' she urged, wondering if he was having second thoughts. They surely wouldn't have offered him the position if they'd had doubts.

Nick turned his attention to the monitor's screen where the email was still displayed and let the cursor hover over the reply button.

'You really want us to move down to Lydford Cross, Hat?' he asked, fixing her with a concerned expression. 'To leave this area and set up home miles away?'

'Of course I do, Nick. Wasn't it *my* suggestion?' she reminded him. 'Ooh, I can't wait to get this house on the market and tell old haggis-bag he can stuff the job – in the politest of terms, of course!'

'Right, I'll accept,' said Nick firmly, returning to his email and clicking on reply. The business with the letter, Hattie's mood swings and her reaction to the job offer still didn't add up and short of asking her outright, he felt no nearer an answer that made any sense. Let sleeping dogs lie, he mused. The sleeping dogs were away with the fairies, so he decided that's exactly where he'd like them to remain.

8

At breakfast the following morning, Nick announced that he'd decided to instruct Samways and Partners.

'Their valuation is probably more realistic,' he observed casually. Hattie's face hadn't shown a flicker of disappointment at his decision, he noted. In fact, she had greeted it with cheerful agreement then gathered up her gardening apron and secateurs and had gone off to arrange the church flowers with Celia Halverson. Nick felt greatly heartened. Only hours before, he'd been in fear of his marriage falling apart. Now, however, he was convinced that the letter was merely the pitiful ramblings of a deluded loser. One innocent smile in the utility room must have been the cause. He could think of no other opportunity. Clearly, Hattie couldn't care a fig for the man.

'We'd like to go on the market at once,' Nick told Brian when he phoned. 'Excellent news, Mr Chesney, and I'm very pleased that you decided to choose a reliable, tried and trusted company like mine.' The unspoken subtext implied, 'and not one of those new cowboy set-ups like Mia Casa.' 'Now, let me see... Yes, I could come and take photos and measurements this afternoon. Would that be convenient? If not, Monday would be fine.'

'Um, well I think so,' replied Nick, remembering Hattie's reaction when he hadn't bothered to consult her. 'But I'm not sure of my wife's plans for later.'

'Oh, I expect the little woman will be busy with her ironing or some such if she's anything like Mrs Samways,' Brian replied, with a certain air of Reverend Collins, of *Pride and Prejudice* fame, about him. Nick boggled at the sort of poor, hapless female Brian had managed to ensnare into holy matrimony: presumably one who was also wedded to her ironing board.

On hearing Brian's rather old-fashioned view of the female sex, Nick saw an opportunity for some innocent amusement.

'Ironing? Oh no, she's more likely to be out in the back garden hacking branches off the apple tree or mending a fence or two. Or maybe she'll have her welding kit out.'

'Her *what* out?' Brian gasped, aghast.

'Her welding kit,' Nick confirmed, 'and quite a sight she is in goggles, with her blow torch at full blast.'

'Oh, I see,' Brian replied, hardly disguising his surprise. 'Well, er… shall we agree a time? I've got a clear diary from one o'clock onwards. Would two be suitable?'

'Um, I think so. I'll text Mrs C and check with her. She's down at the church at the moment.'

'Not with her welding kit?' Brian ventured, incredulous at the bewildering insights into the Chesney marriage.

'Oh no, not the welding kit this time,' replied Nick in an indifferent tone, 'but something just as vital to the life of the church I assure you. So if it's okay with the little woman, I'll expect you at two; if not, I'll call back and we can reschedule.'

'Very well, Mr Chesney. Now let me see, 7 Witchert Close … three-bed semi with en-suite, conservatory, nice views at the back,' he recited, 'and a little cat.'

'You remember the cat do you?' asked Nick, bemused by this surprising detail.

There was a pregnant pause and some throat clearing before Brian answered. 'Let's say my trousers remember, shall we?'

'Ah.' Nick noted the serious undertones then recalled Hattie's hilarious account of the Samways valuation visit in vivid detail and the effect of Jezebel's favourite cushion on the navy pinstripe polyester. 'See you later then.'

Nick couldn't help but have a quiet chuckle before texting Hattie and confirming that the afternoon appointment would be fine with her.

'I can't believe you told him I had a welding kit,' she giggled, stowing away the last of the cat food pouches after their quick supermarket blitz.

'Well, he was asking for it,' countered Nick. 'I mean, he was so pompous and opinionated.'

'Hmm, I know exactly what you mean,' agreed Hattie, 'but if he can sell our house in super-quick time, I'll forgive him all that.'

Right on cue, Brian rang the doorbell as Hattie filled the kettle and set out a plate of digestives.

'Come on in, Mr Samways,' said Nick. 'There'll be tea in the kitchen when you're ready.'

'Oh, just call me Brian. There's no need to stand on ceremony,' he replied jovially, then set off with his clipboard and electronic measure.

Some twenty minutes later he reappeared, looking around nervously at the available seating before risking his trousers a second time.

'Cup of tea, Brian?' offered Hattie, with her most winning 'little woman' smile.

'Lovely thanks,' he replied, lowering his frame gingerly on one of the plain wooden kitchen chairs. He spotted the biscuits and scooped up a couple in one easy movement. 'We'll put the details on the website straight away and post out paper copies to our mailing list clients on Monday.'

'That's all very promising,' commented Nick. 'It sounds like you've plenty of potential buyers lined up already.'

'Yes, indeed, Mr Chesney, there *are* a number of clients looking for this type of property. So, we'll hope to get viewings arranged ASAP.'

'Right,' murmured Nick, catching Hattie's eye and winking.

'We'll have you out of here in a jiffy!' Brian boasted, taking a quick swig from his mug before reaching for another digestive. The plate was looking quite empty already. How did the man manage it? Was it some sleight of hand?

'Now, here's a spare key if you need to show clients around when we're both out at work,' said Nick.

'Rest assured, we'll always warn you first,' Brian promised, tucking the key into his folder.

'Oh good,' said Hattie, 'I wouldn't want prospective buyers greeted by rumpled duvets and my undies.'

'Certainly not,' agreed Brian, blushing deep crimson.

They discussed fees and the selling price over more mugs of tea and then Brian was ready to leave.

'Well, thank you,' he said amiably, heaving himself off his chair after quickly disposing of another digestive with the dregs of the tea.

'Oh, just one thing, Mr Samways – I mean Brian,' began Hattie anxiously. 'Is there anything we should do to improve our chances of selling? I mean, is the colour scheme okay, or should we give the rooms a quick once-over with magnolia?'

'Oh no, don't you worry yourself about such details,' he replied, with his irritating tendency to condescension. 'This is a charming house and you've done it up really nicely. I like a bit of colour myself and if the buyer doesn't like it, it can always be changed. If you want to sell quickly you don't want to waste valuable time painting, do you? The new owners will do that when they move in.'

'Oh, I see,' said Hattie, feeling as if she was being steam-rollered. 'But I've heard about some TV programmes where they give you advice about selling your house, like giving it a makeover and I thought –'

'Take no notice of that silly stuff. I've been in the business for years, when today's TV presenters were in nappies, and I don't have a problem selling properties. Personally, I think this "doing up to sell" is just a passing fad. I mean it'll cost you money to start with,' he pontificated, 'and most buyers look beyond colour schemes. As a matter of fact, I think the lime green and lilac are most attractive, and the rest as well of course.' It was almost as if he was going to pat her hand and murmur 'there, there', but mercifully he didn't.

'It's all about money,' he continued, tapping the side of his nose. 'Those DIY set-ups and the like have probably got nice little earners sorted with the TV companies, mark my words.'

Hattie and Nick nodded mutely. Clearly, Brian was the fount of all knowledge when it came to selling houses.

'I think it's time Celia and I had a little chat,' said Hattie, once Brian had left.

'Oh yes, mustn't forget Josh in all our excitement,' agreed Nick. 'Play down the laundry and decibel problems, old girl, or they'll never agree.'

When Celia Halverson had a fresh snippet of news, it was guaranteed to be on the village bush telegraph in no time. Sure enough, when Hattie and Nick arrived for Matins the following morning, half the congregation already knew about Nick's job offer and the impending move.

'You've been here such a long time,' sighed Hilda Makepeace, queen bee of the Mothers' Union and assistant sides-person, 'but I'm sure we'll manage without you.'

Even churchgoers who'd been around for twenty-plus years were made to feel like insignificant newcomers at times. Established as one of the long-standing members of St Swithin's, you might be forgiven for thinking that Hilda was on the welcoming committee when Noah pitched up with his ark on Mount Ararat.

'But what about Josh?' she continued crisply. 'Fancy getting Toby and Celia to take him on – at *their* time of life too.' Hilda had perfected the knack of combining compliments with subtle snubs. In fact, she had it down to a fine art. Hattie struggled to keep her Sunday-best face, despite Hilda's suggestion that Josh's presence was marginally more risky than a Rottweiler or a tank of rattlesnakes.

'But they're perfectly happy to have him,' she protested hotly. 'After all, they *are* his godparents.'

'Oh, I see,' muttered Hilda with a meaningful sniff. 'Well, maybe that's what made them agree.' She turned to pick up a pile of hymn books and continued handing them out to whoever was following on behind.

At that moment Hattie's mobile sprang to life, playing its merry little tune. Around the church, conversations came to an abrupt halt and furtive glances darted around in search of the culprit. Hilda turned around sharply and tutted, lifting her nose as if something extremely smelly was too close for comfort.

'Oh, bodkins!' gasped Hattie, frantically rooting around in her bag to silence the offending article. Its glowing screen showed the name *Leo*, before she jabbed the 'off' key. Leo? What could he want, she wondered, feeling a deep flush burning her cheeks. In Hilda's estimation, she taken advantage of Celia, shocked the whole congregation and been rude to a church stalwart all in the space of two minutes. Hattie raised her eyebrows and sighed.

'Are you okay, Hat?' asked Nick, who had missed most of the excitement while in a conflab with Toby over the next Playing Field Committee issue.

'That woman!' hissed Hattie when they were well out of earshot. 'She's insufferable!'

'Ah yes: "Love they neighbour",' he chuckled as they sat down, 'all part of the daily challenge, and she's more challenging than most – even Madge!'

Most of the service passed by without registering in Hattie's brain. At some point the vicar must have told one of his famous silly jokes, judging by an explosion of giggles around her, but even that failed to make any impact. Blasted Leo was the cause and forgiving him – as with Hilda – was a virtual impossibility. Then the vicar proceeded to preach on the subject of 'turning the other cheek', which added to Hattie's bad temper and set her thinking about Wednesday's meeting.

Much later, when Hattie had tidied away her patchwork clutter and Nick and Josh were deeply immersed in Sunday sport, she fished out her mobile. Leo's badly timed text had niggled away most of the day. There'd be no peace of mind until she read it.

Did u get the letter?

Letter? Then she recalled Friday's valuation confirmation. Why text her about something so mundane, she wondered.

Yes, received, she texted back – anything to keep him quiet. However, within a minute, another text arrived.

Okay about the letter? it read.

What was wrong with the man? Didn't he have better things to do?

Fine, she texted back, then carried on folding fabric ready for Wednesday evening.

Within a few seconds, the mobile spring into life yet again.

'Gobstoppers!' Hattie snapped fiercely, snatching the phone as if it were a recalcitrant child.

'What's up, Hat?' asked Nick, temporarily distracted from the TV screen.

'It's nothing,' she huffed. 'Cynthia Dacey can be a bit of a pain at times.'

'Oh, right,' replied Nick. 'Thought you two were getting on fine.'

So pleased, was the message on the screen. Hattie jabbed the 'off' button viciously for the second time that day. Text messages from Leo were the last thing she needed after his pathetic performance at the college. Did he really think that he stood the slightest chance of getting their business? Stodgy Brian Samways might grate horribly, but at least he didn't come with any emotional baggage. Out of all the estate agents in the area, what had compelled her to choose *those* two?

*

Nick was feeling perky when he arrived at work the following morning. Arsenal had had their best win of the season so far, and the letter confirming the job offer had arrived before he'd left home that morning. He'd taken it with him to thrust under Madge's nose, if the occasion arose. Hattie had been avidly trawling the Lydford Cross property websites the previous evening and had already compiled a long list of desirable, must-see properties. The trifling Marcello business was history.

'Good morning, Madge,' he called cheerfully, 'and how are you this bright and sunny morning?' All traces of snow had melted away over the weekend and signs of spring were gradually transforming the late winter landscape.

'Oh, mustn't grumble,' she sighed heavily and then proceeded, at great length and grisly detail, to regale Nick about the state of her bunions.

'Too much information!' warned Nick, as his PC started humming. 'Sounds as if you've been living it up at the weekend – dancing and letting your hair down, eh, Madge?'

'What do you mean, "dancing and letting my hair down"?' she snapped waspishly.

'Oh nothing, Madge,' he replied innocently. 'I could have said… er… too much jogging and keep fit.'

Madge huffed and sat down at her desk, scattering a sheath of papers in her wake. There was an alarming similarity with Hattie's recent hissy fit.

'Don't you want to know how I got on last Friday?' he asked with a twinkle.

'Friday? What about Friday?' she muttered, refusing to show the slightest flicker of interest.

'My interview at Lydford Cross of course. Surely you noticed how peaceful the office was without me?'

'And such a peace that passed all understanding,' quipped Madge primly, 'to quote the good book!'

'Oh-ho, that's very witty, Madge.'

Madge peered at the hourglass on her monitor with exaggerated concentration, although Nick was sure she was itching to be first with his news that she could gossip around the building.

'Well?' teased Nick.

'Well, Nicholas Chesney, it's obvious you're like the cat that got the cream, so you'd better tell me because you obviously can't wait.'

'They offered me the post of *senior* accounts manager – subject to the usual medical of course, which should be a breeze. Once that's sorted, I'll be giving in my notice and should start down there at the beginning of April.'

Madge snapped to attention and absorbed the revelation with a mixture of irritation and disbelief. '*Senior* accounts manager? Never!' she gasped. 'Well, you'd better not lord it over me while you're still working in *this* office, and I'll remind you to keep all the drawers as I like them,' she warned him.

'Absolutely, Madge. I promise I won't be messing around in your drawers,' he chuckled. She glared at him, suspecting his usual leg-pull was loaded with smutty innuendo.

'Are you being suggestive?' she snapped, narrowing her eyes.

'Oh no. Not at all, Madge. Nothing was further from my mind. I was just assuring you that your staples and paperclips will be left all ship-shape and Bristol fashion.'

'That's just as well,' she replied, taking a large envelope to the photocopier. 'You can turn your new office into a pigsty for all I care. I pity the poor beggar who has to share it.' The senior status of Nick's new position with the usual added bonus of sole office occupancy and a personal assistant had obviously not occurred to her.

Nick pulled out some files and addressed the most urgent matters that had been awaiting his attention since Thursday. After a few minutes, in which Madge was waging war on the photocopier, to the accompaniment of much tutting and fussing, the phone rang.

'I don't have three pairs of hands,' she muttered, leaving the office in high dudgeon. In the blissful peace that followed, Nick reflected on the turn his career had taken and tried to recall the details of the Bennington accounts set-up. He'd be in charge of two young men in their early twenties and a woman, probably in her mid-thirties. The current senior manager, he understood, was retiring after twenty years with the company. Hopefully his appointment would be welcomed rather than resented. On the bright side, there wouldn't be a Madge clone to snap at his heels all day long.

A quarter of an hour later, Madge bustled back, laden with an armful of files. She dumped them on her desk and sank gratefully into her chair.

'Let me fetch you a coffee, Madge. It looks like you need one,' offered Nick, putting aside his calculations.

'That's very civil of you,' she acknowledged. Nick nipped out to the drinks machine in the corridor and came back with two brimming cups. He left his to cool and gathered up several sheets for copying. On lifting the lid, he saw at once that Madge had clearly forgotten about what she had been doing when the phone rang. Nick removed the sheet and turned it over. What was this? Certainly not accounts paperwork. The sheet was covered in diagrams and labelled instructions and was entitled *Belly Dancing Movements*. Belly dancing? Madge? Nick couldn't think of two more unlikely pairings in the whole of existence. It took an extraordinary effort not to laugh aloud. Of course, there *had* been something strangely familiar about one of the pink-faced ladies he'd briefly glimpsed at the college last week. It was now making sense.

'Er… Madge, is this yours?' he enquired casually, holding up the incriminating evidence. Seeing how snappy she'd been with him that morning he didn't think he owed her any favours.

'What's that?' muttered Madge in between sips of coffee.

'This sheet: it was on the photocopier. Did you leave it here earlier?' The penny took approximately two seconds to drop. With a startled shriek, Madge was out of her seat faster than a prize greyhound. She blushed and snatched the sheet from his grasp.

'Thank *you!*' she snapped, grabbing the envelope that lay abandoned beside the machine.

'Oh, please finish what you were doing,' chuckled Nick, 'and then I'll fetch the copier logbook and cash box so you can settle up.'

Nick may have had his faults, but stealing from the firm was not one of them. With his impending move to senior management, he was even more aware of the importance of setting a good example.

'No, I'll finish later,' Madge insisted stiffly. 'I'll not have you gawping and making snide remarks.' She stuffed the envelope into her shopping bag and returned to her desk.

'I wouldn't do that,' protested Nick.

'Uph!' huffed Madge. 'Think I'd believe that?'

'No, er... I think it's great. And I'm sure it's good for... um... keeping good shape too. Only the other day I noticed how well you looked.' He added the last words more out of determination to relieve Madge of the misery of embarrassment. Otherwise, the atmosphere in the office would be heading for unknown depths.

'Really?' she asked hopefully, sounding less mortified.

'Yes, really.'

'Well, it was Sandra's idea actually,' she admitted after a pregnant pause. 'We *both* go.'

'Oh, I see,' murmured Nick, busy with his copying. 'Are you in a troupe of some sort?' he asked innocently.

'We're not a nightclub act, if that's what you're implying,' she huffed.

'No, no, I wasn't implying anything like that, Madge. I just don't know the collective term for belly dancers.'

She eyed him suspiciously while he pondered on the possible terminology: a wobble of belly dancers? A quivering of belly dancers? A pulsation? A wiggle? An undulation? Even the thought of Madge, Sandra and their classmates – probably all over forty – gyrating, swaying and waggling their derrières was mind-boggling. Then he tried to imagine what they might wear, picturing sequinned harem pants, yashmaks, skimpy tops, filmy, floaty veils and glittering jewellery.

'We do it to keep fit, you know,' Madge said as an afterthought, wanting to give her evening class an air of respectability.

'Undoubtedly,' Nick agreed.

'That girl in Sandra's nephew's company started us on it. She's a qualified instructor, you know.'

After a few moments of confusion, Nick worked out that Madge was referring to Greg of Mia Casa and the delectable blonde who worked there. Into his mind floated the gorgeous Rebecca sinuously wiggling her hips – what a picture!

'Oh yes. The lovely Rebecca!' he sighed, remembering their chat and her saucy wink.

'What did you say?' snapped Madge.

'Oh… er… the *lively* Rebecca. I'm sure she's an excellent teacher,' he replied quickly. 'It's a shame Hattie's patchwork class is on the same night, otherwise she might have liked to join in.' He ambled back to his desk, his mind still filled with tantalising images, and beavered away at his work pile, leaving Madge to her mountain of folders.

'So you're putting your house on the market are you?' Madge enquired at the end of the day, while zipping up her substantial padded jacket that gave her the unfortunate appearance of a Michelin man.

'Yeah, that's right. We had photos and measurements done on Saturday and should be on the website today.'

'Oh Greg'll do a good job for you. Sandra says he's very efficient.'

'Well, actually, we're not instructing Mia Casa. We've decided to go with Samways,' Nick replied somewhat apologetically, realising that in rejecting Mia Casa, a hornets' nest of huffs would be released.

'Samways?' Madge spat in horror. 'That Brian Samways is a proper old woman – so Sandra says.'

Indeed, as Nick had been told at least a hundred times, Sandra had the final word on everyone and everything.

'He's all right, Madge. Although he *does* have some interesting views on the fairer sex.'

Madge shot him a scandalised glance.

'Well, a bit old-fashioned; that's what I meant,' corrected Nick.

Madge dug out a brightly patterned earflap hat that was topped by a jaunty cluster of pink bobbles. 'Well *I* think you've picked the wrong agent,' she continued as she secured the ties under her chin and adjusted the hat for maximum coverage and comfort.

'And I'd wager that Sandra would agree,' replied Nick with a twinkle, but he swiftly turned away so Madge wouldn't catch him breaking into a smirk.

'What's wrong with Mia Casa, that's what I'd like to know? They're two nice young men with a smart office and a pretty girl to help them. What more could you want?'

'Well, it was a difficult decision, Madge,' Nick lied, 'but we can only afford sole agency fees, so we had to plump for one – sort of heads or tails, you know.'

'Heads or tails? Well, that's a very strange way to decide. What didn't you like about Greg?' Madge was clearly affronted on Sandra's behalf.

'Greg? We haven't actually met Greg as it happens. He wasn't in the office when I called and it was the other chap who carried out the valuation.'

'Ooh, the lovely Leo,' giggled Madge. 'So charming, so friendly,' she simpered, momentarily distracted from grilling Nick on his botched decision.

'If you say so,' remarked Nick as he picked up his briefcase.

'It's a shame you didn't meet Greg. You might have made a different decision.' She picked up her bags and bustled from the office with a disdainful sniff, now looking like the Michelin man mutating into a Teletubby. As Nick followed on he decided it wasn't worth wasting his breath when Madge was in one of her moods. It was all down to fate though. If Greg *had* carried out the valuation, Marcello and Hattie would never have met, the letter would not have been written and their lives would have been just as they were before. But the Mia Casa business was over now, Nick reminded himself. Then he reflected on the one rather attractive facet of Mia Casa – Rebecca Vaudin – and the regret of not being able to pursue that brief but stimulating acquaintance. C'est la vie, he thought.

How to buy a house, sell it, clean it, spruce it up, transform it, build it; you name it, there was a programme out there showing you how to do it. Hattie was transfixed and her passion for picking up tips was becoming addictive. Seeing the stunning transformations conjured up with the right expertise – usually some trendy designer – and a few hundred pounds was amazing. She now saw her home with new eyes. It was decidedly lived-in, cluttered and stuck in a nineties time warp. By mid-afternoon, she had drawn up a checklist of jobs to be tackled, as well as a shopping list of stylish accessories to dress the rooms. Top of the list was a cappuccino machine, marked with two large asterisks. Persuading Nick to agree might be a tad tricky, but if the selling process turned out to be slow, she'd have her list ready to flash under his nose. Josh, however, was another matter. He seemed to have a built-in allergy to laundry baskets. The latest one was generously proportioned for a whole week's worth of dirty clothes. Sadly, though, it stood in the corner of his room, empty and unnoticed, while piles of grubby underwear were sprinkled liberally over the floor. Alarmingly, his socks had acquired the disturbing habit of crawling off to the darkest recesses of the room and mouldering there until Hattie had the time and energy to retrieve them.

Over a reviving cuppa and absolutely essential chocolate biscuit, Hattie fine-tuned her list and started to wonder about supper. What bliss it was to be on half-term. With the huge list of jobs, she needed time to get them done and have the house generally spruced up ready for viewings. Just then, the phone rang and someone called Pete started chatting to her like an old friend.

'Sorry,' she cut in, 'but who are you?' Maybe it was a wrong number or one of those irritating marketing calls.

'Pete,' he told her brightly. 'Pete Ingleheart of Samways and Partners.'

'Oh, I see.' That was obviously the crucial information she must have missed in his opening greeting. 'So you're one of the partners.'

Secretly, she'd been harbouring a suspicion that no partners actually existed and that Brian had named his company as part of a sad, middle-aged ego trip. She imagined the Samways empire was really only biscuit-loving Brian and assistant Geraldine Jupp plying their trade in some poky little back street office.

'Yes, that's right. I'm one of Brian's partners. We've some clients who are keen to view.'

'What? Already?' gasped Hattie, blinking with horror at the phone shelf with its assortment of household detritus and coffee mug stains. 'But there's no board up yet.' She was mentally estimating how long it might take to tick off all the jobs on her to-do list and hoped the clients in question weren't too keen. She'd want the house to be looking its best if it was to stand a chance of attracting a quick offer.

'But you're on our website and I've had requests to view tomorrow, if that's convenient with you,' Pete explained patiently.

'Tomorrow? But I haven't even started my spring cleaning.' Hattie was seized with full-blown panic at the thought of strangers trooping around her home, rubbing fingers along dusty shelves and wrinkling their noses at Josh's stray socks peeping under the valance.

'I understood you were hot to trot,' said Pete, keeping upbeat.

'Hot to trot?' echoed Hattie. It sounded like a bad bout of Delhi Belly.

'Now, the Dunnocks are keen to view tomorrow or possibly Wednesday and Mr Bainbridge is asking for the earliest possible appointment. Could we pencil in tomorrow p.m.?' he continued, undaunted.

'Well… okay tomorrow afternoon. That'll give me a fighting chance of getting some jobs done,' she flustered, now regretting all those lost hours of TV watching.

'Excellent! I'll phone back when we've sorted out times. 'Bye for now.'

Hattie slammed down the receiver and dashed upstairs to survey the carnage in Josh's room. It was depressing. As she stood marvelling at his inability to perform the simplest tasks, she mentally composed the riot act she'd be reading that evening. Their own room was only marginally less challenging. Several bags of jumble, destined for a charity shop, were lined up along one wall and the dressing table was snug under its blanket of dust. Earring boxes were scattered around spewing out their contents, together with loose change, safety pins and crumpled receipts. She stuffed the jumble bags into the wardrobe and jammed the door shut. 'Out of sight, out of mind' would have to do. At least Laura's old room was kept tidy for her occasional visit and fortunately, Hattie had remembered to put it to rights after Dom and Tom's brief stay. She sighed. Just getting two bedrooms licked into shape would take ages, unless she was able to enlist Nick and Josh's muscle.

'Of course I'll help,' promised Nick, over his plate of sausage and mash. 'I knew old Samways would come up trumps.'

'And Josh,' Hattie began, in her no-nonsense manner, 'I shall expect your full co-operation.'

'Yeah, right,' he muttered.

'Like using the laundry basket on a regular basis,' she continued, 'instead of festooning the place with your grimy garments in the vague hope that they might find their own way.'

'Chill, Mum,' he sighed. 'No need to be sarky. I get the message, okay?'

'And, Nick, you'd better sort your clothes and think about ditching the things you don't wear any more. I've been through my drawers already.'

'Well, I hope you chucked out the baggy ones with sagging elastic,' he quipped with a chuckle. Josh sniggered and speared another sausage.

'You know what I mean,' snapped Hattie.

'And the TV's staying off until the bedrooms are tidy, match or no match.'

Nick and Josh rolled their eyes in joint dismay.

'She who must be obeyed has spoken, Josh,' intoned Nick with a mischievous grin threatening to break out.

'And once it's done, I don't want you two messing up all the good work, especially in the bathroom,' she threatened. 'I want towels folded neatly and hung back on the rail and no dabs of toothpaste spattered all over the place or odd socks littering the floor. Okay?'

'Yes ma'am!' snapped Nick with a mock salute. 'Message received and understood!'

First came Mr Bainbridge, escorted by Pete Ingleheart. Mr B looked slightly harassed, having parked his battered old estate on the drive. After a brief introduction, Hattie withdrew to check on the progress of her bread-maker. It had reached the cooking stage – perfect! She wedged the kitchen door open so the wonderful aroma could pervade the downstairs at least. Jezebel was on her best behaviour, having been enticed into the utility room by a handful of Seafood Snax, and was settled snugly in her basket. On their way through the kitchen, Hattie heard positive comments and 'Hmms' and 'Ahhs' from Mr Bainbridge, who even managed a weak smile.

The Dunnocks were a different matter entirely. Hattie was convinced she'd never met such an arrogant pair in all her life. For most of the viewing, she kept out of the way, but the little she saw was hardly encouraging. Mrs D arrived clutching a whole sheath of house details that she shuffled haphazardly, dropping sheets as she went, while the poker-faced husband only managed an occasional bored grunt. Keen to view? This pair probably wouldn't know 'keen' if it jumped up and bit them on the nose. She suspected that they'd set themselves a demanding schedule of viewings and 7 Witchert Close was the last one of the day. Mrs D also managed to tut and sniff in a way disturbingly reminiscent of Gloria Preston.

'Not quite as nice as Fir Tree Way,' she observed to her husband, just loud enough to ensure it reached Hattie's ears, as she surveyed the kitchen décor. 'Not sure about the dayglo green on the walls!'

'Cheaper though,' grunted her husband.

How rude, thought Hattie, hoping they wouldn't want to buy her house. Dayglo green, indeed! The paint chart had it labelled at soft spring green. They were probably the sort who'd rip everything out and start again. She couldn't wait for them to leave.

'Good riddance!' she muttered after the door closed and Pete had escorted them back to their car.

As Hattie drove to college the following evening, she hoped that Leo had got the message that she was utterly tired of his feeble excuses, and that he'd have the courtesy to leave her alone. She was also wondering if she'd bump into Madge and Sandra now that she'd learned about their daring foray into belly dancing. The thought of Madge dressed in flimsy pants and a yashmak took some imagining. Although it was school half-term, the college courses continued without a break. In Beginner's Patchwork there was general agreement that a week off would have spoiled the momentum, especially as everyone was so keen.

'It's whirling stars this evening, ladies,' announced Zena with a twinkle. 'Marigold and I will demonstrate how two contrasting designs can produce a really stunning combination,' she added with a raised eyebrow in Marigold's direction. Marigold blushed and giggled like a nervous schoolgirl.

'I think there might have been a double entendre there,' whispered Cynthia knowingly. 'There'll be fireworks at Quaintly tonight!'

With Cynthia's intriguing insights into their private life, Hattie found her concentration waning as the pair cut, pinned and stitched the pieces deftly, producing a striking 3D effect, which the class spent the session trying to emulate, with mixed results.

Although she'd planned a quick getaway, mainly to avoid Leo, Hattie decided to stay behind to quiz Zena and Marigold on likely sources of good patchwork fabric. They were experts after all. Some other students evidently had the same idea.

'We recommend Dobbins and Tippler on the Wendover trading estate, as a matter of fact,' confided Marigold.

'Oh really?' murmured Hattie, trying to work out the quickest cross-country route to the place in question.

'Yes, indeed,' continued Marigold. 'They have an excellent range. Ask for one of their discount cards and you'll get ten per cent off after you've spent fifty pounds.'

Oh great, thought Hattie, wishing they'd all been given this important information on their first night. However, with all the lining, wadding and thread, as well as three more fat quarters, she'd soon be qualifying for discount status. Noting the details in her diary, she gathered up her belongings and set off down the corridor. Most of the classes had finished ten minutes earlier and the exodus of students had now reduced to a trickle. With any luck, Leo and his adoring groupies would have already left the building.

As she reached the college foyer, lost in thought about which flavour of hot chocolate she'd be whipping up for a bedtime treat, she was disturbed to see Leo standing and staring in her direction. Seeing the huge grin plastered all over his face was even more annoying. Couldn't this man get the message?

'Ah, Hattie! Good to see you,' he called warmly, coming towards her.

'You weren't waiting for me, I hope,' she replied irritably, recalling the previous week's garbled ramblings about wrong bags and forgetting her name. 'I thought I made my wishes quite clear last Wednesday.'

'But Hattie, you said the letter was fine. Why are you so upset?' he asked tenderly.

'Letter? You mean the letter about the valuation? I really don't know why you bothered to text me about that,' she snapped.

'No, no... not *that* letter... the *other* letter. You know, the one *I* wrote,' he explained patiently, gazing at her with his dark brown, puppy eyes.

'Leo, I don't know what you're talking about,' she retorted, remembering that Nick had opened the post.

'But Hattie, you surely saw the other letter in the envelope?'

'I didn't open the post on Friday, Leo!'

'But it was addressed to *you* Hattie. I wrote a letter explaining *everything*. Every time I've tried to explain, something has happened. It was so frustrating.'

They gaped at each other in horror, each considering the possible repercussions of the ill-fated letter.

'Oh gremlins! Nick was home *before* me on Friday; he'd just driven back from his interview. He'd already opened the envelope! The valuation letter was on the table.'

'But I addressed the envelope to Mrs H. Chesney,' he protested with a sinking feeling in his stomach. 'It was meant for *you*.'

'Oh, so you managed to remember my name perfectly well last week.'

'What do you mean?'

'Last Wednesday? Remember? You were rambling on about wrong bags and forgetting my name and all that rubbish,' she snapped, stopping short of mentioning the mysterious Alex who seemed to have figured as a major player in the drama.

They stood in gloomy silence, both momentarily lost for words, although Hattie was spoilt for choice at the possibilities she could launch in Leo's direction. Had Nick read the letter? Whatever Leo had written wouldn't have made any sense to him, yet he hadn't mentioned a second letter. Surely, if he *had* seen and read it, he would have said something; he would have challenged her about it. She needed to know exactly what Leo had written.

'Leo, tell me what you wrote,' she began sternly, as if in the classroom, 'No... first of all, how did you address it?'

'I *told* you – Mrs H. Chesney.'

'No Leo, I didn't mean *that*. I meant, how did you start the letter?' Please God, let him not have written anything soppy like "Dearest Hattie".

'Er..."Dear Hattie", I think.'

'You *think*?'

'Yes, I'm sure it was "Dear Hattie", then I described what happened at the station. That's why I texted you. I wanted to know that you'd read my explanation and understood why I didn't contact you.'

'I see,' said Hattie grimly, wondering if he'd owned up to his relationship with Alex. She took a deep breath. Leo had meant well, although as far as she was concerned it was still a stupid thing to do. However, there was a slim chance that it was still undiscovered.

'Leo, where exactly did you put the letter? Did you fold it inside the printed one or was it separate?'

His brow furrowed in thought as he tried to recall those particular details.

'Er... it was folded separately. I tucked it in after Rebecca had put the other one in the envelope.'

'Ah, so the letter might still be there. Now I wonder where Nick put the envelope. It wasn't on the table, so maybe it's in the waste bin or the wheelie bin, and the rubbish goes out tomorrow,' she gabbled, more to herself than to Leo. 'If I'm quick enough...'

She scooted off at top speed towards the door.

'But don't you want to know what I wrote?' he called.

'Of course, but let me find out first,' she called back.

The familiar TV football crowd roar greeted her as she arrived home. The chance of Nick disturbing wall-to-wall sport for rubbish disposal was as unlikely as Madge switching to lap-dancing.

'Hi!' she called, popping her head around the sitting room door. Judging by the expressions on their faces, Josh and Nick weren't going anywhere for the time being.

'Nil-nil in extra time,' Nick told her, 'so it looks like penalties.'

Even Hattie knew that a penalty shoot-out was likely to give her enough time to sort through a couple of bins.

'Just making hot choc, Nick. Fancy a cup?' she called over the crescendo of cheers and groans. 'I'll bring it through in a mo.'

'Yeah, thanks! Great!' he said, his eyes glued to the screen.

As soon as the kettle was set to boil, Hattie seized the waste bin and tipped the contents on the floor. The absence of slimy banana skins and soggy teabags confirmed that Josh had at last learned to differentiate between food and paper waste. Feverishly, she sorted through the mess, checking all the envelopes in turn for clues. As she reached the bottom of the heap, she came across a long, white envelope. Turning it over, she recognised Leo's handwriting, addressed just as he'd said. With the elegant Mia Casa emblem in the bottom, left-hand corner, she understood why Nick had opened it. He'd quite reasonably assumed it was intended for the attention of them both. She shook the envelope hopefully and peered into its corners. It was empty.

'Knickers!' she cursed, ferreting through the heap again, hoping to find the missing letter.

Approaching steps made her start with guilt.

'Mum, Dad says he's gagging for a hot chocolate,' announced Josh, on his way to the fridge for a spot of quick foraging.

'I doubt those were his actual words. Okay, won't be two ticks,' she promised, springing up quickly. 'Want some, Josh?'

'Gross!' he mumbled, slipping back to the TV with a half-finished carton of juice.

Hattie grabbed two mugs and spooned in several generous measures of chocolate powder, while frantically considering her next move. Like it or not, a careful search of the wheelie bin might be her only hope. If Nick had found the letter he'd have said something by now – surely. He and Josh were literally poised

on the edge of their seats and groaned in frustration as she momentarily moved across their field of vision, bearing Nick's bedtime
drink.

'Mum, we can't see,' Josh whined, flapping her out of the way.

'Don't mind me!' she snapped, quickly returning to her
rubbish pile. Methodically, she examined every piece of paper
before dropping it into the bin. There was no letter, but instead
a nasty sinking feeling in her stomach. Now she had to face
the possibility that Nick had found and read the letter, but was
keeping quiet about it. But why? That was the baffling bit. If
the letter was simple, straightforward and informative – if Leo
was capable of that – why hadn't Nick produced it and challenged her?

'So you know this chap then! Why didn't you say so?'

What would she have said? Perhaps she might have pretended
she hadn't recognised him to start with, then admit they'd had a
bit of a brief fling years ago at uni, which ended abruptly. There'd
be some embarrassment maybe, but then they'd laugh it off and
it would be all over. Leo Marcello equals past history, equals
sorted, done and dusted and a few other clichés. But – and this
was the scenario that gave her the worst sort of sinking feeling
– what if Leo's letter wasn't quite as straightforward as he'd
suggested? What if he'd slipped in a few little details hinting that
their fling had been more like a grand passion? If Nick discovered that, he'd naturally be curious why she'd been so silent about
it all those years. Hattie sighed deeply and glugged down her
not-so-hot chocolate. Perhaps she'd go out and sort through the
wheelie bin, although after a hard day's cleaning, two hours'
concentrated cutting and stitching then five minutes of emotional
turmoil with Leo, she barely had the energy for grappling with
black bin bags. Still, what was the alternative?

She drained her mug and reluctantly picked up the rubbish
bin. Out in the garage the temperature felt several degrees below
freezing. Without jacket and gloves, the job of sorting and sifting
would be finger as well as mind-numbing. She lifted the wheelie

bin lid and surveyed the huge stack of neatly tied bags as well as stray detritus that had been lobbed in separately.

'Oh faggots!' she snapped and slammed down the lid. What was wrong with the men in her life? Why couldn't they communicate? 'And why don't you?' a small voice in her head asked her. 'Because I'm too scared,' she replied.

9

Hattie woke with a splitting headache – the sort you'd expect after glugging half a bottle of cheap red plonk – but, of course, this headache had nothing to do with over-indulgence and everything to do with guilt.

'Happy Birthday Nick.' Even that took a superhuman effort.

'Prezzie time?' hinted Nick hopefully as he peeled off his pyjamas.

'Sorry, Nick, but I've got a headache,' said Hattie, completely misreading the signs. 'Oh… yeah, of course,' she added, quickly retrieving a wrapped parcel and card from her wardrobe shelf. 'Sorry… thought you meant –'

'Aha!' said Nick with a twinkle. 'Well, *that* can wait until later.'

'Maybe,' Hattie replied, willing herself to rise above the gloom that seemed to have settled over her like an overcooked sago pudding.

'Good-oh,' said Nick, once he'd ripped off the paper. 'What would we do without Amazon wish-lists?'

'I thought you'd prefer a new copy, although the slightly used ones were incredibly cheap.' It was so easy to add to Nick's growing library of Arsenal books with a couple of clicks of the mouse. At least he'd get something he actually wanted and it saved her trawling the local stores for the usual boring 'gifts for men'.

'And a juicy steak at the Feisty Ferret tonight, followed by afters at home will make a great end to the day,' chuckled Nick as he wandered into the en-suite. 'Better book a table, eh, just to be on the safe side.'

Bins emptied, family despatched, dishwasher swooshing, Hattie stood in her kitchen, her head still throbbing and her conscience giving her the third degree. She tried to recall Nick's mood on Friday: he'd been tired and had gone for a lie-down before the job offer email arrived. What had he said? Something about traffic? Her memory of the day offered no clues, so she turned to her patchwork.

By mid-morning, she had completed a misshapen, whirling-stars square, after unpicking and re-sewing sections that she'd managed to pin together the wrong way. She was about to start again when the phone rang.

'Pete Ingleheart here, Mrs Chesney.'

'Oh hello, Pete,' she said, wondering if he was about to report some positive reactions to Tuesday's viewings.

'Mr Bainbridge has just phoned and asked for a second viewing.'

'Really?' gasped Hattie, the sago pudding cloud of gloom miraculously melting away. 'When?'

'Well, this afternoon, if at all possible. He's very keen, Mrs Chesney.'

'This afternoon? When exactly?' she probed, realising that she'd be grabbing her Marigolds and spray polish as soon as the call was over. They agreed on two o'clock, which propelled her into feverish clearing, cleaning and tidying By five to two, the house was ready for viewing and another batch of dough was rising in the bread-maker. The emptied wheelie bin had been returned to the garage and some obliging crocuses had popped up on the lawn to give the perfect kerb appeal. Hattie sat sipping freshly brewed coffee in the kitchen while Pete carried out the viewing. Mr Bainbridge may have been keen, but his expression barely hinted at unrestrained joy. Pete's idea of keen was quickly losing all credibility. Mr B, however, *was* busy making notes as Pete showed him through. Despite his deadpan expression, there was a hint of promise.

'I'll be in touch,' Pete told her with a brief wave, but the phone stayed silent for the rest of the day.

The Feisty Ferret was a cosy, thatched pub which oozed rustic charm. Its restaurant had a reputation for an imaginative menu and had featured regularly in the *Bucks Herald*'s food and leisure supplement over the years. It was the sort of place that attracted the farming community as well as discerning diners in their 4x4s. The car park was unusually full when they arrived. Sure, the food had always been good, but on an average weekday you wouldn't expect the place to be packed solid.

'Good thing I booked a table,' commented Hattie, wondering if she'd missed a special promotion in the local rag.

'Oh no,' groaned Nick. 'Look!' Along one wall of the car park a banner was slung with the following invitation: *Under new management. Gaz and Jodie invite you to try their new menu!!*

Nick was immediately rattled. He considered anything needing two exclamation marks to be suspect. 'I hope Gaz and Jodie are keeping up the pub's good reputation,' he commented, suspiciously.

As they pushed open the bar door, loud, pulsating music hit their eardrums. Gaz and Jodie had certainly made their mark. Not a hunting horn, farming implement or quaint old milk churn could be seen. Instead, framed photos of A-list celebrities and sporting memorabilia plastered the walls. Two enormous fruit machines, which flashed, rattled and beeped, were also holding court at one end of the bar, while a cluster of excited youths fed them with fistfuls of coins. In a corner, two old gents sat sipping pints of mild and ruminating mournfully on the passing of time.

'Oh hollyhocks!' groaned Hattie, hoping the restaurant might have been excluded from Gaz and Jodie's ruthless reordering. The words 'new menu' now took on a whole new meaning.

Drinks in hand, they were shown through to the restaurant, where a large space was now set apart for dancing, with clusters of tables around the edge. Several of these were already occupied. At the far end, on a small stage – a notable innovation – a group was setting up and exchanging noisy banter with a party at a nearby table. Judging by what was being wired up and plugged in, the musical accompaniment for the evening was promising to be anything but calm and restful. Hattie and Nick exchanged worried glances as they chose a table near the door.

'I'll be back to take your order,' promised a young waitress, whose skirt resembled a broad belt. Hattie frowned as she studied the girl's features, but couldn't think why they were so familiar.

'Oh, it's Mrs Chesney, isn't it?' said the girl, giggling. 'Thought I recognised you.'

'I'm sorry but –'

'Tanya Preston,' put in the girl. 'You taught me in Year 6.'

No wonder, she thought, noting the low slung neckline – just two inches south of decent – and high spiky-heeled shoes of Gloria's eldest precocious offspring. Tanya couldn't be older than sixteen, but strutted about like a twenty-year-old.

'Oh yes, right,' replied Hattie, summoning a wan smile. 'Jolly good, Tanya. We'll see you in a few minutes when we've chosen.'

'Okay Mrs Chesney,' she simpered, and sashayed off, buttocks swivelling provocatively.

'Very tasty,' murmured Nick with a smirk.

'What, Gaz and Jodie's new dishes?' asked Hattie, turning her attention to the menu.

'No, dish-of-the-day Tanya,' he chuckled, following the girl's exit with an appreciative stare.

'Stop it, Nick. She's only sixteen! Don't be so disgusting!' she snapped, quickly scanning the evening's offerings. Several more customers piled into the room and bagged the few remaining tables as the band launched into their first number. With an excited whoop, two scantily clad females jumped out of their seats and started gyrating to the beat.

'Oh, this is awful!' Hattie despaired. Burgers, pies, sausages and various battered offerings seemed to be the general theme. 'I don't think Jodie and Gaz have heard of jacket potatoes or salads.'

'Never mind, lasagne's still on offer,' murmured Nick, noting the presence of steak and chips on the menu. 'Perhaps the puds will be better.'

The band was well into its third or fourth number when Tanya, now busily chewing gum, returned to take their order. Compared with Tanya in her skimpy little outfit, Hattie felt like an overdressed frump in her roll-neck sweater and cord trousers.

'I'll have the lasagne please, with salad garnish. No chips,' she announced crisply, 'if the kitchen can manage it.'

Tanya's lip started to curl as she detected a sideswipe at Gaz and Jodie's culinary expertise.

'And I'll have…' began Nick. It was then that Hattie spotted him and gasped.

'What's that, Hat?' Nick asked, snapping his attention from Tanya's cleavage to his wife's ashen face.

'Oh… er… nothing. You go ahead and order.'

'Yeah, well, I'll have the steak – medium rare – with all the trimmings,' he told Tanya with a broad smile and a sly wink.

'Right you are, Mr Chesney,' replied Tanya confidently. 'And wine?'

'Oh, just a half-bottle of house red to keep on the right side of the traffic cops.'

Meanwhile, Hattie was wondering how Leo managed to appear in the room. After a twenty-six-year absence from her life, he seemed to be popping up with alarming regularity. Just a few tables away, she could just see him through a forest of heads. There were four others at the table, all happily chatting together. Hattie noted two women and started speculating on their status as far as Leo was concerned. Wife? Girlfriend? Mistress? She was sure he hadn't seen her. If he had, he certainly wasn't looking in her direction.

'You okay, Hat?' asked Nick, after Tanya had strutted off with their order.

'Nothing… honestly,' Hattie faltered, relying on her blossoming talent for impromptu improvisation. 'I just remembered I'd promised to pop in to see Wilf today.'

'Hey, don't worry, old thing. Wilf's hardly with-it these days. I don't suppose he noticed,' he assured her, patting her hand. 'Nice girl, that Tanya,' he continued, taking a sip from his half of lager. 'Polite, engaging, quite different from some teenagers.'

'You don't fool me, Mr Eyes-on-Stalks,' muttered Hattie accusingly. 'You almost had your nose in the girl's cleavage, and she's brazen, just like her mother!'

'Well, I could hardly ignore her, could I? That would have been rude.'

Several minutes of mind-numbing pop numbers passed by before Tanya reappeared.

'Enjoy!' she announced brightly as she placed their plates before them. Nick's was covered by a monstrous slab of steak and a pile of glistening chips.

'You bet – ouch!' Hattie's well-aimed kick under the table quickly wiped the leer from Nick's face. 'Can't a chap enjoy his birthday?' he grumbled, once Tanya had gone.

'Within reason,' Hattie told him primly, tentatively sampling a glutinous forkful. 'Yuck! Too much salt. How about your steak?'

'Wonderful!' he said, grinning.

By now, the lights had been dimmed, the room pulsated with a heavy rock beat and many of the clientele had flowed onto the dance floor. Once the last of their plates had been cleared, Nick pushed his chair back and swivelled round to watch. From amongst the dancers, a familiar head of blonde curls came into sight.

'Well I never!' he breathed, a smile playing on his lips. It was Rebecca from Mia Casa, with her arms wrapped around some lucky bloke. Remembering the huge rock that sparkled from her left hand, he supposed the lucky bloke in question to be her fiancé.

'Come on, Hat. Let's dance away some of those wicked calories,' he urged, grabbing her by the hand. He planned to steer his way around the floor so he could view the lovely Rebecca from a closer vantage point. Meanwhile, Hattie had lost sight of Leo, but guessed he could be somewhere in the mêlée. The words 'letter', 'Nick' and 'Leo' started whirling round her brain and she started imagining a showdown on the dance floor.

'Oh, come on, Hat; you know you like a bit of a bop.'

'But I'm not dressed for dancing,' she protested.

'Don't worry. You look great. Now come and humour your husband on his birthday.'

The white chocolate and hazelnut cheesecake had settled snugly in her tum, threatening extra inches on her waistline and a shock for the bathroom scales. Action was imperative. 'Okay,' she finally relented and slipped her neck-purse securely over her shoulder. Nick pulled her to her feet and set off in the general direction of the blonde bobbing curls. He could see her cheeky grin over her partner's shoulder. Wow, he thought to himself, imagining Rebecca in a floaty belly-dancing costume. Then several other couples moved across his line of vision and Rebecca and partner were hidden from view. With some nifty footwork, he manoeuvred around the edge of the floor, which was now packed solid. Then the band started 'Lady in Red', a song that took Hattie back to her student days. It was *their* song. Had Leo forgotten? As she moved, she caught a brief glimpse of him chatting and laughing. They'd smooched to that song, Leo humming gently in her ear and making her feel special. That time had now come back to haunt her. Was that his wife or girlfriend? She couldn't work out her age from a back view, but guessed she was younger than Leo. Just the sight of him turning on his Latin charm was like a knife twisting in her stomach. He'd been like that with her once.

Through the seething mass of humanity, Leo and partner turned at the very moment that Nick executed a quick move, giving Hattie quite a different view. She glanced up at Nick, dreading a sulky scowl, but instead she saw the smile of a self-satisfied birthday boy. Phew, she breathed, safe in the assumption that he hadn't yet spotted Leo. When the last chord of 'Lady in Red' floated away and a soft sigh went up from the floor, Hattie made a determined effort to head back to their table. Inside her roll-neck she had cooked up quite a heat. Never mind a cool St Clements, a gallon of water would do very nicely, she thought.

'No, not yet, Hat,' insisted Nick in her ear as the group stepped up a gear into a more lively number.

Before she could protest, he steered her with single-minded determination to within a few feet of his goal. What a stunner, he thought, taking in the immaculate make-up, glitzy earrings and strappy, soft-draped top. Poor old Hat, by comparison, looked a bit crumpled round the edges. Spotting a small gap, he steered closer to his prey, but by then Rebecca and her partner had also moved. Instead of gorgeous Rebecca, his gaze landed on Leo Marcello, the sneaky letter-writing wife snatcher. If the lovely Rebecca *was* his fiancée, what was he doing writing letters to other men's middle-aged wives? Nick glanced down at Hattie, whose forehead was beaded with sweat, and guiltily compared her with Marcello's partner. There really was no contest. If he were to have his time again, he'd definitely aim for someone in Rebecca's league. There was something about blonde hair and dimples that pressed all his buttons.

'We'll just take a break now,' announced the vocalist as the last chord drifted away. A chinking of glasses signalled an imminent stampede to the bar.

'Thank heavens,' gasped Hattie, melting into her chair and gulping her drink.

'Same again?'

'Please – and with lots of ice.'

So far so good, she thought, grateful for the subdued lighting. While they'd been on the dance floor, candles had been lit on every table, casting flickering shadows over the whitewashed walls. Nick made a sprint for the bar, hoping to elbow his way past those who were already waving cash and cards at the frantic bar staff. Then he saw her again, playfully nuzzling the ear of a much younger man. Nick watched them, transfixed and felt a pang of jealousy as the man planted a predatory hand on Rebecca's pert little bottom and started to stroke it. This one had to be the fiancé. Nick switched his attention back to the bar. Discovering that Rebecca was not Marcello's property was a relief.

Meanwhile, as Hattie sweated inside her roll-neck and fantasised over ice-cubes, a deep, male voice whispered her name. With a startled cry, she turned and discovered Leo already too close for comfort.

'What a pleasant surprise,' he added.

'Oh, gobstoppers!' she snapped. 'Go away, Leo. Nick'll be back any second.'

'Ah, Hattie! Your charming little expletives,' he teased. 'How I love to hear them.'

'Leo,' she hissed, 'go away!'

'But I wanted to know if you found the letter?'

'No, Leo, I didn't find the letter. Are you sure you put it in the envelope?' she demanded, nervously watching for Nick's return.

'Of course I did.'

'That means Nick, who opened the envelope, also read your letter. Oh great!'

'But that's not my fault. It was addressed to _you_!'

'I know it was,' she continued, through clenched teeth. 'I found the envelope at the bottom of the waste bin, the Mia Casa crest was a giveaway. It's not surprising Nick thought it was meant for both of us. Honestly, Leo, didn't you think? Anyway, you'd better go back to your girlfriend. She'll be wondering where you are, and Nick will be back −'

'Girlfriend? What do you mean? I'm just here with some friends. The young woman you saw is here with her fiancé.'

Then Hattie caught sight of Nick through the stream of drinkers and diners.

'Go! Go now!' she hissed urgently. Like an obedient puppy, Leo turned and made straight for the gents.

Nick had not been impressed with the bar service, especially Jodie, who must have been relying on her fake tan and facelift rather than expertise at the pumps. She'd never heard of a St Clements and the squirt of lemonade on his bitter top had gone all over the place. It was a shambles.

'There you go,' he muttered, sinking to his seat and taking a grateful swig. 'God, what a crowd! Looks like half of Aylesbury Vale's here, judging by the crush in the bar. Seen anyone we know?' he asked casually.

'I'm not sure,' she lied, taking a gulp and then whizzing the ice cubes around her glass in a distracted fashion. 'But it *is* rather crowded. It's a shame this place has changed such a lot.'

'Yeah,' agreed Nick, 'the bar service is not exactly up to speed and I'm not sure if I like the class of people this place is attracting now.'

'Hmm, I know what you mean,' she agreed, avoiding his eyes and hoping that Leo's exit from the gents had not been spotted. 'We won't be coming here again though, so who cares what they serve up.'

'Bad vibes, Hat,' remarked Nick with feeling, gulping down his pint thirstily.

Hattie couldn't think why he'd said that, but decided not to pursue it. When Tanya Preston had been around, he'd been like a dog with his tongue hanging out. Even the performance on the dance floor was Nick on rare top form. But now, he was a different man and Hattie had a shrewd idea why.

'We'd better be off pretty soon,' he said after he'd drained his glass. 'And I'm still waiting for my other prezzie,' he added, summoning a smile.

'Other prezzie?'

'*You* know, Hat. Remember this morning?'

'Oh yeah,' she replied nodding, trying to match his mood.

Then, on the way home, the unexpected happened, just as

Hattie was wiping the real and metaphorical sweat from her brow.

'Saw that estate agent this evening – well, I think it was him,' Nick observed levelly.

Hattie froze while her heart set up a rapid pounding that echoed right up in her eardrums.

'Really?' she squeaked, unable to control her voice. 'What, biscuit-loving Brian?'

'No, not him. That other one .'

Hattie shot Nick the briefest of glances, but his eyes were fixed on the road ahead.

'What, you mean Pete Ingleheart?' she improvised lightly.

'Pete Ingleheart? Never met him. No, the other one. *You* know, the Italian bloke.'

Hattie found it interesting that Nick couldn't bring himself to say Leo's name, although it had come up in conversation on several occasions.

'Oh, him,' she replied wearily, adding a long yawn for good measure.

'Hmm, so you didn't spot him then?'

'No, I didn't,' Hattie lied, calling upon her creative streak, 'but now I come to think about it, I think I spotted Penny Mullinger, the receptionist at the vet's.' The chance of Nick knowing Penny Mullinger was as likely as snow in the Sahara.

'I don't know the woman, but –'

'Careful, that was a badger!'

'Where? I didn't see it.'

'Phew! That was close.'

'My sentiment exactly,' Nick replied with an edge to his voice that Hattie chose to ignore, although she suspected that the name Leo Marcello featured in the subtext.

'There you are, Hat,' said Mark, handing her a bottle of Pinot Noir and a bunch of freesias. 'It's really kind of you to invite me, what with your house sale and all that.'

Nick was busy opening cans of beer while Hattie checked the progress of supper.

'No trouble, Mark. Always pleased to see you, especially with Fliss and the boys away. Sorry it's nothing more exciting than pizza and chips. We're creatures of habit in the Chesney household.'

'My favourite,' chuckled Mark indulgently. 'It makes a change from Fliss's posh frozen dinners.' Nick and Mark wandered through to the sitting room leaving Hattie sprinkling salad greens on their plates.

'Anyway, here's to the new job!' Mark raised his glass. 'So, when do you start?'

'Um, well, I think it should be the beginning of April. The medical's on Monday and if that's okay, I'll be handing in my notice straight away. I can hardly wait,' he told him with feeling. 'The sooner I can get away from old Madge the better. She really does my head in.'

'Did I hear mention of dear Madge, by any chance?' giggled Hattie. 'Oh and mine's a G and T Nick, if you can manage that. I'll give Josh a shout.'

'Try a loudhailer!' he suggested with eyes to heaven. 'God only knows what he's playing up there.'

'Ours are the same,' chuckled Mark.

'Really?' gasped Hattie, her assumption about the Tarrier boys blown to smithereens. 'But not while they were with us.'

'Hardly,' replied Mark. 'They were on strict instructions. Any trouble and they'd have forfeited their allowances. Hit 'em where it hurts, I say.'

Hattie wasn't sure if this was a gentle sideswipe at their parenting skills, but let it pass. 'Delicious,' she murmured, taking a sip from her glass.

'I don't know what the Halversons will think of their beloved godson when he takes up residence,' reflected Nick. He went on to fill in all the details of their planned move while Hattie did a creditable, mimed supper invitation at Josh's open door.

'So, no offers on the house yet?' Mark asked when the first course was over and after they'd exchanged the latest news of Fliss's mum and Samways's efforts.

'No, but we had someone round for a second viewing yesterday,' enthused Hattie, finishing her first glass of wine and pouring some more. 'The trouble was, I couldn't tell how keen he was. Some people are good at hiding their feelings.'

'Whereas some are quite transparent,' remarked Nick pointedly.

'Meaning?'

'Oh, er… lots of people, old girl, but if the cap fits…'

Hattie glared at Nick who was enjoying extra male company and was behaving accordingly.

'Pudding anyone?' she asked tartly. 'I know Josh has hollow legs but as for you two: verging on legless, I'd say,' she snapped.

'Very witty, Hat,' laughed Mark. 'Don't worry. I'll surrender my car keys until I've had at least three cups of your strongest black coffee. Most inventive, this crumble,' he added, pushing unidentified lumps around his dish.

'Just old satsumas,' Hattie volunteered.

'Old being the crucial word,' sniggered Nick. 'They add a certain something to an apple crumble, especially when they've passed their best.'

'Like the rest of us!' Mark chuckled, pushing some of the segments to one side. 'I'll have to pass on this secret to Fliss. Perhaps she'll persuade Myscha to knock up one for us. We usually get those sinister little cloves that lie in wait for the unwary diner until you bite on them.'

'Yuck! Disgusting!' commented Josh dourly between mouthfuls. 'Mum's banned from using them. They turn my stomach.'

'Well, we'd better warn Celia about your delicate insides, Josh, when we go round later. She wouldn't want you to become ill would she?' Hattie added with a hint of sarcasm. 'So Myscha's a cook. I thought she just cleaned and tidied.'

'Ah well, now Fliss's into serious health and fitness – and I mean big time, she's finding it just a bit too busy for much home cooking. Mind you, I think this health kick is part of her way of coping with her mum's decline. She certainly appears to be bene-fiting from it – the exercise I mean. There's a real glow about her and if it helps the rest of her life, then I'm pleased for her. I'm not much use to her at the moment. It's full-on trade fairs for me for the next two months.'

'So, how was Germany?' Nick asked, once they had the house to themselves.

'Weather-wise, you mean? Cold, very cold, if you really want to know: snow, ice, blizzards, the lot! Mind you, I was staying in a very convenient hotel right by the exhibition complex, so I didn't have to set foot outside once.'

'Lucky for some,' replied Nick. 'It's a shame my job doesn't come with foreign travel, although I believe Bennington's are pushing into Europe now, so who knows.'

'Hmm, well there are drawbacks mate, so don't be too keen until you know a bit more. Living out of a suitcase with no home comforts can lose its appeal, even though there's plenty of attrac-tions on offer – if you know what I mean,' said Mark, rolling his eyes and chuckling.

'Yep, I can imagine. So, did you go by yourself or was there a team of you?'

'Well, we always have at least two at these trade fairs, so I took Si, as a fairly new recruit. Said he knew some German. Well, I asked him and he said he did, but I think the lure of Munich's nightlife had more to do with it.'

'Ah, I can see a great big "but" coming along.'

'Did he know some German?' sighed Mark, with a shake of the head. 'Not unless you count 'Borussia Mönchengladbach' and 'Franz Beckenbauer'.

'Oh, footie fan then?' Nick chuckled. 'You have to credit him with a bit of cheek.'

'Bit?' spluttered Mark. 'A whole cartload of it would be nearer the truth. Spouting the local club's name and a footballing legend is hardly the sort of vocab for dealing with clients is it?'

'Oh, I don't know,' said Nick, grinning.

'So it started me thinking. You see, I can get by quite well in German, French and Spanish but some of our sales reps haven't a clue. Now that we're building up our European client base, we need to improve our team skills. Si thought that speaking English with a phoney German accent would do – the plonker!'

Nick sniggered and helped himself to another can.

'So I hit on this idea of a quick training course in basic business language so we can set a better example. A few of them have a GCSE in French, but *"ou est la plume de ma tante"* is not exactly smart business lingo.'

'But I thought *everyone* spoke English. Fancy another?' he offered, picking up another can. Mark shook his head.

'I know you sort of expect everyone to speak it, but we Brits are basically lazy sods. Anyway, I heard there was a course at one of the local colleges.'

'What, at Wycombe?'

'No, Aylesbury. It's not a business language course, but one for holiday-makers – conversational Italian,' he explained.

'So you have Italian contacts as well?'

'Oh yes, we've several clients around Milan. Anyway, I thought to myself: how about finding out if this course could be tailored to business conversation? So I went to meet the tutor at the college a couple of weeks ago and I think we might be in business. The tutor was up for putting together a course for us, as long as I draw up a list of phrases we'd need.'

'Brilliant, so you'll provide the students and the company pays for the course. That's very neat.'

'Oh, I expect they'll open it up to the general public as well, but if we guarantee a dozen students, that'll make it viable.'

Then Mark remembered the Hattie connection and the conversation he and Fliss had had after their evening at The Four Seasons. 'I gather Hat's doing a course there as well. In fact, I saw her that evening.'

'Oh yeah, Hat and her patchwork! She's loving it. I think it's taking her mind off the stresses of moving. Did you see her at the college then? She didn't say.'

'No, I was only at the college a short time, seeing the Italian tutor, who *is* Italian, as it happens.'

'Italian?' quizzed Nick. 'A woman or a bloke?'

'A bloke, mid forties, suave, sophisticated, the type that women drool over. No, it was afterwards that I saw Hat, in The Four Seasons.'

'Oh yeah, I seem to remember she arranged to have coffee with a new friend from the class one week. That was probably the night.'

'Well, Fliss and I popped in for a quick drink –'

'Fliss too?'

'With one of our cars in dock and Fliss desperate to top up her tan at the new solarium, it meant the little wife dropped me off and then collected me later. So, there we were having a nightcap and that's where we saw Hattie, but not until she was leaving. But she didn't see us.'

'Oh, that's a shame. You could have all met up. I think her friend is called Cindy. No, not Cindy… er, Cynthia. Cynthia Dacey.'

'Cynthia Dacey? Yes, we know Cynthia by sight. The Daceys live in the next village and Donald umpires for the Bledlow cricket team. Small world isn't it?' he reflected. 'Funnily enough, the Italian tutor, Leo Marcello, was there too, after his class of course. It's amazing how many people you know can turn up in the same place at the same time.'

Nick gulped at the mention of Marcello and the fact that he'd been in exactly the same place as Hattie. Was it a coincidence or was he stalking her?

'Hmm, Marcello. Oh yes, now I know who you mean. He did a valuation for Mia Casa, but we think he overpriced us. That's why we decided to go with Samways.'

'Ah yes, I noticed their board outside. I gather their valuations are usually on the conservative side. You're wise to be realistic though. If you're not, you could be on the market for ages.'

'Which is what I – I mean, *we* – don't want,' snapped Nick, wondering if the appearance of Leo Marcello was *really* down to chance?

'Good morning, Mrs Chesney,' said a female voice. 'Samways and Partners calling. We've three lots of interested buyers who'd like to view your property today.'

'Oh goody!' replied Hattie. It was Saturday and Nick had woken up in a filthy mood. Hattie was baffled. He'd seemed cheerful enough when she and Josh had set off for the Halversons, but when they arrived home, Mark had left and Nick was online and communicating only in grunts. By the time she had finished discussing the timetable for the day with Geraldine, he was already flicking through the sports channels.

'Er, Nick,' she began tentatively. 'There's three viewings today.' No reaction.

'So… it might be wise to turn off the TV when people arrive.'

'Whatever for?' he asked gruffly as he scrolled down the listings.

'Well, it… um… gives the wrong sort of ambience, and we –'

'The *what?*' snapped Nick, fixing her with a disagreeable scowl.

'Ambience,' replied Hattie, remembering some of the points gleaned from her recent viewing. 'We need to give our prospective buyers a calm atmosphere.'

'Who says?'

'Well, on one of the house selling programmes – '

'Oh God!' he groaned. 'So, some opinionated house-styling guru has been filling your head with a lot of rubbish!'

'It's not rubbish, Nick,' she protested. 'If you want to sell this house as much as *I* do, just turn the TV off when they come in the room at least, okay?'

For a moment, the tension in his shoulders seemed to ease and Hattie wondered which part of her speech had been the key.

'If you say so,' he muttered.

Hattie donned her pinny and assembled her bread-making ingredients. Next, she shoehorned Josh out of bed with the promise of eggy bread, a smoothie and the reminder that he was expected at Tarrants Garage within the hour. Despite Hattie's feverish efforts to present a calm and orderly home to the viewers, by the end of the day, none had showed enough interest to make an offer.

Monday morning dawned dark and gloomy to match Nick's mood. Before work, he went for his medical at the village health centre. No problems there, he was told, but decided he'd wait for a firm offer before typing his letter of resignation. While colleagues were telling him how lucky he was to have landed the new job, his thoughts were consumed by a different letter and exactly where Leo Marcello figured in his wife's life – if at all. His accountant's brain still couldn't make the figures add up.

For Hattie, the children that morning were more than usually uppity. Like the staff, they resented being back at school after a week's break, but she was happy that the morning passed without incident. She was even happier when the morning was over and she was back at home, in the conservatory, balancing a plate of sandwiches and a cereal bar in one hand and her mug of tea in the other.

'Bliss,' she sighed, slumping on the sofa and hoisting her feet onto the newspaper pile on the coffee table. Halfway through her first sandwich the phone rang. 'Oh no! Go away!' she groaned, suspecting it to be some foreign call centre with yet another tempting offer for switching their energy supplier. On the other hand, it just might be Samways wanting to book in another viewing. Abandoning her lunch, she raced to the hall.

'Good afternoon. Brian Samways speaking.'

'Oh hello, Brian. Sorry I took so long. Just back from school.'

'Yes I wondered if you might be at work. I tried earlier,' he explained. 'We've had an offer from Mr Bainbridge.'

Hope sprouted wings in Hattie's breast. 'And how much is he offering?' she asked tentatively, preparing herself for some derisory figure followed by days of bartering and a mounting phone bill.

'As a matter of fact, he's prepared to pay the full asking price.'

'Oh wow!' shrieked Hattie gleefully, bouncing up and down like a five-year-old at a funfair.

'Thought you'd be pleased, Mrs Chesney,' replied Brian confidently. 'The only thing is, he hasn't actually sold his house yet, but assures me that there's a first-time buyer who's very interested. He's expecting an offer any day now, so...'

'Ah, I see,' murmured Hattie, deflating like a pricked balloon.

'So I suggest we keep your house on the market for the time being because we might get another offer from someone who's in a position to proceed,' Brian proposed.

'Okay,' murmured Hattie, preparing herself for yet more grubby fingers on her knick-knacks and tedious hours of dusting and cleaning. 'But won't Mr Bainbridge be put off?' she asked anxiously. If it were up to her, she'd take the house off the market at once.

'No, he understands the position completely,' Brian assured her then rabbited on at length in estate agent jargon about offers, firm or otherwise.

'I'm sure you're right, Brian.'

As soon as the call was over, she gobbled down the rest of her lunch and then texted Nick; news like this was sure to lift the gloom. She then decided that a little online browsing might be useful. Trawling through several websites, she earmarked a list of likely possibilities within their price band: 'The Old Bakery', 'Knapp Cottage', 'Walnut End', 'The Privets', 'Holly Lodge' and 'Juniper Croft' – such delightful names. If only Mr Bainbridge's first-time buyer would get a move on.

Nick still hadn't replied to the text, but that might have been because of meetings. He had very definite views about intrusive bleeps and ring-tones at work, and kept his personal use to a minimum. Dismissing any negative thoughts, she picked up the phone and dialled the first of five Lydford Cross agents. Nick might say she was tempting fate, but they had to start their search some time. The next job was to set up a folder for the house details that would be plopping through the letterbox in the morning. One of the agents had even offered to send a map of the area. Maybe a trip to Lydford could be planned for Saturday. She was full of hopeful optimism until the memory of Nick's black mood came flooding back. Over the weekend, it had been like walking on eggshells and poor Josh had been on the receiving end several times.

'Turn down that racket!' he'd snapped, flinging the door open, glaring and then stomping downstairs to immerse himself in yet more sporting highlights.

'What's up with Dad? He's being a right pain,' Josh had grumbled to his mum.

'Pressure at work, I expect,' Hattie had told him. It sounded plausible, even if she didn't believe it herself.

When Nick arrived home that day, he was still as tight-lipped as ever. In fact, normal conversation seemed to have come to a complete halt, but Hattie was determined to keep the lines of communication open even if *he* wasn't.

'So, how did the medical go?' she asked brightly, plonking a mug of tea in front of him. 'No problems were there?'

'No,' he yawned. 'All straightforward.'

Several minutes passed as he slurped his tea, sighed and flicked aimlessly through the Sunday sport supplement.

'Did you get my text?' Hattie asked casually after she'd finished feeding the ravenous and indignant Jezebel.

'Oh… er… yeah,' Nick muttered, flicking and rustling the pages as if they were the cause of his black mood. 'Has Bainbridge sold then?'

Hattie's heart sank. Now here was a challenge. How exactly could she set the scenario in the most promising light?

'Well,' she began in a positive tone, 'he hasn't sold quite yet, but there's a first-time buyer who's poised to make an offer any day I believe.'

'So his offer doesn't mean a thing, does it!'

Nick wandered into the sitting room, mug in hand, and soon the usual sounds of Sky Sports could be heard. Hattie gazed out of the window, but there was nothing to see, except a lone star, low in the sky and the red and green flashing lights of a plane on its way out of Heathrow. Even the sight of Wilf twitching his curtains in pursuit of gnome nobblers would have provided a welcome diversion, but in all likelihood he was glued to *The Weakest Link* and drooling over Anne Robinson. Wretchedness and despair started to swamp her and a tear trickled down her cheek. How long would Nick carry on like this? Leo had accused her of deceit. Perhaps if she'd told Nick at the beginning, she wouldn't be in this torment now. She imagined the conversation that never was.

'You'll never guess, Nick; I've just met an old flame from uni.'

'Oh really? Where was that?'

'Well, the chap from Mia Casa as a matter of fact – Leo Marcello, who came to do the valuation before I had to dash off to see Fliss.'

'Small world! What a coincidence!'

Yes, she mused dismally, it could have been just as brief and straightforward as that. Naturally, she would not have told Nick everything, like her secret plan to marry Leo and settle down on his family's estate in Montelugia. He really *would* feel second best if he knew that.

Supper was as cheering as a power cut on Christmas Eve. The only sounds were the clattering of eating irons and the hum of the fridge until Josh belched loudly. Hattie thought he was trying to make a not-so-subtle point. Nick chewed slowly as he turned over in his mind all the moments in the past two or so weeks that had caused him to wonder. At first, he'd been convinced that Hattie's stroppy behaviour was down to women's troubles. But there was something else and for some reason, the name Leo Marcello kept dropping into his mind. Convinced that the man was only a deluded loser, he'd not bothered to finish reading the letter. At the end of the meal, however, he'd made up his mind: he had to read the whole letter and try to find out exactly what was going on.

'Bit of a headache,' he muttered, getting up from the table. 'Think I'll go up and have a doze.'

In the privacy of the bedroom, Nick reached into his underwear drawer and brought out the crumpled letter.

Dear Hattie,

Because of the deep love I have had for you, I have been so sad that the recent chain of events has prevented me from telling you what you have wanted to hear.

When I arrived late at the station and you had gone...

She was meeting him at a station? What station and when? Where were they going? He flung the letter down on the bed and started pacing the floor, shaking his head in disbelief. After a minute or two, he stopped and eyed the letter nervously before picking it up.

I searched through my bags to find your number, but it wasn't there. I was sure I had it in one of the plastic bags I'd filled when I moved out of Alex's flat. The trouble was, the bag with your number was identical to one full of rubbish. Alex must have got rid of the wrong bag in the rush to move out.

My God, thought Nick incredulously, one woman kicks him out and he's already trying it on with another man's wife.

I wanted to phone you, I promise you, but I had no number. I tried searching through telephone directories at the station, but I became confused about the spelling of your name — if there was an 'h' in it or not. I'm so sorry.

Not very bright, concluded Nick, considering he could have always used his mobile. Who bothered with directories these days?

I had the tickets and everything and the villa was ready for us. I was truly wanting to be with you. Believe me, dear Hattie, you were not a passing whim.
   Sincerely yours Leo

Tickets? Villa? This sounded serious, although one or two points didn't seem to make sense. One thing was clear: they – or more likely *he* – had made plans. Nick re-read the letter, puzzling over it and concluded that Hattie had seen enough sense to pull out at the last minute. It was a real shocker. He sat down on the bed forlornly, with his head in his hands. How could this have happened? This was much worse than he'd imagined. After a while, he re-folded the letter and replaced it in its hiding place. Now all he could do was lose himself in the oblivion of sleep.

Two days passed without a glimmer of hope: no viewings, no news on the Bainbridge front and no lifting of the domestic gloom. For Hattie, the possibility of seeing Leo at college seemed a better prospect than coping with a monosyllabic, grunting grouch at home. Perhaps she'd make a special effort to be pleasant to Leo and find out exactly what he'd written. The saga had dragged on far too long.
   'Hello, Hattie,' Cynthia greeted her cheerily. 'How's things with you?' She was unpacking her bag and proudly laying out completed squares in pretty pinks and greens on the worktable. By Hattie's estimations, Cynthia must have been soft-pedalling on the domestic chores to manage such an amount of sewing.
   'Oh, Cynthia, they're wonderful and such stunning fabrics too,' Hattie gasped, seeing several versions of the whirling star with not a wonky seam between them.
   'You're too kind, dear,' she replied modestly. 'So, any progress with the house sale?'

Hattie started to unpack her work and tried to put on a bright, positive manner. However, the pretence was proving difficult to sustain. When Nick had commented acidly about some people's transparency, it hadn't taken many guesses to work out that he meant her.

'Well, there's someone who's prepared to pay our full asking price, who's expecting an offer on *his* house any day now,' she told her.

'That's very good news then,' replied Cynthia. 'I bet your husband's thrilled.'

'Nick? Ah, well, I'm sure he is, but he's not saying much about it at the moment. The trouble is, I'd like to go and have a look at some cottages but, well, it's difficult,' Hattie faltered, temporarily losing a grip on her emotions.

Cynthia studied Hattie's expression with interest. The sparkle she'd seen in earlier weeks had disappeared. 'Is this house business getting to you?' she asked sympathetically. 'I know it can be so stressful waiting for things to happen.' However, before Hattie could reply, Zena clapped her hands authoritatively to signal the start of the session. What a relief! Another few moments and Hattie, heedless of Cynthia's blabbermouth reputation, might have revealed feelings best left hidden. In the blink of an eye, or the click of a tongue, Hattie and Nick's marriage would have been the hot topic around Bledlow Ridge. Given the geography and appetite for chitchat, her sorry tale would soon reach Fliss's ears. While they watched the week's demonstration, she had time to invent a suitably neutral reply based on headaches and job pressure; in other words, nothing that would appeal to Cynthia's gossipy nature. The moment of danger had passed.

Later, as they cut out little cardboard hexagons for the tumbling blocks design, Hattie had upgraded Nick's headache to a migraine. In addition, she invented a suitably dramatic incident with a difficult pupil. Predictably, anything centred on anonymous children with learning or behavioural difficulties did nothing to fuel Cynthia's imagination. All she managed were a few sympathetic murmurs, before bragging about her grandchildren's achievements. With the session drawing to a close, Hattie was planning a loo dash to avoid an embarrassing encounter between Cynthia and Leo. Momentarily, the additional Madge factor had slipped her mind.

'Bye Cynthia!' she called brightly, leaving her companion to the waiting Donald. Once in the loo, she splashed her face with cool water, carefully patted it dry and then touched up her lip-gloss. The thought of meeting Leo suddenly set her stomach churning in an alarming way. A group of giggling girls with glowing complexions burst through the door as Hattie was about to leave. Could these be apprentice belly dancers?

As she reached the foyer, she spotted the jolly Sorrento pair, which meant that Leo had finished his class and could arrive any minute. Students were passing by in groups as she waited impatiently for him to appear. The longer she waited, the more she felt like the lone, black sheep in the flock: odd, awkward and obvious. Quickly, she unzipped her folder and started rummaging. It had worked perfectly when she wanted to avoid an encounter with Ms Brewster, after all. To any casual observer, she was merely checking her belongings. Then she had second thoughts. It was probably a stupid idea anyway, so she re-zipped her folder and grasped the handle ready to go. It was then that she saw him rounding the corner, in conversation with two girls who had all the appearance of groupies. They giggled and simpered, gazing at him with adoring eyes. How could she attract his attention? There was only one way.

'Leo!' she called, setting off towards him purposefully, intending to speak to him away from the main thoroughfare.

'Hattie!' Leo exclaimed. 'How good to see you.'

The groupies glowered at Hattie, realising their time with Leo was about to be curtailed. 'Ciao,' they giggled, with much fluttering of their lashes.

'Ciao,' he replied, flashing one of his dazzling, top-drawer smiles.

Hattie watched them as they wandered off, sniggering as they went. The last conversation she'd had with Leo was the tense, bad-tempered one at The Feisty Ferret six days before. Why was it, she wondered, that he seemed so patient and forgiving after all the accusations she'd thrown at him? As she prepared to spill out her misery, she studied his handsome features that bore no sign of animosity, but simply genuine concern. It was so different from Nick's dismal coldness. Even her suspicion about the mysterious Alex seemed to have diminished.

'What is it?' Leo asked gently, seeing Hattie chastened and vulnerable.

'It's Nick,' she told him despondently. 'He's been in a filthy mood since Friday. I think he must have the letter.' She shook her head forlornly and closed her eyes. 'He's hardly speaking to me and Josh. It's awful,' she gulped.

'It was so stupid of me,' began Leo regretfully.

'What do you mean?'

'The letter,' he sighed. 'What I'd do to turn back the clock.'

'Me too,' agreed Hattie, recalling so many decisions that seemed right at the time.

They regarded each other remorsefully, sharing the same sense of helplessness.

'But you *do* want to know what I wrote, don't you?'

Hattie glanced back towards the central foyer area. 'Of course I do, Leo, but... Oh no! It's Madge!' she breathed in horror, trying to move out of sight of a group of chattering ladies who were making their way to the door. *These* were obviously the belly dancers, and out in front was the bubbly blonde girl she recognised seeing through Mia Casa's window on the day of the snow storm. Could she be the one she'd seen dancing with Leo at The Feisty Ferret?

'Oh hi, Leo!' the girl called. Madge and Sandra eagerly looked in his direction. He smiled and waved, but to Hattie's frustration, did not stand still enough to provide a shield from their beady eyes.

'Hi, Rebecca!' he replied.

Yet again, Hattie dodged out of their eye-line and dived into her folder.

'Sandra,' Madge remarked with interest, 'there's a woman cowering behind Signor Marcello. I thought for a moment she had a passing resemblance to Mrs Chesney.'

'I'm sure I don't know, Madge,' replied Sandra. 'Cowering did you say? How odd!' She craned her neck to get a better view. 'Or maybe it's nothing of the sort, but just your suspicious nature.'

Hattie stood her ground, gazing down at her boots while Leo and Rebecca exchanged banter. Why was he prolonging her agony?

'See you tomorrow!' called Rebecca, within a step of the door. Only Madge and Sandra remained, still speculating on the hidden female until Rebecca went to stir them from their reverie.

'Come on, Madge,' she said, taking her arm companionably. 'We're going back to Wendy's for coffee. Are you coming too, Sandra?'

'It's okay, Hattie. They've gone,' murmured Leo when the last of the group had left the building.

'But you didn't exactly help, did you, Leo?' Hattie reminded him reproachfully, but without her usual waspish sting.

'Rebecca saw me first, Hattie. She's my colleague, but they've gone now. Anyway, who's this Madge?'

'Nick's work colleague,' replied Hattie dramatically, rolling her eyes. 'I just hope she didn't spot me. I can just imagine the effect on Nick if she tells him she's caught us chatting.'

Leo studied the little he could see of Hattie's face under her woolly hat, with its brim folded down over her eyebrows, almost touching the folds of her matching scarf.

'She'd have to have very good eyesight if she did,' he chuckled. 'There's not much showing in between all your layers.'

'Well, let's hope her talent for recognising casual acquaintances at twenty yards is on a par with her suitability for belly dancing,' she quipped.

'For your sake, I hope so too,' said Leo.

Hattie recalled her collision with Madge on the corner of Goose Street and how quickly she'd been recognised. There was a pause and then she said, 'Leo, I daren't be late, but can we meet somewhere, sometime?'

'Of course. Just text me, okay?' He smiled at her and tenderly squeezed her hand. 'I'm sorry, believe me.'

'Thanks.' Hattie picked up her folder and set off towards the door, marvelling over Leo's capacity for forgiveness.

'Ciao!' he called, as she pushed the door open. He was still standing there, watching her, a smile just lifting his lips.

'Ciao!' she answered, managing her own smile. He bowed in his usual way then blew a kiss, instantly turning her insides to jelly. As she stepped outside, into the bitter evening chill, a hot flush spread to her cheeks. Back in the car, ready to start the engine, she replayed in her mind the scene in the foyer and realised that she had at last forgiven him. Whatever his reasons for what did or didn't happen on 13th July, she was ready to hear them. The root of bitterness inside her had withered and died.

10

'Post!' announced Madge, bustling into the office with a bundle of envelopes.

'Hmm,' muttered Nick, already busy checking his emails.

'What's up with you?' she snapped. 'Cat still got your tongue? You've been like this all week.' She started sorting through her pile, setting aside those for Nick's attention. 'Here's one marked "Private and Confidential – Mr N. Chesney",' she announced, holding the envelope aloft.

'Thank *you*, Madge,' said Nick curtly, getting up from his desk to retrieve it.

'Oh we *are* speaking this morning, are we?' she commented caustically, which ignited the smouldering blue touchpaper of Nick's temper.

'Any work to do, Madge, or are you planning to spend the whole day making personal comments at the company's expense?'

Madge harrumphed back to her desk, having dumped the two separate piles of mail. Nick tore open his confidential envelope, which was, as he'd guessed, the official job offer. Evidently, this had been triggered by the successful medical at the beginning of the week. Just as he'd anticipated, he was due to take up the new position at the beginning of April, once he'd handed in his letter of resignation. The content of the letter in his underwear drawer, however, was crowding his mind with increasing regularity and plunging him deeper into despair. It was after the evening with Mark that things had become worse, and now it felt as if he was at the bottom of a dark pit without a lifeline. At work, there was generally enough to keep his mind occupied, but at home, it was easier to let football take over. Consequently, the gulf between himself and Hattie was growing ever wider. As she'd prepared to set off for college the previous evening, he was plagued with the thought that she might be meeting *that* man. As far as he could make out, Marcello had attempted to steal Hattie away once before, so what was stopping him from trying it again? When she'd arrived home he'd looked for clues, but all he saw was a face as miserable as his own.

As he folded the letter, Madge's voice brought him out of his dark thoughts.

'You need to lighten up, you know,' she told him. 'Whatever's bothering you –'

'Who said anything's bothering me?' he snapped before she could finish.

'Just about anyone who sees you.'

'And who asked for *your* opinion, Madge?' he asked, stone-faced.

'Suit yourself,' she huffed. 'I feel sorry for your wife if you're like this at home.'

'And how do you know what I'm like at home?'

'I don't, but if she's getting the same treatment, then I don't blame her if she goes and…' She stopped short, realising that her suspected sighting of Hattie the previous night might have been mistaken. However, if it *had* been her – and there *was* something odd about her behaviour – it reminded her about the same shiftiness on the day of the snowstorm collision. Winded or shifty, Madge couldn't decide. On the other hand, Sandra might be right. It might not have been her at all.

'If she goes and *what*, Madge?' Nick demanded frostily.

'Nothing, but just remember: actions have consequences,' she snapped cryptically.

It was the perfect moment, Madge decided, to embark on her next task, which involved photocopying, stapling and then distribution, leaving Nick to sulk and simmer. The battle lines were drawn. In the past, there'd been the occasional pot shot between them, although the exchanges had been of a light and trivial nature. Now it felt like open warfare and Nick was thoroughly fed up with her snide comments and opinionated pronouncements. Turning to his PC, he opened a new document, typed a few short lines then printed and signed it.

'If you're down near Human Resources, you could drop this in for me,' said Nick in his best business-like delivery. Madge eyed the sealed envelope, predicting what it might contain. For a few seconds, she was tempted to tell him to do his own dirty work.

'With the greatest of pleasure' she replied frostily.

Ah! How sweet the sound of the ding-dong chimes on the call-minder, thought Hattie as she lifted the receiver. It was a relief to be home after battling with the taxing demands of 4R and playground duty at the end of a difficult week. Sweeter still was the voice she heard – Brian Samways – sounding either confidently optimistic or optimistically smug. Either way, he wasn't sounding like the bearer of bad tidings. Eagerly she dialled his number.

'Ah hello, Mrs Chesney,' he began, purposefully. 'Mr Bainbridge has secured a buyer, so it looks like all systems go.'

'Oh, that's good news,' she replied, a warm glow of relief easing the stresses of work and home. This was bound to snap Nick out of his bad mood.

'So, we'll cancel the viewings we'd lined up for the weekend and get everything moving,' continued Brian.

'Great,' replied Hattie, mentally removing several hours of cleaning and tidying from her to-do list, and working out a strategy for her own house-hunting

'Now,' said Brian after an embarrassed cough, 'Mr Bainbridge would like his partner to look at the house, so perhaps we can use one of tomorrow's cancelled slots?'

'Ah, right,' Hattie replied, adding back the cleaning and tidying and working out how she could still achieve her goals with the least disruption to family life. Up to now, she'd assumed Mr Bainbridge was a lone purchaser, so it seemed odd that his partner hadn't figured in the viewings before now. What if the partner hated the house?

'So, can we agree on nine thirty?' breezed Brian.

Hattie agreed. In truth, she would have agreed to anything to keep their precious buyer happy.

'Good news, Nick,' called Hattie, beaming, as soon as he was through the door. 'Mr Bainbridge has a buyer for his house and would like to bring his partner to have a look tomorrow. Isn't that great!'

His Arsenal mug was ready and the kettle was warming up nicely.

'Not too early I hope,' he sighed wearily, registering zero reaction to the news.

'Well… er…' Hattie started, choosing her words carefully. 'They'd like to come at nine thirty.'

'Nine thirty? That's indecently early! They'll have to come later,' he snapped irritably, dumping his briefcase and draping his jacket on the nearest chair. Hattie eyed him cautiously and chastised herself for her childish haste. Tea, chocolate biscuit *then* news, she reminded herself.

'Er… I think they're a bit restricted and they particularly asked for an early slot,' she improvised earnestly. 'So, I don't think we ought to put them off by being difficult.'

There were a series of grunts as Nick loosened his tie and dropped it on top of his jacket. Hattie waited a moment for the odd word, but in the absence of any, interpreted the grunts as, 'Oh, all right. If you say so.' He had picked up the local free paper and was leafing through it idly. At this rate, the chances of any viewings in Hants seemed as likely as Hilda Makepeace handing out bingo cards with the hymn books.

She sighed wearily and dropped a teabag into the waiting mug. Nick, however, had other things on his mind. He left the room without a word and soon the predictable sports channels had him in their stranglehold.

'Blasted football!' she muttered peevishly, wondering what ploy she could use, short of stripping off all her clothes, to jolt Nick back into the old cuddly and good-natured version. With Josh's imminent arrival home, a striptease was definitely out of the question. Realistically, goose bumps on saggy white flesh on a February afternoon wouldn't be wildly appealing even to the most hot-blooded of men. It had to be food after all.

'Here you are, Nick. Nice cup of tea and chocolate chip cookie.'

Grunt, zap, sigh. Not very promising, decided Hattie, feeling as if she'd just stepped into a lion's den and found her name on the menu.

'Are Arsenal on TV tomorrow?' she asked casually, hoping to work out a scheme that wouldn't fall foul of Premiership action on the box.

'Yeah,' replied Nick. 'A seven forty-five kick-off.'

'Oh great!' breathed Hattie, half to herself. Nick blinked at her quizzically. 'I... um... sent for some house details the other day, Nick,' she continued tentatively. 'Would you like to have a look at them later?'

'Maybe,' he mumbled through a mouthful of chocolate chips and crumbs, but with his eyes firmly glued to the TV. Progress, thought Hattie gleefully. Words were a definite improvement on grunts.

'There are a couple of cottages I'd love to have a look at before it's too late,' she mentioned casually.

Instantly, his head swivelled away from the screen. 'Too late? Too late for what?' he demanded, a cold, piercing glint in his eyes.

'Too late for buying of course. Before someone else snaps them up. What did you thing I meant?'

The tension in the room fairly sizzled as his eyes locked into hers.

'Oh, I was just wondering if you had other plans, that's all.'

'Other plans? I wouldn't suggest house-hunting if I had other plans.'

'Er... I was just wondering if you were thinking of going abroad.'

'Abroad?'

'Yes, abroad,' he answered. 'Don't keep repeating everything I say like some performing parrot.'

'Where did you get *that* idea?' snapped Hattie in protest. 'I thought we'd decided to put our holiday plans on hold, what with the job move and everything.'

'Oh, so you weren't thinking about a nice little villa some-where?' sneered Nick, his eye contact turning glacial.

'Vi... No, I just told you, Nick.

'I see,' he remarked, turning his attention back to the screen.

Remembering the business of the missing letter, Hattie guessed it might have triggered his cross-examination.

'Yes, we agreed,' she reminded him, 'just after the weekend away.'

'I just wondered if anything had changed since then.' It was almost a throwaway remark, but there was so much sarcasm in his voice that it shook Hattie to the core. She took a step closer towards the sofa, her heart aching with the pain of so many distressing days, angry looks and now this bitter exchange.

'Nick, believe me, the plans we made when we went away are still the same as far as I'm concerned,' she insisted calmly. 'Look, I'm keen to start looking at houses, so what's to stop us going tomorrow after Mr Bainbridge and partner have gone? It's not my turn to do the church flowers and – oh, I forgot – there's the weekly shop to do. Oh gremlins!' Ditching the supermarket run on the way home hadn't been such a great idea after all.

Nick grunted then noisily slurped his tea, a habit that drove her mad.

'Well, if you're prepared to take care of that, seeing as you're the one who's so keen on house-hunting, then go ahead.' He still didn't look wildly enthusiastic, but the fact that he was now managing whole sentences was encouraging. Back in the kitchen, she started her shopping list. Admittedly, battling around a super-market single-handed wasn't her ideal Friday evening's enter-tainment, but if it was a means to an end then she'd gladly do it.

'Is there a bus through the village?' enquired Mr Bainbridge's partner, who turned out to be female and stuck in a 1970s, Laura Ashley time warp. Maybe she, like Zena, loved searching through charity shops, in her case for vintage frills and flowery prints.

'Oh yes,' replied Hattie brightly, taking every opportunity to confirm that their house was the perfect choice. 'There's a bus stop at the top of the road and buses come through every hour.'

Mr Bainbridge and partner beamed. This was a first from a man who had managed little more than a vague smile on his two previous visits.

'She doesn't drive,' he informed Hattie confidentially. Deciding to buy the house had evidently freed his tongue.

They moved through to the utility room, where Jezebel was abruptly roused from her slumber by a piercing squeal.

'Ooh! A Sheila Maid!' giggled Vintage Lady excitedly. Jezebel shot out of the cat-flap, her hackles hoisted at ninety degrees.

'A what?' asked Hattie, momentarily perplexed.

'Up there!' Vintage Lady pointed. 'Ooh, Vince, I've always wanted one of those!' she exclaimed. 'Is it staying?' she asked with pure lust in her eyes.

Hattie glanced fondly at her precious clothes hoist that she knew would suit some lovely cottagey kitchen. 'Um... well... I'm not absolutely sure whether it's staying,' she began, then seeing the disappointed expression, quickly added, 'but I'm sure we might come to some arrangement.'

Vintage Lady beamed and rubbed her tiny hands together in glee. 'Nice shrubs. Nice view,' she commented, peering out of the glazed door to the garden.

'And very nice apples from the tree,' pointed out Hattie, in the same vein.

'Scrummy!' commented Vintage Lady with a giggle. They trooped upstairs, Vintage Lady clomping in her 3-inch platform boots.

'Nice tiles,' she commented, poking her head round the bathroom door. 'Blue, my fave colour. Very groovy, don't you think, Vince?'

'Then there's plenty of storage in the master bedroom,' Hattie informed her confidently, leading the way.

'Oodles!' exclaimed Vintage Lady, opening a door and inspecting the shoe racks. 'Brill for the boots, don't you think, Vince?'

Vince had metamorphosed back into his former self, but nodded benignly.

Hattie found little to say about Josh's room, but Vintage Lady seemed transfixed by the posters that always made Hattie shudder.

'Very Goth,' she breathed in wonder, inspecting Josh's individual choice of décor.

'Indeed,' agreed Hattie, teetering on the brink of a giggle.

At the front door, they each pumped her hand enthusiastically and thanked her with beaming smiles. It looked as if they were completely smitten, which was just the encouragement Hattie needed for the day ahead. In fact, she was so encouraged that she had to restrain herself from clasping Vintage Lady to her bosom in a friendly hug.

House hunting with Nick, Hattie decided, was depressing. Was he trying to sabotage their plans? If so, he was certainly an expert. If she had to be honest, though, the two they'd viewed so far were not the picture postcard properties of her dreams. The first was stunning from a distance, until they spotted the leering local who inhabited the untamed wilderness next door and the cottage's own minuscule courtyard garden. Number two could have been the ideal country hideaway if you wanted to live in a field, surrounded by a thicket of brambles. The owner's junkyard garden and crumbling lean-to kitchen weren't exactly inspiring either. Knapp Cottage, however, was a much brighter prospect, although Hattie's heart sank when she realised she'd overlooked one important detail on the agent's details.

'Ah, ground-floor bathroom. Not so ideal,' she added, frowning.

'Unless we ditch this pie-in-the-sky cottage rubbish and go for a nice, safe new-build,' Nick suggested matter-of-factly, knowing that would rile her.

'Oh, Nick, how can you say that?'

Nick shrugged and opened the car door. 'Just being realistic.'

However, on being shown into the cottage by proud owners Jo and Terry Dunbar, they were pleasantly surprised by the abundance of original period features.

'We're relocating to Portugal,' giggled Jo, sleek in linen pedal pushers and a Guernsey sweater. 'Got inspired by *A Place in the Sun – Home or Away*. Away's definitely more us!'

'Wow!' exclaimed Hattie, noting the smart kitchen fittings and gorgeous granite tiles. 'And what an adventure for you both.'

Nick wandered around with a neutral expression as Hattie inspected the impressive storage and built-in white goods.

'Terry favoured a villa in Italy to start with,' Jo trilled. 'But then we plumped for the Algarve – better for the golf, you know.'

'Indeed,' smiled Hattie. 'Good choice.'

She went over to the sink and gazed out at the back garden where a neat vegetable patch and greenhouse claimed a quarter of the space. The bathroom, however, was far from ideal, leading off from the back porch, adjacent to the kitchen.

'I wouldn't fancy trekking down here in the middle of the night,' grumbled Nick when their guide had moved out of earshot.

'Shush, Nick,' whispered Hattie. 'Let's see if there's space upstairs for an en-suite.' As they went to find out, Hattie felt the mobile in her pocket spring to life, then play its merry tune.

'Master bedroom,' announced Jo, beckoning Nick inside.

Hattie paused to check the incoming text. 'Leo,' she breathed, sensing her accelerating heartbeat. 'What now?'

'Lovely views over to St Wilfred's Tower,' Jo continued, waving her arm and pointing in a westerly direction. Nick nodded.

c u soon? the message read, but Hattie jabbed the 'off' button, quickly dropped the phone into her bag and joined the guided tour.

'Emergency message?' probed Mrs Dunbar. 'Heard your phone and – my, you *do* look flushed.'

'Oh, nothing,' she laughed airily. 'Just one of those silly library reminders.' She fanned herself wildly with the agent's details as Jo and Nick stared, each with puzzled expressions.

'Life's too busy to read a book sometimes,' Hattie gabbled, making a circuit of the room, 'so they end up texting me before I've hardly started.' She strode off down the little passageway and discovered a second bedroom with a promising layout for a tiny en-suite. 'Perfect,' she breathed, feeling less flustered and definitely more in control. 'Just the place for an extra loo,' she pointed out as Nick appeared at the door. 'And right above the lobby cloakroom downstairs, so the plumbing would be a breeze.'

'Yeah, probably a five-grand breeze on top of a price we can barely afford.'

'But, Nick, they're so keen to tee off in Portugal. I'm sure we could negotiate.'

Jo was by now brewing tea in the kitchen, so Nick and Hattie re-traced their steps and made their way to a back terrace, where a grapevine rambled up a rustic-style pergola. It was here that the Dunbars had put a matching bench seat. Nick and Hattie sat for a while to enjoy the view of meadows beyond the back fence.

'Oh, Nick, this is so lovely, don't you think?'

'Well, it's better than the last place,' he agreed grudgingly.

'Nick, it's a whole world away from the last place. Okay, so it's thirty thousand more, but worth every penny. I just love it.'

'What, with the bathroom stuck onto the kitchen? Can't imagine you legging it downstairs at two in the morning.'

'We already discussed that. So, could you see yourself living here?' she asked, detecting the odd positive vibe amongst the objections.

'More to the point, can you?'

'Nick,' she protested, linking arms and snuggling up to his stiff, unyielding shoulder, 'what part of "I just love it" don't you understand?'

'Hmm… well…'

'I know it's not perfect, but we could be looking for months and still not find the perfect property. There'd always be some problem with, say, the size of the garden, or out-dated kitchen or too far from your work, or —'

'A ground-floor bathroom,' finished Nick.

'But setting that aside?'

'It's not bad.'

Praise indeed, thought Hattie. Was the iceberg really melting at last?

Just then Jo appeared to announce that tea was made.

'We just love your cottage,' Hattie told the pair as they sipped something smoky flavoured and nibbled Hobnobs, 'but there're a few points to consider.'

'How long have you been on the market?' Nick asked, wondering where he could safely tip the contents of his mug. Several spider plants looked likely candidates.

'Since Wednesday,' Terry answered, 'but we're hoping for a quick sale.'

Very little was said as they drove home, but Hattie's mind was bubbling over with ideas for Knapp Cottage. Over coffee, in church the following morning, she updated Celia on their day out and their dilemma.

'You need to talk to Harry Nuttall,' she suggested. 'He

converted one of our garages into a granny annexe a few years ago and several other jobs over the years – such a terribly nice chap too. Just a minute, I'll find you his phone number. I'm sure he wouldn't mind giving you some idea of costs.'

Warned by Celia that Harry started work very early, she decided to call him at eight the following morning and arrange a time to quiz him about their hypothetical project. As she noted the number beside the phone, she hoped that nobody had already secured Knapp Cottage for themselves.

In the seclusion of the conservatory next morning, Hattie tapped in Harry Nuttall's number, while Nick munched toast in the kitchen with Five Live for company.

'On what?' Harry asked, after Hattie had introduced herself and her predicament.

'Suite,' she added, then to make it clearer, 'En-suite, with a loo and shower.'

'Ah, one of them little bathroom jobbies,' replied Harry after a short pause. 'Yes, missus, I knows the sort you mean.'

'So when could you come and advise me? I need an estimate as soon as possible.'

The cogs in Harry's brain whirred slowly, accompanied by heavy breathing and even heavier throat clearing. 'Reckon I can come by after work, missus, 'bout five.'

'You're a star, Harry. 7 Witchert Close,' gushed Hattie, ecstatically. 'Many thanks.' Before pressing the 'off' button, she scrolled through her latest texts and saw the one from Leo that had set her pulse racing and her heart careering into overdrive.

C u soon? he'd written, but she hadn't yet replied. The dilemma of choosing a risk-free rendezvous was still unresolved. She remembered the last glimpse of him, blowing a kiss. Could she cope with another meeting or should she wait until Wednesday? She tapped in his number, hoping Five Live would keep Nick distracted long enough.

'Hi,' Leo answered, 'how nice to hear from you, Hattie.' It

sounded as if he was smiling. Might he still be in bed, she wondered, or fresh out of the shower with a towel around his waist, or...? She silently chastised herself for letting her thoughts stray into forbidden regions. 'Leo,' she began, lowering her voice guiltily, 'sorry I didn't reply but we were in the middle of viewing a cottage at the time. I was wondering if we could meet this week.'

'Viewing a cottage? Does that mean you've sold your house?'

'Well, yes... we have. Amazing isn't it? So quick too!'

'Oh, I see. I guess that's wonderful news for you both.' Leo, however, didn't seem to be entering into the spirit of their good fortune, judging by the tone of his voice.

'So, when do you suggest we meet, and where?'

Leo had also been considering the tricky subject of possible meeting places, preferably where one of Hattie's friends or acquaintances wouldn't suddenly pop up and send her running for cover. Hattie was at a loss as well. Lonely hillsides might seem ideal until a local walking group came tramping by. So maybe look for a handy crowd? Short of football crowds, Hattie couldn't think of anywhere safe. She was about to suggest dropping in at his office when she remembered that Leo's colleague, Rebecca, was Madge's belly-dancing instructor. The possibility of stray comments could not be risked. If Madge and Nick were embroiled in office warfare, the sniff of clandestine meetings – however innocent – would be perfect ammunition. However, if Leo came to her home, someone was bound to drop by without warning. Pubs were definitely out of the question and her suggestion of the library had been, of course, quite silly.

'Maybe I could meet you by the bus stop at the end of my road,' she whispered, hearing Nick moving around upstairs. 'It might be safer to keep on the move. I could always come in disguise. How about this afternoon or any time on Wednesday?'

There was a pause at Leo's end that coincided with footsteps down the stairs at Hattie's.

'Well,' he replied, accompanied by the sound of pages being turned, 'I could manage three this afternoon. How about that?'

'Yes, that's fine… right, Harry, I'll see you later,' Hattie improvised as Nick wandered into the far end of the sitting room and
signalled that he was off to work.

'Harry? Who's Harry, Hattie? Whatever do you mean?'

'Don't worry, Leo. I'll tell you later. Must dash.'

At five to three, Hattie set off for her bus-stop rendezvous feeling
like an undercover agent on a secret mission. An uncommonly
high proportion of her neighbours were washing or unloading
cars, cleaning windows or twitching curtains. All this activity added
to her sense of guilt, although for all *they* knew she was just off
to do some shopping. She had trawled through her wardrobe to
find her most nondescript clothes, which she'd layered thickly,
giving her the appearance of a suet pudding. Traffic on the main
village road was busy, so she turned away from the steady stream
and studied the bus timetable intently, hoping no bus would appear
and offer her a ride. Stuffing her hands in her pockets, she edged
around the back of the bus stop to watch for Leo's car. As she
checked her watch and noticed that the hands made a perfect
right angle, two short and possibly illegal horn hoots sounded
from a car across the road. It was Leo.

Quickly, she nipped across through a break in the traffic and
slid into the passenger seat beside him. Just a brief, low-key smile
passed between them as Leo set off and headed towards the dual
carriageway.

'Very cloak and dagger, Mrs Chesney,' commented Leo as
Hattie pulled her hat brim well over her eyes and hunched low
in her seat.

'Self-preservation, Signor Marcello.'

'Hmm… right… you wanted to know why I didn't call you
after we missed each other at Victoria Station,' he began.

'Yes, Leo. That's the bit I found so difficult to understand.'
When someone claims to have loved passionately and devotedly,
why would they let a minor inconvenience like a dodgy lift cable

sweep away their life's plans? That thought had plagued her ever since the day of the Goose Street meeting.

'Well, first I wandered around the entire station searching for you, then I looked through my bags for the phone number and address you'd given me. I remembered that it was written on a Monet postcard and that I'd put it in a carrier bag with your letters, photos and some special mementos. I was sure the plastic bag I was carrying was the one with the card, but as soon as I turned it out I realised it was the one with old essays and notes – the one I'd intended to throw away.'

Hattie gasped. 'Oh no, you mean you threw away the wrong bag? That was rather careless, wasn't it, Leo?'

'No, I'm sure it was Alex's fault,' he sighed.

'Alex?' repeated Hattie suspiciously, remembering Leo's burbled ramblings at college. 'What did she do? Was it deliberate?' she asked, narrowing her eyes.

'She? What do you mean, *she?*'

'Okay. Correction. What did *Alex* do?' sighed Hattie in frustration. 'My mum always picked me up on that sort of thing. *She's* the cat's mother and all that,' she added, realising that she had also taken Laura to task about the use of *that* particular pronoun.

'Oh, Hattie,' Leo sighed, shaking his head, 'Alex was – I mean *is* – a man. Why did you assume Alex was a girl? Didn't you ever know my other flatmates at Birmingham? Ah no, I remember now, Alex took over Mike's room when he dropped out.' In fact, he and Hattie had always met well away from the mess and noise of the basement flat, which frequently overflowed with visitors, unwashed dishes and splitting dustbin sacks.

She shrugged, relieved that at least there had been no deliberate sabotage plot hatched by a jealous rival. 'Do go on Leo.'

'I remembered him loading a whole lot of boxes and bags of rubbish into his car and taking them to a tip.' Leo explained. 'It was all a bit of a rush.'

'I see,' sighed Hattie, 'so keen old Alex rushed around the flat grabbing plastic bags for the rubbish dump. Wasn't that rather a stupid place for storing important stuff?' She recalled the letters she'd written to him and the photos they'd taken and was sad to think they'd all ended up trashed on some council tip. She was even sadder to think that the Monet postcard, with its vital information, had suffered the same fate.

'Hattie, believe me, I thought I had it with me.'

A moment of silence hung in the air while Leo changed gear and turned off the main road. 'So,' continued Leo, 'I realised that there was no way of contacting you. No address, no phone number and no one else I could ask. You see, I didn't know any of your friends well enough to get in touch. My friends and your friends didn't exactly mix did they? Can you imagine how I felt?'

'That makes two.'

'I was so frustrated about everything that had happened that morning. All I wanted was to be with you.' He glanced at Hattie who had pulled her hat clear of her eyes and was gazing at him with a mixture of regret and frustration.

'So, you hadn't had second thoughts about us?' Hattie asked sadly, realising yet again how she'd misjudged him. 'I imagined you'd decided that I wouldn't fit in with your life in Italy, or even that there was some other girl out there waiting for you.'

Leo sighed heavily and shook his head. 'No, Hattie, it was nothing like that. This is the truth.'

'Okay, Leo, I believe you. Of course, we all have mobile phones now. If we'd had them then, there wouldn't have been a problem.'

'Ah, yes – the mobile phone,' he reflected philosophically. 'What a difference that would have made.'

'So, what then?'

'I wasn't giving up that easily. I tried to trace your parents' phone number, although I didn't have an address to help me.'

'Hmm, I see. What did you do?' By now she was feeling guilty that she had given up so easily. Admittedly the hour waiting at the station had been costly in terms of damaged pride and disappointment, but if only she'd waited longer.

'I found the nearest library and started searching phone directories. You see, I remembered you came from Hampshire – somewhere near Winchester, Southampton, or was it Salisbury?' He had come to a temporary pause in his account as he reached a crossroads. 'The trouble was – oh, this sounds so ridiculous – I was confused about the spelling of your name.'

'Oh, Leo!' Hattie exclaimed, sounding horribly like Mrs Chesney the schoolteacher.

'I wasn't sure if it was Morris or Morrish,' Leo admitted awkwardly. It was then that Hattie recalled the incident in the college classroom.

'Ah, so *that's* what you meant when you kept on about whether there was an "h" or not. I thought you'd totally lost it, Leo. I mean, Hattie starts with an "h" after all.'

'You see,' he continued apologetically, 'I hadn't had to write your full name before. The spelling had never been important – Morris, Morri*sh*: they sound the same when you say them quickly and there were so many Morrises in those directories.'

'Oh, Leo!' Hattie exclaimed again, trying not to sound too exasperated. 'I realise it's too late to remind you, but my name was Morri*sh*,' she told him, 'and it's fairly uncommon. I expect there were barely half a dozen Morrishes in those directories.' She slumped further in her seat, amazed that one little 'h' had made such a difference to her life.

'I know it must sound a really feeble excuse, but it's the truth'

In the pause that followed, Hattie let Leo's words sink in. He wasn't two-faced, hadn't changed his mind or given up on her. It was his memory that had let him down.

'So, did you try any of the phone numbers?' she asked tentatively, calculating that even the student heir to a wine estate in Tuscany might be short on spare change for phone calls.

'Yes, but I couldn't try *all* of them, could I? So I decided to write down the ones in a place called Ringwood,' he continued, 'because I had a feeling your address was somewhere beginning with an "R". So, I tried all those, but of course…'

'Ah, I see,' Hattie sighed. 'Well, the "R" was right, but my home was in Romsey.' Although she couldn't help feeling just a bit annoyed with Leo for his vague memory for names, rotten spelling and poor grasp of Hampshire geography, she couldn't help feeling sorry for him as well. Hattie sighed, and for a few moments there was silence, apart from the sound of the engine.

'And then what?'

'Well, because I had no way of being sure of the correct spelling of your name, because I didn't know where to find you and most of all because you weren't still waiting for me at the station, it seemed to me that everything was stacked against us.'

'Oh if only I had stayed at the station,' she murmured.

'Yes, if only,' Leo sighed. 'By then I was starting to come to terms with the thought that you'd changed your mind. I could have stayed on in England, I could have tried every conceivable way to find you, but at the back of my mind would have been the stark reality that you and I were not to be. With the last of my small change I phoned my parents, told them I'd be coming alone but that I wouldn't arrive for another two days. Then I changed my ticket, checked into a hotel and waited until the next day to catch a train. It gave me a chance to cool down. I was angry, upset, disappointed and struggling to understand why everything had gone so horribly wrong.' He shook his head sadly.

'Because I didn't wait,' she sighed.

He nodded and murmured something that was lost in the sound of the engine. He had changed direction several times as they'd been travelling and now, peering over the dashboard, Hattie could see that they were approaching the village from the north.

'When I arrived home, I became involved with the vineyard and then, after a few months, I started going out with a girl I'd known since childhood. I hadn't seen much of her because of being at an English boarding school, but we'd been casual friends when I'd returned home for the holidays. Her family lived in

Montelugia. In fact, her father had a flourishing building company, and Gina had studied interior design at college. She used to set up show-homes by choosing and organising the décor, carpets and fittings.'

'Oh yes. You see a lot of that sort of thing on the TV channels these days,' commented Hattie, recalling her recent viewing. It sounded like the perfect job, choosing gorgeous fabrics, paint and plants without costing yourself a penny.

'Well, after a year, we became engaged and then a year later we were married.'

Despite the passage of time, Hattie couldn't help feeling slightly jealous of the unknown Gina who had taken on the name of Signora Marcello that she'd considered to be her preserve.

'Our son, Alphonse, was born three years later and then our daughter, Simone, two years after that.' Leo paused again and shook his head sadly. It didn't take many brain cells to work out that his life had taken a dive and that he was no longer the happy family man of twenty years ago.

'So why are you in England, Leo?'

'Gina and I started to grow apart. We wanted different things… We had different values… I didn't realise quite how different until we'd been married for a while. She suddenly developed an alarming shopping habit – only the best for Gina; only the best for Alphonse and Simone.'

'And what about *you*, Leo?'

'Well, money's not everything, Hattie, but to keep her happy I never begrudged Gina anything. The trouble was, no matter how much I gave her, she always wanted more. I think she had some dream of being a grand lady, a lady of property, with her children at the best and most exclusive schools with all the trappings of a wealthy lifestyle.'

Hattie started to feel distinctly uncomfortable. It was almost as if Leo was echoing her own private agenda from the heady days of their romance. Wasn't that the same dream she'd had for herself all those years ago? Perhaps she and Gina were twin souls.

But Hattie was convincing herself that she wouldn't have been quite so greedy.

'So did you start arguing about it?'

'No, we just grew apart, because I realised no matter how much Gina had, she'd always want more.'

Gina struck Hattie as a nasty gold-digger, which she would never have been.

'She seemed to treat me as a money machine rather than the man she loved,' continued Leo. 'Whenever I challenged her about this, she'd fly into a rage. She said I was mean and that she was entitled to a generous allowance after all the hard work of building up a huge client base. I think Gina saw herself as some sort of glorified ambassador for the wine trade, strutting around in her ruinously expensive designer clothes.' And ruinously high designer heels, speculated Hattie privately.

'Oh dear,' she murmured, wishing she'd had the chance to add one or two designer labels to her own modest wardrobe, instead of charity shop and chain store bargains.

'Then she started looking elsewhere for male company. She denied it, of course, but when she returned from some trip, supposedly with a girlfriend, there was something about her that told me she was cheating on me. After another year or so of that, she asked me for a divorce, on the grounds of incompatibility of all reasons. Naturally, she demanded a very generous settlement.'

'Oh, Leo, how awful!' gasped Hattie, already predicting this revelation. 'Was it a shock?'

'Well, no. It wasn't really. I'd been rather expecting it – dreading it as well,' he admitted with resignation. 'We were divorced two years ago.'

The car was slowing down, so Hattie struggled into an upright position to see that they were approaching her bus stop.

'Oh, we're back.' There were so many questions that she was longing to ask, such as how did he end up as an estate agent, and in Aylesbury of all places? But there wasn't time. 'I don't know what to say, except I'm sorry I was so hateful to you that first day. It was a shock.'

'You understand then?' he asked gently, fixing her with a look that was having a strange effect on her insides.

'Yes, I understand and I'm sorry how it's worked out for you, but I'm not sure I could have been a better wife,' she sighed then immediately regretted voicing her own secret wish. A crimson blush spread across her cheeks, a sure sign that her internal thermostat had passed the danger mark. How could she assume that he'd ever considered marrying her? She needed to make a quick exit before any more classified information tried to surface.

'Well, I'll never know,' Leo sighed wistfully, unaware of Hattie's embarrassment.

'Bye, Leo. Must dash! Expecting a conflab with a builder soon.'

'Goodbye, dear Hattie,' Leo replied to her departing back, almost adding a resigned 'as usual' until he realised there were precisely ten minutes before a scheduled valuation appointment in Weston Turville.

Hattie didn't dare check if anyone had seen her emerge furtively from Leo's car. Pulling her hat well past her eyebrows, she beetled off home, hoping her little jaunt had not been witnessed by any of the local blabbermouths. Once inside, she checked her muffin stash and selected a tangy blueberry one for a change which would provide enough comfort to help her digest Leo's unfortunate story. Someone up there seemed to have made doubly sure she ended up as Mrs Chesney rather than Signora Marcello, but that, as she reminded herself again, was history. Even sadder was the fact that Leo was now separated from his children, although how that happened, she was yet to learn.

Harry Nuttall was expected around five, but the appointed hour passed and she decided to plough on with the sausage toad batter regardless. The oven was heating up nicely with the sausages turning golden brown and the batter was glooping thickly in the bowl when the doorbell eventually rang.

'Oh conkers!' she cursed, wiping her hands and disentangling her legs from Jezebel's best attempt at cupboard love. 'Come in, Harry,' she said. The stubbly-faced senior citizen seemed to have spent most of the day in a cement bin.

''Ow do, missus! Best take me boots off I s'pose,' he announced meekly, removing first his battered cap and then his heavy-duty footwear. Judging by the gaping holes in both heels, she concluded that there might not be a Mrs Nuttall, or only one who shared Hattie's views on sock repair.

'Come through to the kitchen, Harry. I'm just in the middle of getting supper organised. How about a cuppa? Builders' brew okay for you?'

'Well, thanks kindly, missus,' replied Harry, following on behind. Hattie whipped out the dish of browning sausages from the oven and covered them in the waiting batter. With the toad-in-the-hole set to finish cooking, she organised a mug of tea and offered a ginger nut

'Now, about my idea for adding an en-suite to the cottage, Harry... I'm hoping you can give me some advice,' she began.

Harry slurped his tea, his brow wrinkled in thought. 'Now, what cottage would this be, missus? I thought you was wanting one of those little bathrooms in this 'ere 'ouse, but I see you've bin and sold it like. A bit strange, I'm thinking.' He paused to dunk the biscuit then sucked contentedly at the soggy crumbs. At once, Hattie detected a major misunderstanding.

'No, it's not for *this* house, Harry. It's an en-suite for *this* cottage,' she explained, passing the details of Knapp Cottage across the kitchen table. 'And I've drawn a rough diagram of the first floor showing where I'd like the en-suite to go. I just need an idea of the cost of this sort of work.'

Harry took the sheets and studied the glossy picture intently. He then scribbled for a while on the back of Hattie's sketched plan with a well-chewed pencil, breathing heavily and scratching his weathered scalp. When he was satisfied with his work, he wrote a figure, which he circled with a flourish. Hattie peered at the figure with a gulp and calculated that Harry's estimate would easily supply Josh with a good second hand motor... although it was less than Nick's estimate.

'There you are, missus,' he said genially. 'I reckon that would just about do it, depending on your fixtures and fittings, like.'

'Oh, so this doesn't include them?'

'No, no, missus. That's up to you. Them warehouse places could fix you up for five 'undred or you could blow a few thousand on them so-called designer ones. Gawd knows why – a lavvy's a lavvy after all. Mind you,' he muttered darkly, thrusting his stubble closer than Hattie would have liked, 'that's what *I* would charge, but you needs to be careful; other folk might try to fleece you.'

'Oh right. Well, thank you, Harry. Do have another biscuit before you go.' This seemed a meagre reward for sharing his wealth of experience, but he declined it all the same. Considering the work involved, Harry's estimate was really not unreasonable and just about kept the purchase of Knapp Cottage at an affordable level if the Dunbars were open to offers. How to convince Nick was another matter entirely.

'Right, Jezebel,' she said as she filled her bowl, 'we'll wait until the master's full of sausage and batter before sharing our interesting news. You have to soften them up first – not that you need to know that of course.'

'What's that, Mum?' came a voice. 'First sign of madness, talking to yourself.' Josh dumped a bulging rucksack on the floor and then removed a carton of juice from the fridge.

'I'm not talking to myself, Josh. I was talking to Jezebel.'

'Same thing. She's not into conversation in a big way,' he observed in between gulps.

'Is this the pot calling the kettle black? Didn't think your effort in that area was particularly outstanding. Do we see a sea-change at last, I wonder?' Hattie retorted.

Josh mooched away from her, taking more thirsty gulps. Could it be, she wondered, that there was a slight flush to his cheek, or was it a trick of the light?

'How much?' Nick exclaimed when Hattie finally found the perfect moment to mention Harry's estimate. He was replete with second helpings of sausages and fruit crumble. Josh had also slunk away upstairs. Hattie pushed Harry's circled figure across the table and galvanised herself for Nick's current favourite topic of new-builds.

'But I could spend that on trading in the Astra and upgrading to a better model,' he spluttered.

'I expect you could,' agreed Hattie. 'Not that you've mentioned that recently, I recall. So it can't be that important.'

Nick stirred his coffee and gazed vacantly at Harry's handi-work. 'Well, it seems a lot to pay for an extra toilet,' he complained, 'when you could buy somewhere –'

'I know! I know! But do you really intend driving down every Saturday and forking out for all that extra petrol when we've already found a cottage that's virtually perfect?'

The clink of Nick's spoon was joined by the sudden roar of the boiler, which indicated that Josh was paying another visit to the shower; that made twice in one day, which was indeed rare.

'Look, Nick, I'd like to put in an offer,' Hattie proposed, stroking his spare hand. The look he gave her bordered on suspicion.

'Are you sure?'

'Positive. Absolutely love it!'

'Hmm, well, we don't have to splash out on the luxury end of the market; a bog-standard suite would do.'

'Splash out? A bog-standard suite?' chortled Hattie. 'Oh, Nick, that's very droll.'

'What?'

'Never mind. What shall we offer?'

'Now, bear in mind that we're in tricky times, so… we'll offer fifty thousand under the asking price for starters.'

'Nick, that's very mean. They've only just gone on the market after all.'

He drained his cup and shrugged. 'Fifty thousand under and not a penny more.'

11

'It's for you; sounds like your wife,' announced Madge tersely, having grabbed the receiver on the first ring. It was almost time for lunch and after a particularly fraught morning of meetings, Nick was looking forward to a break.

'Hi, Nick. I've just had a call back from the Knapp Cottage agents. I'm afraid our offer's been rejected.' It had been no surprise to Hattie, who had phoned during mid-morning break with what she considered a very cheeky offer.

'Oh, I see,' murmured Nick, trying not to give Madge-of-the-flapping-ears too many clues. 'Well, we could always improve on it I guess,' he added reluctantly.

'I should jolly well think so! They've been on the market barely a week!' she retorted hotly. An abrupt pause in the lunchtime chatter registered in Hattie's ears, warning her that half the staff were avidly following the Chesney house purchase negotiations. Cupping her hand around the mobile, she shuffled over to the photocopier corner. There was a pause while Nick doodled on his message pad.

'Well, all right,' he relented with resignation. 'Try another ten.'

The on-going antics of Sally's class kept Hattie fully occupied that afternoon, with scarcely a moment to wonder about the outcome of their second offer. She drove home with an odd mixture of feverish excitement and ominous foreboding. If they'd been pipped by a few measly thousand, she'd have plenty of choice phrases for Nick's arrival home. When she arrived, she saw the light flashing on the phone, indicating a message.

'Oh, hello. This is Patrick O'Donnell from O'Donnell and McLaverty. Please would you call us at your earliest convenience.'

Hattie punched in the number and waited for Patrick O'Donnell to pick up his phone.

'I'm sorry, Mrs Chesney,' he explained, with starchy aloofness, 'but my clients are still not inclined to accept your offer.'

Not inclined, thought Hattie mutinously, not *inclined?* This O'Donnell fellow was short on charm and a few other qualities.

'Oh, I see,' she murmured, smarting from his high-and-mighty tone. 'The trouble is,' she continued firmly, 'the only bathroom is in a most inconvenient position – practically in the garden in fact.'

'I'm fully aware of the bathroom's location, Mrs Chesney,' replied O'Donnell smoothly. His manner was speedily advancing from irritating to infuriating.

'We've consulted a builder about the cost of installing an en-suite in the front bedroom, and have included that cost in our budget.' She felt on firm ground now, but how much more would Nick be prepared to pay to secure that little piece of heaven?

'I see,' droned the agent, obviously unmoved by Hattie's reasoning. 'So will you be making another offer?'

'I certainly hope so. After I've consulted with my husband of course.' If it had been up to her, she'd have offered the full asking price, without all the quibbling over an extra few thousand. At least the cottage was still available.

By the following day, Hattie had finally worn Nick down to offer another twenty thousand and this gave them the desired result. Then a call to Pigeon, Grimes and Company, their solicitors, meant both sale and purchase were underway. Anyone who bumped into Hattie had to agree they were exceedingly fortunate

251

to have achieved so much so quickly. The prophets of doom, however, waxed lyrical about their own tales of woe.

Oh fiddlesticks, thought Hattie. It doesn't have to be like that.

The pounding of the rain on the conservatory roof sounded like giant peas bouncing off a bass drum, as Hattie packed her patchwork ready for session number six.

'I could run you in,' offered Nick, looking up from his paper. That was the second sentence he'd managed since arriving home. The first one had been, 'Oh, thank God for that!' when she'd given him the news of their successful offer. However, the odd look on his face made Hattie suspicious. Maybe *his* offer was not purely out of concern for her safety on the road.

'Whatever for? Why waste petrol on two journeys, unless you're planning another football-watching session at one of Aylesbury's watering holes?' She cringed inside as she remembered the embarrassing business of the fictitious encounter with the bolshie caretaker.

'No match tonight, Mum,' Josh volunteered as he flicked through the innumerable channels.

Nick shot him an irritable glance. Could it be, Hattie wondered, that he was planning to check up on her? She imagined him standing guard outside the classroom and then escorting her down the corridor with a sack over her head to ward off unwelcome male attention.

'I just thought... It's pretty atrocious out there...'

'And you think I can't handle my car? Is this some male thing? Oh dear, women drivers!' she fumed, mimicking his voice.

'I just wanted to make sure everything was okay, that's all,' he grumbled, head down, addressing the Premier League fixtures section.

'I see,' she snapped waspishly. 'And which one of us has managed to incur points on our licence?' She knew it was a bit below the belt, but Nick's fake concern for her safety had certainly touched a nerve. Her remark was met with stony silence which she took as her cue to leave. If Nick was doing the grumpy old man impression again, she was best out of it.

The rain that lashed against the windscreen for the first ten minutes of her journey had reduced somewhat by the time she reached the college car park. On the way, she had reflected yet again on the likely cause of Nick's mood – that dratted letter – which had never been mentioned, even obliquely. Although she now knew the substance of it, she hadn't actually *seen* it herself. It was possible that Leo had used the odd phrase that might not have gone down well with Nick. Perhaps, just for the last time, she should find out.

On arriving in the college foyer, she texted him, suggesting a quick coffee, but not in The Four Seasons, just in case the Tarriers were in the vicinity. As she set off down the corridor, her phone hummed into life with Leo's reply.

C u @ Bar on the Corner, Market Row, Leo.

Hattie smiled as she pocketed her phone. Armed with all the facts, she might even be able to pluck up courage and finally confront Nick about the innocence of the letter. It was amazing how relaxed she felt about meeting up with Leo after all the painful angst of recent weeks.

'See you next week and happy stitching,' said Hattie to Cynthia, quickly sweeping her work into her folder and grabbing her coat after another busy patchwork session. She was determined to nip out ahead of the rest of the class, hoping to avoid bumping into Madge and co, and arrive at the Bar on the Corner in good time.

The rain was now a relentless drizzle as she hurried along the canal path and across into the Market Square. By the time she'd reached Market Row, her hair resembled rats' tails and a glance in her handbag mirror confirmed that her carefully applied mascara had now turned into panda eyes. The Bar on the Corner, fortunately, went in for low-lit ambience and even better, had just a handful of complete strangers chatting over glasses of wine and mugs of coffee. Hattie quickly attended to her eye make-up disaster and hoped Leo wouldn't be delayed by the giggling groupies or the Sorrento timeshare pair. However, five long minutes passed and Hattie was on the point of giving up when she heard the door open. It was Leo, slightly out of breath and clutching his briefcase. Soon they were sipping cappuccinos and Hattie's rats' tails were steaming nicely.

'Well, this is pleasant, Hattie,' Leo murmured, relaxing into the soft leather of a neat little sofa. 'But no doubt you have an ulterior motive.'

'Naturally, Leo. You don't think I make a habit of arranging clandestine meetings with strange men just for the heck of it, when I could be enjoying the peace and tranquillity of my own fireside?'

Leo gave her a quizzical look.

'About the letter...'

'Not *that* again!' he sighed in frustration. 'But, Hattie, I told you everything on Monday.'

'What you told me on Monday was about losing the phone number. Can you remember what else you wrote, bearing in mind that Nick has read it and he's in a filthy mood most of the time.'

Leo carried on sipping his coffee, his brow furrowed in thought. 'When I wrote the letter, I wasn't expecting anyone else to read it.'

'Obviously not.' She studied his expression, which suggested a degree of mental discomfort.

'Well,' he began awkwardly, 'I wanted to assure you that I hadn't had doubts about our relationship – that you weren't just a passing whim, or something like that.'

'I see.' Hattie considered Leo's reply carefully, trying to imagine what effect that might have had on Nick.

'And it was obvious that you were referring to something that had happened ages ago?'

'Of course. I just wrote about what happened at the station on that day, what had gone wrong and why,' he told her with a shrug.

'So there's no reason why he should be particularly upset then?' she replied frowning. 'Unless he realised that I'd deliberately avoided mentioning you when we first met.'

A moment passed while Hattie spooned up some froth thoughtfully.

'How can I say?' Leo protested softly. 'I mean, some people can get upset easily, but others have thick hides.'

'Thick skins, Leo.'

'Oh yes, thick skins. You could say anything and they wouldn't mind.'

'Hmm, well, I think Nick is generally somewhere in the middle, although he may have shifted to the sensitive end of the scale just recently,' she reflected. 'Do you know, apart from being on his best behaviour when we were viewing houses at the weekend, he's been freezing me out for most of the past two weeks. Leo, please think carefully about anything else you might have written. Sorry to keep asking.'

Leo shook his head and tried to picture the letter. Then, with a sudden jolt, he remembered his opening phrase. After all, he'd been at the receiving end of Gina's infidelity, so he knew how it felt when he'd suspected she'd been spending time with other men. But this was different.

'But Hattie, what I wrote simply referred to the relationship we had as students. Are you suggesting that your husband thinks we're conducting some sort of affair?'

'Affair? Of course I'm not! Well, I hope he doesn't! Why do you say that?' Hattie gasped, feeling a flush prickle around her neck and onto her cheeks.

'I may have written that I'd had a great love for you,' he admitted solemnly, looking deep into her eyes.

Hattie swallowed nervously as her stomach and heart lurched in unison. Leo's pronouncements seemed to be from another era, one of chaperones, formal marriage betrothals and dowries. He could have stepped straight out of a Jane Austen novel.

'Had?' she asked.

'Yes, Hattie, *had*,' he stressed, trying not to let his exasperation show. 'I've already *told* you. I was referring to our former relationship, something you've kept secret from the rest of the world.'

'Oh, I see. So he can't possibly think we're embroiled in some steamy affair?' He shook his head.

She couldn't help feeling just a tad disappointed that he was no longer owning up to any feelings for her, considering the way he'd just been fixing her with his 'come hither' eyes. 'Well, Leo, if you must know, I was so upset about the way it ended between us that my only way of dealing with it was to pretend it had never happened. I'm ashamed to say that when Nick and I started going out, I told him I'd never had any serious boyfriends before him. Not because I'd not loved you, Leo, but because of what happened. I didn't want him to think I was going out with him on the rebound.'

'And now your husband will have discovered that we were, as they say, an item.'

'Precisely, and he'll know that I deliberately lied to him, something I've become an expert at recently.'

'Hattie, believe me, I'm not lecturing you, but I think it may have been Mark Twain who said, if you always tell the truth, you'll never have to remember what you said.'

'You mean, like remembering what story you made up?'

'Indeed. The truth is the truth is the truth, and always will be.'

'Who said that?'

'I just did.'

'It's not always as easy as that,' Hattie replied forlornly, 'but to use another saying, I'm now in a tangled web, woven by my own lies and I'm struggling to find my way out.' She sighed regretfully. 'Oh, if only…'

Leo laid a comforting hand over hers. 'Take courage, dear Hattie. If your husband loves you, he'll forgive the lies. I'm sure he will.'

'Are you? You don't know him, Leo. Do you know, I've even started wondering about that recently; about him loving me, I mean. I've found myself thinking, if Nick loves me and sees how keen I am to move, then surely he'll stop behaving like this. But whatever I do or say doesn't seem to make any difference.'

Leo squeezed her hand and smiled. 'He's a lucky man, your husband.'

Hattie squeezed his hand in return. 'Thank you, Leo. You're very kind.'

For a moment, their eyes locked together in a meaningful exchange. Then she realised that wasn't helpful. In her vulnerable emotional state, she shouldn't be indulging in significant glances or hand squeezes, no matter how innocently intended. She should go home at once, so she gathered up her belongings and buttoned her jacket.

'I never did hear what happened to you – after Victoria Station,' he said after draining his mug.

'Sorry, Leo, but I must go.'

'I'll come with you. My car's parked at the college too.'

As they walked back, Hattie told him about au pairing in Holland, the postgraduate course at Winchester and how she'd met Nick. Now, at least, all the gaps had been filled. Not telling Nick about Leo had been just a tiny deception at the time, but the trouble was, she was now living with the consequences.

As she drove home, she considered Nick's moodiness yet again. So she'd had a serious boyfriend before meeting him – so what? But as the relationship hadn't come to anything, why should he be so upset? Or maybe Nick was angry because she'd lied? Well, if *that* was the reason, he could hardly claim an unblemished past. Leo, on the other hand, seemed to have an endless capacity for patience and understanding. Did she now have the courage to confront Nick about the wretched letter and more to the point, would he let her?

After all the lies that had passed Hattie's lips, feigning sleep the following morning was easy. Nick had been in bed when she'd returned home the night before, so there was no inquisition on the theme of, 'What time do you call this? I was on the point of calling the emergency services!' Even after she heard his car pull away, she kept under the comforting weight of the duvet, languishing in the freedom of a day without bickering kids and staffroom politics. Jezebel, desperate for breakfast, however, had other ideas. She paced up and down, purring loudly and pausing every so often to nuzzle Hattie's cheek.

'Oh Jezebel,' she groaned. 'Give it a rest, do.' But by then, even Hattie was desperate for caffeine and calories. As she munched on banana chips, sunflower seeds, plump, juicy raisins and toasted oat flakes, she reviewed Leo's gentle lecture. He was right, of course. She was a wimp of the first order – not that he'd ever use that sort of language. The best bit of their conversation, however, was that he hadn't had second thoughts about their relationship, neither had there been the malicious meddling of a rival or pressure from the Marcellos back in Montelugia.

When Nick and Josh arrived home, a semblance of family life was maintained, although lips were still tightly sealed and the pressure-cooker tension hovered silently in the wings. Josh, however, seemed quite perky.

'Could anyone run me over to the Zed Shed tonight?' he asked, with no sign of a mumble. Nick and Hattie's mouths dropped open in disbelief. Had Josh finally emerged from his chrysalis?

'Zed Shed?' repeated Nick irritably. 'What's that when it's at home?'

'Isn't it some sort of night club or disco on one of the Aylesbury industrial estates?' put in Hattie.

'Yeah. Anyway, any chance of a lift over? I'm meeting someone.'

'And now he tells us! What, one of your loud-mouthed mates?' Nick asked suspiciously, remembering some of the less-savoury ones who'd been in trouble over illegal substances.

'No, Dad,' said Josh shyly. 'I'm meeting, um…'

'A girl!' giggled Hattie. 'Ooh, Josh, are you *really* meeting a girl?'

Josh blushed bright red but munched on regardless.

'What's she called then?' asked Hattie mischievously. 'Tell me and I'll run you in.'

'She's called Tamsin, as it happens.'

'Tamsin? Hmm, nice name. Any chance Tamsin's parents could drop you back – share the load, you know?'

'Sorry, Mum. She lives over Aston Clinton way, but when I've passed my test –'

'It'll be a ruddy miracle,' muttered Nick, rolling his eyes.

'When I've passed my test,' continued Josh, undeterred, 'it'll be different.'

'Not in my Astra, you won't,' warned Nick.

'Okay, Josh. I'll do it, as long as you clear up, load the dishwasher and leave the work surfaces *pristine!*'

'Oh great! Thanks, Mum.' A huge grin lit up his face as he grabbed a cloth and swabbed the draining board.

As it happened, it wasn't until almost eleven that Hattie met Tamsin. After dropping him off, she'd spent most of the evening speculating on the subject of multiple piercings and black lipstick and how she'd cope if the girl favoured nose chains. Knowing Josh's music and décor preferences, the possibility of a Goth girl seemed highly likely. She turned off the engine and sat a-quiver with pent-up excitement. Knots of teens and Josh look-alikes were clustered near the Zed Shed entrance, which was lit up like a Christmas tree, with rhythmic lightshow effects flashing from a multi-coloured neon sign. Hattie's instruction to Josh was to be outside at the agreed pick-up point at eleven on the dot, or future ferrying favours would be withdrawn. Josh had five minutes to keep her faith alive.

As she waited, her attention was drawn to the adjacent building. It was a smart new fitness centre, still open for business, even at that late hour. Why anyone would want to pound the treadmill or lift weights when any sane person would be reaching for slippers and hot chocolate was beyond Hattie's comprehension. Of course, Fliss swore by exercise and starvation diets and, as a result, managed to achieve a stick-like profile on a par with celebrity WAGS. Was Hattie jealous? Certainly not! Well, maybe just a smidgen. She glanced at the gleaming entrance as the occasional fitness freak trotted out, glowing with the effects of an evening's energetic workout, then switched her attention back to the Zed Shed. Still no sign of Chesney Junior. Glancing again to her right, she noticed a slender female in animated conversation with a tall, male companion. Although the pair was half in shadow, the female was unmistakable.

'Fliss,' she breathed in surprise, grabbing the door handle. She was outside on the pulsating tarmac when a second double-take was needed. Surely that wasn't Mark! He'd never struck her as fitness club material. Whoever he was had plenty to say for himself and Fliss was hanging on every word.

Hattie glanced at her watch, which showed only two minutes until Josh's deadline. Nevertheless, she set off in Fliss's direction. If Mark was making an attack on his middle-age flab, that would be truly newsworthy.

'Hi, Fliss. Is that you?' she called, emerging from the darkness of the Zed Shed car park. Fliss started in surprise and turned abruptly.

'Hat!' she exclaimed. 'What are you doing here?' The man quickly strode off – obviously not Mark.

'Doing my devoted mummy duty,' Hattie replied, 'and His Nibs is cutting it very fine.'

'Oops, poor Josh,' giggled Fliss. 'I'll leave you to it, Hat. I must be off.'

'I thought for a moment that was, er…' began Hattie, searching for sight of Fliss's erstwhile companion.

'Oh, just a chap who… er…' mumbled Fliss, fishing around for her keys.

'Not Mark then,' chuckled Hattie. 'Thought that was unlikely.'

'Oh yes. Given a choice between a bag of toffees or a week's free membership to this place, the toffees would always win. Oh, there's Josh!'

'Great! Spot on time too. Well, better be off. Note the girlfriend!' she whispered. 'Indeed,' replied Fliss conspiratorially and then set off to find her car.

Despite the lateness of the hour, Hattie was buoyant. Josh with a girlfriend was a different animal from the former monosyllabic version. He was cleaner too, although the possibility of providing a free taxi service was not so welcome. Fliss's late-night appearance at the fitness centre, however, gave her plenty to think about. Did sane-minded people *really* do that energetic stuff at such ungodly hours? Evidently, they did.

It was another wet Friday: a day when floors became slippery, mud-spattered health hazards and soggy socks steamed on classroom radiators; a day that Hattie was pleased to see the back of when it was finally time to go home. The merry ding-dong of the call-minder awaited her attention when she arrived. It was Brian, sounding unusually sombre.

'Ah, Mrs Chesney, thank you for returning my call,' he began.

'That's okay, Brian,' she chirruped brightly. Catching up with their house sale progress was far more pleasurable than marshalling muddy kids in muddy classrooms.

Brian cleared his throat noisily. 'I'm afraid there's been a setback with your house sale.'

'What sort of a setback?' asked Hattie apprehensively.

'Well, it's quite a serious problem actually: Mr Bainbridge has withdrawn his offer.'

'What? Why?' gasped Hattie angrily. She felt like adding, 'How dare he!'

'I'm afraid he didn't say,' apologised Brian, 'but don't fret, we'll organise more viewings straight away.'

'Oh, right,' murmured Hattie despondently. Just when she thought she'd finished with all the cleaning and tidying, the whole process was starting all over again. 'The trouble is, we've made an offer ourselves. What are we going to do?'

'Don't do anything yet. After all, we may find you another buyer this weekend.'

'Oh, I *do* hope so. It would be a shame to lose Knapp Cottage.'

'Now don't you worry, Mrs Chesney. We'll do our utmost to get things moving.' And he did. Before five o'clock, there were two viewings booked for the following day.

When Nick arrived home, the two promised viewings did little to offset the disappointment over the lost sale.

'Thought it was too good to be true,' he muttered dismissively, flinging down his briefcase.

'What do you mean?'

'Well, that woman he brought... I wasn't sure about her. In fact, I think she was just putting on a show with all those stupid remarks.'

'Really? Well *I* thought she was quite keen – she loved my clothes airer.'

'Lusting after your clothes airer is one thing,' Nick pointed out cynically, picking up his mug. 'Wanting to live here is entirely different.' He gulped the tea thirstily and then dumped his mug on the drainer.

'But why let two whole weeks go by? If she didn't like our house, why didn't she say so? It's most unfair,' remonstrated Hattie, upset by Nick's know-it-all attitude and their fickle buyers.

'Two weeks was the time it took to find another property. I'd have thought that was obvious.'

'And there we were, going off looking for a cottage, making an offer... And there's poor Mr and Mrs Dunbar with their plans for moving to Portugal.'

'As if *I* care,' remarked Nick dismissively, picking up his abandoned briefcase and stumping off.

Hattie was in despair. Despite Brian Samways's best efforts, the weekend brought no hopeful development of any sort. On Monday morning, the *Sold, Subject to Contract* board was amended, announcing to the world in general that the Chesneys were back to where they'd started. By Wednesday, however, Nick had reached a significant decision. For over a week, he'd had an uncomfortable nagging thought buzzing around his mind like an annoying bluebottle. Although he wasn't big on confrontation, he realised the best solution was to take action. Sometimes, leaving things unsaid and questions unasked only made matters worse. He'd decided to make his move at lunchtime, and maybe even grab a bite to eat in town rather than sit around with the same crowd in the staff canteen.

'You're off early today,' remarked Madge, looking even more severe in a recently shorn and tightly permed hairstyle, which did nothing to flatter her square-jawed face and strong features.

'Just a few errands, Madge,' he replied airily, refusing to discuss his private affairs. 'So if you feel the need to catch up on your belly dancing in your lunch break, you've the whole office to yourself. Better keep your kit on though; we don't want to hear of any heart attacks!'

Madge glowered back frostily. She'd lost half a stone since starting the classes and was proud of it.

By the time Nick was within a few yards of Mia Casa, he started to have second thoughts. Could he keep his cool? Slowly, he sidled up to the window, pretending to study the houses on offer. Peering between the display, he checked to see who was there and was pleased to note Rebecca Vaudin at her desk, gazing at her computer screen with great concentration. The sight of her pretty features furrowed in thought was all he needed, and a gentle sigh escaped his lips. Almost as if she'd sensed his gaze, Rebecca suddenly looked up and blinked. There was nothing for it but to go in.

'Can I help you?' asked Rebecca, smiling in response to his obvious glance of appraisal. Despite the cool March day, she was wearing a close-fitting, V-neck sweater that left very little to the imagination. The animal instincts in Nick reacted promptly and a slight blush appeared on Rebecca's cheeks, aware that his eyes were locked onto her cleavage.

'Er... um... I need to see someone,' replied Nick, meeting her gaze.

'Mr Allanby's available,' she suggested helpfully.

Ah, thought Nick, the elusive Mr Allanby! However, it was evident that he was cloistered away in a private office. Would he ever meet this so-called property dynamo?

'Thank you, but it's Mr Marcello I need to see,' replied Nick, hoping he'd made his request sound as business-like as possible.

'Signor Marcello is due back from a viewing very soon, if you don't mind waiting,' said Rebecca, fluttering her eyelashes, before turning her attention to her screen.

'Er, that's fine by me.' Nick found a chair that was conveniently placed close to Rebecca's desk. As she navigated from the page in front of her by a deft click of the mouse, her earrings swung gently and sparkled in the glow of the down-lighters. Nick studied the beads and then admired the gentle curve of her neck. She paused for a moment, once more meeting Nick's gaze.

'There are more comfy seats in the interview area,' she suggested, indicating the back section of the office that Nick remembered from his first visit.

'No, this is fine,' he assured her with a grin, 'but don't let me stop you working.'

'Well, there's not a lot to do at the moment actually. I was just checking on holiday deals,' she admitted guiltily.

'Business quiet, is it?'

'Oh no, it's going well, but Wednesdays tend to be quiet – half day closing and all that.'

'Oh, I see.' He unzipped his jacket and stretched out his legs lazily. 'Tell me, do *you* ever have a chance to go out and conduct viewings or does Mr Allanby keep you chained to your desk all day long?' Nick chuckled, enjoying his attempt at light relief.

'Chained to my desk? He's not into bondage,' replied Rebecca stiffly.

'Well, of course not!' flustered Nick in confusion. 'Er... um... I didn't mean to imply...'

Rebecca giggled, seeing Nick's embarrassment. 'Just teasing,' she told him. 'No, we all take a turn. We work as a team here.'

'Glad to hear it,' replied Nick, already imagining her shapely form ascending stairs, followed by keen potential buyers. 'I believe you know my work colleague, Madge, a short, er... solidly built lady with a rather severe haircut. She goes to your dancing class at the college – full of eastern promise and all that!' he said with a chuckle.

Rebecca blushed again, ever so slightly. 'Yes, that's right. So you and Madge work together do you?'

'Well, not exactly *together*. We just happen to share the same office space. So, how did you start belly dancing?'

Rebecca swung round in her chair, stretched her arms and then cupped them behind her neck. 'Ah,' she sighed, 'the same old question... Well, it happened by accident actually. I was on holiday in Turkey and of course, it's part of the scene there, especially in the bars and nightclubs. You could even have a few free lessons at the hotel, so my friend Jess dared me. It was just a laugh, but I rather took to it,' she giggled fetchingly.

'Bully for Jess!' put in Nick and then regretted showing his age. People didn't use phrases like that any longer. 'But didn't you have to learn a lot more for the college course?'

'Well naturally, but I've been belly dancing for a few years now. It's a great way to keep fit.'

'Yes, I can see... I mean, I can imagine it is,' chuckled Nick, 'what with all that wiggling of the hips. I can't imagine old Madge shaking her chassis though; she's built more for striding than swaying.'

Rebecca was saved from making further comments by the sound of the door opening and a cool blast of air.

'Ah, Signor Marcello,' she said, turning to Leo, 'this gentleman's waiting to see you.'

265

Leo could only see the back of Nick's head and so he drew level with a welcoming smile before realising who he was. There was a sense of déjà vu.

'Oh, Mr Chesney… would you like to come to the interview area?' Leo asked politely, his smile fading fast, although their last encounter at the college had been amicable enough.

Nick got to his feet, notions of belly dancing now replaced by a sense of foreboding. Leo led the way and sat down at the desk, inviting Nick to take the soft leather chair facing him. Nick hesitated, looking back to where he'd just been waiting and estimated the likelihood of their conversation being overheard.

'Er… is there somewhere more private?' he asked, looking and feeling distinctly uncomfortable.

'Is it really necessary?' asked Leo. 'Greg, Rebecca and I all work together and −'

'Well, I'd prefer it, if you don't mind. It's not about selling houses.'

'I see.' Leo pursed his lips, pushed back his chair and indicated a rear office that led from the interview area, separated by a glass partition. 'Now, what can I do for you?' he asked politely, once they'd both sat down.

'It's about my wife,' stated Nick boldly.

'And?'

'I think you know why,' insisted Nick frowning.

'Please explain, Mr Chesney, and then we can be clear why you've taken the time to come here.'

Nick stared at Leo, trying to work out if the man was being sarcastic or just plain clever. 'You wrote a letter to her − a love letter. Don't deny it,' said Nick, speaking as levelly as possible. 'You were planning to run off with her.'

The immediate look of utter disbelief on Leo's face gave Nick the scent of victory and galvanised him for his second attack − his trump card. 'I saw it with my own eyes!'

'What?' gasped Leo, incredulously. 'Run off with your wife?

266

Mr Chesney, whatever gave you the idea that I was planning anything so unlikely or ridiculous?'

'Because it was all there in the letter – the tickets, the villa, the whole sneaky plan,' Nick snarled, wishing he'd brought the evidence to thrust under the man's nose.

'What?' Leo shook his head in disbelief at Nick Chesney's skewed interpretation of the ill-fated letter.

'Oh, so you're denying it are you? Well, perhaps I'd better come back with it tomorrow and we can continue our conversation then,' he snapped, starting to leave.

'Wait, Mr Chesney. Please let me explain. I think we need to establish the facts. There has been a complete misunderstanding,' protested Leo, also springing to his feet.

'Misunderstanding?' echoed Nick sarcastically. 'The only misunderstanding was that my marriage was safe from unwanted predators.'

Leo sighed and shook his head again. 'Please sit down, Mr Chesney, and allow me to explain. Do allow me that, at least.'

Nick hovered awkwardly then sat down, his confidence fading fast.

'Mr Chesney, I knew your wife many years ago. We were friends.'

'Friends?' laughed Nick unpleasantly. 'You think I'm stupid? That letter didn't strike me as a chummy little note between friends, so don't you try and pretend that's all it was.'

'We were good friends at university and yes, we were very fond of each other; in fact, I'm sure we loved each other.' Leo was doing his best to stay unruffled.

'At university? So this has been going on behind my back for years, has it?'

'Certainly not!'

'But that letter said you had tickets and a villa and then some stuff about some girl called Alex running off with a phone number. Jealous was she? Some floosy was she? Or your wife?' spat Nick, refusing to believe there'd been any misunderstanding on his part, other than being unaware of a whole secret area of his wife's past.

'No, no, no,' breathed Leo, shaking his head, 'you don't understand. It was about something that happened *twenty-six* years ago. Hattie and I missed meeting up at Victoria Station when we'd planned to go and spend some time on my parents' estate in Tuscany.'

'Oh yes?' Nick commented suspiciously.

'Yes, that's the complete truth, I promise you. Hattie and I lost touch and hadn't seen each other until the day I turned up to value your house. It was a shock for both of us to meet so unexpectedly after such a long time. I started to explain what had gone wrong on that day.'

'I *knew* there was something funny going on in the utility room… the two of you in there with the door closed. And there was Hattie acting the innocent too.'

'I started to explain,' began Leo patiently, once more, 'but there wasn't the time to go into everything. In the end I decided to write the note.' He leaned back in his chair, his face impassive.

'And this Alex?' challenged Nick.

'Was a man, not a girlfriend or anything else like that,' replied Leo patiently. 'We shared a flat together in Birmingham. He didn't run off with the phone number either. In his frenzy to clear up, one of my bags was thrown out by accident.'

'Oh right… I see,' said Nick, digesting this new piece of information. 'So I suppose Hattie thought you'd stood her up.'

'Something like that,' replied Leo.

They sat in silence, having reached stalemate. Then Nick recalled meeting him at the college, the sighting at The Feisty Ferret and Mark Tarrier's account of his meeting with Marcello after the evening class.

'So you're telling me that you only saw my wife when you came for the valuation?' he probed.

'It was the first time since our student days, Mr Chesney.'

'And since then?'

Leo hesitated, choosing his words very carefully. 'Well, I have been aware of your wife at the college on a couple of occasions. I'm tutoring a language course on Wednesdays, but I had no idea that Hattie was doing a course there until I happened to see her one evening.'

'Hmm,' mumbled Nick, considering the man's reply and trying to decide how much of it he was prepared to believe. 'So she doesn't know about your letter then,' he reflected.

'Mr Chesney, you have already admitted to having it in your possession. Why don't you speak to your wife about it?'

'I just might,' replied Nick thoughtfully, getting to his feet once more. 'She's either a scheming bitch or —'

'This house move,' Leo cut in, 'was it *your* idea?'

'No, it was hers actually,' conceded Nick.

'There you are then, Mr Chesney. She'd hardly suggest something like that if she wasn't committed to you.'

'I suppose so,' Nick sighed in resignation, 'she's always on about it.' He looked at his watch and then turned to go. 'Right, I'll be off then.'

'I hope your move goes well, Mr Chesney,' said Leo, assuming his property agent's role once more.

'Well, it's not looking so good at the moment. The buyer's withdrawn his offer.'

'Oh, I'm sorry to hear that,' replied Leo sympathetically. 'If there's anything we can do to speed your move, please do give us a call.'

Nick narrowed his eyes and studied Leo's expression.

'I'm sure Greg would be more than happy to handle your house sale,' Leo added quickly.

'Oh right… might just consider that or your other colleague, Miss Vaudin, of course,' Nick replied, convinced that he was now emerging from the meeting in the stronger position. Considering the possibilities of more contact with the lovely Rebecca cheered him as he made his way to the door. Lost in thought, imagining her dressed in belly dancing garb, he narrowly avoided colliding with the girl herself, who was also leaving.

'Oh, sorry… miles away,' he apologised, enjoying the proximity of Rebecca and the musky aroma of her perfume. 'On your lunch break are you?' he asked, following behind and closing the door as he went. 'Perhaps you can recommend somewhere I can get a decent sandwich. I usually end up in the staff canteen.'

'Well, I usually pop into Maggie's.'

'Maggie's? Don't think I know the place. Are you going there now?'

'Well yes,' she replied with a twinkle.

'Is it okay if I tag along?'

'Sure.'

Nick grinned to himself as he fell into step beside her.

'Did your meeting with Signor Marcello go well?' she asked. 'I think you'll find our commission rates very competitive.'

'Yeah, very competitive. Mia Casa might well be getting our business if things don't change in the next week or so.'

Rebecca led the way down a narrow alley and then across a wide, cobbled square, which was surrounded by a mixture of period properties and bland, modern buildings. Maggie's had smart, olive-green paintwork and matching window boxes. Inside, there was jolly green bunting strung across the bay window, after the fashion of the trendier eating places. Nick was surprised he'd never noticed the place before, but considering his usual routine, maybe it wasn't so surprising

'Very tasty!' affirmed Nick enthusiastically, taking in the tempting array of baps, ciabattas, sandwiches, cakes and pastries, as well as homemade soup, pots of salad and bowls of fresh fruit. There was also a steaming coffee machine, which filled the air with a delicious aroma of freshly roasted beans.

'What a treat! Let me buy you a coffee,' he offered, reaching for his wallet. 'That's if you've time to stay.'

'Oh, well, that's very kind.' She smiled gratefully.

They queued to place their orders and Nick was soon chewing

on his ciabatta and studying the ring on Rebecca's left hand. 'Beautiful ring you're wearing; exquisite.'

'Oh, thank you, Mr... er...'

'Call me Nick.'

'Thank you... Nick,' she giggled. 'We both agreed on diamonds, although Darren thought white gold would look the business. I wanted a ring like my mum's.'

'Must have set him back a packet,' observed Nick thoughtfully.

Rebecca stretched out her left hand and gazed proudly at the diamond cluster. 'Well, he can afford it. He's the top rep in the region, selling office supplies. His Christmas bonus paid for my ring.'

'So, have you fixed a date for the wedding?'

Rebecca paused and sighed. 'Well, not yet. We're saving up for it, but it might take a while and we haven't decided where to have the ceremony. Darren's set his heart on a beach in Cuba,' she explained as she pushed crumbs round her plate.

'Wow! That's a bit different.'

'Hmm,' Rebecca agreed hesitantly, 'but I wanted something really traditional, for my parents' sake I suppose. They wouldn't think we were properly married if it happened on a sandy beach with no bells or cute choir boys.'

'Oh dear. It sounds like one of those episodes of *Don't Tell the Bride,*' chuckled Nick. 'Well, people can get married anywhere they like these days.'

'Yes, I know,' she sighed. 'It's just that Darren and I have such different ideas. I hope we can sort it out soon.' For a few moments, she toyed with a piece of lettuce and her usually bubbly exterior became reflective.

'If your Darren has any sense, he'll forget about Cuba and book the church, especially with the prospect of such a lovely bride.'

Rebecca blushed at Nick's words, which were accompanied by a wink.

'Perhaps I'll forget I saw that,' she giggled, picking up her mug.

'I'm sure it'll work out for Darren and me. Probably too many TV programmes putting silly ideas in his head.'

'It happens,' agreed Nick. He glanced at his watch. 'My God, is that the time? Well, I'd better dash and see if I can catch the trading estate shuttle bus.' He zipped his jacket and stood up to go. 'Must try Maggie's again... Maybe I'll even see you in here?'

'Maybe,' replied Rebecca, opening her eyes wide and then returning the wink.

From a table in the far corner, Celia Halverson happened to look up from her prawn and avocado salad and caught a glimpse of Nick's profile as he left his seat. She craned her neck to find out who he was speaking to. Might it be Hattie or one of his work colleagues? The blonde girl at his table was certainly not the former and possibly not the latter, because she remained there after Nick had left.

'Well I never!' she murmured under her breath, her eyes wide in undisguised interest.

'What's that, Celia?' asked Hilda Makepeace, a morsel of pavlova on its way to her waiting lips.

'That's Nick Chesney isn't it?'

'Where?'

'Just at the door. I'm sure it's him. But who was his companion?'

Hilda skewed round in her seat and peered over her specs in the direction of Celia's gaze. 'Where was he sitting, dear?' she whispered, the scent of intrigue reaching her nostrils.

'Just over by that monstrous cheese plant... with a blonde girl.'

Hilda pushed her chair back to get a better view, the pavlova momentarily forgotten. 'Really?' she replied with a smirk. 'And Nick Chesney was at her table? Well I never!'

'Oh dear,' murmured Celia, full of regret. She had known Hilda long enough to appreciate her appetite for gossip and inability to keep it to herself. 'It was probably all very innocent... or I may have been mistaken,' she improvised, trying to sound dismissive.

'Not necessarily, Celia. Although I wasn't really paying attention, I *was* aware of a couple sitting down at that table about ten minutes ago, when I went to fetch another napkin. They came in together, that I *do* know, but I didn't take much notice of them. These specs aren't any good for those sorts of distances.'

'Oh dear,' groaned Celia, spearing a piece of avocado. 'I do hope there's nothing unsavoury going on. Hattie and Nick are such a devoted couple.' She shook her head, admonishing herself for speaking her thoughts aloud. 'Now, Hilda,' she warned her friend, 'there's absolutely *no* need to mention this to anyone – especially not to Hattie. Nick was probably having a working lunch and if he chooses to have it in Maggie's, there's nothing wrong in that. Whether he decides to tell Hattie about his lunchtime arrangements is up to him.'

'Yes, dear,' murmured Hilda with a self-satisfied smile. 'I'm sure you're right.'

12

Nick arrived home that evening, whistling, humming and oblivious to Hattie's frazzled state.

'Is this my husband I see before me?' she intoned sceptically.

'Ah, the thought of bidding a fond farewell to Madge and co in three weeks' time doesn't half give a chap a lift,' he chuckled.

'Lucky old you,' she sighed. 'I've worked my socks off today, scrubbing, dusting, tidying and baking. Then Mr and Mrs Couldn't-Care-Less phoned up ten minutes before they were due to arrive – ten minutes, I ask you! – to say they'd just put in an offer for some place in Thame, so they wouldn't be coming after all.'

'Never mind, Hat. Can't win 'em all,' he quipped, picking up the local free paper and wandering out of the kitchen, still humming.

The thought of Knapp Cottage being snapped up by cash buyers exercised Hattie's mind greatly. Nick, of course, had made it perfectly plain that he'd be happy to settle for a smart, modern box-of-a-house with plumbing in all the right places. No wonder he was so cheerful, thought Hattie mutinously, as she drove to college for the penultimate patchwork class. However, a couple of hours spent learning the finer points of joining techniques were a welcome change from Nick's moods swings.

*

'Now, ladies,' announced Zena after her appraisal of their home-work. 'Gather round while Marigold explains how to assemble your work.'

The class obediently took up their positions and silence descended as Marigold prepared to launch into her introduction.

Deep inside Hattie's jeans pocket, her mobile hummed and bleeped into life.

'Oops, sorry,' she muttered, seeing Marigold's lips pursed in disapproval. She pulled out the offending article and glanced at the display:

Must c u urgently, Leo.

What could he want? Hattie surreptitiously edged back from her front row position and quickly texted back a reply: *Bar on corner after class, ok?*

Trying to follow Marigold's patient demonstration began to prove very difficult.

'Are you feeling unwell, dear?' Cynthia whispered, noting Hattie's pale appearance and look of confusion.

'No... er, nothing really... My son's idea of a joke I think,' she improvised quietly. 'I'll sort him out when I get home.' She tucked away the phone and forced her attention back to Marigold.

'It's very important to lay out all the patches first and swap them around until you're happy with the arrangement. And *do* try to achieve a balance of colour,' she emphasised, indicating one of her own quilts, which was draped over a tall display board. The class murmured and nodded like a flock of obedient hens.

'On a quilt this size,' interjected Zena, 'you'll need to cut sixteen cornerstone pieces.'

'Indeed,' agreed Marigold, smiling at her friend, 'but do remember not to choose a fabric that's too busy.'

The class murmured and shook their heads in unison, apart from Hattie, whose mind was full of Leo Marcello. Back at their worktables, they measured and sliced cornerstones and sashings, while keeping up a flow of companionable chatter. When the classroom's clock hands approached finishing time, Hattie was ready for a quick exit. As she scooted down the corridor, safely away from Cynthia's prying eyes, she read Leo's reply:

Ok c u soon.

His urgent need to see her was alarming and her heart was pounding rapidly as she reached the corner of Market Row. A quick glance inside confirmed that the clientele, as before, was safely anonymous. As far as she could recall, Fliss had another Cornwall visit planned sometime soon and Mark was due to fly off to Sweden. It would be sod's law if either of them turned up and caught her in a cosy tête-à-tête. Now act casually, she reminded herself. She took a deep breath, pushed open the door and headed straight for the table they'd occupied the week before.

'May I take your order?' asked a spotty youth who had slouched out from behind the counter, pad in hand.

'Not quite yet. Just waiting for a friend,' replied Hattie briskly, hoping the lad wasn't one of Josh's mates from college. There was certainly something vaguely familiar about him. She drummed her fingers on the table and willed her heart to slow down, but she seemed to have no control over that part of her body.

A gentle thud signalled activity at the door. Yes, it was Leo, smiling and looking as devastating as usual.

'Let *me* buy coffee this time,' she offered, springing to her feet.

'But it was *my* idea to meet,' he protested softly, joining her at the counter. A tray of muffins sat prominently at the front of the counter under a glass dome, distracting Hattie by their mouth-wateringly indulgent proportions. A wistful sigh escaped her lips.

'No, *I* insist,' she replied, trying to decide which one of the beauties in front of her was destined to add some much-needed comfort to her lurching stomach.

'And *I* insist,' whispered Leo, placing a hand on her shoulder. 'Put your purse away.'

'Very well,' she sighed, wondering whether Leo's offer included anything more sustaining than a regular Americano. It seemed greedy to take advantage of his generous offer. However, a particularly chunky lump of chocolate was cheekily winking at her over its pleated white paper case.

'And a muffin?' added Leo, his voice much closer than before.

'Hmm, that would be heaven,' she sighed. 'This nice plump chocolate one here,' she added, pointing to the one in question, 'would go down a treat.'

Seated back at their table, she watched his every move, filled with a mixture of anticipation and dread.

'Why did you want to see me?' she asked nervously, as soon as they were sipping coffee and tucking into muffins. Leo brushed away a tray crumb from the corner of his mouth and then leaned on the table, his fingers intertwined.

'Your husband came to see me today,' he began quietly.

'What!' Hattie exclaimed, dropping her muffin in shock. It caught the edge of the plate and rolled back into the centre. 'When? Why?'

'Because of the letter... he as good as accused me of planning an elopement.'

'He did *what?*' Hattie breathed, aghast at Leo's words. 'I don't believe it!' She picked up her mug with trembling hands and sipped the steaming liquid tentatively.

'He admitted he had the letter, but it was obvious that he'd completely misunderstood it. He thought the tickets and the villa referred to a plan we'd cooked up recently.'

'The tickets?'

'Sorry, Hattie. Of course, you've not seen the letter.'

'No, *that's* the problem,' she hissed, hoping she'd not been overheard by the bar staff, especially the one with rampant acne.

'Never mind,' Leo sighed, placing a hand over the one she'd been waving about wildly a few moments before.

'So what did *you* say? I really can't imagine Nick in confrontational mode, especially with a relative stranger.'

'I told him we'd been going out at university and that we'd lost touch when our plans went wrong.' He peeled the paper case from his blueberry muffin and tore off a hunk. Hattie picked out a chunk of chocolate and popped it on her tongue. Suddenly strains of 'Lady in Red' could be heard through the speakers and their eyes met for a brief moment. Hattie remembered when it had been played at The Feisty Ferret and how she'd felt that evening.

'I told him that I'd started to tell you when I came for the valuation,' continued Leo, after a significant pause. 'Then decided to write a letter to explain what had happened.'

'And how did he react?'

'Oh, he seemed to accept it, but then he wanted to know if I'd seen you since, because of that time at the college, I suppose. Remember that evening?'

'How could I forget?' Hattie gulped guiltily. 'There was I flying at you like a deranged harpy!'

'Don't worry, Hattie. You weren't to know,' he assured her. 'I had to admit that I'd seen you at college a couple of times and left it at that. In other words, I lied for you.'

'But you did it for the *right* reason,' she protested. 'Nick doesn't need to know it took so many failed attempts to sort out our unfortunate past.'

'I'm sure you're right,' agreed Leo, reaching across the table again and squeezing the hand that wasn't dealing with the remains of a chocolate muffin.

'Most definitely,' sighed Hattie, sure that her conscience was now absolved of any duplicity. 'I thought there was something different about him when he came home this evening. He was humming and whistling and said it was because he was looking forward to his new job, or rather leaving his current one.'

'Well, there you are! It sounds as if our talk has cleared the air.' He smiled reassuringly at her and took another mouthful of muffin.

'Hmm,' agreed Hattie, 'but to think he suspected we were about to run off together. How crazy! No wonder he was in such a filthy mood for so long.'

Their eyes locked in another look of the deep and meaningful variety, recalling the steamy nights of passion of their student days. Leo shook his head and withdrew his hand while Hattie spooned the remaining sprinkles from her mug.

'I'll need to be off home now, Leo. Good mood or not, Nick might get uppity if I'm back late, even if I told him I was having coffee with a fellow student.'

'Your friend Cynthia, I presume?' teased Leo, getting to his feet and buttoning his overcoat.

'The very same,' giggled Hattie, grabbing her work folder and winding her scarf around her neck.

As before, they walked back to the college car park together and Hattie was feeling calm and relaxed until *it* happened. They'd paused as she was fishing out her car keys, when Leo suddenly leaned forward and kissed her lightly on the forehead.

'Leo!' she gasped, startled by his display of emotion. 'Lady in Red' had a lot to answer for, and Leo's kiss seemed to kick into life all the feelings that were waking from hibernation.

'That song... It reminded me...,' he faltered.

'Me too... Oh, Leo,' she moaned softly, sinking forward onto his chest. Then she was aware of a hand on her back, stroking it gently.

'I'm sorry, Hattie,' he whispered, 'I remembered how it was and just couldn't help myself.'

She relaxed into his embrace, enjoying the aroma of his cologne. This shouldn't be happening, she told herself, but allowed the moments to pass anyway. Nick hadn't been so hot in the kisses and cuddles department just recently. In fact, she couldn't remember the slightest display of affection since their weekend away.

'Oh, Leo,' she moaned again, her body suddenly seized with a powerful desire. She tilted her head to meet the gaze of his 'come-hither' eyes. A second later, their lips touched, briefly at first and then in a long, lingering kiss that set her head spinning. 'Red alert! Red alert!' screamed a voice inside, but Hattie was past caring. This was what she'd longed for, ever since Leo had turned up with his clipboard on that Thursday morning in January, although it had taken her this long to admit it.

'Oh, Hattie,' he breathed guiltily when they drew apart. 'I'm sorry. Go home to your husband… It was wrong of me… Please forgive me.' He turned away abruptly, setting off for the far side of the car park.

'Leo!' called Hattie tearfully, her body shaking, but all she could hear was his retreating footsteps. Every move, every glance, suggested that he still loved her and every fibre in her body seemed to agree. She unlocked the door and sank into the seat.

'Oh God, what a mess,' she whimpered forlornly.

What do you do when you arrive home after a moment of wicked passion with an old flame? In Hattie's case, it was a quick dash upstairs and straight to bed, in an attempt to feign total exhaustion. She was good at this. When Nick followed a few minutes later, her slow, regular breathing gave no clue that she was pretending. However, in the night, when she found sleep impossible, she'd re-run the car park embrace dozens of times and guiltily enjoyed every single one. Then her imagination had strayed into no-man's land and pictured a full-blown affair, glamorously illicit and abandoned, like the perfect ending to *Brief Encounter*. Just the thought of it gave her little shivers of pleasure. What would Nick say if he could read her thoughts? But when she tried to picture his disapproving face, it was replaced by Leo's smouldering eyes

The arrival of a damp and gloomy morning did nothing to restore Hattie to a state of calm. Furtively, she peered from the edge of the duvet as she heard Nick noisily yanking open drawers, and then snapped her eyes shut. It was the rattling of the drawers that prompted her to think of the letter and where she might find it – his underwear drawer! Of course! Why hadn't she thought of that before now? Just to see it would resolve some of the frustration that had been quietly building up over the last few weeks.

After what seemed an age, the sound of doors slamming announced the departure of Josh and Nick in quick succession.

'It has to be here,' she muttered, rummaging through the muddle of socks, hankies and miscellaneous items, until, at the very back, there was a rustle of paper. Eagerly, she pulled it out and unfolded the single sheet. Of course, she knew the substance of it, but the opening sentence made her sigh with pleasure. Yes, he had *truly* loved her and wanted her to know he hadn't had doubts about their relationship. It was just as he'd told her during their clandestine car ride. Had it not been for that moment of reckless abandon the night before, she would have now felt relieved and free to enjoy the future, wherever it took her.

'Oh, Leo,' she sighed, shaking her head and wondering why she hadn't given him a sharp slap round the face, rather than succumbing to his Latin charms. The trouble was, she reminded her pricking conscience, her wifely loyalty *had* been tested to its limits by Nick's relentless moodiness. There was only so much a girl could stand, no matter how pristine her twenty-six years of marriage. Admittedly, there'd been the cheeky student who'd pinched her bottom and then cornered her in the stockroom. Nevertheless, that was ages ago and he wasn't her type at all – gorgeous in his classroom gear, but fresh off the sports field, he exuded aromas that were a real turn-off. Then there was the dishy TV repair man, who had a smile that melted matronly hearts at ten paces, but who turned out to be in a confirmed gay relationship – not that Hattie would have indulged in more than some gentle flirting. In fact, her fidelity had never been seriously tested in all those years, not until now.

She replaced the letter in its hiding place, realising she'd have to conquer her inner turmoil or her whole world might come crashing down. Could she dare confide in Fliss? She fished out her phone and started to tap in the number. No, poor Fliss had enough to deal with, she decided, and jabbed the 'off' button. What about Celia? Definitely not. This was *not* the sort of subject to share with her. Recommendations for builders and handymen were one thing; matrimonial problems were quite another. Maybe Sally at school? Hattie wandered over to the window and gazed vacantly out onto the road where a car had just pulled up next door. The world seemed to be up and going about its business, but here was Hattie Chesney still in her nightie and in danger of losing a grip on her life. In other times and cultures, this might signal a spot of self-flagellation or a dose of the hair shirt – it *was* Lent after all. Maybe even a bit of self-denial on the chocolate front? No, she decided, that would be too depressing for words.

Dropping her gaze to Jezebel, who was yowling for her breakfast, Hattie noticed, with mortification, an accumulation of fluff on the bedroom carpets. She must have missed this room completely in her feverish cleaning for the fickle viewers the day before. Perhaps it was a good thing they had decided not to turn up after all. By a process of elimination, that also meant that the en-suite had been missed as well, *and* the full basket of dirty washing. What was happening to her? The keen-eyed cleaning twosome on TV would have a field day in the Chesney household now that her attention was being hijacked by a certain Signor Marcello. A few hours spent with the vac and duster would hopefully be punishment enough to purge lustful thoughts from her fertile imagination. However, as she thirstily downed a mug of tea, following a long spell of cleaning, Leo's dark, smouldering eyes still haunted her. The gloom outside had now darkened by a few shades to a threatening muddy purple, but Hattie zipped herself into her oldest padded jacket and set to with fork, trowel and secateurs. Gardening, however, with zero opportunity for conversation, was even more useless in banishing Leo from her thoughts.

'Hell's bells!' she cursed, jabbing at an obstinate dandelion root. 'Blasted man!' The roughly severed root came away in her hand, leaving the rest lodged firmly underground, ready to put in another appearance of shoots, leaves and flowers when her back was turned. 'Damn you, Leo!' she muttered, flinging the roots into her bucket. 'Why didn't you stay in Italy? Why did you have to pitch up in Aylesbury Vale of all places?'

A sharp gust of wind swept across the garden, disturbing a scattering of crisp, brown, beech leaves that had been freshly dislodged from a nearby hedge by its new young shoots. Jezebel's head pushed open the cat-flap, followed by the rest of her lithe body, and she started to pursue the leaves with glee, pouncing and then batting them with her paws. Her appearance signalled feeding time, that was certain, so Hattie wearily struggled to her feet and cleared up ready for her next chores. All day she'd tried to convince herself that the Leo effect could be easily ignored, but who was she fooling? It was no good; she'd fallen for him all over again – totally, utterly, completely.

'That's all I need,' groaned Hattie, as a tractor and trailer lumbered out into the road ahead. She was already running ten minutes late, and the prospect of a rescheduled day with Norma's little darlings without time to draw breath did nothing for her confidence. In the night she'd slipped in and out of fitful sleep, her fertile imagination conjuring up variations on the guilty car park scenario.

'You forgot to sign your last supply form,' Gail had told her when she'd called the day before. 'Could you pop into the office first thing so I can deal with it straight away?'

'It's eight twenty eight, and almost time for the news headlines,' a chirpy voice on the car radio reminded her.

'Oh kippers!' Hattie cursed, grinding her teeth. The tractor lumbered on along the narrow country road, spattering clods of mud as it went. Feverishly she reviewed her instructions for the day and hoped that Val Tribbeck, the trusty teaching assistant, wouldn't have fallen foul of some nasty bug.

'Phew, you're cutting it fine,' remarked Gail, looking more flustered than usual, as Hattie flew into her office, pen in hand.

'Don't state the obvious,' she muttered, 'my patience is down to the reserve tank and if you spotted a steam cloud over the ring road, it came from my ears!'

'There's one or two things I was going to-' began Gail.

'Later Gail,' Hattie gasped. 'It'll be red alert down in Early Years any second.'

She dashed into the corridor, wishing there'd been time to grab a quick coffee, when an apparition in Harris tweed blocked her way.

'Leaving us soon, I hear, Mrs Chesney?' said Angus with a half-hearted smile.

Hattie stopped in her tracks, remembering her request for a reference. She nodded mutely, imagining the scene on the far side of the complex. 'Well, we'll see how you get on today,' he said, a sinister glimmer visible under his bushy brows.

As she rushed through the building there seemed to be an unusual air of feverish activity. Something was afoot. In Norma's room Val Tribbeck was busy with worksheets.

'Oh Hattie,' she gasped, looking unusually pale and harrassed. 'It's Ofsted! We've had half an hour's warning!'

Hattie's anxiety level cranked up a couple of gears. 'Hide the scissors, quick,' she hissed, wondering if someone in a suit was about to appear.

'No can do. We're down for cut and stick. I think Ofsted would smell a rat if we ditched it. It's down on the plans.'

Hattie rolled her eyes and sighed. 'Okay Val, that's the bell. Better fetch the little angels, and point out Lorretta will you? I need all the help I can get!'

'So far, so good,' she whispered to Val as break approached. No wet pants, no fights, no tears and – fingers crossed – no black marks on the Ofsted report, thought Hattie nervously. A formidable woman loitered by the coat pegs with a clipboard, making notes.

'Miss! Miss! Look what I found!' shrieked Rooney Cornfield, rushing up with a clump of hair.

Hattie stared at the clump in alarm. 'Yours? No, silly me,' she chuckled nervously, surveying the lad's shaven head.

'Gilbert's I fink, miss,' he announced proudly, wiping his snotty nose on his sleeve. 'Found it in the Wendy 'ouse.'

'Gilbert's?' gasped Hattie, recalling the class guinea pig. It had to be Lorretta.

'Scissor alert in the Wendy house, Mrs T,' she hissed urgently. Val, however, was grappling with the children's snack boxes.

'Right, sit down Rooney,' said Hattie as calmly as she could. She strode over to the Wendy house, her heart hammering wildly. It was time to put an end to Lorretta's fun.

'Out of there at once, young lady, and bring Gilbert with you!' she ordered severely.

'Is this what you're looking for?' The curtain parted and a permed head appeared. The inspector had beaten her to it. Hattie gulped in horror, any hope of a reference rapidly diminishing. One hand grasped a squirming Lorretta, while the other cradled a quivering Gilbert.

'I've made a note,' the woman warned as she passed the creature over. 'A career in hairdressing maybe?' The inspector led Lorretta back to where the rest of her classmates were devouring their snacks, and then left.

'Right young lady,' said Hattie sternly 'there's to be no more snipping or I'll be telling Mummy. You wouldn't like that, would you?'

'No, miss,' replied Lorretta, her bottom lip quivering. 'Mummy says naughty girls have big smacks an' no telly.'

'So, you'll be a good girl now, won't you?' Lorretta nodded her head vigorously.

Compared with Lorretta and the scissors, the rest of the day was a breeze.

Mick Hayhurst steered the elderly couple out of the front door and raised his eyes to heaven. It was Saturday and the third viewing of the day, and the couple's repeated tut-tutting and head-shaking indicated that an offer was as likely as Nick giving up football for Lent.

'Too many stairs,' complained the man.

'Try a bungalow,' muttered Hattie fiercely under her breath.

'I don't like that lilac,' sneered the woman, on entering the sitting room.

Nick simply kept his head down, mainly in the weekend sports pages. Hattie's TV ban did nothing to help his temper.

'Lovely house!' another couple had enthused earlier, then admitted that theirs wasn't yet on the market. Time-wasters, Hattie thought despondently.

In church the following morning, Hilda Makepeace made a beeline for Hattie in the mêlée following the service.

'Coffee, dear?' she asked with an unusually bright smile.

'Yes, thanks,' Hattie replied, scanning the pale offerings on Hilda's tray. Someone was evidently rationing the grains that morning to save the pennies. She selected the darkest one and noted the absence of biscuits. Being Lent, the Mothers' Union had obviously vetoed such extravagant treats until Easter Sunday. Hattie tentatively sipped the ditch-water-dull brew, made worse by the absence of a ginger nut or even a modest rich tea. Hilda stood her ground, her face still fixed in a frozen grin.

'Now, how are you all?' she enquired wistfully, allowing her grin to fade just a fraction.

'Oh, we're all fine, thank you,' replied Hattie, bravely swallowing another mouthful. The coffee grains that had found their way into the cup seemed to have given up the will to live. Meanwhile, Hilda stubbornly refused to move, having cornered Hattie between a pew-end and the church bookstall.

'That's good, and when does Nick start his new job?' she probed, tipping her head to the side like a sparrow full of springtime *joie de vivre*.

'Er, the beginning of April… Not long now.'

'And will he be commuting every day, the poor dear? Such a long way for him.'

'Well, he *could* stay with his parents during the week to save time and petrol.'

'Hmm,' murmured Hilda, her face now a picture of gloom and despondency, 'that can be a mixed blessing.' She was either play-acting or had found the grimace too much to sustain.

'How do you mean?' asked Hattie, bemused by Hilda's concern.

'Well, my dear, sometimes it's "out of sight, out of mind",' she confided in a whisper.

Hattie blinked in surprise and then noticed there was a dewdrop hanging from Hilda's nose. Hattie gazed at it, transfixed, as Hilda tapped the side of her nose enigmatically, then gasped in horror, trying not to notice any splashes as it dropped onto the waiting cups.

'Yes, dear, you understand my drift, I can see,' she continued darkly. 'My sister's husband almost went off the rails when he was working away. It turned out he was entangled with the area manager's secretary.'

'Oh goodness!' exclaimed Hattie, wondering if another dewdrop would soon appear.

'Yes, dear. It's as well to keep an eye on them when they reach a certain age. Your Nick's at a dangerous time in his life, you know,' she added mysteriously.

'What, a mid-life crisis you mean?' Hattie was becoming distinctly uncomfortable about her own wild behaviour in the college car park and started to feel rather warm around her neck and ears.

'That's exactly it! A mid-life crisis! One glimpse of a pretty young secretary and all thoughts of their middle-aged wife miles away, can fly right out of their heads.'

Why was it, Hattie reflected, that Hilda had managed to make the words 'middle-aged' sound so unappealing?

'Come on, Hilda,' Celia interrupted briskly, bearing down on the twosome with steely-eyed determination. 'Don't stand there hogging the coffee. We're all gasping.' She went to grab the tray from Hilda's grasp, but Hilda resisted.

'All right, dear. I was having a little chat with Hattie here,' she remarked in a hurt tone.

'Not spreading scandal and gossip are you, Hilda? Surely, you were listening to the vicar's sermon not ten minutes ago, about the tongue being like an untamed beast. "Death and life are in the power of the tongue, and they that love it shall eat the fruit thereof!"' quoted Celia sternly.

Hilda glared at her friend and stuck out her chin stubbornly. Hattie watched in horror as another dewdrop hit the tray.

'Gossip? No, not at all, Celia,' Hilda snapped. Then she leaned closer to Hattie and added ominously, in barely more than a whisper, 'Just remember what I said, dear. I'd keep an eye on that husband of yours if I were you!'

Hattie was speechless as Celia virtually dragged Hilda away. Whatever could all that have been about? Peering down at the loathsome liquid, she decided she'd wait until she was home before satisfying her thirst. The chances of it containing random dewdrops were too ghastly to contemplate.

While she was puzzling over the surprising conversation and wondering where she could surreptitiously abandon her cup, Evadne Proctor, another stalwart of the Mothers' Union, sidled up to her.

'Hello, Hattie,' she began with a cheerful smile. 'I hope you won't think I'm speaking out of turn...' which was a clue that she was about to do just that, 'but my cousin and her husband viewed your house yesterday and...' she hesitated and averted her eyes nervously, her lips moving silently.

'Oh, really?' Hattie had a shrewd idea which of the visitors she was referring to – the final, depressing pair.

'And... er... the interior décor, dear... It's a bit wild I gather,' she murmured in almost shocked tones.

'Wild?' exclaimed Hattie. Evadne's wide-eyed expression and pursed lips suggested the possibility of nude murals or black walls at the very least. 'Do you mean the delicate shade of soft lilac in the sitting room?'

'Very risky, Hattie,' she commented in a superior manner. Most likely Evadne and her cousin would consider any colour other than magnolia to be risky or indeed wild, thought Hattie. 'My cousin was put off straight away. Not a wise colour when you're trying to sell your house, you know.'

The previous day's viewing and the bad-tempered biddy's pronouncements came flooding back into Hattie's mind. 'Oh dear. What a shame. But it's nothing that a pot of paint can't remedy,' she replied promptly. 'We'll probably repaint the cottage *we're* buying. It's not a problem.'

'Ah well, Letitia wouldn't want the bother of all that. She wants to be able to move straight in,' Evadne continued, 'and... er...'

Hattie wondered what else was coming, as indeed there seemed to be something still bothering the woman.

'And the fluorescent green in the kitchen too!' she gasped, shaking her head.

'No, not fluorescent green, Evadne. Honestly! It's a very chic shade of pale lime, not *at all* fluorescent,' Hattie flustered, 'and no one else has commented on it.'

'Nor have they agreed to buy your house.'

'Well, there *was* someone.'

'*Was*, yes, but no longer, obviously,' Evadne continued, full of self-importance. 'Very risky, as I said before. If I were you, I'd go and buy some tins of nice, tasteful, magnolia paint. *Everyone* likes magnolia, you know,' she advised with a sniff.

'I had a feeling you were going to mention magnolia,' Hattie replied levelly, 'but I mustn't keep you, Evadne. Here, why don't you have this coffee, which I haven't had a chance to drink? It's nice and weak.' She passed the cup to Evadne with a smile and neatly sidestepped her with a passing comment that cousin Letitia might soon find a suitable property.

On the way home, Hattie started to wonder if Evadne's unwelcome comments might have had more than a grain of common sense in them. She also recalled some of the daytime TV, house-selling shows, with their preference for bland paint schemes.

'Are you sure it's really necessary?' Nick asked with a sigh. 'Just because that busybody Evadne Proctor says we ought to redecorate; I don't see why we have to go to the expense of a complete makeover on the say-so of that old bat of a cousin of hers who was rubbishing the place yesterday.'

However, as the day wore on, Hattie remembered some of the other tips from the house-selling programmes, such as de-cluttering, putting spare furniture into store and keeping pets out of the way during viewings. At the time, she hadn't seriously considered taking this sort of action, but now, in the light of zero progress, she was beginning to see her home in a new light. If Hattie needed any more distractions from Leo, who kept popping into her mind unbidden, then embarking on a major redecoration project might be the answer.

Over supper, she put forward her case yet again, emphasising her willingness to devote every spare minute to the task.

'Look, Nick, the sooner we sell, the sooner you can put an end to the commuting. I know Brian Samways pooh-poohed the idea of redecorating, but anything to speed the process by making our home appealing to a wider market surely makes sense.' All the phrases she'd heard on TV were now tripping off her tongue effortlessly. 'I could rope in Fliss as well. I'm sure it would give her something different to think about, and the job would be finished more quickly.'

'Well, if you put it like that... Okay, go ahead,' he agreed resignedly. 'I suppose I could do a bit in the evenings as well.'

'Great! I'll buy the paint on the way home from school tomorrow and make a start straight away.'

By Wednesday teatime, not a sign of soft lilac or pale lime was to be seen. The bedrooms were next on the agenda, but would have to wait; it was the day of her final patchwork class and Hattie only had time to make a quick call to Fliss before setting off.

'Hi, Fliss. How's things?'

Fliss sighed, obviously finding it difficult to sum up her feelings. 'Well, Mum's condition is deteriorating rapidly,' she told her friend forlornly. 'I was speaking to Dad earlier. The doctor doesn't give her more than two months at most.'

'Oh, Fliss, that's awful. I'm so sorry. When are you going down to see her?'

'Well, I'm waiting until the end of term. It'll be much easier then. Mark's just flown off to Sweden and he'll be away about a week.'

'You know we'll have the boys again if you want to go before then.'

'I know, Hat, but I think it's better if we all go together.' Hattie could almost hear the unspoken phrase, 'to say our goodbyes', and shivered involuntarily. 'Sure... I understand.' She paused, wondering if her own cry for help was that important. 'Um... Fliss, do you fancy coming over tomorrow and lending a hand with a paintbrush?' she asked then gave the edited highlights of Evadne's snide comments.

'Course I'll come,' chuckled Fliss. 'It's just the sort of diversion I need at the moment. I can be over around ten.'

'Brill,' giggled Hattie. 'I'll look forward to it.'

Partly constructed quilts and throws were draped over every available surface in the patchwork room. Hattie's was even further from being finished than she'd hoped, thanks to the pressing needs of redecorating. With Marigold's assistance, she hoisted her effort over a freestanding display board and was encouraged by the compliments her work received.

'Super effort, Hattie!' gushed Marigold, clapping her hands together in girlish glee. This was doubly amazing: Hattie's quilt was the least completed in the class and Marigold had actually remembered her name. She flushed with pleasure until she realised that, as a teacher, she'd always learned the names of the most troublesome pupils long before those of the quiet, orderly ones. All that breathless last minute arriving, sloppiness with the cutting wheel cover and intrusive mobile bleeps must have had something to do with that.

'That's very kind of you,' she replied modestly, 'but it's still a work in progress, as they say.'

'And *I* think it's coming along *really* well,' added Cynthia, once Marigold was swept away by Zena to appraise some of the other efforts. 'Those colours are just stunning.'

Hattie considered Cynthia's quilt to be stunning as well, but in a more understated way. She'd obviously been beavering away since the last class and had joined all the rows of patches with contrasting rectangular sashings with cornerstones between, as well as adding a narrow outer border. Being a cot quilt, it naturally needed less time than Hattie's double-bed sized one.

'At the rate I'm going, it'll be a miracle if it's finished by the time we move, unless we're on the market for the next year,' replied Hattie gloomily as they took their seats for the final teaching session.

'Now, ladies,' Zena began, silencing the last of the chatter with a commanding glance, 'once the patches have been joined, as many of you have done already, next comes the task of *hand* quilting.'

A ripple of apprehensive murmurs spread around the gathering, accompanied by furrowed brows.

'However,' Marigold cut in, 'before Zena demonstrates the stitching, I will show you how to prepare for this stage.' She turned aside and picked up a roll of wadding and a length of plain cotton fabric. 'You'll need to cut wadding and backing fabric to fit your quilt, like so,' she continued and proceeded to show one she'd made earlier. Then followed Zena's painstaking demonstration of quilting stitches that were executed with a very short and sharp needle, before the two of them showed the class how to finish the quilts with bound edges.

'Now, before you all try out the stitches for yourselves, I have an announcement,' declared Zena, a mischievous grin hovering on her lips. 'The college is holding an open day next Wednesday and has invited us to attend − a free session of course. Marigold and I thought it would be lovely to turn it into a sort of end of term party, as well as a chance to display our work, finished or not. What do you think, ladies?'

A chorus of 'oh yes' and 'great idea' rippled around the room.

'What about the other evening classes?' one lady piped up.

'I'm sure I'm correct in saying that most of the practical ones will be putting in an appearance,' Zena assured her. Everyone was invited to bring an edible contribution and Zena and Marigold promised to supply fruit juice and low-alcohol fizz.

'And finally,' announced Marigold with an air of excitement, 'we'd like you all to know that we're hoping to put on a display to the public at Quaintly Manor: our − I mean *my* − home.'

Cynthia and Hattie exchanged meaningful glances.

'Yes, it's so exciting,' Zena continued, slipping an arm around Marigold's waist. 'We've been approached by a local children's charity. We haven't finalised the date yet, but as soon as we have, we'll be in touch.'

'Always wanted to nose around Quaintly,' confided Cynthia.

'I hope they're not expecting us lot to have our quilts ready for the great event,' murmured Hattie. 'Charity event it may be, but I'd rather dance around the staff car park starkers than let the local busybodies pull my work to pieces.'

'The mind boggles!' spluttered Cynthia, tears of mirth running down her cheeks.

Hattie was determined to avoid Leo that evening. The previous Wednesday's moment of weakness had had a sobering effect on her as the days had passed, and she resolved to do all she could to avoid any repetition. Nick had also emerged from his former grouchiness and although he wasn't exactly back to hugs and kisses, things were definitely looking up. In fact, he'd even managed to summon up a smile and the briefest of pecks on the cheek, which was progress indeed. She was strolling down the corridor with Cynthia, indulging in reciprocal praise, when she spotted

Madge and her dancing companions streaming out of one of the sports halls.

'Madge! Yoo-hoo, Madge!' she called, quickening her steps. On hearing her name, Madge smiled and hurried over to join them. After introductions were made, they continued on their way to the main entrance, exchanging highlights of their various activities.

'And Rebecca says we're good enough to put on a proper performance,' bragged Madge proudly.

'As opposed to an *im*proper one!' murmured Cynthia with a chuckle.

'What's that you said?' snapped Madge.

'Nothing. I was just clearing my throat.'

'A public performance? Ooh, really?' giggled Hattie, trying to imagine Madge all decked out in harem pants and a skimpy top, with acres of middle-aged belly on display. Would the public be ready for such a treat, she wondered.

'But not a word to your other half please,' she stressed. 'I could do without suggestive comments from him, even if he hasn't long left to plague me with his warped humour.'

Hattie rolled her eyes at Cynthia who was still wearing a broad grin after entertaining thoughts of assorted female figures casting off veils to the delight of gawping males.

'Ah, you'll not have to put up with Nick much longer now,' chuckled Hattie.

'Just over two weeks and counting,' replied Madge grimly.

'That bad?' gasped Hattie. 'I mean, he seems to be busy with lots of extra meetings out of the office, lunch times and all.'

'Extra meetings? What extra meetings? I'm sure I don't know what you mean,' Madge snapped, clearly miffed. 'If there'd been extra meetings, *I* would certainly know about them.'

'Oh really?' questioned Hattie, trying to recall exactly what Nick had told her. 'I'd assumed Nick was having briefings with his replacement and some of the managers.'

'Well, as it's Rafiq Hussain taking over, I can't see that any more than a few memos are needed and the odd five minutes here and there – unless he's choosing to spend his lunchtimes with Rafiq as a special favour.'

'Oh, I see.'

'And probably end up talking football, if *I* know anything about those two,' she huffed.

'Yes, I expect that's it,' concluded Hattie. 'Nick making it sound so important, just to impress me!'

'Exactly!'

By this time, they'd reached the main entrance and there, right on cue, was Donald waiting for Cynthia, who scuttled off with a cheery goodbye. Hattie was all for following on until Madge grabbed her sleeve and started jiggling around excitedly.

'Oh coo-ee! Signor Marcello! Coo-ee!' she exclaimed, uncomfortably close to Hattie's ear.

'Pilchards!' she muttered crossly, trying to pull free from Madge's grasp.

'Oh, I *must* introduce you to him, Hattie; he's *such* a charming gentleman,' she asserted, beckoning Leo over. Some weeks earlier, she had wondered if it had been Hattie she'd spied chatting with the handsome signor, but hadn't been absolutely sure. The woman in question had been acting furtively from what she could tell and was wearing her hat so well pulled down that it obscured most of her face. 'Signor Marcello, you may not remember me, but I was at the Mia Casa opening do with my friend Sandra – Greg's Auntie Sandra,' she simpered. 'We do belly dancing with your Rebecca, but Sandra couldn't come tonight on account of her bunions. I told her she's asking for trouble wearing those shoes.'

'Pleased to meet you again, er...'

'Madge,' she supplied, blushing scarlet and giggling as Leo took her hand and kissed it lightly.

'Ah, young Rebecca... Such an asset to Mia Casa,' reflected Leo genially, 'and her fiancé's a fortunate man indeed.'

All the while, Hattie was gazing at the remaining straggles of students emerging from the adjoining corridor, trying to decide what to say and summoning up her repertoire of acting skills.

'Let me introduce you to Hattie Chesney. Her husband is my work colleague, but not for much longer, thank goodness.'

'Ah, yes, we *have* met, haven't we, Mrs Chesney?' remarked Leo cordially, taking her hand and giving it the same treatment as Madge's. He gazed intently into her eyes, keeping hold of her hand, which had an alarming effect on her stomach. 'I had the pleasure of carrying out a valuation at Mr Chesney's invitation,' Leo told Madge.

'Oh yes, of course… Mr Chesney *did* mention it. How silly of me not to remember.'

'So good to meet you again, Mrs Chesney,' Leo said, squeezing her hand gently before letting go, his eyes conveying much more than any words.

'Er… yes… um… pleased to meet you again,' flustered Hattie, wishing her heart would stop pounding so energetically.

'Well, I must be going now. Good evening, ladies,' he replied and with his characteristic bow, he was off.

Madge glanced at Hattie and rolled her eyes. '*So* Mr Darcy, isn't he? What a dreamboat!' she sighed softly.

'Darcy without the aloofness I would say,' agreed Hattie wistfully, recalling that 'dreamboat' was exactly how Fliss had described him.

'Ooh, if only I were twenty years younger,' mused Madge, watching him stride to the door.

'Ah yes,' murmured Hattie under her breath. 'If only…' Her stomach turned several somersaults, signalling Leo's complete mastery of her emotions. How was it possible that with one glance of those eyes, she imagined abandoning all decorum, tearing off his clothes and having her wicked way with him? Obviously her imagination hadn't included the college foyer for an act of such daring indiscretion but, with the right time and place, she felt she could have surrendered her matronly reserve in a riot of unfettered passion. Madge would not stand a chance. Dream on, sister!

'Ah well, Madge. I must be off too,' she announced. 'See you at Nick's leaving do, no doubt.'

13

'Oh, this is such fun!' exclaimed Fliss, pausing to wipe a splash of paint off her cheek.

'Fun it may be,' replied Hattie, 'but we're on a tight timescale with this. I told the agents there weren't to be any viewings while we were redecorating, so we've agreed to be finished by the weekend.'

'No pressure then!' giggled Fliss.

They had been hard at work all morning and, after a quick sandwich and coffee, it was time to tackle Josh's room.

'Think we need a bit of music,' said Hattie, selecting a favourite Abba album. In the lead up to the second chorus of 'Dancing Queen', they were suddenly aware of the insistent ringing of the doorbell.

'I'll go,' called Hattie, putting her brush carefully aside on a pile of old newspapers. 'It's bound to be for me!'

'Perhaps it's Jehovah's Witnesses again,' suggested Fliss, with a grin, as Hattie rushed to answer the door.

It was Hilda Makepeace on a mission.

'Oh, hello, Hilda. This is an unexpected pleasure, but I can't invite you in as I'm in the middle of some painting.' Why was she being so nice to the woman after her strange pronouncements about mid-life crises and the fatal attractions of nubile young secretaries?

Hilda cleared her throat noisily. 'Ah, Hattie, would this be your

298

glove dear?' she enquired, producing a black glove with an embroidered sequin motif.

'Yes, it is. Thank you so much, Hilda. Where ever did I lose it?'

'In church, dear. I spotted it under one of the pews when I was clearing up on Sunday morning.'

'You must have good eyesight, Hilda.'

'Oh yes, dear. I have *very* sharp eyes. Nothing gets past me, I assure you,' she said with a knowing wink.

Hattie blinked in surprise. Hilda wasn't known for her winking. In fact, she didn't seem to have mastered it yet because it was more of a distorted grimace.

'Oh well, that's a good thing if you're on church cleaning, I suppose.' Fliss was in full voice by now and Hattie wished Hilda would buzz off so she could get back and join in the fun. How much longer would this boring conversation continue, she wondered? Where was it actually going, for goodness' sake?

'Hmm, well it's a useful gift in all *sorts* of situations, my dear. It's amazing who you see when you're out and about – all sorts of people in all *sorts* of very surprising situations.' Hilda rolled her eyes this time, having given up on her unsuccessful winking.

Hattie went cold inside, hoping Hilda hadn't been sneaking around the college car park. She tried to imagine what evening class could tempt Hilda away from her fireside and her telly on a dark night: flower arranging? No, she was an expert already. Chinese cookery? No, Hilda was most certainly a meat and two veg person. Badminton? Definitely not! Perhaps she'd never been anywhere near the college.

'Oh really?' replied Hattie brightly, yet trying to convey boredom with the subject of Hilda's sightings. 'Well, it takes all sorts, they say.'

'And some aren't known for their discretion or morals, my dear,' she murmured darkly, with eyes raised.

Hattie was suddenly feeling very hot under the collar, although in truth she was only wearing a T-shirt.

'Take the clientele of Maggie's Sandwich Bar, for instance,' she added, lowering her voice and quickly glancing around in case someone was eavesdropping on their conversation.

'Maggie's Sandwich Bar?' Hattie echoed. Surely Maggie's wasn't a hotbed of scandal and vice, she thought, even though it might be a bit on the bohemian side. At least she hadn't been spotted in the college car park in Leo's arms.

'The very same, dear. It's amazing who you see in there of a lunchtime.'

'You don't mean an MP with his mistress?' suggested Hattie with interest.

'No, no not MPs... Someone *much* nearer home,' she breathed, her eyes wide in horror. 'I was only saying to Celia when we were in there yesterday, there's that young Nick Chesney *again*, as I live and breathe.' She nodded knowingly, her eyes now having gone through their full repertoire.

'And what's so amazing about that?' Hattie asked stiffly, wondering what revelation Mrs Beady-Eyes might be about to reveal. 'He's very busy with lunchtime meetings at the moment.'

'Oh, is that it?' replied Hilda with a wan smile and a raise of her shaggy eyebrows. 'So the pretty, young, lunchtime companion is his secretary is she?'

'The who?' asked Hattie, puzzled by this unexpected disclosure. Hilda had probably witnessed some perfectly innocent meeting and blown it out of all proportion. This was obviously what all that mid-life-crisis-keep-an-eye-on-your-husband stuff was all about. 'Oh, I expect that's Rafiq's PA,' she improvised, knowing it wouldn't mean a thing to Hilda, but would still sound convincing.

'Well, that's fine then,' replied Hilda. 'I'm sure the cosy little chats are just company business, but it was just the two of them we saw. Maybe this... er... Raffy person was unavoidably detained, as they say.' She laughed in a decidedly humourless way. 'Ah well, I'd better not hold you up.'

'No... there's lots to do here, but why don't you pop in and see Wilf next door? I'm sure he could do with cheering up,' Hattie suggested, closing the door abruptly. 'Stupid, nosy cow!' she muttered, glaring at the closed door and secretly hoping that Hilda's ears were as sharp as her eyes. She then stomped upstairs, her fists clenched and her imagination full of painful and undignified images of what she would like to do to Mrs Hilda-Beady-Eyes-Makepeace, given half a chance. She returned to Josh's room, muttering furiously under her breath.

'What's up, Hat?' gasped Fliss, quickly dismounting the stepladder and turning down the CD player.

'Nosy cow!'

'I only asked,' protested Fliss, mortified.

'No, not *you*, Fliss,' laughed Hattie, weakly. 'Hilda Makepeace. She was probably born with a wooden spoon in her mouth, already programmed with instructions on how to stir in one easy lesson.'

'I think she must have perfected the art, if your expression is anything to go by.'

'You'll never guess what she's just told me,' continued Hattie, shaking her head in disbelief, 'about Nick.'

'What about Nick?' gasped Fliss, the colour draining from her cheeks.

'She's just enlightened me that Nick passes his lunchtime – with a pretty young woman in Maggie's Sandwich Bar!'

'Really? Is that all?'

'All? She made it sound as if he was having an illicit affair with the woman. She was even wittering on the other day in church about men having mid-life crises and how Nick's at a dangerous age and how I should keep an eye on him! Now she's inferring he's been meeting this woman on a regular basis and that she and Celia Halverson have been witnesses!'

'What? Surely not! You mean she came round specially to tell you that?'

'Basically, yes. Although she sneakily disguised it as her Good Samaritan act of returning a glove I'd dropped in church last Sunday,' Hattie fumed. 'I wouldn't put it past her to have deliberately whipped it off the pew while I was being lectured on the advantages of magnolia colour schemes by know-it-all Evadne Proctor.' She paused for breath and started pacing the floor, recalling Hilda's particularly annoying facial expressions. 'Yes, I bet that's what she did, to give herself the perfect excuse to come round and spread her malicious lies and gossip.'

'Well, there could be some perfectly innocent explanation,' suggested Fliss. 'I mean, I've seen the odd surprising incident before that might have looked, maybe a bit... um... unusual, but could have been just down to my own misunderstanding. Mark says I sometimes read too much into things.'

'What sort of incident?' asked Hattie warily.

'Oh nothing really... Well, okay... like when I spotted you in The Four Seasons that night, remember? It might have seemed odd at the time, being there all by yourself, but then it turned out you'd been having a coffee with your chum Cynthia. To the outside observer, something quite innocent could be misunderstood. I expect that's the case with Nick.'

Hattie turned aside to pick up her paintbrush, suddenly feeling awkward about the Four Seasons incident. 'I'm sure you're right,' she agreed. 'I mean, it was only the other day that Nick was telling me he was having extra lunchtime meetings in the run up to leaving. Now here's Hilda-Beady-Eyes-Makepeace suggesting there's some hanky-panky going on. How ridiculous! Who'd plan a meeting in a sandwich bar if they were up to something illicit? I expect it was just company business.'

'Exactly so,' agreed Fliss, giving her a hug. 'There now, Hat. Calm down. This Hilda Makepeace has obviously got a vivid imagination.'

Hattie sighed deeply. 'Time for a cuppa, Fliss?'

'Spot on! Just what I was thinking myself.'

'And a muffin?'

'Not for me,' giggled Fliss, patting her washboard-flat stomach, 'but I think you need one.'

Saturday arrived and 7 Witchert Close was once more ready to greet the viewing public. The magnolia transformation and drastic de-cluttering was complete.

'You need to give your prospective buyers a clean canvas for their imaginations to work on,' Fliss had spouted, sounding ominously like one of the TV house experts. She had always favoured the pared-down minimalist look.

'But it looks so stark!' Hattie had wailed, surveying her sitting room gloomily. The walls were bare except for two prints. The only other accessory, on the glass-topped coffee table, was the library book of American quilts.

'No, not bare, Hat. It looks restful, stylish and much more chic, and not that tired shabby chic you had before. Just see if I'm right.'

Fresh coffee was brewed, the bread-maker churned out loaves, vases of daffodils added splashes of colour and Jezebel sulked in the garden, on the other side of a locked cat-flap. However, the two couples, shown around by an eager Pete Ingleheart, gave no clue to their reaction to the restful, but bland, décor. Hattie was hoping her hard work would tempt an offer from one of the couples.

Nick said nothing. Like Josh, he seemed to be in a world of his own, although less gloomy than of late. All the while, Hattie was now plagued by images of Nick and the mystery woman.

By four o'clock, just two hours after the last viewing, the house was settling back into its comfortably lived-in state. Sky Sport once more reigned and discarded slippers and newspapers were scattered on the floor. Even Jezebel had been allowed back indoors and was curled up contentedly on her favourite kitchen chair. Hattie was just beginning to exhale the tension that had gripped her all day when the phone rang.

'Hello again, Mrs Chesney. Pete Ingleheart here.'

Hattie's heart missed a beat. 'It was one of those "good news, bad news" moments. Yes, Mr and Mrs Judge loved the house, but sadly, their offer was derisory.

'Typical cash buyers!' growled Nick irritably when Hattie reported the conversation to him.

'I know it's a bit cheeky,' began Hattie, realising it was a lost cause.

'Cheeky? It's a downright insult!' he glowered.

'All right, I'll phone back and tell Pete we need a better offer.'

'If Samways can't come up with better results,' snapped Nick, 'I'll be thinking of trying other agents – and you can tell them that from me!'

Other agents, thought Hattie with interest. It sounded as if Mia Casa might get their chance after all. The prospect of Leo doing the honours with the keen house-hunting public was quite a delicious one.

Hattie had plenty of reasons for keeping her head down in church the following morning, Hilda Makepeace, Evadne Proctor and Celia Halverson being three of them. She was on coffee duty with Daphne, the vicar's wife, and quickly suggested that she'd stay in the kitchen and serve from the hatch rather than do the rounds with the tray. Daphne was more than happy with this arrangement, being a naturally chatty person. When Celia smiled benignly at her as she returned her cup, Hattie gave her no opportunity to chat as she whipped it away and turned back to a sink full of waiting crockery. If Celia had an opinion about Nick's lunchtime activities, Hattie certainly didn't want to hear it, until she'd made her own investigation. Perhaps her husband's out-of-work interests were already the subject of conversation at all the village coffee mornings. She could picture Hilda and Evadne hunched over their knitting like crones beside the guillotine, picking over the juicy titbits of the Chesney household's affairs. If that were so, she'd have accepted any offer just to get away from all the scandal-mongering and backbiting.

Arriving home the following day, worn out by a morning with the lively Year 3 classes, she instinctively checked the phone for messages. Sure enough, Pete Ingleheart had left one just an hour earlier, asking her to call him back. Was there some hint of a breakthrough in his voice, she wondered as she listened to his brief message a second time? Were the Judges so smitten by 7 Witchert Close, and so desperate to take their furniture out of store and settle into their own home, that they'd seen reason and offered a much better price? Unfortunately not.

'And is that their final offer?' asked Hattie, seeing the light at the end of the proverbial tunnel guttering and fading.

'Yes, I'm afraid so. Mrs Judge was adamant that the kitchen and bathroom would have to be replaced, and that would have to be reflected in their purchasing budget.'

Hattie replaced the receiver, feeling bleak and cold inside.

'Just because they're cash buyers,' she fumed, 'they think they can play nasty, sneaky games with us.' Jezebel, her only companion on that grey afternoon, slinked around her legs and then wandered through to the utility room, chirruping as she went.

'Oh, crumpets!' she snapped, reflecting on the call. She followed behind the little cat, who sat expectantly beside the open shelf that stored her extensive menu of pouches and pussy treats. 'You're a greedy girl,' Hattie scolded, but couldn't resist the insistent yowling and sprinkled a handful into an empty bowl. 'Oh, what are we going to do?' she sighed, watching Jezebel wolfing down the treats. Did Nick really mean he wanted to switch agents? Perhaps he'd been doing a recce round the town already?

Later on, while Hattie was working at her patchwork and cheering herself up with a bar of orange milk chocolate, the phone rang.

'Ah, good afternoon, Mrs Chesney. Archie Pigeon speaking. I thought I'd give you an update on Knapp Cottage.'

'But I thought we'd agreed to put everything on hold,' Hattie exclaimed, dreading a mounting conveyancing bill for a property that might soon be out of reach.

'Don't worry, Mrs Chesney,' replied Archie smoothly. 'I just wanted to check a few things and I'm afraid I've unearthed some information that might change your view of the property in question.' He paused and cleared his throat. 'In fact, what I've discovered will most definitely change the view of anyone standing in the back garden.' There was a sound rather like an embarrassed chuckle. Was Archie trying to be funny? If so, she didn't warm to his humour.

'I'm afraid it's been going on for several years too.'

'Really?' The man was making no sense at all. 'Do enlighten me,' she begged, trying to keep the frustration out of her voice.

'It appears the owners of the adjacent property have applied for planning permission to erect a single-storey building in their garden.'

'You mean a garage?' That didn't sound too awful.

'No, nothing as straightforward as that; they have divided off a section of their extensive garden and are applying for planning permission for a bungalow.'

'A bungalow? Where exactly?' Hattie demanded, wondering if the Dunbars were privy to this unfortunate development.

'According to my information, it would be directly opposite the back door.'

'Where there's a rustic bench seat on a terrace surrounded by a pergola,' recited Hattie, 'and a rambling grapevine...'

Archie cleared his throat again in the stony silence that followed.

'And where there's likely to be uninterrupted views of washing lines and brick walls!' snapped Hattie. 'Do the Dunbars know about this proposed blot on the landscape?'

'Oh, yes, indeed they do. In fact, it seems that their neighbours have applied for planning permission several times over the past five years and each time the Dunbars have contested it. However, there's no knowing if the neighbours might eventually be successful.'

'What? You mean all the time they were showing us around their cottage and pointing out the view to some tower or other, they knew their neighbours were planning to build something slap bang in the middle of it and obliterate it? Why, that's down-right dishonest!'

'Oh, I wouldn't go as far as saying that, Mrs Chesney. It's more a case of being economical with the truth. You see, it's not defi-nite that the bungalow will go ahead, so they probably decided to say nothing and hope any objections they raised would call a halt to it – yet again.'

'Hmm, I see,' replied Hattie, fuming, 'and it seems they've become so fed-up with this on-going saga that they've decided to move to Portugal and leave the new owners with the problem.'

There was another silence at the end of the line.

'I'll send you the information to show you what is planned,' suggested Archie.

'Yes... you'd better send it. I expect Nick will want to see for himself, but it sounds like we will have to withdraw our offer... unfortunately,' she said, with a heavy heart.

Pushing open the door of Maggie's Sandwich Bar two days later, Hattie quickly checked again to make sure there was no sign of Hilda, Celia or Nick, with or without a pretty young companion. She'd already sauntered past the window, pausing supposedly to read the menu several minutes earlier. A few early lunchtime customers had already filled some of the tables and because of the layout, it seemed possible to be tucked away out of sight behind various pillars and vegetation. Hattie then noticed some open stairs curving up to a gallery, which overlooked the main eating area. She was wearing an old hooded jacket and had tucked a pair of sunglasses in her pocket. This was to be her sleuthing disguise. She had also brought her latest *Country Crafts* magazine, which she thought might come in handy, to hide behind at least. She daren't risk being spotted.

After choosing a large coffee, a tuna mayonnaise baguette and a chocolate chip cookie, she nipped up to the gallery and managed to find an empty table. It was in a perfect position, giving an excellent view of most of the floor below. On went the sunglasses and she propped the magazine against the menu stand, shielding her from the customers below. The decision to spy on Nick was made even before she and Fliss had finished Josh's room, not that she had mentioned it to her friend. Of course, there was always the chance that Fliss might also wander in. After all, her hours seemed to be very flexible.

Several minutes passed, during which the downstairs part of the café gradually filled, although there were still a few seats in the gallery. What if Nick came upstairs? Would he recognise her in the old hooded jacket and sunglasses and if he *did*, what would she say? Frenzied thoughts whizzed around her head as she visualised all sorts of awkward and embarrassing scenarios. While she was deciding on some emergency strategies, a hiatus at the door announced the arrival of two familiar figures clutching bulging shopping bags – Celia Halverson and Hilda Makepeace. 'Oh no,' breathed Hattie. A gloating Hilda was someone she could do with avoiding. Would they attempt the stairs with trays and shopping bags? Possibly not, especially as there were still seats below.

Celia and Hilda were still at the counter dithering over rolls, salads and choices of soup when two girls clattered up the stairs and homed in on her table. With great relief, Hattie smiled a welcome, safe in the knowledge that Hilda and Celia could no longer join in a cosy little threesome. Hilda would know *exactly* why she was there. She sipped her coffee and kept an eye on the comings and goings below, feeling every inch the private investigator. By this time, quite a queue had formed behind the two ditherers who were now poking around in their purses for the correct money. Then they bumped and jostled their way towards the back of the café and settled themselves at a corner table, having rearranged their chairs to give a good view of the door. She was certainly seeing Celia in a new light, a person she wouldn't have linked with such behaviour.

More minutes passed as she slowly nibbled her baguette and sipped her cooling coffee until a familiar figure was seen at the door. Her heart started hammering furiously and she started wondering what had possessed her to stoop as low as the snooping Hilda. She adjusted her magazine and pulled her hood forward a fraction, despite the fact that she was now cooking up quite a heat inside her jacket.

Was he alone? A cluster of satisfied customers were leaving just as he arrived so there was a slight pause before a young woman could be seen behind him. It was hard to tell if they'd come together as they stood at the counter. There was certainly no chat or light-hearted banter. However, a glance in Hilda and Celia's direction confirmed their excited interest. Hilda actually clapped her hands together in glee and nudged her friend as she whispered in her ear. The girl behind Nick in the queue must have been the one they'd seen before. Hattie studied her with interest, although there wasn't much to see from her back view. She wore a smart, raspberry-pink beret and a silvery grey jacket with a high collar. She was also *very* slim, Hattie observed with a sigh. If only she would turn her head a fraction, but her attention was on the food choices.

Nick finished paying and looked around for a seat. Hattie quickly held up her magazine higher and peered surreptitiously around one edge. Raspberry Beret was still at the counter and still gave no clue to her identity. Then, momentarily, Hattie's heart skipped a beat as Nick turned around and glanced up at the gallery, and then checked out the rest of the ground floor. She gazed blankly at an article on needle felting and prayed he wouldn't decide to come up the stairs. No, he was moving over to a table almost directly below, where a young couple were getting up to leave. Hattie sighed with relief and swallowed a mouthful of coffee. At last, Raspberry Beret picked up her tray and stood gazing across the seating in Hilda and Celia's direction. Maybe she hadn't come in with Nick. She was certainly acting the complete stranger. Or maybe this was part of an elaborate charade.

Then several things happened at once. First of all, Hattie's attention was claimed by a blob of tuna mayonnaise that landed in her lap. Next, someone from behind the counter chose that moment to come through to the front with a fresh tray of cutlery. Then three chattering women lurched past on walking sticks, a young mother with a baby under her arm tried to lug a pushchair into a space between two tables and, before Hattie knew it, Raspberry Beret had managed to somehow emerge from the mêlée and arrive beside Nick's table, still with her back conveniently facing the gallery. There was the slightest suggestion of blonde hair poking out from under her beret and in the brief moment as Nick invited her to take a seat, Hattie thought she had seen her somewhere before, but the glimpse was too brief to be sure. She lowered her magazine and studied the scene playing out below her. She could see Nick's face clearly, but not that of the girl who sat with her back towards the underside of the gallery. Hattie ground her teeth in frustration.

Well, what a pretty sight, she thought cynically. Nick and the girl, still wearing her beret, were chatting away like old, established friends. Judging from Nick's body language and animated manner, Hattie noted, he was turning the charm full on, and his companion seemed to be reacting to it very favourably. Even from a back view, she could tell as much.

'If you only knew!' she muttered angrily. At once, the animated chatter at her table stopped abruptly and Hattie turned to see the two girls staring at her quizzically.

'Sorry. Got carried away... A bit of surveillance you understand,' she murmured, lifting her sunglasses as she spoke. The girls rolled their eyes in amazement.

'Really?' whispered one, with green hair-streaks and multiple piercings, picking up Hattie's air of subterfuge.

'Oh yes,' whispered Hattie, recklessly taking on the persona of an experienced private detective. 'There's a fellow down there, wife and two kids, playing fast and loose with his secretary. Same old story! The wife will have something to say about this!'

She nodded her head, pushed the sunglasses back on her nose and made the pretence of scribbling some notes on the page of her magazine. The two girls leaned towards the gallery rail and watched open-mouthed as Nick delivered what looked like the punch-line to some story or joke he was telling. Predictably, the girl doubled up in laughter and nearly choked on her lunch. Quick as a flash, Nick leapt up from his seat and frantically started patting her back to dislodge some rogue crumbs.

'A proper Sir Galahad,' murmured Hattie. Once the coughing and spluttering had subsided, she found herself willing Nick to remove his hand from between the girl's shoulder blades. But no, it just stayed there and began some slow massaging of the general area, while he leaned and said something in her ear. Glancing towards the back of the café, Hattie spotted Hilda all a-dither, pointing out to Celia what she could see of the recent excitement. Nick was really chancing his luck, Hattie decided, with this downright brazen behaviour. How could he? What a nerve! She picked up her pen and scribbled a few notes for her fascinated witnesses. However, the girls had by now chewed their way through jam doughnuts and were now giggling over texts on their iPhones. Hattie's play-acting was no longer interesting enough to keep their attention. What had Nick said about lunchtime meetings, thought Hattie, apart from implying they were boring and that Madge wasn't involved? Admittedly, the girl *could* be part of the changes at Padgett and Bicton, although she just knew she'd seen the girl before, and not at the firm's Christmas do. If only she'd had a better view of her face before she sat down. Hattie fished out her mobile and tapped in Nick's office number. This was one way of checking out the truth of the situation.

'Is that Madge? Hattie Chesney speaking. Is Nick around?' she asked, lowering her voice and ducking down behind her magazine.

'Oh hello, Mrs Chesney. No, sorry, he's out at lunch at the moment. He left the office about half an hour ago. Is there a message or will you call back?'

'Er... um,' floundered Hattie, realising she hadn't concocted a reason for her call. 'No, it can wait. Is he having a lunchtime meeting with Rafiq, and the secretary?'

'No, he's not with Rafiq because I've just seen him at the coffee machine just down the corridor. Which secretary did you mean?' Madge was sounding quite shirty. She'd evidently caught her at an awkward time.

'Um, would Rafiq have a secretary or a PA?' Hattie asked tentatively.

'Rafiq? Goodness me no! He has to type his own letters just like the rest of us. It's only the top nobs who have PAs. They can't afford such luxuries for the rest of us ordinary mortals.'

'I see. Well, it's not that important and you don't need to mention I called. He'll only think it's some emergency, which it's not.'

'I understand, Mrs Chesney. I've more than enough to do as it is,' she huffed. 'It's all right for those who only work part-time I'm sure.'

Ah well, pondered Hattie, Nick's cover is well and truly blown. She lowered her magazine to check the situation, but it looked like Raspberry Beret was preparing to leave. Hattie pushed her magazine into her bag, then, positioning her mobile carefully, took a picture. This was more for the girls' benefit than anything else. Sure enough, they were gazing at her open-mouthed and despite her annoyance at Nick's very public behaviour, she couldn't help enjoying her little charade.

'You need evidence,' she murmured.

'What, for court you mean?' asked the one with Gothic over-tones.

'Well,' confided Hattie, leaning across the table, 'let's hope it doesn't get as far as that.' She pocketed her mobile and gathered her belongings.

By now, Nick was preparing to leave and was helping Raspberry Beret with her jacket. Then he went ahead and opened the door, the very epitome of chivalry. When was the last time he'd made such a gesture for *her* benefit? The answer was, a very long time ago. Now she was in a quandary. Should she follow on behind Nick and the girl at a discreet distance and risk being seen by Hilda and Celia? She really didn't want to give Mrs Beady-Eyes any more satisfaction than she had already. Perhaps her hooded jacket and sunglasses would conceal her identity well enough to make an anonymous exit. Without further hesitation, she quickly nipped down the stairs and left Maggie's without a backward glance. Once outside, she realised she may have waited too long, as there was no sign of Nick or the girl in any direction. Which way to go? Maybe back towards the town centre? She crossed the square and glanced up the narrow alleyway.

'Yes!' she breathed, the scent of the hunt in her nostrils. At the far end, they'd stopped and were chatting. Hattie moved to one side and leaned against the wall, hoping she wouldn't be noticed. Then the girl turned in one direction and Nick in the other and they were both gone from sight. Perhaps Raspberry Beret was one of Nick's colleagues who was off to do some shopping. Whoever she was, she had managed to conceal her identity and this was causing Hattie great irritation. All she'd seen was the briefest glimpse of a profile, and a tiny wisp of fair hair, but even so, there was something familiar about her apart from the beret. She'd never seen such a sleek fashion statement on the head of anyone in her current circle of friends or acquaintances. Where might she have seen her? The bank or possibly the library or even the college? But not with the hat of course.

There was no time for hanging around. She hurried up the alley and carefully checked in both directions before emerging. The shuttle bus that served the industrial estate had stopped a few yards to the right on the opposite side of the road. There was every chance that Nick would be getting on board. Hattie removed her sunglasses, pulled her hood well down and set off after the girl who by now was a good way down the busy main street. Some 100 metres further on, her quarry paused at a shop window, giving Hattie a chance to gain some ground. She was determined not to lose sight of the distinctive headgear, which now bobbed along ahead of her.

'Oh, hello there, Mrs Chesney,' came a young female voice close by. Hattie snapped out of hunting mode to see the familiar figure of Tanya Preston, almost as scantily clad as on the night at The Feisty Ferret. Her irritation grew by a few more degrees as she remembered Nick's brazen drooling that evening.

'Tanya! Well I never! Not at school today?' she asked, wondering if Gloria knew her precious daughter was parading her burgeoning womanhood around the streets of Aylesbury.

'Study leave!' trilled Tanya with a pout that any WAG would have been proud of.

'Oh, really? So you've left your study to give your poor brain cells a bit of a rest, eh?' retorted Hattie dryly.

Tanya shifted her weight from one 4-inch wedge heel to the other and frowned at Hattie's reply, trying to work out if there had been a trace of sarcasm in it.

'Yeah, well, you can't keep at it all day can you? Stands to reason.'

'Indeed,' agreed Hattie, aghast that this depressingly dull exchange had sabotaged her pursuit. 'Must dash!'

Where was the bobbing beret? All Hattie could see was a trickle of pedestrians in muted greys, beiges and sombre navies. Not a speck of raspberry wool was in sight.

'Oh, cowpats!' she muttered in frustration. Maybe the girl worked in one of the shops or offices nearby, but even Hattie in her keenness to track her down, wasn't in the mood for too much browsing. She sauntered along aimlessly, glancing in the windows of boutiques and building societies, hoping to spot the girl, until she saw Mia Casa up ahead. No, she thought, I mustn't go any further. The temptation of seeing Leo was so strong, but that would have to wait until later. She turned abruptly and walked back towards the multi-storey car park, reviewing the scene in Maggie's. So, Nick was spending his lunch breaks with a twenty-something stick insect with a penchant for stylish headgear, but with his new job starting soon she didn't think there was much to worry about. Who was she though? Perhaps I'll never find out, she told herself as she headed off to buy snacks for the patch-work party.

'Tiring day at the office, Nick?' asked Hattie casually as she ladled out goulash from the slow cooker. On the subject of lunchtime encounters Hattie had decided to stay mum. After all, her own behaviour had hardly been exemplary of late.

'Yeah,' he replied wearily. 'Lots of loose ends to tie up, you know.'

'More meetings do you mean?'

'Oh well, there's plenty of those, and it's almost the end of the tax year as well.'

He tucked into his food, so Hattie had to wait a few moments before she could lay her carefully-planned trap.

'What a bind,' she commented sympathetically between mouthfuls. 'And through your lunch break again?' Hopefully Madge hadn't accidentally mentioned her phone call.

'Hmm... bit of a pain, but I have to have everything sorted before I hand over to Rafiq.'

'Poor you,' she murmured, putting on her most understanding expression. 'You'll be ready for a change of scene after all those dull meetings in dull old boardrooms.'

'Yep, I certainly will. Rafiq can rabbit for England once he gets going. You sit there wondering when he's going to draw breath.'

'Ah, but it's probably because he's anxious to do a good job. You'll just have to forgive him for taking up your valuable free time.'

'I guess so.'

'Anyway,' said Hattie brightly, still picturing the lunchtime scene at Maggie's, 'you'll soon be away from all that.'

They were well into rhubarb crumble and custard when Nick started to discuss the arrangements for his leaving do the following week.

'I've booked The Four Seasons,' he announced. 'You know where that is, do you?'

Hattie's pulse set up a fierce gallop. 'Yes, that's where Cynthia and I had coffee a few weeks ago.'

'It'll be straight after work next Wednesday. It was the best time for everybody and the company is paying for the buffet.'

'That's very generous.'

'Well, I *have* been there a while,' he continued, 'but they're not paying for the bar.'

'Well, maybe Madge will buy you a drink – for old time's sake.'

'I won't hold my breath.'

'Oh, I don't know. Of course, if you buy *her* a drink, she might just throw caution to the wind and give everyone a demo of what she's been learning at college.'

'God, what a horrible thought!'

'Gross!' added Josh, scraping around the crumble bowl for the last dregs.

'Mind you, I've nothing against belly dancing per se,' commented Nick, grinning. 'Those detergent ads on the telly are very tasty, very full of eastern promise. You know the ones I mean?'

'Oh yes,' replied Hattie, 'but I've seen some of Madge's dancing chums and it's mainly the crimplene slacks and perm brigade.'

'Really?' Nick sounded disappointed.

'Except their teacher of course. I caught a glimpse of her one night and she's in a different category altogether,' Hattie told him.

'Oh… er… yeah. Madge is always banging on about Rebecca this and Rebecca that. Sounds like she's quite an expert.'

Nick scraped round his dish and cast a disappointed glance in Josh's direction.

'Any more calls from Samways?' he asked.

'Unfortunately not. It's all gone horribly quiet ever since that offer from the Judges.'

'Well, it's just not good enough,' he announced, throwing down his spoon. 'So I've made a decision.'

'Really?' Hattie hadn't seen him so animated since... Well, actually, it hadn't been that long – five hours ago in Maggie's to be precise.

'I've decided we should let that other company see if they can do any better.'

'Other company?' asked Hattie in surprise, wondering how Nick had changed his mind about Mia Casa. After his confrontation with Leo, it sounded highly unlikely.

'Yes, you know, the one with the stupid name. They did the valuation, but I thought it was a bit OTT.'

'Hmm, maybe it was.'

'Anyway, old Madge's been wittering on about why didn't we choose dear Greg's company. I think Sandra's been on at her, so I thought I'd let them have a shot.' Nick leaned back in his chair and folded his arms across his chest, smug self-satisfaction plastered over his face. Josh sniffed noisily, picked up his dish, dumped it on the draining board and then started rifling through the fridge. Hattie sat open-mouthed in amazement, marginally more surprised by Josh's thoughtful gesture than Nick's willingness to do business with Mia Casa.

'What? You've decided to give them a call, or shall I do it? I could phone and speak to Greg first thing in the morning.' This was quite an about-turn for Nick, although the prospect of Leo escorting people around the house was quite pleasant, in a bitter-sweet sort of way.

'No, it's all arranged,' he announced matter-of-factly, and with that he dumped his dish and escaped to football heaven.

'Well, thanks for telling me,' murmured Hattie, distinctly niggled by Nick's high-handed attitude.

'Chill, Mum,' muttered Josh, wiping his mouth on his sleeve after draining half a carton of strawberry smoothie. 'Dad's just showing he's an alpha male.'

'You think so? Well, I wonder how he managed to squeeze this change of plan into his jam-packed day.'

As she cleared the table and loaded the dishwasher, one positive thought lodged in her mind: Nick must have forgiven Leo for his letter and that meant she was now out of the doghouse for her deliberate deception.

14

Open Day at the college was going swimmingly. Throughout the evening, while the Beginner's Patchwork group sipped elderflower cordial and nibbled on crisps and assorted finger food, a steady trickle of would-be students wandered in to admire the work on display.

'Just think, ladies,' Zena told a cluster who were admiring Cynthia's completed cot cover, every square neatly hand-quilted, 'you *too* could produce work like this in just one eight-week course.'

'We've some sign-up sheets here if you want to book in for next term,' added Marigold with a wodge of them in her hand.

'We'll also be running an Advanced Patchwork Course for those who wish to continue with their learning. Both courses can be booked at twenty-five per cent off if you fill in a form tonight.'

'Will you be signing up?' Hattie asked Cynthia later on.

'Not sure,' Cynthia replied wistfully. 'The twenty-five per cent discount is tempting, but Donald's threatened to confiscate my bank card if I spend any more on all this.' She sighed ruefully as she carefully removed her quilt from the display board and folded it up.

'But the fabric doesn't have to be brand new,' Hattie reminded her. 'How about trawling the charity shops like Zena and Marigold?'

'Oh yes,' chuckled Cynthia, 'then I can tell everyone I'm making *vintage* quilts; sounds much better than second-hand, doesn't it.'

'Well, I hope it goes well,' Hattie replied as she packed her own unfinished one. 'Might I see you at Quaintly if the charity day goes ahead?'

'Wouldn't miss it for the world!' murmured Cynthia with a wink.

As she bustled over to Marigold to collect her form, Hattie quickly went into the corridor to send a very important text: *Meet 4 coffee?* Nick's change of heart about Mia Casa had been exercising her mind most of the evening. She was dying to know more and spending time with Leo, even briefly, was a tempting prospect. He generally replied fairly promptly, but by the time Hattie reached the entrance hall, there'd been no word from him. All around her, there were students and visitors chatting and giggling, with an air of end-of-term excitement, while she stood there waiting, like a spare part.

'Yoo-hoo, Hat!'

That was Fliss's voice. What was *she* doing there? With Fliss around, the chance of a cosy chat with Leo was disappearing fast. Her heart sank at the prospect.

'Fliss, fancy seeing you here! Don't say you're here signing up for next term. I hear the belly dancing is very popular,' chuckled Hattie, pushing aside her frustration.

'What? Belly dancing? God no! Not *my* thing at all. The thought of sharing a room with a dozen perspiring matrons is *not* my idea of a fun evening. Give me the fitness club any day,' she chuckled with a grin. 'No, I'm just here on another of Mark's errands.'

That explained why Leo hadn't replied. She glanced over Fliss's left shoulder and saw him rounding the corner. 'Of course, the language course.'

'Yes, that's right,' replied Fliss, lowering her voice. 'I've just spent a wonderful hour or so in the company of the delectable Signor Marcello.' Turning around, she spotted him just a few feet away. 'Look, here he is now. Let me introduce you, Hat… unless you've already met him,' she teased. 'Ah, now I remember, you were out in the garden, weren't you?'

Hattie's insides went into meltdown. 'Signor Marcello, meet my friend Hattie.'

'Oh...yes, Signor Marcello,' murmured Hattie, holding his gaze, 'we did meet briefly, didn't we, when you came to carry out a valuation.'

'Charmed to meet you again,' murmured Leo, bowing and taking her hand, and kissing it gently. In her mind, she replayed her previous wicked fantasy of tearing off his clothes in unrestrained passion. Just the gentlest brush of his lips was enough to set her heart pounding and ignite a bright blush on her cheeks. Fliss studied the two of them carefully and noted with interest the change in Hattie's complexion.

'Signor Marcello − Leo, that is,' explained Fliss, flashing a provocative smile in his direction, 'has been tying up a few loose ends. Mark's away until the end of the week, so I've been the messenger again. Not that I'm complaining of course. It takes my mind off Mum's situation.'

Leo nodded and smiled.

'Oh... sorry, Hat. Are we holding you up? Were you waiting for someone?'

'Er, no problem,' flustered Hattie. 'I think she may have gone already.'

Before Fliss could continue, Hattie was aware of a small body bustling past her.

'Ah, Signor Marcello!' It was Madge, rosy-cheeked and glowing from her recent exertions. She offered a chubby hand and was rewarded with the usual Leo treatment, giggling like an embarrassed teenager. Then she glanced at the two women she'd just pushed past. 'Oh, it's Mrs Chesney again! Catching up on the house-selling arrangements are you?'

Hattie shot a startled look in Leo's direction. He, on the other hand, was obviously bemused by Madge's words.

'Ah-ha,' murmured Fliss, as Madge's excited chatter continued unabashed.

'I must say, I *was* disappointed when you decided to let that stodgy Brian Samways handle the sale, but it'll be *much* better now that you've got Mia Casa involved.' She flushed with a confident smile, as if she was claiming credit for the change of plan.

'I'm sorry but I'm not with you,' Leo faltered. 'I didn't know about this.'

'You didn't know?' Hattie asked Leo. He shook his head. 'That's odd, oh well I expect it's just in the early stages.'

'I expect Greg will tell you in the morning,' Madge continued. 'He *is* the boss after all.'

'Well actually…' Leo interrupted, trying to put the record straight, but Madge blundered on, unaware that her understanding of the Mia Casa set-up was wildly off-course.

'Sandra's so proud of him. Mind you, he had a wonderful start with his schooling, so it's no surprise is it.'

'No, it was just an ordinary state school.' Leo tried to say.

'Oh no! Sandra told me he was at a *very* posh school in Somerset, because his dad worked there,' she announced defiantly. 'Perks of the job and all that!'

'As a groundsman,' muttered Leo softly to himself.

'And where *is* Sandra this evening?' asked Hattie, sensing a need for a change of subject. 'Still having problems with her bunions?'

'Oh no, she's gone to the ladies',' Madge replied in not-too-hushed tones. 'Waterworks trouble.' She nodded her head sagely. 'Well, I must be off. The girls are going for a drink at The Four Seasons. Ooh, looks like they might have gone without me!'

'Bye, Madge. Till next week then,' said Hattie.

Madge wrinkled her nose. 'Oh yes, the leaving do. Well, I expect so.' She gathered up her bag and rushed off, leaving the perplexed trio and an awkward silence.

Fliss raised her eyebrows and turned to Hattie. 'Ah, so that's the famous Madge I've heard so much about.'

Hattie nodded and glanced in Leo's direction, aware that Madge's blustering had irritated him. 'Now you understand how it's been for Nick over the past year,' she told Fliss with a chuckle. 'Not an ideal work situation, I can tell you.'

'Now, anyone for coffee? But not in The Four Seasons I think,' Fliss suggested brightly, 'Unless you've got different plans, Hat?'

'Um, no… coffee would be great. What about you Signor Marcello?'

Leo shuffled his feet and then glanced at his watch. 'Well, I guess I've some time and what could be better than to spend it with two such charming ladies?' he replied, recovering quickly.

Fliss simpered and fluttered her lashes.

'Stop drooling,' Hattie hissed in her ear, 'or I'll have to tell Mark you're not to be trusted as a messenger.'

Fliss giggled and linked arms with her friend. 'Ah, Hat, what it is to be a loyal and devoted wife! Didn't you know that the occasional eye-feast is just the sort of tonic you need from time to time,' she whispered as they set off, 'and if you're pretending to be immune to that sort of treat, then my granddad was a blobfish!'

'What's a blobfish?'

'A ball of slime that lives at the bottom of the ocean.'

'Well, I hope Signor Marcello didn't hear you describing him as an eye-feast.'

'What if he did? He's hardly going to be offended.'

He was on his way to the door, but just then turned and smiled. 'Let me lead the way, dear ladies. There's a rather good coffee bar I know where we can enjoy a drink without the company of the… er… person with the high opinion of my business partner,' he suggested and with a flourish, opened the door and then set off in the direction of The Bar on the Corner.

'Hope I haven't hijacked your evening, Hat,' whispered Fliss.

'No, not at all,' replied Hattie a little stiffly.

'Only you seem a bit put out.'

'It's just this business about the house sale,' Hattie improvised. 'Seems odd that Madge knows more about it than Signor Marcello.'

'It strikes me,' Fliss commented, 'that old Madge was hatched from the same mould as Mrs Makepeace.'

'Nosy and opinionated you mean,' chuckled Hattie, as they followed Leo.

'Well, this is cosy,' commented Fliss with a grin as they settled around a table that Hattie and Leo knew very well. 'I haven't been here for ages. How about you, Hat?'

'Um! Oh yes… once or twice,' she answered, avoiding Leo's gaze. 'So how's Mark's trip going?' she asked, determined to keep any conversation strictly on neutral subjects.

'Well, of course he's worn out as usual. These trade fairs are all about making contacts, attracting good orders, all the usual networking stuff. The poor love comes back absolutely shattered.'

The conversation continued along the same vein for a while, Leo sitting silently, engrossed in his own thoughts, until Fliss made a dash to the ladies'. This gave Hattie her opportunity.

'So, Leo, how is it you haven't heard that Mia Casa is now handling our sale?' Hattie demanded. 'Nick waited until we'd finished supper and then announced that it was all sorted. And now we know he's told Madge too.'

'Well, I wasn't aware of your house coming on our books,' Leo replied, mystified.

'That much is obvious,' said Hattie a touch irritably, 'and there was I thinking he'd actually spoken to you, you know, got over the letter business and everything.'

She took a sip of coffee and sighed. 'He's really fed up about Samways and had decided, in his own words, to "let that other lot have a go". He was quite huffy with me, as if they were *my* choice. To be honest, neither of us were all that impressed by Brian Samways and I'm not just talking about his capacity for demolishing the contents of my biscuit tin.'

'I see.'

Hattie held Leo's gaze for a moment more than was good for her heart. All the usual reactions kicked in: the pounding, churning, light-headedness and rapid breathing, as if she'd just survived the Oblivion experience at Alton Towers.

'Dear Hattie,' murmured Leo, moving his hand a fraction closer to hers, 'I sometimes wonder if that husband of yours really knows what a treasure he has.'

'Oh no, no… I'm not the perfect wife, I assure you. Look what happened last time we…' she protested, shaking her head, in an attempt to rid her memory of the car park kiss.

'How can I forget?' he murmured warmly.

'I'm shameless, that's what I am. The trouble is, after twenty or so years of marriage, things can get a bit samey, but it doesn't mean we've fallen out of love.'

'You don't sound very convinced,' he said gravely.

'Well, someone *did* tell me the other day… It may be nothing, but there's this mischief-making old bat called Hilda Makepeace.'

Fliss had returned unnoticed. 'Oh, Hat, you're not telling Signor Marcello about that scandal-monger are you? Goodness, you two must have been getting on like a house on fire if you're revealing the family skeletons to a virtual stranger.'

Hattie blushed and took a quick gulp of coffee. Leo's hand, meanwhile, went back in his pocket where he fished out his mobile and pressed the 'off' button.

'Well, er, I can't think how it came up,' asserted Hattie with a shake of her head.

'Signor Marcello,' giggled Fliss, 'you wouldn't believe it; poor Hattie had this annoying old busy-body knocking on her door last week, saying that her husband was spending his lunchtimes with a bright young thing in Maggie's Sandwich bar – ow!'

Hattie had managed a well-aimed tap under the table.

'Fliss, please… No!' she hissed. Despite the background music, however, Leo had heard every word.

'Maggie's Sandwich Bar? I believe my colleague Rebecca goes there for her lunch most days.'

'Oh really?' asked Fliss eagerly. 'This sounds interesting.'

'And does she have a raspberry pink beret?' asked Hattie.

'What?' exclaimed Fliss, shooting a puzzled glance.

'Well, yes, I believe she does,' replied Leo, non-plussed by Hattie's questioning.

'And a silvery grey jacket?' Hattie continued.

'Er… yes, I think so.'

The two women exchanged horrified glances.

'Rebecca the belly dancer, the Mia Casa girl... Now it's all making sense. Of course! I've seen her at the college too!'

'Ah-ha!' gasped Fliss. 'So you went to Maggie's then. I must admit I was tempted, but hadn't quite found the time. Oh, how yummy!'

'What? *You* were going to spy on him?' snapped Hattie accusingly.

'Well, isn't that what *you* were doing?'

'I *am* his wife after all, Fliss. I *needed* to know.' The two friends glared at each other.

'Ladies, ladies, please calm down,' Leo begged. 'It appears that my colleague was conducting business in her lunch hour – not the usual practice, I admit – but I'm sure it was all quite legitimate.'

'You think so?' asked Hattie hopefully. 'Then why didn't she share her news with the rest of the office when she returned?'

'And how many lunch hours did it take to arrange that?' Fliss asked, tapping her finger on the table. 'Half a dozen?'

'We don't know how long it's been going on, Fliss. We've only got Hilda Makepeace's say-so,' Hattie protested.

'And *yours* now, it seems,' Fliss reminded her, with a lift of her neatly shaped brows.

'Hmm, well that only accounts for two lunch hours.'

'But you said Hilda implied it was an on-going source of entertainment,' argued Fliss with a smirk.

'And Hilda might be prone to gross exaggeration,' retorted Hattie.

'Whatever,' said Fliss dismissively. 'Anyway, it proves your Nick is a dark horse. The sooner he's shipped off to Lydford Cross the better, by the sound of it.

'I'm sure there's nothing to worry about, Mrs... er... Chesney,' Leo assured her.

'Oh, please, call me Hattie, Signor Marcello. It's so much friendlier.'

'And you can call me Leo,' he replied, playing his role to perfection.

'As if you didn't know already!' Fliss murmured under her breath.

'What's that Fliss?'

'Oh, nothing, Hat. Oh no!' Her mobile was singing to itself inside the cavernous depths of her shoulder bag. 'It's only Tom,' she announced, scrolling down the text. 'Just checking up on his mum and wondering when she'll be home. It comes to something when your teenage sons start checking up on you!' She glanced at her watch. 'Is *that* the time! Must dash. Nice to meet you again, Leo. I expect Mark will be in touch sometime soon. Do keep me posted, Hat.' She gathered up her belongings, flashing a knowing smile in her direction.

'Oh, I'll certainly do that,' promised Hattie.

'And don't do anything I wouldn't,' Fliss giggled, making a hasty exit.

'Fliss isn't known for her discretion, as it happens, and there was once some rumour about her having a fling with a gardener. It was ages ago, when the children were small,' confided Hattie. 'I'd gone over to have coffee with her when Josh was still preschool and dropped into Bledlow Post Office for something on my way home. I remember overhearing two women on the other side of a display unit have a giggle, then Fliss's name was mentioned with a lot of speculation about a mystery man with a mower. I don't know who the women were, but I remember being quite shocked, so I stopped browsing, grabbed Josh's hand and left. Of course it could have been someone's wild imagination. When I broached the subject with Fliss later on, although she dismissed it as village tittle-tattle, I had a feeling there was more than a grain of truth in there somewhere.'

Leo nodded solemnly.

'So when she says don't do anything I wouldn't... Well, you get the picture?'

'Hmm, I think so,' replied Leo, frowning.

'Oh, I'm sorry, Leo. Of course I shouldn't be boring you with all this. Fliss would say I'm just as bad as Hilda Makepeace,' apologised Hattie. 'So it's Mia Casa to the rescue then,' she added after a pause.

'Ah yes, I'm to have the dubious pleasure of trying to sell your house any day now,' he said with a sigh. This time his hand reached hers and gave it a squeeze.

'Don't look at me like that, Leo. It's not good for my heart.' She pulled her hand free.

'Your heart, Hattie?'

'Yes,' she told him briskly. 'There's a danger of it being broken all over again.'

'I'm sorry. I didn't mean to – '

'You don't need to apologise and I really should be going,' she murmured, fastening her jacket. 'It's been a rather emotional roller-coaster of a day.' She picked up her work folder, slung her bag across her shoulder and shot a quick smile in his direction. 'I'll see you... er... well...'

'Oh, let me escort you,' offered Leo. 'My car's back at the college too.'

'Are you worried that the Gatehouse thugs will get me?' she asked warily.

'Well, Canal Walk can sometimes attract the rougher element, I've noticed.'

They walked in silence, Hattie speculating on her chances of telling Leo to keep his distance. Could she, would she or was she on the inevitable slide down the slippery slope of unfaithfulness? The trouble was, knowing that Nick was indulging in some extra-marital distraction himself gave her a convenient loophole of her own. So there they were again, just like two weeks before, facing each other as Hattie paused, car keys in hand. They held each other's gaze, both seeming to hold back from what they knew was out of bounds.

'Thank you, Leo,' said Hattie softly, reaching out and touching his arm.

'For what?'

'For being here for me; for being a friend.'

'Oh, to be more than that,' he sighed with feeling, shaking his head.

'Twenty-six years too late, Leo. You know that,' she reminded him.

'But not for this...'

Before she could protest, he had drawn her tenderly close to him, and his mouth found hers. A deep desire grew, low down in her stomach and spread rapidly, consuming her until she felt weak and dizzy. All she wanted was to remain wrapped in his powerful embrace, while the memory of their long-ago intimacy replayed in her mind in all its splendour.

'Oh, Leo. Dear Leo,' she gasped breathlessly, pulling away from his mouth and reaching up to enclose his head in her hands and lose herself in his searching gaze. He leaned towards her again, his arms gripping firmly around her waist, when the shrill sound of her mobile brought them abruptly back to earth. Hattie jumped away guiltily and turned to unlock the Clio.

'You'd better go, Leo. I don't know what came over me,' she faltered, trembling. 'I expect Nick's wondering where I am.'

'It wasn't your fault,' Leo protested. 'Good night, sweet Hattie.' He turned and set off to find his car, while she felt hot tears coursing down her cheeks; whether out of shame or regret, she did not know. Of one thing she was certain: where guilt was concerned, she and Nick were both as bad as one another, giving her every reason to follow her heart.

'Good morning, Mrs Chesney.'

Hattie needed no introduction to the young woman at the door with the smart briefcase and efficient smile. The raspberry pink beret and silver-grey jacket were uncomfortably familiar.

'Oh, good morning,' Hattie replied in a fluster, 'and you are...?'

'Rebecca Vaudin from Mia Casa. Greg Allanby phoned earlier I believe.'

Even if there hadn't been another reason, Hattie took an instant dislike to the girl, with her brisk and condescending tone.

'Oh yes, he did, but didn't say who'd be calling. Well, you'd better come in,' replied Hattie, utterly deflated. And to think of all the effort she'd made, imagining Leo would be the one who would be calling.

Rebecca swept in with wafts of something exotic, making her feel distinctly homespun by comparison. Catching sight of her own reflection in the hall mirror, she wondered what Leo saw in her. Despite her best efforts, it was not an inspiring sight. Miss Vaudin, however, was strutting around on vertiginous heels as if she owned the place. No prizes for guessing what she and Nick had been discussing over coffee and baguettes at Maggie's the day before.

'So, my husband phoned your office yesterday to fix things did he?' asked Hattie casually, once Rebecca had completed the ground-floor measurements and taken photos. 'He's so busy at work at the moment; I didn't imagine that he'd found the time to call into your office.' Hattie watched carefully to see how she'd answer, but the girl was quick to turn away, scribbling on her clipboard all the while – a very sneaky move, she thought.

'Possibly,' Rebecca replied indifferently.

'Well, let's hope your company can find a buyer,' Hattie commented. 'Shall we go upstairs?' However, Rebecca was already on her way.

'These posters will have to come down,' she observed disdainfully, pointing at Josh's walls. 'They're not a good selling point you know and make the place look cluttered. It's a small enough room as it is.'

'Right, I'll see to that.' Hattie could imagine how Josh would greet the news.

'I don't think I'll bother to take a picture in here; it might put buyers off.'

This girl was much worse than the ones she'd seen on TV. On completing the family bathroom details she had yet more to add to Hattie's deflating self-esteem.

'I'd advise you to invest in some new towels; white or cream would be advisable – matching of course,' she sniffed haughtily as she cast a final eye around the room.

Hattie felt mortified. She had put out fresh, fluffy, two-tone blues ones that morning, but obviously these weren't good enough for Miss Vaudin. 'Really?'

'Definitely,' confirmed Rebecca, 'and I suggest you update the light-fitting. It's rather tired you know. *Too* eighties!'

She flounced out leaving Hattie open-mouthed in disbelief. Count to ten, she told herself, her hands clenched into tight fists. By the time she'd recovered some self-control, Rebecca was already in their bedroom, having a good nose around before taking pictures and noting dimensions.

'Too many knick-knacks on the dressing-table,' she told Hattie, 'and I should put away all those cheap toiletries. Of course designer perfume is absolutely fine, if you've got any, that is.' By the tone of her voice, she doubted the existence of such a luxury in the Chesney household. 'Ditto the towels in the en-suite,' Rebecca continued with a smile that was more of a self-satisfied smirk, running her finger along the windowsill for evidence of dust. Hattie turned and stormed out silently. This girl was the limit!

'I'll be downstairs in the hall when you've finished up here,' she told her, knowing that if she heard any more nit-picking remarks, she'd be in serious danger of throttling that pretty little neck.

'We'll be sending out texts to everyone on our database in the next few hours,' Rebecca informed Hattie, 'so I'd advise you to prepare the house for viewing.'

The fact that there was a Samways 'For Sale' board outside seemed to have momentarily escaped her.

'You may wish to employ professional cleaners to give the place a *proper* overhaul and don't forget to ditch the knick-knacks if you're serious about selling.'

'But my friend Fliss says the downstairs is fine.'

'Is your friend a property consultant?' asked Rebecca tartly.

'Well no –'

'Exactly,' rapped Rebecca, 'so if you take my professional advice you'll do everything I've suggested. Here, have this list and if you need any numbers for reliable domestic cleaning companies, I can give you a couple.'

Next came the vexed subject of the selling price, until Hattie reminded her of the Samways valuation.

'What a shame,' she commented. 'I see Signor Marcello gave a higher figure and I'm sure we could achieve that if the house was properly presented. Oh well, we'd better stick with your current price.'

Hattie nodded and made an obvious show of checking her watch, hoping Rebecca would take the hint and leave.

'Well, I'll be off,' she said, closing her briefcase, 'so you can make a start on my list.' There was a brief smile, which did not reach her eyes, as she strutted out to leave Hattie fuming and in desperate need of caffeine and calories. Her blood had cooled down somewhat when the phone rang half an hour later. It was Nick, sounding very perky.

'Hi, Hat. Have Mia Casa done their stuff yet?'

'Most definitely,' she informed him grimly.

'What's up, Hat? You sound a bit upset.'

'A bit upset?' she mimicked. 'It's not surprising after the lecture I've had to endure. It feels as if I've been through a mangle!'

'Oh, wasn't Mr Allanby happy with the house? I mean, he hadn't seen it before, had he?'

'Mr Allanby? No, it wasn't Mr Allanby; it was his blonde little cutie-pie Rebecca Vaudin.' As soon as the words were out of her mouth she regretted it. 'She picked holes in *everything*! Told me to buy new towels, if you please, take down Josh's posters, ditch the bathroom light-fitting, put away Jezebel's dishes – she obviously doesn't have pets – and she insinuated that any less-than-designer perfume should be kept out of sight.'

There was a stony silence at Nick's end.

'Who does she think she is? Some TV house-styling guru?'

An embarrassed cough, a sure sign that Nick was searching for the right words, could be heard after a brief pause.

'Well, I'm sure she meant it for the best,' he replied, not sounding as perky as before. 'I mean, she's an agent trying to sell our home. Perhaps it's good to have an objective opinion.'

'But, Nick, she was so superior about it and it didn't sound very objective to me. It sounded like a personal attack. This is a family home, for goodness' sake, not a state-of-the-art apartment on Canary Wharf!'

'Calm down, Hat. It sounds like you're getting it all out of proportion. Now, how about popping along to your favourite store and buying the towels Rebecca suggested?' ventured Nick. 'And if you see anything else that would brighten up the house, then go ahead and splash out, okay? No need for good old cheap and cheerful either.'

'No need for good old cheap and cheerful? Well you've certainly changed your tune!' Hattie snapped angrily.

'Oh sorry, Hat. Er, someone's just turned up in the office. I really must go. See you!'

The line went dead before Hattie could reply.

'The bitch!' she cursed and slammed down the phone. It was quite clear that the girl had bewitched Nick and nothing she said was going to make the slightest bit of difference. Still, Hattie was never averse to a spot of retail therapy and after another sustaining milk chocolate digestive, she set off feeling ready to punish the bank account, seeing as Nick had given his blessing. It wouldn't be the usual out-of-town chain store either. Seventh Heaven was the designer homeware outlet that she visited infrequently and only for wishful browsing. Quite simply, the prices were beyond her usual budget, but if Nick meant what he'd said, then she'd take him at his word.

Three hours later, she sank gratefully onto a comfortably squashy sofa in the store's café area, surrounded by yummy mummies and plum-in-the-mouth county types who probably treated the place like most mere mortals treated Tesco. Dumping down her bulging carriers, she loosened her jacket and slipped off her shoes for a few moments. Bliss!

'Um… a Danish and a cappuccino please,' she told the smiling waitress who had arrived surprisingly quickly beside her. Despite Rebecca's snooty pronouncements, Hattie had had a wonderful time splashing out in the shop of her dreams. She'd tracked down sumptuous, snowy towels, a sleek light-fitting, pretty lined baskets for bath essentials and some smart stripy mugs to add to her growing collection. There was also a new bathroom roller blind, tea towels – even nicer than the ones at Rosehill Garden Centre – and washing-up brushes to replace the tatty ones she'd made do with for too long. There was nothing like a shopping trip to lift her spirits. However, if Rebecca had her sights on conducting all the viewings, how would Hattie cope?

'There you are madam.' Glistening with a thick layer of icing and a sugary glaze, the pastry seemed to cover most of the plate. It took care of most of a day's calories as well, but Hattie was past caring.

'Scrummy!' Hattie breathed. She'd make a point of leaving a tip. The service was certainly impressive.

'Hi, Hat. Fancy seeing you here! Any room for me?'

Hattie jumped guiltily. Fliss swore by regular detox and considered pastry consumption to be the eighth deadly sin.

'Fliss, what a lovely surprise! Yes, do come and join me!' She hastily swept away the pastry flakes that clung to her jacket and took a sip from her mug. Fliss, predictably, was clutching a bottle of plain mineral water. If only it had been someone like Cynthia who just happened along, thought Hattie; someone who wouldn't quiz her but would be happy to chat about the finer points of hand-quilting or Donald's latest plans for the garden.

'So, what brings you here?' Fliss asked eagerly, eyeing up the bulging carriers. 'Has Nick unlocked his wallet for once? That must have been a piggy I saw doing a loop the loop outside a moment ago.'

'He's not *that* bad,' protested Hattie. 'I'd rather have a thrifty husband than one who boozed and gambled and ran up horrendous credit card bills.'

'Of course, but there *is* a happy compromise and I see that he's found it at last.'

Hattie then recounted the humiliating events of the morning and Nick's phone call. The timing had been uncanny.

'Sounds like he's feeling guilty,' concluded Fliss. 'By letting you loose on a wild spending spree, he's attempting to make up for his passing dalliance with the delightful Rebecca. It's probably all very innocent though.'

'You think so?' asked Hattie earnestly. She was feeling far from innocent about the two car park clinches with Leo.

'Absolutely.'

'The trouble is,' continued Hattie glumly, 'we're likely to be seeing a lot more of the delightful Miss Vaudin. I've a shrewd idea she's taken charge of our house sale and I bet she'll be checking up on me as part of her to-do list.'

'Oh, bad luck, Hat.' She paused to pour some mineral water into a glass. 'Actually, on the subject of Mia Casa… what about the sexy signor then?' She shot a sideways glance at her friend after taking a sip. Definitely some guilt there, she decided with a faint smile.

'How do you mean?' asked Hattie guardedly.

Fliss chuckled. 'Oh come on, Hat. Even a blind man could have noticed the chemistry between the two of you. I mean, the glances you were exchanging last night *and* the body language.'

'What glances? Can't a girl enjoy the company of a dishy bloke and give her flirting techniques a little outing once in a while?'

'Hmm, I'm not sure it's just that. What about all that stuff you were telling him when I came back from the loo? It's not the sort of chat you tend to have with a stranger, so don't you try and pretend otherwise.'

'I don't agree, Fliss,' retorted Hattie. 'Sometimes it's much

335

easier to talk to someone you don't know well, and I was still so irritated by Nick's lunchtime performance.'

'If you say so,' sighed Fliss. She turned her attention to her water, while Hattie munched a few more calories. 'And after I left?' she asked lightly.

'Well, we chatted for a short while…'

'And?'

'That's all. I had to get back, so we left and went our separate ways.' She shrugged as she said it, but was careful to avoid Fliss's gaze as she licked the tip of a finger and dabbed up the rest of the crumbs on her plate.

'So did he escort you?'

'Fliss, what part of "went our separate ways" did you not understand? Is this the Spanish Inquisition or something?'

'No… just curious. So did he? He's wonderfully old-fashioned. It's just the sort of thing I can imagine him doing.'

'Well, it was just a matter of collecting our cars from the college, so naturally we had to go the same way to start with. That's about it.'

'Oh, you disappoint me, Hat. There was Naughty Nicholas in Maggie's with Rebecca the belly dancing queen, giving you the perfect excuse for a steamy grapple on the signor's back seat. I would if that had been Mark!'

'Fliss, what a suggestion! Climbing into the back seat of Signor Marcello's car was the last thing on my mind.'

'Or steamy grapples?' Fliss giggled.

Put like that, Hattie registered the sordidness of her fall from grace. Nick's very public meetings with Rebecca were just that – public – in contrast with Hattie's secretive acts of unfaithfulness. Shame stiffened her resolution to end them at once.

'You speak for yourself, Fliss. Anyway, what brings you to Seventh Heaven today?'

'Oh, changing the subject are we?' she giggled again. 'That's a sure sign there's something you'd rather not discuss. Fair enough…' and she went on to describe her latest idea for giving the extension a quick makeover. It was clear that she was trying to keep her mind occupied with more cheerful subjects rather than dwelling on her mother's declining health.

'I picked up some great ideas on the TV the other day,' she enthused. 'Just see what I've found. They're the perfect colour.' She then proceeded to bring out some stylish cushions and opulent throws.

'Wow, Fliss! I could revamp the whole of my wardrobe for the price of these. Mark must have landed a few prestigious orders on his latest trip, judging by some of the tags.'

'It helps.'

'Even with Nick's new job, I can't imagine ever being able to justify splurges like these,' she sighed wistfully, fingering the deep pile of one of the throws. 'But I guess money isn't everything…'

'No, it's not,' agreed Fliss, becoming reflective. 'I'd rather have my mum at the peak of health than wasting away with that awful disease.' She nodded sadly, all the joking and jollity sucked from her like a burst balloon. Her shoulders suddenly sagged and her head was in her hands.

'Oh, Fliss.' Hattie felt helpless watching her friend. Fliss shook her head slowly, a single tear trickling down her cheek. Hattie moved across and put a comforting arm around her, squatting beside her seat.

'Sometimes it feels so overwhelming,' Fliss whispered, choking back the sobs. 'Do you think there'll ever be a cure? It's horrible seeing someone you love so much shrinking and losing all their strength.'

'It must be dreadful… I can't imagine…' Suddenly the bleeping of her mobile cut in and rudely interrupted them. 'Blasted thing!' she cursed, rummaging in her pockets. Fliss blew her nose noisily and then carefully wiped around her eyes with a clean tissue. Hattie moved away to take the call, although nowhere in Seventh Heaven's upmarket café was exactly suitable for quiet phone conversations. Squealing spoilt brats and their mummies abounded.

'Important?' asked Fliss, who had by now regained her usual poise.

'Brian Samways. He's rustled up some prospective buyers who want to view tomorrow.'

'Does he know you're with another agent?'

'Oh yes, and he wasn't very impressed. He's got views on new companies like Mia Casa that he's more than willing to air.'

'Judging by your expression, Hat, I suspect they may be ones you wouldn't want to repeat in the hearing of Rebecca and co.'

'Indeed,' giggled Hattie. 'The word "cowboy" featured in them, I seem to remember.'

'He should be jolly relieved he's still in with a chance. Well, it's time to go I think,' she said, her eyes glazing over. It was obvious that she found house-selling deliberations as scintillating as an income tax return.

'Guess so,' agreed Hattie, 'the house won't clean itself.'

Twenty-four hours later, Hattie was spitting nails.

'You work your Marigolds to a frazzle,' she told Jezebel, who sat expectantly with whiskers twitching, 'and then they decide not to come.'

It wasn't until she'd arrived home that the news of the cancelled viewing came. Not long after, Nick arrived home to find her, feet up, eyes closed and no nearer to unpacking the shopping or starting on supper.

'All in, old girl?' he asked cheerfully, exuding an air of spring-like optimism. Hattie jolted to attention. 'Must have dozed off.'

'Any news of today's viewing?'

'Cancelled,' she told him glumly, flicking the kettle switch and popping a teabag into his Arsenal mug.

'Never mind. We've two booked in for tomorrow,' he announced brightly.

'But how come?'

Nick loosened his tie and started pulling things out of bags.

'Becky phoned this afternoon,' he replied, opening the fridge door with an armful of yoghurts.

'Becky?' queried Hattie. Then the penny dropped. 'Oh, Rebecca Vaudin. Of course! But why didn't she call here?'

'She did, but you weren't in, so she tried the office number I'd given her, for emergencies.'

'Ah, I see.' Of course, it made sense. But even so, it rankled.

On the dot of nine-thirty the following morning, as Hattie was swilling the downstairs loo with bleach, the phone rang. It was Pete Ingleheart.

'Good morning, Mrs Chesney. Geraldine has passed me a note about a Mrs Piles wanting to view today. Would eleven o'clock be okay?'

'Mrs *Piles?*' repeated Hattie, stifling a snigger. 'Eleven o'clock? Um… that's fine.' Piles? she chuckled to no one in particular once she'd replaced the receiver. 'I'd change my name by deed poll rather than be saddled with that, to Miles or…'

'Biles?' Nick put in, looking surprisingly smart for a Saturday and smelling suspiciously of aftershave.

Hattie ignored his remark and also chose not to ask what had happened to his favourite jeans.

'Sorry about the delay, Mrs Chesney,' said Pete as he ushered in his client ten minutes later than expected. 'Let me introduce Mrs Pil-*es*.' He raised his eyebrows as if to emphasise his earlier mistake. This time he pronounced the name 'Pill-*ez*'.

In swept an elegant, forty-something woman. She had short, dark hair – and not a grey hair in sight – cut in a fashionable wedge with a long fringe. She was ultra-slim, about a size 8 Hattie estimated enviously, and was very stylishly turned out. Why would such a woman be interested in 7 Witchert Close? She seemed a more likely candidate for something smart, modern or detached.

'Spanish,' whispered Pete, behind his hand, as his client strode into the sitting room to discover a delighted Nick. He abandoned his sports supplement, sprang out of his seat and seamlessly took on the persona of the welcoming host. Mrs Piles, who'd appeared rather distant on arrival, soon started to show signs of a slow thaw at Nick's full-on charm offensive. Hattie, however, retreated to the kitchen and settled down with a cup of coffee, her Sudoku book and Jezebel for company, leaving Pete to conduct the viewing in relative peace, aided and abetted by Nick. On their way through the kitchen a few minutes later, he flashed an encouraging smile and surreptitious thumbs-up, then returned later for a brief word while Mrs P revisited upstairs accompanied by a drooling Nick.

'Think she likes it,' Pete murmured encouragingly. 'Looking for a second home, but we're off to Chapelford next. Got a few more to see. I'll let you know if you're still in the running.'

'Oh, right. Okay,' whispered Hattie, hearing footsteps on the stairs, 'but a second home *here?*'

'Kids coming to Oxford probably,' Pete ventured on the way out.

'It figures,' agreed Hattie. 'It's just half an hour's drive away.'

Later that day, Nick was almost hopping from foot to foot in eager anticipation of Rebecca's imminent arrival.

'Now, you've got the bread-maker going, haven't you, Hat?'

'That's the second time you've asked me and the answer's still yes.'

'And the coffee-maker?'

'Nick, I'm not a total numskull. *Yes!* Now clear off and leave me to vimming the taps for the umpteenth time,' she snapped. 'I'm not having some snooty cow tell me how to clean my house,' she muttered under her breath

At exactly two-thirty, the doorbell rang and Nick was ready with a beaming smile. In tottered Rebecca on the same killer heels, followed by a diffident-looking couple and their small toddler.

'Right, shall I lead the way?' said Nick. There was the sound of footsteps on the stairs and then muted voices from above. Hattie peered round the kitchen door to find an empty hallway.

'Don't mind me,' she muttered crossly, 'I'm just the skivvy.'

A few minutes later Rebecca strutted into the kitchen, followed by tight-lipped parents and their pouting toddler.

'Okay Hat?' said Nick brightly as he followed on.

'Waa!' shrieked the child, from the utility room, after a loud feline yowl signalled the end of Jezebel's afternoon nap.

'No Bertie,' scolded the mother half-heartedly. 'Leave the pussy cat alone.' She was not very convincing. Escalating shrieks bounced off the walls.

'Nasty, vicious creature!' snarled the father, following the loud clatter of the cat-flap.

Rebecca strode back into the kitchen. 'That cat will have to go!' she snapped, hands on hips, giving her most officious stare.

'She most certainly will not,' retorted Hattie, glaring back. 'Anyone who pulls Jezebel's tail deserves what they get!' The shrieks in the utility room subsided and out marched Bertie and parents wearing disagreeable scowls.

'Shall we go back to the hall then?' suggested Rebecca stiffly, with an air of desperation. After the family had made a hasty exit, she returned to dish out the blame, which she was clearly laying at Hattie's feet.

'If you had taken my advice and put the animal in the garage for the afternoon, this would never have happened!'

'Jezebel was minding her own business, which is more than I can say about some people...'

Before Rebecca could form any kind of response to this, the sound of the doorbell was heard, followed by an embarrassed cough from Nick.

'Your next clients have arrived, Becky,' he called. 'Shall I let them in?'

Rebecca turned away abruptly and marched back into the hall. The second viewing was like a breath of spring air and the would-be buyers were exactly the sort of people that Hattie liked – child-free, polite and appreciative.

'I'll be in touch, Nick!' called Rebecca as she left.

'Yeah, see you then, Becky!' Nick called, lingering at the door as the sound of an engine was heard. 'That all went quite well,' he commented as he ambled back into the kitchen with a satis-fied grin.

'You think so?' replied Hattie grimly, her mind still occupied with Rebecca's outburst and her reaction to it. Not one of her best moments. 'Or perhaps you weren't aware of Miss Vaudin's bitter attack on poor Jezebel.'

'What bitter attack?'

'She told me to put her in the garage – and Jezebel was the innocent party! Didn't you see that noxious infant in action? Poor old Jezebel, minding her own business too.'

'Oh, Hat, you're making a mountain out of a coal hill.'

'Mole hill actually and I'm not. These people come in and wreak mayhem and that… that… *woman* blames *me*!'

'She's very conscientious. She was probably worrying about her clients,' he retorted defensively.

'And good riddance to them. Bertie and his parents can take a running jump as far as I'm concerned.' She threw down her scouring pad and reached for the biscuit tin.

'Well, I didn't notice much. Just a kid doing what kids usually do.'

'Really? Well, I suppose you were too busy drooling over Miss Vaudin and following her around.' She fished out a bourbon cream and bit into it hungrily.

'Well, Rebecca didn't seem to mind. I thought she liked me being there.'

'And it's all Rebecca this and Becky that now I notice,' commented Hattie pointedly.

'Why not?' replied Nick airily, pacing the floor with hands in pockets. 'People don't stand on ceremony these days.'

Hattie grunted peevishly and went to fill the kettle. 'Well, I thought it sounded much too chummy,' she replied, fixing Nick with a knowing look.

'Really? I just wanted to make her feel welcome.'

'Which you certainly did. In fact, she felt so welcome that she started to act as if she owned the place!'

The bread-maker beeped loudly to signal the end of baking time.

'Sounds as if you're jealous, Hat!' chuckled Nick.

'Oh, and of course you know nothing about jealousy do you, Nick?' The comment hung in the air between them and for a few seconds, there was complete silence as Hattie stared out of the window at nothing in particular.

'Time for the half time scores,' Nick muttered and retreated to the safety of the sitting room.

'Touché,' murmured Hattie to herself. 'One nil I think.'

Monday morning arrived and with it a text message.

Must c u. Leo.

Hattie felt a shiver of delight at the sight of his name.

When? she texted back, trying to ignore the pricking of her conscience.

ASAP, he replied.

After one - @ mine? she suggested, feeling unusually daring.

OK.

'Hattie, sweet Hattie,' Leo sighed as she opened the door to him two hours later. He gathered her into his arms and fixed his lips onto hers as soon as the door closed. Hattie's well-intentioned distraction tactics – a cup of tea being the first on the list – flew out the window. Inviting him to her house had been a BIG mistake. Aylesbury library would have been safer – fewer smooching opportunities there. The curtain-twitchers of Witchert Close might well have been having a field day.

Hattie's first feeble struggles petered out within his masterful embrace and at the delight of the first proper kiss since their last guilty grapple in the college car park. Nick, by contrast, was still only managing the odd, occasional, passionless peck on the cheek. Hattie's sensible side struggled to remind her that sliding down the slippery slope of temptation might be fun at the start, but a painful crash-landing at the bottom was inevitable. However, on this particular Monday afternoon in March, her sensible side had only a fingertip hold on the cliff top of reason, with no hope of rescue from above or below.

'Oh Leo,' she murmured, once he had surfaced for air and was planting delicate kisses around the nape of her neck. Shivers were running up and down her spine in an alarming way.

'Hattie, cara, I can't stop thinking about you.' He used to use that endearment all those years ago and in her imagination, they were students again.

'Hmm,' she sighed contentedly, revelling in the moment of illicit tenderness.

'And you?' he murmured, after a pause. Then Hattie registered that his remark had a question mark at the end. 'Do you think of me?' he continued, stroking her back gently until her insides turned to jelly.

'Of course, Leo,' she replied, nuzzling his cheek. 'You always seem to be popping into my mind – in the classroom, in the car, in bed...

'I thought it was too late, but maybe not,' he whispered with even more passion.

Alarm registered in Hattie's brain. Did he mean what she thought he meant? She loosened her hold on him and drew back to study his expression. Mentioning 'bed' was another BIG mistake.

'What do you mean, Leo?'

He put his hands on her shoulders and gazed at her with intensity. 'Hattie, dear one, I think of you all the time. I *love* you. I *adore* you.'

Hattie stood speechless. Where was this leading? 'Really?' she gasped, scarcely believing her ears.

'And you, cara?' he asked again, imploringly.

Half a dozen possible answers presented themselves, but she

shied away from revealing how besotted she was. If she told him exactly how she felt, what would happen next? There had been nothing half-hearted about the way she'd responded when his mouth found hers. It seemed as if the slippery slope was made of ice and she was clinging to the side wearing fluffy slippers. But what about Nick in all this? Her mind was in turmoil as she held Leo's gaze. His look of intense longing was startling. In the murky gloom of the college car park, his face had been in shadows, but the stark daylight revealed a depth to his feelings that she had scarcely imagined.

'Oh, Leo, I *told* you; I'm *always* thinking of you.'

'But cara, do you *love* me, or were those kisses just meaningless trifles?'

'Oh, Leo, you're so Jane Austen,' she sighed, shaking her head in wonder.

'Jane Austen?'

'I mean, so Mr Darcy.' It was Leo's turn to shake his head. 'But what do you mean by meaningless trifles?'

'What do you think I mean? Is it not obvious?' he implored, moving his hands to gently cup her cheeks. 'I *want* you Hattie and if your kisses were for real, then I know you want me too.'

Hattie ran a quick mental inventory on the state of her bedroom and her underwear. Could he mean what she thought he meant? Had she deliberately led him on and given him the idea that they could resume where they left off twenty-six years ago? Despite Nick's moods and current diversion, did she seriously want to give up on their marriage for a mad moment of unbridled passion? The naughty voice in her head was screaming, 'yes please!' while her sensible side was still clinging on for grim death, telling her not to be so stupid. The trouble was, Leo was the answer to any jaded housewife's prayer, and the perfect chemistry between them couldn't be denied. If Nick was the bread and spread in her life, Leo was like the fresh cream éclair or double choc chip muffin. She found it impossible to refuse éclairs and muffins when they sat on a plate, just asking to be taken and devoured. She needed time.

'Come into the kitchen, Leo. It's much cosier in there,' she said, taking him by the hand and leading him into a room where the possibility of full-scale passion was limited by a lack of suitable soft surfaces. Despite having all those fantasies about tearing off his clothes and having her wicked way with him, when reality struck, there were plenty of boring reasons that stopped her. Her sensible self had obviously been winched to safety and was back in control. So what next? She released his hand and made a move towards the kettle.

'Ah, you English, always the cup of tea,' Leo sighed with a hint of exasperation, correctly guessing Hattie's intention.

'What do you mean?' she asked, pausing to turn off the tap.

He took a step toward her, resting his hands on her shoulders once more and fixing her with his smouldering dark-brown eyes.

'Hattie, cara, I have just asked you an important question, but all you do is stare back at me and then decide it's time for tea. I have been thinking about us: how it was, how it should have been and how it could be in the future – *our* future – but you say nothing.'

'*Our* future?' gasped Hattie, realising with shock that Leo hadn't been merely hinting at a quick romp in her bed, but more of a long-term relationship.

'Yes, *our* future, the one that fate took from us. Dearest Hattie, I keep remembering what you said about not wanting your heart broken again. Believe me, I don't want to break your heart. I want the chance of the life we both hoped for. Tell me, cara, do you love me? I need to know. I need to hear,' he implored.

'Oh, Leo, of course I love you. I can't deny it,' she confessed. 'I've tried fighting my feelings, for Nick's sake, but every time I see you, and every time we're together, I just can't help myself. It's like being offered a chocolate muffin – I just have to have it.'

Leo looked puzzled.

'I don't suppose I'm making much sense,' she added with a sigh.

Leo turned to gaze out of the window, seemingly lost in thought. The kettle had boiled and Hattie found teabags and poured water.

'So, I'm like a chocolate muffin am I?' he asked with the suspicion of a smile. 'But a chocolate muffin only gives a few moments of pleasure. Is that all you want? Are you teasing me, cara? You return my embraces and kisses and say that you love me, but maybe I'm just a passing whim to distract you from a husband who no longer appreciates you.'

Hattie's face fell. 'No, Leo, don't say that.'

'Don't say what?'

'About me teasing you and the chocolate muffin thing. You obviously don't realise what chocolate does for me.'

'Well, it was you who started the muffin theme.' Leo shrugged and shook his head.

'Okay, I know I did, but what I meant was,' she paused to search for the right words, 'that I find you irresistible, desirable…' To emphasise her point, she moved towards him and reached up to plant a kiss firmly on his mouth, but a strident sound suddenly issued from within his jacket and she jumped back guiltily.

'Oh no,' Leo sighed tetchily, reaching for his mobile and checking the message. 'It's Rebecca. Excuse me a moment. I'd better call her.'

He retreated into the hall and from the sound of his side of the conversation, he should have been somewhere else.

'Yes, yes, I *know* what time it is. I had to stop for petrol and then there was something else I had to do… Yes, I assure you, Rebecca. I'll be there as arranged.' He paused and raised his eyebrows in exasperation. 'No, no, I'm not late… Right, I'll see you later… Yes… Okay. Goodbye.' He replaced his phone and returned to the kitchen. 'I'm so sorry, but I must go.'

'Well, well, and I used to be the one who was always dashing off,' she teased with some relief.

'But we'll finish this conversation, cara… promise me,' he murmured softly.

'I promise, Leo,' Hattie replied, wrapping her arms around him and leaning against his chest.

The kitchen still smelt faintly of his cologne as Hattie stood in a state of shock, revisiting the last few minutes in her mind.

'Oh, flapjacks!' she cursed. The teabags were horribly stewed by now, so she dumped them in the bin, tipped away the disgusting liquid and flicked the kettle switch once more. 'Caffeine and calories,' she told Jezebel, who had strolled through from the utility room now that she was sure of some attention from her mistress.

'What's a girl to do?' she said, stroking Jezebel's head as she butted into Hattie's hand. 'Faced with a plate of muffins and a loaf of value, sliced white, there's really no contest.'

15

'Here you are, Hat. G and T for you,' announced Nick magnanimously, 'and a port and lemon for you, Madge.'

'Thank you, Nicholas. That's very kind,' giggled Madge, taking a delicate sip.

'Well, for old time's sake, eh, Madge?' he chuckled, giving her a playful nudge. 'And if we're lucky, might you give us a shimmy later on?' he teased, waving his arms and swivelling his hips playfully. Madge stared at him, frowning, and shook her head dismissively.

'I'm sure I don't know what that's supposed to mean,' she retorted primly. Then, turning to Hattie, she started to quiz her about their house-move progress. Hattie felt acutely uncomfortable. After all, it was *she* who had jokingly suggested Madge might be persuaded to give them a demo. What had she been thinking?

'Well, we had calls from both agents today, which were very promising,' she told Madge, pleased to give her some attention. 'Some people who viewed last Saturday want to take a second look.' At this, Nick took the hint and went to join a group of colleagues at the bar. Madge visibly relaxed and took another sip.

The Four Seasons was almost full to bursting, with most of the Padgett and Bicton office staff who'd turned up for Nick's farewell bash. The usual array of finger food was spread around the area commandeered by Nick's colleagues who wolfed it down eagerly between lagers, beers and glasses of wine.

'That *does* sound like progress,' agreed Madge with a broad smile, 'and I'm pleased that young Greg's company has found you a possible buyer. Did Greg do the viewing himself?'

'No, it wasn't Greg. We haven't *actually* met him yet,' Hattie told her with a shake of her head. 'Miss Vaudin seems to have taken over our case, if that's what you call it.'

'Oh, Rebecca you mean?'

Hattie nodded, trying to show some enthusiasm.

'She's my dancing teacher you know,' Madge added, lowering her voice modestly.

'Yes Madge, I've seen you all together at college from time to time,' Hattie smiled patiently and reached for a crisp.

'Such a lovely girl too,' commented Madge with a sigh. 'So bright and enthusiastic, although she can be a bit strict at times.'

'Hmm,' agreed Hattie, her teeth gritted behind closed lips. She would have used a different word.

'And Sandra says Greg's so pleased with the way she's taking more responsibility.'.

'She certainly has a strong sense of … er… knowing her own mind,' replied Hattie, hoping she was being convincing. 'So Sandra keeps you up to speed with Mia Casa then?'

'Oh yes. Greg's her closest family and they live just round the corner. She never had any family of her own, you see. She thinks the world of him.'

Hattie sat politely listening and sipping her gin and tonic. At times Madge was rather like a CD stuck in repeat mode.

'Oh look, there's Rebecca now! Well, what a coincidence,' she giggled, '*and* the charming Signor Marcello.'

Hattie snapped out of her stupor, her eyes riveted to the door. Miss Bossy-Boots Vaudin was brazening her way in, with Leo following on behind a little awkwardly. Madge started waving at them enthusiastically, while Hattie wished a convenient hole would suddenly appear. There were too many tricky associations and unfinished conversations for her comfort, and Nick's farewell do certainly wasn't the right time or place. She was still trying to make sense of her feelings for Leo and spending time in Rebecca Vaudin's company would be one meeting too many.

As if fitted with some sort of homing device, Rebecca made a beeline for her table. Leo saw her and hesitated for a moment. A continuation of their recent conversation looked mercifully unlikely.

'Hi, Madge!' called Rebecca greeting her like one of her closest chums. Almost as an afterthought, she added, 'Oh hello, Mrs Chesney. Leo and I were just passing by after work and we happened to spot you and Madge in here. Come on, Leo, there's a seat by Madge.' Looking around with an air of innocent interest, she remarked to no one in particular, 'There seems to be a bit of a party going on. I hope we haven't gate-crashed!'

'No problem, Miss Vaudin,' replied Hattie with her best fake smile. 'It's my husband's farewell do. Most of those drunken males propping up the bar are his work colleagues.'

'Really? Well, I'm sure he wouldn't mind if we hung around for a while.' She peered towards the bar and having spotted Nick, went to join him.

'Lovely to see you again, Signor Marcello,' sniggered Madge, patting the space beside her. 'Room for another here, especially someone as handsome as you,' she told him with a saucy wink and a hiccup. The port and lemon was having a surprisingly quick effect. Leo gave a brief smile and sat down as bidden. Just then, loud guffaws erupted from the group at the bar. Judging by the body language, Stan Burke had just told one of his famous dirty jokes. Rebecca, however, didn't seem in the least put out and was joining in the general hilarity. In fact, for a latecomer, she was the centre of attention, with Nick playing the perfect host.

Hattie watched the scene playing out in front of her: Nick ordering a drink and passing it to her, while still managing to wrap a friendly arm around her shoulder. He certainly was a smooth operator.

'Come and join your dancing pupil, Becky,' he was heard to

say, guiding her over, his hand still clamped around her shoulder. 'Oh, er, hello,' he added, noticing Leo for the first time. 'Budge up, Madge.'

There was a general shunting around the curved sofa until Hattie found herself opposite Leo. Madge's giggles were verging on hysterical and her glass was empty. She tapped it gently, smiling in Nick's direction. Nick, oblivious to Madge's hint, was gazing adoringly at Rebecca's profile.

'Well, this is great, isn't it?' he commented, taking a swig.

They all sat eyeing each other for a few moments and judging by the awkward silence and furrowed brows, all but Madge were working on their own coping strategy. Then, noticing Leo without a drink, Nick quickly supplied him with one, as well as a refill for Madge.

'Vol-au-vent anyone?' offered Hattie desperately, grabbing a plate and passing it around. Everyone obediently took one. Munching on a vol-au-vent, after all, gave a good excuse not to have to engage in mindless social chitchat. Madge, however was in a world of her own, glugging her port and lemon merrily, her face now flushed.

'Hmm, this is really tasty. Better than the usual,' she remarked with appreciation.

'Only the best for you, Madge,' said Nick with a twinkle.

'So when does the new job start?' enquired Rebecca, as if unaware of Nick's timetable, when Hattie suspected they'd been sharing a table at Maggie's only hours before.

'Monday morning – April the second as it happens,' Nick supplied dryly.

'Ooh, not April Fool's Day then,' giggled Madge, now well on the way with her second drink and considerably relaxed.

'Here, have a sausage roll, Madge.'

'No, no, mustn't indulge. You know what they say: a moment on the lips, a lifetime on the hips.' Judging by the size of Madge's, stopping at one vol-au-vent was probably wise, thought Hattie.

The slow jazz number, which had provided the ideal

wind-down after work, came to an end and, after a brief pause, a track with a Bollywood beat issued forth from the speakers. Nick perked up from the languid appreciation of his pint and Rebecca's cleavage.

'Hey, that sounds just the ticket for a bit of shimmy and shake, eh, Madge? How about it, Becky?' he added, giving her shoulder a squeeze.

'No, Nick!' Hattie mouthed fiercely in Nick's direction. It was amazing, in a worrying sort of way, thought Hattie, how Nick could behave in the company of beer-swilling mates and a few inches of exposed female flesh.

'Come on, girls! Let's have a bit of action, for old time's sake,' he cajoled, leaning across and giving Madge a playful nudge, his arm ever-so-slightly brushing Rebecca's breasts. Rebecca simpered into her azure cocktail.

'You *are* naughty Nick,' she giggled coyly.

'Yep! Naughty Nick, that's me,' he quipped. 'Now, what do you say, girls? Come on! Give us a quick demo while the music's playing. I've heard so much about the old belly dancing. You can't deny me a little taster, seeing as I'll be off to pastures new.'

Dream on, thought Hattie, shaking her head and taking another crisp.

In a flash however, Madge abandoned all decorum, grabbed Rebecca's arm and pulled her to her feet, and before the astounded crowd, they started gyrating and wiggling their rear quarters in a very suggestive way. Leo watched open-mouthed, his expression wavering between disbelief of Madge and appreciation of Rebecca. Nick, however, was joining in with the catcalls and whoops from his mates at the bar. Hattie, on the other hand, felt a wave of embarrassment for Madge, who wasn't built for graceful moves. It didn't take much imagination to guess she'd be the subject of snide comments on the Padgett and Bicton grapevine the following day. For now, however, she was enjoying every second of the attention.

The whoops and catcalls turned to raucous cheers, then, before anyone knew what was happening, Rebecca sprang onto the low table, almost spearing a vol-au-vent with her killer heels. This drew gasps, whistles and a roar of approval from most of the customers, who crowded forward for a better view, recording the moment on their iPhones. Nick, however, was enjoying his ringside seat.

'Get 'em off!' yelled Stan Burke, leering, who seemed to think that Rebecca was about to treat them to a striptease.

Hattie rescued the plates and her bag and made for the door, head down and mortified by the display behind her. Rebecca's minuscule skirt left very little to the imagination and the sight of Nick ogling her thighs was too much. She dumped the food on the nearest table and reached for the door handle. A strong masculine hand covered hers.

'Allow me,' said a velvety brown voice in her ear. It was Leo.

A wave of cool evening air hit her face. 'Not *my* idea of a jolly evening,' she muttered furiously, heading off towards her car. Leo was quickly behind her, matching her step for step.

'Not mine either,' he agreed.

Hattie turned sharply to catch his expression. She wasn't entirely convinced. She'd caught the expression on his face when Rebecca had leapt on the table.

'What a display!' she huffed. 'It was Nick's fault. He suggested it! In fact, he teased Madge about her belly dancing from the moment she arrived and was rather too quick to buy her a second drink. Do you think he deliberately spiked it? She said it tasted better, or did she say it tasted different?'

They carried on walking, Hattie turning over the suspicions in her mind.

'She'll probably regret it in the morning,' predicted Leo.

'Hmm,' agreed Hattie sombrely, 'especially when the bush telegraph goes into overdrive.'

'I expect Rebecca will laugh it off in her own way. According to Greg, she's rumoured to earn a bit extra as a lap dancer, but I don't know if it's true.'

'After this evening's display, I wouldn't put it past her. And by the way, she's meant to be conducting a second viewing for us tomorrow. I think I'll make myself scarce,' she vowed, then slowed down and fished in her bag for her keys. She had found a convenient parking space in a side road that was mostly lined with small, industrial lock-ups and seldom used in the evening – the ideal place to park now that the college had finished. As far as she was concerned Nick could get himself home in his own time if he was sober enough, or leave his car overnight and take a taxi if he wasn't.

'Cara,' murmured Leo, reaching towards her, 'we've an unfinished conversation, remember?'

'I know,' replied Hattie. 'Sorry, Leo, but this isn't a great time for talking and even if I tried, I'm not sure I could put one clear thought after another.'

'Your husband –'

'...is just like a little boy at the end of term,' finished Hattie with irritation. 'School's out and he's pushing the boundaries, big time! Did you see the way he was drooling over Rebecca? It was disgusting!' she snapped.

'Hmm, well, what I was trying to say was, your husband doesn't appreciate the treasure he has.'

'But, Leo...'

'Yes, cara, *you* are the treasure.'

'You've said it before and it's sweet of you, but as *I* said, after so many years, things can become a bit samey. You must know that; *you* were married.' She fumbled her keys. 'Look, I think I need to get home. It's not that I'm avoiding our conversation; it's just not the time, especially after witnessing that awful display by Nick and his drunken mates.'

'What you need,' insisted Leo firmly, cupping her chin and tilting it towards him, 'is this.'

Yet another Wednesday evening, thought Hattie dreamily, as their lips met. What was it about Wednesday evenings? A moment later, she was jolted back to reality and the risk of being discovered. This time there was no comforting cover of darkness to hide their guilty pleasures. She pulled away with embarrassment and quickly checked for passers-by. What if Nick had suddenly been overcome with remorse about his boorish behaviour and had come looking for her? But no, all was quiet except for the drone of a lawnmower in a nearby garden and the brisk steps of a sprightly pensioner taking her Jack Russell for an evening stroll at the far end of the road.

'No Leo,' she groaned awkwardly. 'Not a good idea. Not here!'

'I have another suggestion,' he whispered smoothly. 'My apartment is not far –'

'No!' she gasped, although the thought of escaping to his cosy pad – and knowing Leo, it *would* be – was very tempting. 'Look, I need to get home. Not that I'm not enjoying your company, but I'm not good company myself at the moment.'

'But you promised we could finish that conversation,' he implored.

'Okay, let's sit for a few moments,' she sighed, unlocking the car door. He really could be quite pushy when he wanted to be, thought Hattie, despite looking like an obedient puppy dog following behind Rebecca earlier on. No, she reminded herself, pushy was not the best word to describe him; masterful, yes – that's how he was. He embodied the best attributes of a gentleman as well as the desire for plain speaking. The obedient puppy version was his way of dealing with girls like Rebecca Vaudin, who were definitely the worst sort of pushy.

As he settled beside her, she steeled herself for what he might be about to say. It wasn't that she didn't want to hear his passionate declarations; it was more to do with her fury over Nick. His stupid behaviour had put her in a bad mood and had spoiled the whole evening. There were so many emotions swirling around inside, making her weak, vulnerable and likely to react in exactly the wrong way. It was obvious from their Monday meeting that Leo was pushing their relationship up several notches and, to her shame, she had been ready to blurt out how she felt. She started to feel hot and sweaty around her neck and wound down the window for some cool air. Dratted flushes, she fumed silently. They probably didn't help her emotional turmoil.

Leo reached for her hand and pressed it to his lips. Little ripples of pleasure ran up and down her spine and a fluttering of butterflies cavorted around her stomach. Leo seemed to be an expert at pressing all the right buttons. All at once her irritation melted. He looked up with a questioning gaze.

'So, dearest Hattie, do we have a future?'

Hattie gulped. 'A future together, you mean?'

'Of course, cara. Montelugia is a beautiful place to live…'

'Montelugia?' She recalled how he used to describe his home, the place she dreamed would be hers too. 'But, Leo, your job… Mia Casa.'

Before he could reply, a shriek and resounding sobs burst upon the evening air.

'Oh my God!' gasped Hattie, looking around. 'Has the Jack Russell been mown down?' The pensioner was no longer in sight. 'Perhaps her bag's been snatched. I wouldn't trust the layabouts around here.'

There was a sound of hurrying footsteps, mingled with heart-rending cries.

'Goodness! Someone's in serious trouble!'

Leo was out of his seat in a flash, his metaphorical armour burnished and trusty charger at the ready to rescue the damsel in distress, whoever she might be. Hattie followed suit, wondering if her hazy first aid skills were going to be needed. They didn't have long to wait. A short, dumpy body, red in the face and choking back sobs, came careering into sight, scarf and bag flapping wildly.

'Madge,' groaned Hattie.

Her moment of glory had ended sooner than they'd predicted. Rooted to the spot, they watched aghast as she faltered and came to a halt and then collapsed into renewed wailing, her head in her hands. She obviously hadn't seen them.

'Whatever shall we do?' Hattie whispered.

'Poor lady,' murmured Leo sadly. 'She needs comforting.'

'That's not all she needs,' muttered Hattie bitterly, remembering how easily Madge had been egged on. Alcohol and Madge did not go together well, especially if the alcohol had been deliberately spiked. Madge fumbled in her bag for a tissue, dabbed at her eyes and then blew her nose. She moved a step closer, still unaware of her audience. Black smears could be seen where her mascara had dribbled down her cheeks. Leo leaned closer to Hattie, not wanting their voices to startle her, when Madge at last looked up and jumped in alarm and embarrassment.

'Oh no!' she wailed, confused and humiliated by the turn of events and struggling to regain her composure. Hattie felt helpless as she met Madge's gaze, aware that Leo was close beside her, his hand resting on her shoulder and his lips all but brushing her ear. For a moment, it was hard to say who was more embarrassed by the meeting. For Madge, the scene in front of her caused her momentarily to forget her tears.

'Hattie… and the handsome signor?' she blubbered in bewilderment.

Hattie knew she had to take action. 'Madge, whatever's up?' she asked sympathetically, putting some distance between herself and Leo and a comforting arm around Madge's shoulders.

'It was Stan Burke's fault!' she howled, dabbing at her eyes.

'Stan Burke? What happened?'

'Nasty, slimy creature!' spat Madge with a shudder. 'Hands all over the place… coarse and crude… Women aren't safe when he's around. No wonder his wife left him!'

'Oh poor you,' sighed Hattie, giving her a reassuring squeeze, 'and I'm sorry Nick was so awful as well. He really was so stupid!'

'He wasn't so bad,' sniffed Madge.

'I'm not so sure,' Hattie told her. 'I've a shrewd suspicion the port and lemons might not have been all they seemed.'

'You mean I was drugged?' she snapped, glaring.

'Well, I wouldn't go that far, and I've no proof, but let's say that taste you mentioned might have been down to something stronger.'

'The beast!' breathed Madge.

'I may be wrong, Madge, and even if I'm not, he probably didn't mean any harm,' finished Hattie lamely, scarcely believing her last comment.

Leo, who had been silent up to now, stepped forward and said, 'May I escort you home, Madge?'

Madge blushed, obviously delighted with his suggestion. She hesitated, lips pursed and eyes cast down. 'Oh no, it's fine, thank you all the same,' she murmured, 'my car's just over there.'

Hattie and Leo exchanged worried glances. The words 'she's not in a fit state to drive' must have sprung to both their minds simultaneously.

'It's no bother, honestly. I could drive you in your car,' pressed Leo gently.

'But... what about you? How will you get home?' Madge flustered.

Hattie and Leo exchanged glances again.

'I'll follow on behind then drop Signor Marcello back. It's no bother, Madge. You've had a nasty experience after all, and I feel partly responsible, on behalf of Nick, of course.' The fact that she'd foolishly planted the dancing demo idea in Nick's mind had been playing on hers most of the evening.

'Thank you,' said Madge graciously, accepting at last. 'It's so good to see a friendly face after that... that... bear garden!' She gave her nose a hearty blow.

'Oh... er... yes,' stuttered Hattie, hoping that Madge's imagination wasn't working overtime. 'I was upset by Nick and his crowd as well. I just had to get out. Signor Marcello wanted to make sure I was all right.'

'Ah, what a gentleman,' commented Madge. 'A breath of fresh air after all that groping, grasping, leering and laughing. Oh, how am I going to face them all tomorrow?' she wailed, then broke down and dissolved into tears.

Leo and Hattie looked on helplessly. Groping and grasping? It sounded as if the raunchy dancing had stirred up some less savoury masculine tendencies. The thought of being groped by Stan Burke made Hattie shudder.

'Come on, Madge,' she said gently, taking her by the arm, 'let's get you home for a nice cuppa and a sit down with the TV for company.'

Madge sniffed and stuffed her tissue into her pocket. 'A chocolate bourbon and my "Songs from the Shows" CD,' she murmured, letting Hattie lead her. 'Mine's the blue Honda over there.'

'Right, I'll be right behind,' promised Hattie.

A sheepish smile spread over Madge's face as Leo started the engine, and before long she was safely returned to the comfort of her little two-bed terrace.

'Will you come in for a coffee?' suggested Leo, as he opened the passenger door outside a smart apartment block on the east side of town, some twenty minutes later. Hattie weighed up her options and decided to err on the side of caution.

'No, tempting though it is, I think I'd better be off.'

'Till another time then, cara,' he murmured, touching her mouth gently with his.

As Hattie drove, she pondered over Leo and the surprising news that his future apparently did not involve estate agency in a Buckinghamshire town. Added to that, there was still that unfinished conversation and the astounding suggestion that he wanted her to leave Nick and settle in Montelugia with him – for good! The thought of that sent alternating shivers of terror and delight coursing through her body. The whole idea was almost too much to contemplate.

Hattie's plan for the following day was to switch off her mobile phone, drive to her favourite fabric shop and leave the two estate agents to conduct their follow-up viewings in peace and quiet.

Jezebel would be shut safely in the utility room and Miss Bossy-Boots Vaudin would jolly well have to lump it! At breakfast time, she'd been careful to say very little about events at The Four Seasons. 'I had a headache' was the only excuse she gave when Nick casually remarked that he'd realised eventually that she was no longer there. No prizes for guessing where his attention was, thought Hattie. Judging by his demeanour, he was nursing the mother of all hangovers and had arranged for a colleague to pick him up that morning.

'Didn't want to risk being breathalysed,' he mentioned ruefully. Hattie raised an eyebrow and carried on loading the dishwasher.

Her visit to Dobbins and Tippler near Wendover was very successful. She now had everything she needed to finish her master-piece. Feeling particularly pleased with herself, she decided to stop off at Rosehill Garden Centre to buy some early bedding plants. Even if the day's viewings eventually led to a sale, she still felt responsible for keeping the garden well-tended and colourful. As she loaded the trays into the Clio's boot, she checked her watch and realised that half an hour more out of the house should ensure that it would be empty on her return. The tearoom beckoned with plates of scones and flapjacks, piped music from Vale FM and Melanie Makepeace with a sneer that she'd inherited from mother.

'Oh, hello, Mrs Chesney,' she breezed with a half-hearted smile, 'and how's the house sale going?'

Mother had evidently been passing on titbits of gossip.

'Getting there,' Hattie replied levelly. She had absolutely no intention of giving Ms M any clue to pass on and be speculated over by members of the extended Makepeace clan.

'Husband keeping well?' probed Melanie, as she dispensed hot water into a teapot.

'Absolutely, and yours?' Hattie snapped back absentmindedly. 'Oh sorry; of course, you haven't got one,' Hattie added, realising her faux pas.

'No, best off without one. Some men just can't be trusted,' she said with a gleam in her eye.

'Crumpets!' breathed Hattie, *sotto voce*. Hilda was bound to have told her daughter about her sightings in Maggie's Sandwich Bar. Why else would she have made that comment?

'Crumpets, did you say? No, none left, sorry, but we've a few teacakes.'

'Yes, a teacake, thanks.' Not that she intended to order one, but Melanie was hardly to know that Hattie's use of 'crumpets' was more of a curse than a request.

'Toasted?'

'No, just as it is. I can't stay long.' Spending any more time than necessary in Melanie's company was to be avoided at all costs now that Nick had unsurprisingly emerged as a subject of conversation.

'Right you are.'

Hattie grabbed her tray and fled to the furthest table. As she sipped her tea, it seemed a safe moment to check for texts and messages. Fliss's name came up as a missed call. She had also left a message to call her as soon as possible. That was two hours ago.

'Fliss? Sorry, I didn't have my phone switched on. I've been out most of the day.'

'Yes, I worked that out. I tried calling your home number, but some strange woman answered. Thought I'd dialled the wrong number first of all,' said Fliss, sounding bleak and distant.

'Strange woman?' There could only be one candidate: Rebecca Vaudin. No one else would have the cheek to answer someone else's phone when they were just meant to be conducting a viewing. 'Ah, yes... Miss Vaudin.'

'The belly dancer of Maggie's Sandwich Bar fame?' quizzed Fliss.

'The same, but I'd rather not talk about *her*. So, any news?'

'It's Mum,' Fliss replied, sounding tearful.

'Oh!' What do you say to someone when you both know their mum is dying?

'Dad phoned earlier. I've got to go down. Mum's suddenly taken a turn for the worse.' She dissolved into tears, choking back sobs.

After a pause, Hattie said, 'I'm so sorry, Fliss. Is there anything I can do?' What she wished she could do was put her arms around her and give her a hug.

'I don't think so, Hat, but I appreciate your offer. I've already spoken to Mark and he's taking time out, or rather he's going to work from home. The boys break up tomorrow, so I can take them, although it'll be upsetting for them, but...'

There was a silence, followed by a sniff and some throat clearing.

'I see.'

'Apparently, it's a very aggressive cancer. Mum may only have a few days or a couple of weeks at most.'

'I'm so sorry,' murmured Hattie. 'I'll say a prayer for you.' It seemed the right thing to say, although she knew Fliss's brushes with religion were infrequent and sceptical.

'Thanks.'

'Keep in touch, Fliss. We'll all be thinking of you.'

Returning to her teacake, which was curling round the edges, she took a small bite and swallowed her tea, which was now rather cool, and reflected on her own situation and Nick's, both with ageing parents. Moving to Hampshire had definitely been the right decision, but now that Leo had his own agenda, life was too complicated for words. If she could have turned back the clock, knowing what she now knew, would she have behaved differently?

'She's what?' shrieked Hattie. Several heads turned and conversations were temporarily suspended in the staffroom. 'Wow! I can't *believe* it!' It was all she could do to stop herself jumping up and down in ecstasy like the six-year-olds she taught each Tuesday afternoon. Act your age, not your shoe size, she told herself firmly, despite the mounting excitement. 'Really? The full asking price?' She paused as Brian burbled on pedantically about it being subject to a satisfactory survey report. 'Yes, yes, of course. I understand she'll need one, although I'm not aware of anything… Yes… of course we'll accept.'

'So it's happened at last,' commented Sally warmly, as Hattie jabbed the 'off' button, her mind buzzing. 'That must be such a relief.'

'Hmm, yeah… it's great, although I'll try not to count my chickens, especially after last time.'

Hattie picked up her lunch box and chewed on a stick of celery. Yet again, her thoughts went back to Wednesday evening, Leo's bombshell about returning to Montelugia and his offer of her very own one-way ticket. No, she thought, I can't even entertain the idea. Nick may not be the perfect husband – was there such a thing as perfection in a man? – and his lunchtime fling with Miss Bossy-Boots might be a bit peeving, but it was bound to be different once they had moved. It would be back to the two of them, happily settled in their new home, with Nick on a better salary, able to splash out on the accoutrements of a senior manager's lifestyle. But then she re-lived some of her steamier moments with Leo and found it difficult to dismiss her longings. He was, no doubt, a real dreamboat, and – more significantly – he loved her.

'You look thoughtful, Hat,' said Sally, noticing her friend's abrupt mood change. 'I expect there's so much to get sorted now.'

'Yes, small details like somewhere to live,' agreed Hattie, flippantly. She dug in her shopping bag, brought out a handful of house details and started to thumb her way through them. By the time the bell sounded for the end of lunchtime, she had picked out four likely properties to view the following day, as long as Nick could be persuaded to sacrifice his precious Saturday sport fix. Hmm, she thought, that would need careful handling.

Hattie was busy forking out Jezebel's supper when the first call came. Dumping the dish on the floor she grabbed her pen and diary, expecting to speak to one of the Hampshire agents she'd contacted earlier.

'Mrs Chesney?' began a female voice that seemed strangely familiar.

'Er yes?'

'Rebecca Vaudin speaking. I'm just calling to say we've had an offer from Mr and Mrs Perry.' A broad, self-satisfied grin lit up her face as Hattie started to prepare her response.

'Oh, but we —' she began, but Rebecca carried on regardless.

'The offer is just five thousand short of the asking price, but I think it's very reasonable in the current climate,' she continued undaunted. 'So we'd strongly advise you to accept it. You *have* been on the market for a while after all.'

'Oh, but you see it's really not —'

'And I honestly don't think haggling over the odd five thousand is wise when you have keen buyers who are ready to move quickly.'

Hattie listened and savoured the moment when she could at last get a word in edgeways and deliver the killer blow. Oh, sweet victory, she mused gleefully. At last Rebecca paused for breath.

'We've a buyer!' replied Hattie with a giggle.

'That's right,' gushed Rebecca, completely misunderstanding Hattie's reply. 'So pleased you're prepared to accept what is a really good offer.'

'No, you don't understand. What I mean is, we've *already* sold the house... to someone else.'

'What?' snapped Rebecca. 'You've sold your house? But when did *this* happen?'

'Oh, earlier this afternoon actually. Brian Samways called me in the lunch hour. His client has offered the asking price and naturally I accepted,' Hattie told her airily.

'But why didn't you inform us of this development?' Rebecca demanded stiffly.

'I've been teaching all afternoon and only got home a few moments ago.'

There was a pregnant pause and a sniff. 'I see. Well, if your buyers can't get a mortgage or if they decide to pull out...'

'She's a cash buyer actually, from Spain – a second home,' Hattie informed her smugly, enjoying every second. It certainly more than made up for all the grief she'd been given over her interior décor shortcomings.

'Hmm... right... well, I'll have to disappoint the Perrys then.' Rebecca's remark sounded more like an accusation of deliberate sabotage.

'Yes, you will,' agreed Hattie. 'Their offer was too little, too late. Goodbye, Miss Vaudin.' And good riddance, she thought, replacing the receiver, hoping fervently that Mrs or Señora Piles wouldn't do a Mr Bainbridge on them.

'Why didn't you call me about the offer or tell Samways you needed to consult me first?' commented Nick, after Hattie had gleefully told him.

Her mouth gaped in amazement. 'But, Nick, what was there to consult you about?' she asked incredulously. 'It was a firm offer of our asking price. It doesn't get any better than that.' She stood in suspended animation over the kettle as Nick dropped his briefcase on the floor, loosened his tie and stuffed his hands in his pockets, pouting peevishly. Hattie stared in disbelief. Where was the whoop of joy, the triumphant punch in the air, the celebratory cartwheel? Er, perhaps not the celebratory cartwheel, Hattie thought, but maybe a smidgen of a smile might be in order. Wasn't this the moment they'd been waiting for?

'Well, in the light of the later call, it might have been good to compare the offers, the situation of the prospective buyers, you know.'

'What? I can't believe what I'm hearing! She's a *cash* buyer... And anyway, I didn't know there was going to be another offer and nor did you!' she finished with exasperation then turned her attention to the contents of the freezer.

Nick picked up the free newspaper and flicked through the

pages in a desultory manner. He was finding it difficult to rid his mind of Madge's taunting jibes. She hadn't turned up the day before, which was no surprise after the spectacle she'd made of herself, but that morning she'd swept in, bolshie and belligerent as ever. She was also gunning for Stan Burke after his offer to try out her 'love handles'. Most of the day, however, she'd been engaged in decamping to Janice and Rhoda's office down the corridor. Someone at last had managed some joined-up thinking and had worked out that that was an obvious place for Madge. It was right next to the stationery store, over which she needed to cast her beady eyes. Maybe, though, Rafiq had insisted that taking over Nick's role did not necessarily mean taking on his office co-habitee. After lunch, an odd remark had triggered a volley of pent-up sniping.

'Well, it's a good thing the age of chivalry isn't completely dead,' she declared enigmatically.

'What's that, Madge?'

'Some of the male gender know how to treat a lady,' she continued haughtily as she gathered up the last of her belongings from the desk.

'As opposed to old Stan, I suppose,' sniggered Nick.

'Don't even mention that man's name in my presence!' she snapped, carefully lowering an overgrown fern into a plastic carrier. 'No, if it hadn't been for the charming Leo...' Madge paused and blushed. 'Well, your dear wife was also grateful for his concern after that... that...bear garden!' she added frowning.

'Really? I thought Hat had a headache. That's what she told me.'

'Um, well... all I know is, he was on hand to bring a little comfort into our lives, and they *both* helped to get me home safely, which is more than I can say about some people.' She turned and marched out of the office, leaving Nick without a farewell, but with the same odd niggle that he'd experienced twice before.

'Your tea's getting cold.' Hattie's voice pierced through his reverie. Nick picked up his Arsenal mug and was reminded of a particularly crucial match the following day. Sky Sports was showing it live and Steve, the warehouse manager, was coming to watch. It was the least he could do after Wednesday night's lift.

'Ah right, but I wish you'd phoned me about those offers. I'd have liked to have been involved, that's all,' he muttered peevishly, ambling out of the kitchen.

'Oh, and Nick…?'

'What?'

'It's okay to do some viewings tomorrow I guess? We ought to try and move things along now.'

'You can go if you like, but I've already made plans.'

'What *plans*?'

'There's an important match on and Steve Dyball's coming over.'

'Football!' fumed Hattie. 'Always blasted football!' She yanked open a drawer fiercely and rummaged around for the garlic press. 'We need to sort out somewhere to live, Nick. Surely, you don't want endless months of travelling up and down to Lydford Cross each day, using up all that expensive petrol.' Appealing to the use of his wallet generally did the trick, but on a few subjects Nick was hard to shift, football being the top of the list. When she'd been in labour with Josh, Nick had famously divided his time between mopping her brow and watching the football results in the visitors' room.

'But it's a cup match, Hat,' he complained, reappearing at the door with a hard-done-by expression. 'And they're playing Chelsea. Can't you sort out the viewings yourself next week? I mean, you've broken up now, haven't you. You've got all the time in the world. I'm sure you can make the right choice.'

'That's rich!' snapped Hattie. 'Just a moment ago you were complaining about not being involved, and you know I'm a nervous driver when I'm out of my home patch. If Lydford Cross has a one-way system like Abingdon, it'll freak me out!'

Nick didn't answer.

'Are you saying you're refusing to go to Hampshire tomorrow?'

'Well, I've already said…,' he said, yawning.

'But I've arranged some viewings.'

'You've what? But why didn't you consult me? Doesn't my opinion matter?'

'But you just said –'

'You *assumed*,' Nick rapped, 'and you know what happens when you assume anything; you make an ass out of u and me!'

'Ha, ha! Yes, very clever, Nick. I suppose you learnt that on one of those training courses Padgett and Bicton like to use. But I simply thought you'd want to get it all sorted out as quickly as possible. Don't you want to move?'

'Course I do. It's obvious. I've got this job now, so of course we can't stay here,' replied Nick, shrugging.

'You don't exactly sound all that keen,' observed Hattie. 'Maybe football's more important to you. I've often felt I come a poor second place when it comes to Arsenal's matches.'

'Of course you don't, but I was looking forward to it and so was Steve and how was *I* to know there'd be an offer today?'

'Exactly!' she snapped.

Nick then recalled Hattie using those same words only minutes before, because he suddenly became distracted by something out of the kitchen window. Hattie spread garlic puree over a pizza base then levered off the lid from a jar of pasta sauce and covered it thickly.

'But you'll be able to listen to it on the car radio. There'll be endless highlights as well and if you really can't bear the thought of missing a single second, we can record the whole thing. I'm sure Josh can be trusted not to interfere with the setting. It's our *future* I'm concerned about, Nick,' insisted Hattie, 'but you don't seem to think it's as important as some stupid football match!'

'Our future? Oh, don't be so melodramatic, Hat!'

'I'm not being melodramatic. We planned this back in January and it was going to be our chance to get out of a rut and have a fresh start, a different sort of lifestyle, a new future, if you think there *is* one, that is.'

Nick turned sharply. 'What do you mean by that?' he demanded, glaring at her. Hattie opened the fridge and took a deep breath.

'Oh, nothing! But what am I supposed to think when you obviously rank my needs lower than Steve Dyball's.'

'Oh, for goodness' sake, Hat! I only said I wanted to watch Arsenal in the semi-final. I wasn't inferring we had no future – unless you've got your own agenda?' He fixed her with an enquiring gaze that, coupled with the memory of Leo's declarations, brought the guilt flooding back.

'No, of course I haven't,' she asserted fiercely, although her insides were swirling like her washing machine's final spin. 'You're the one who's being melodramatic now!'

'That's fine then!' He wandered back into the hall while Hattie wrenched open another drawer in search of the cheese grater.

'Ouch!' The tip of a paring knife pierced the tender skin under her thumbnail, producing fat drops of blood. Squeezing firmly to staunch the flow, she felt a few rogue tears and an enormous weight upon her. Oh Leo, she thought, what have I done? What's become of me? What would the rest of Witchert Close think if they knew there was a scarlet woman in their midst? Is this how Eve felt after the serpent had pointed out the finer points of apples in the Garden of Eden and she'd grabbed one with both hands? Was the glorious juice of forbidden fruit dripping down her own chin? More to the point, were the crumbly remains of a proverbial chocolate muffin still clinging to her lips? Hattie was mortified. One little kiss and her life was in disarray. One little kiss? Oh well, maybe not just one, she reminded herself. A quiet sob was the only audible sound of her despair.

'Okay,' Nick called from the hall.

Hattie jolted back to reality. 'Wh, wh, what's that?' she stammered.

'I said okay... you win... *we'll* go down to Hampshire tomorrow,' he called wearily. 'I'll text Steve and tell him we've got other plans.'

16

Nick was not in the best of moods as they travelled south the next morning. Madge's last enigmatic insinuations were still giving him some bother. It wasn't just what she said that was the problem; it was the way she said it, complete with the rolling of eyeballs, raising of eyebrows and pursing of lips. On the subject of lips, Hattie's were more tightly closed than he'd have expected, but he put that down to the fall-out following Wednesday evening. As far as he was concerned, it was just a bit of fun, and if a bloke couldn't enjoy the sight of a nice pair of thighs and a saucy bum waggling – all in the name of culture of course – then it was a pretty poor show. Hat could really do with loosening up a bit. In fact, sad old Madge could teach her a thing or two in that department – aided and abetted by the vodka shot of course! That had been one of Stan's more inspired suggestions.

He was still turning round the jumble of thoughts, including Arsenal's chances in the match, by the time they were pulling in at their first appointment of the day. A neat little redhead with a clipboard was hovering as they got out of the car. Definitely a Saturday girl, thought Nick, and nice legs too. Looking up at the house, he started to wonder if they were at the right address. The agents had obviously spent time cropping and enhancing the picture and what have you, before publishing the finished document, carefully cutting out the bits they didn't want the punters to see. The property was beside an alleyway, with a long narrow garden leading up to a tired-looking front door. Adjacent to the alley was a vacant garage – not a promising setting. Vacant garages with boarded up windows usually attracted vandals and graffiti aficionados like flies. Nick bit back the question he needed to ask and decided to let the girl do her stuff first.

As she showed them in the front door, the sight that greeted them was hardly inspiring: faded and peeling paintwork, sinister damp patches, mouldy, stained carpets and a smell that shouted trouble. They learned that the previous occupier had not long passed away – maybe in one of the depressing bedrooms. Nick shuddered. Even the resident spiders seemed to have lost the will to live, judging by the numerous dried-out corpses that littered the window ledges. The bathroom and kitchen were even worse. This was definitely a 'rip it all out and start again' project with too many zeros in the bill. Why were they there? He shook his head in disbelief. To his utter amazement, however, Hattie was cooing over the period features, as she called them. Every so often she'd come out with cries of 'Oh, how quaint!' or 'It's got so much potential!'

'Potential for complete demolition,' muttered Nick darkly, but the redhead and Hattie had moved on by then.

'Oh, Nick, come and see!' she called. He caught up with her, hoping there might be just one redeeming feature to make the journey worthwhile. 'Original sash windows *and* look at the ceiling roses!' she trilled. Nick could only see evidence of wet rot and large flakes of paint hanging on for dear life. 'Just like on *Homes under the Hammer!*' she added gleefully.

'The garden's very secluded,' announced the redhead with a bright smile. She struggled with a hefty key and two rusted bolts before leading them out to a small patch of knee-high weeds bordered by a towering leylandii hedge. Nick's heart sank even lower.

'Leylandii... Oh God!' he groaned.

'Stops prying eyes,' whispered Hattie, 'and it's not too tall. About eight feet I should think.'

'They can grow to *fifteen* feet in as many years, as it happens.'

Hattie chose to ignore this snippet of horticultural info. 'Ooh, a pond!' she gasped, teetering on the edge of a stone lip and narrowly avoiding a shoeful of slimy sludge. 'And look,' she carried on undaunted, 'isn't that a grapevine coming out of that sweet little greenhouse?'

'Er, yes... I believe it is,' agreed the redhead tentatively, scanning her notes. 'Gardening's not one of my strong points.'

'Greenhouse? What, you mean that rotting apology for a shed?' All Nick could see was jagged, glass-edged frames and a tangle of unruly branches covering most of the roof. 'Not much room for barbeques.'

'Which we have about once a year.'

'Or a chicken run.'

'Oh... well...' Hattie's face fell.. 'So, maybe homemade wine might be a better project than hens.'

Ten minutes later, they were back at the front door.

'What about that empty garage?' Nick asked, waving in the direction of the neglected showroom and forecourt. Even at a distance of 20 yards Nick had now spotted yellow *Proposed Development* notices stuck to the windows. The redhead blushed, gulped awkwardly and shuffled her papers in embarrassment.

'Ah... well, actually there's planning permission for housing, which is really good for the area... really smart, affordable dwellings,' she assured them.

Nick decided it sounded suspiciously as if her firm had landed a deal to sell them too. 'What sort of affordable dwellings?' he pressed.

'Um... er,' she started, glancing down at her notes. 'One and two bedroom maisonettes, I believe.'

'And how many are they planning to squeeze onto the plot?' prodded Nick suspiciously. Hattie groaned.

'I believe it's thirty,' answered the girl, as brightly as she could.

'Well, I don't think my wife and I will be taking this any further.

In my opinion, this is an overpriced dump right next to a building site!'

'Nick!' gasped Hattie, in a 'how-could-you-say-that' sort of tone. She was struggling to find something encouraging to say, but the redevelopment news seemed to overshadow any positive thoughts. 'Not quite what we were looking for,' she agreed lamely with an apologetic smile.

'Right,' replied the redhead, knowing when she was beaten. 'Let us know if you want to view another property.'

Nick had a few choice words to describe the agent's details as they drove to their next appointment. 'And if you hadn't got the message, Hat, we're not property developers and I'm *not* looking for a project!'

They negotiated miles of twisty country lanes and eventually found Kittwhistle Buildings, a terrace of former estate-workers cottages, circa 1900 – according to the agent's flashy folder – on the outskirts of a moderately sized village. At first glance, this was a much more promising prospect, but the absence of an agent was less so.

'Are you sure it was half past?' Nick asked, having driven like a maniac, narrowly missing several agricultural vehicles on dangerously tight corners.

'Of course I am,' sighed Hattie, checking her watch yet again.

After a further fruitless five minutes, they decided to make themselves known, as they'd happened to spot someone opening a first-floor window. With the timetable Hattie had planned for the afternoon, they couldn't risk hanging around for dilatory agents. Nick switched off the pre-match round-up he'd been following.

'I'm not impressed!' he fumed, slamming the car door shut. He strode up the garden path, ducking under overhanging tree branches and pushing past unruly shrubs, Hattie trotting along behind.

'The bell doesn't seem to be working,' he muttered, irritably. Another minute or so passed without a sign of anyone wanting them to view the house.

Hattie surreptitiously peered in at the front window that was partly obscured by a mature honeysuckle, but there was no one in sight.

'Better knock 'em up,' Nick decided, grasping a quirky metal knocker shaped like a grinning gargoyle. Immediately, a loud barking started up nearby. Nick and Hattie exchanged horrified glances.

'Sounds like the hound from hell!' gasped Hattie. 'Jezebel wouldn't be impressed.'

'Probably have her for breakfast!' quipped Nick. Suddenly the door opened.

'Yes?' ventured the middle-aged occupant, wearing a paint-smeared smock, a jauntily knotted neckerchief and brandishing a large parsnip and a tin of sardines.

'We've an appointment to view,' explained Hattie, thrusting the house details towards the bemused vendor, who hurriedly stuffed the sardines into a trouser pocket.

'Supper?' The words slipped out before Hattie could stop them. She blushed.

'No. Still-life composition,' growled the owner. The paintbrush behind his ear and smudge of burnt umber on his cheek were obvious clues that Hattie had missed.

'So sorry to keep you waiting,' came a voice from the direction of the shrubs, accompanied by much puffing and panting. It was the agent. Introductions over, Gavin was straight into viewing mode, once he'd pocketed his mobile. Number 5 Kittwhistle Buildings was as quirky as its name and owner and altogether a much better prospect than the previous property, apart from the worrying canine presence.

'Neat wood-burner,' observed Nick as they made their way through, noting its interesting pot-bellied appearance.

'Gorgeous!' enthused Hattie, sighing. 'Dado rails too!'

'Now the music room,' announced Gavin importantly, leading the way through a side passage that was described on the agent's particulars as a morning-cum-garden room, due to the large expanse of glass in the ceiling and the upper half of the outside wall. Elderly spider plants hung at irregular intervals and the odd fern and aspidistra spilled out of cracked vases.

'Music room? Not art studio then?' muttered Nick to himself.

'With a mezzanine!' Gavin informed them with a flourish as he opened the door. Nick and Hattie gazed up at a wide piece of wood, well above head height that ran along the entire length of one of the walls.

'Mezzanine?' quizzed Nick. 'But it's just a glorified shelf.'

Hattie sensed an emperor's new clothes moment. 'Shush, Nick!' she warned him nervously.

'But it is,' stressed Nick. 'I think it's a case of poetic licence,' he added, frowning.

'You mean artistic?' giggled Hattie.

'Ready for the kitchen?' Gavin asked. 'It's quite a feature, as you will have seen from the details.'

'Wow!' breathed Hattie as they took in the beamed, vaulted ceiling. 'This is something else!'

'Hmm, it *is* a bit different,' agreed Nick, 'but a bit short on storage.'

'But look at this smashing little larder,' Gavin pointed out, grabbing the handle of a minuscule, built-in cupboard in one of the corners.

'Ah,' sighed Hattie, 'wonderfully vintage!'

'Just about room for the cat's food,' added Nick, the cool voice of reality amid the fanciful ramblings of his companions. 'And there's not even room for a table. The layout is all wrong.'

Gavin stood tight-lipped as Nick and Hattie went head-to-head over dining arrangements. He gave an embarrassed cough. 'Ready to see the garden?' he offered, indicating the back door. From the kitchen windows they peered out at a low hedge that contained a postage-stamp-size garden.

'Where's the rest of it?' asked Nick. 'The details mentioned a hundred and twenty feet if I remember correctly.'

'Ah yes! You see, it's just beyond the access road that runs along the back of the whole terrace,' explained Gavin, indicating a stretch of gravel that separated the hedge from a further section of trees, grass and outbuildings.

'I'd like to see the upstairs first, if you don't mind,' said Hattie, hearing renewed barking from next door's hound.

Gavin led the way back through the garden room and into the sitting room to access the ochre-painted stairs that led up to a good-sized landing.

'Two generous doubles and a –'

'Box room,' finished Nick, cutting Gavin short.

'On no! It'll take a single, no trouble,' retorted Gavin stiffly.

'I take it you mean a single cat bed,' remarked Nick.

'Shush, Nick! Don't be so embarrassing,' hissed Hattie.

Off the landing was an L-shaped bathroom, the end wall of which formed part of the stairwell.

'So sweet,' breathed Hattie with a faraway expression, until she noticed the empty arched hole in the wall that overlooked the stairs, 'but no glass!'

'Er… no,' explained Gavin, lowering his voice. 'Mr Ireby lives here alone, so he's never seen the need to glaze it, but it wouldn't take much to fix.'

'But there's no frame in place,' pointed out Nick, 'and specially cut glass comes at a premium, and there's no ventilation, except the gaping hole. That's a grand's worth of work there.'

'Fixing an extractor fan would be a cinch,' Gavin told them.

'Hmm.' Nick looked far from convinced.

'I can't wait to see the garden,' enthused Hattie, having spied more of it from the landing window.

Gavin quickly led them out of the cottage, through the gate and across the gravelled road to an area of land that marked the nearest boundary of the long, narrow garden. 'This gravelled road was used for delivery vehicles originally and there's a turning space at the back of number ten,' he indicated with a wave of his hand.

'Ah, the summerhouse,' Hattie declared, temporarily dismissing all the other shortcomings.

'Yes, it's impressive,' agreed Gavin, 'and a perfect rustic hideaway.'

'Did the owner have to get planning consent? I mean, it's twice the size you'd expect to see on a plot of this size.'

'Er... not absolutely sure on that point,' replied Gavin, a brief flicker of doubt crossing his face.

'And what about the missing glass?' gasped Hattie, spotting numerous empty frames.

'I've just had one of those déjà-vu moments,' murmured Nick in Hattie's ear. As he studied the vaulted roof and then the galleried upper room, he realised that only a fraction of the whole building was weather-tight.

'Ah yes,' said Gavin, picking up the disappointed vibes, 'Mr Ireby bought the glass, but hasn't quite managed to fit all of it, but it wouldn't take long, I'm sure.'

'Why doesn't he do it then?' Nick glowered, seeing piles of dusty panes in decomposing cardboard boxes. They had both now gleaned that Mr Ireby was a master of unfinished projects and, by the state of the overgrown borders and clogged pond, was not much of a dab hand when it came to gardening.

Gavin either ignored Nick's comment or was too wrapped up with his mobile. He had wandered further up the garden and was obviously busy with more pressing concerns.

'Yes!' he exclaimed, not quite under his breath, clenching and brandishing his fist in a triumphant gesture. 'Get in there!'

Nick snapped to attention. Could it be that young Gavin was checking on the semi-final when he should have been extolling the few virtues of the Ireby domain, if any remained?

'Come on you blues!' Gavin sang softly, betraying himself in Nick's eyes as one of the enemy. Nick huffed and shot an irritated glance at the navy suited back.

'Well, what do you think?' enquired Gavin cheerfully, once through the front gate.

'Um... well... quite unique,' affirmed Hattie.

'But clearly unfinished, which is not reflected in the price,' added Nick in clipped tones. Chelsea supporters weren't quite the scum of the earth, but they came a close second. 'So we'll have to think about it. But I wouldn't hold your breath.'

'Two down, two to go,' sighed Hattie, trying to revive her flagging spirits, as they set off for property number three. Nick growled. News from the match had done nothing to improve his temper.

When they reached 29 Michaelmas Lane, his mood matched that of the male resident who sat sullenly in his conservatory with a mug of tea and a long-suffering expression. His wife tried hard to compensate for her spouse's lack of welcome and bobbed in and out of sight as a Brian Samways look-alike conducted the viewing. At first sight, it was a handsome Victorian villa, although Nick thought it overpriced once they had discovered that all was not as it seemed. In addition, the gloomy individual in the conservatory didn't look in the mood for negotiating.

True to form, Hattie had put on her rose-tinted glasses yet again.

'What a gorgeous kitchen!' she trilled and then, 'Oh, what a wonderful grate; it must be original,' she commented, admiring the focal point of the sitting room.

'Yes, that's correct,' agreed the agent, 'and lovingly restored by the current owners, I believe.'

'Not bad, eh, Nick?' Hattie chuckled, until they were taken into the bedroom at the rear of the house and gazed out in horror at the steeply terraced garden. The agent's details had not mentioned the crucial nature of the layout of this important feature, but had used phrases such as 'well-established' and 'abundance of shrubs and perennials'.

'Oh, God! Can't say I fancy lugging a mower up there,' Nick groaned.

'Quiet!' Hattie warned in a whisper, hoping the bobbing female hadn't heard his comments about her husband's horticultural pride and joy.

'Oh, so you'd manage to heave it up all those steps would you then?' he hissed.

Hattie shrugged and followed the agent, who was now tapping his foot impatiently on the polished oak floorboards of the landing.

'Oh, what a view!' she breathed once they'd been led out through the back door and up the well-manicured terraces to the western boundary of the property.

'Great! Especially for sunbathing,' agreed Nick with the slightest suggestion of a grin. 'All the neighbours would have a wonderful view of all your flabby bits from here.'

'Stop it!' she snapped furiously, jabbing him swiftly in the ribs and scowling in embarrassment.

As they drove off, Nick pointed out that he'd noticed some suspicious sections of rotting timber in the conservatory and that the attic conversion probably contravened building regulations.

'Oh, don't be such a wet blanket,' she groaned. 'There's a gorgeous kitchen, the rooms are all good sizes and the garden is *so* pretty. I love it!'

'It's expensive, needs work and I don't want a hernia lugging a mower up all those steps.'

'Oh, Nick,' she said wearily, wondering if they'd ever find somewhere that wasn't spoiled by noisy livestock, overgrown gardens, unfinished glazing or various stages of rot.

'Oh no! Not another one-way system,' groaned Hattie as they arrived in a small market town of fine Georgian buildings, some forty minutes' drive from Nick's new workplace. 'And where are we supposed to park?'

The centre seemed to boast a plentiful supply of thirty-minute parking bays and diligent traffic wardens. Nick clenched his jaw and muttered oaths as he circled the town, hoping to find some-where convenient and free. Eventually, he gave in and followed the signs to a car park. The nearby toilet block was streaming with water and soggy litter – not an inspiring start to their final appointment. When Hattie returned from her loo dash, Nick turned off the car radio, tight-lipped and short on conversation. She realised questions about football scores were best avoided.

'I'm afraid I can't show you the cellar,' apologised Ricky, who was conducting the viewing of The Laurels, a handsome late Victorian villa. 'The vendors have blocked the doorway with boxes.'

'Are you sure you can't open the door just a fraction, so we can take a peep?' Hattie suggested with an encouraging smile. She'd been looking forward to exploring the cellar. Ricky shrugged and pulled the door open to reveal a pile of packing cases. The study was just as bad.

'Don't these people want to sell their house?' Nick harrumphed. He knew he was safe to express his opinion, as they'd seen a woman slip out of the front door just minutes before the appointed viewing time.

'Oh yes, they're wanting to sell. They're splitting up, you see.'

'Oh, I'm sorry to hear that,' said Hattie sympathetically.

Despite the cellar and study blockages, the rest of the house met their expectations: the spacious kitchen/diner led out to a south-facing garden, which was level and easily maintained, and there was off-road parking to the rear of the property. It wasn't quite the chocolate box cottage that Hattie had dreamed of – but it certainly had potential. Splitting up, she thought, that's what Leo is suggesting I do. It was, to use an over-used cliché, a big ask.

'Poor kids,' she sighed, as she surveyed the toys in one of the rooms, then went to catch up with Nick and Ricky who had already reached the top floor. 'Wow! This is more like it!' she exclaimed. 'What do you think, Nick?'

The entire space was taken over as a bedroom, with the back windows giving splendid views over rooftops to the meadows and wooded areas that stretched for miles beyond the ring road. Pigeons clustered on the branches of an imposing oak, two gardens away in one direction, and the pinnacle of the church spire could be seen in the other. As Nick and Hattie took in the view, Ricky absented himself with a 'See you downstairs when you're ready'.

Hattie wandered to the front end of the room and gazed down into the street below, watching the locals as they ambled or bustled past. The sight of a dark-haired man strolling along the street momentarily reminded her of Leo, who was, of course, plying his trade in a different market town.

'Well, Hat?'

'What? Sorry... miles away...'

'Nice home, eh?' Despite the gloomy news on the football front, Nick suddenly felt very positive.

'Oh yes, great... Actually, quite a lot better than I expected.' Her mind was indeed miles away, imagining Leo back in Montelugia and trying to imagine what it would be like if she never saw him again. She sighed softly.

'Another great view,' came Nick's voice, very close this time, as he put an arm around her shoulder and gave it a quick squeeze. He had amazingly rediscovered his touchy-feely side. 'Just imagine, Hat. It would be like a fresh start. I like this house; the garden's just about right for us, the bathroom's in the right place and forty minutes' drive to work is fine by me.'

Hattie felt an ache inside as she absorbed Nick's words. It was odd. He seemed to have suddenly morphed back into his old mellow self and the grumpiness had completely melted away.

'It's a lovely house,' she agreed wistfully and tried to imagine them living there, getting stuck into a new routine and making new friends.

Back downstairs, Nick was keen to register their interest.

'I guess it must be difficult for your clients,' he told Ricky, 'but my wife and I are seriously interested and don't want this house move to drag on too long.'

'I understand, Mr Chesney, and divorces can drag on as well,' Ricky agreed.

Hattie gulped guiltily, trying to rid her mind of images of Leo leading her across the sunny slopes of a hillside vineyard to a secret love nest where they'd make passionate love.

'But I can assure you that Mr and Mrs Elliot are ready to move out as soon as they can. You see, they were badly let down about six months ago. They were on the brink of exchanging contracts, when the buyer at the bottom of the chain changed his mind.'

'We've a lot to digest, but we'll get in touch as soon as we can,' Nick promised as they left The Laurels. 'Fancy a cuppa?' he asked Hattie as they set off towards the town centre.

Hattie could scarcely believe Nick's change of mood. His team was losing and they'd trailed around four properties, yet he was more cheerful than he had a right to be.

'Come on, Hat. I'll put another 50p in the meter and we'll check out one of the town's teashops – they seem to have enough of them. Who knows, we might be getting to know some of them a bit better in the future.'

'If you say so, Nick,' she replied, beaming. 'I'm ready for a Danish pastry, or even a chocolate muffin.' The trouble was, whenever Hattie thought about muffins now, her mind went back to the evening at The Bar on the Corner when she and Leo stood choosing muffins, and her heart ached longingly.

'So, shall we make an offer?' Nick asked once they'd settled at a table in The Nosebag, with a pot of Earl Grey and two custard Danish. 'You know, I think I've found a place I could happily move into. So, what do you think?'

'Hmm, we could try.' Hattie chased some pastry flakes around the plate with a wet finger and popped them in her mouth.

'You sound a bit doubtful. Don't you like the house?' Nick stared at Hattie, frustrated by her change of mood. Okay, so maybe it wasn't the twee little cottage of her dreams, but it was pretty damn close to perfect, considering the other places.

'No, it's not that. It's just a bit unsettling, this moving business.'

'Well, it was *your* suggestion in the first place. Remember what you said on that weekend away? You said we were stuck in a rut...'

'I know! I know! Okay,' she agreed, smiling, 'let's put in an offer.'

'Great! At last we agree on something,' chuckled Nick.

Looking up, she gave him a warm smile. After all, the poor man needed some encouragement on the day his beloved team's chances of FA Cup glory had been stymied.

'I know I've been a bit of a so-and-so recently, Hat.' He reached across the table and patted her spare hand. 'Not been the best husband.'

'You mean last Wednesday?'

'I was a prize prat. I'm sorry.'

'It's okay, Nick, I haven't been quite myself at times.' Holding his gaze longer than usual, she tried to fathom his sudden change.

'Yeah, ladies of a certain age!' he chuckled. 'And all those hormones on the blink!'

'They've got a lot to answer for,' she agreed. It seemed a convenient answer, with maybe just an element of truth.

'So, moving here really could be the fresh start we both need?' He paused to drain his cup. 'Tell you what, Hat; I'll call Ricky straight away and put in an offer. There's no sense in hanging around.'

'Coffee dear?' chirped Hilda Makepeace imperiously in church the following morning, struggling under the weight of a full tray. Hattie peered at the pale penny-pinching brew and put aside her natural instinct to refuse a mug.

'Why not?' she replied airily. 'We've something to celebrate, after all.'

'Oh really?' Hilda lifted a cynical eyebrow.

'Hmm,' continued Hattie. 'We've accepted an offer from a *cash* buyer and have found the perfect Victorian townhouse.'

'I see.' Hilda digested the information with her usual facial gymnastics. 'And what does your husband think of the prospect of moving away?' she asked. 'This area holds so many attractions after all,' she added knowingly, her lips pursed like a dog's bottom.

Hattie could read the old busybody's subtext, but refused to be ruffled. 'Well, as he's due to start his new position tomorrow, he can't wait to move somewhere much closer,' she retorted brightly. 'Out with the old, in with the new, as they say!' she added.

'Hmm, that's what we were wondering about,' murmured Hilda enigmatically. 'Gerald once threatened to trade me in for a newer model until I reminded him that no one else would put up with his foul embrocation and his feet. That and my jam roly-poly told him which side his bread was buttered.'

'Oh really?' The use of the word 'once' in Hilda's surprising disclosure was the only point that raised a doubt in her mind.

'You'd better still keep an eye on him, dear,' Hilda advised as she moved away.

Hattie returned a tight smile. 'And you can take a running jump,' she murmured under her breath. Now that Nick had turned back into the good old Nick she knew and loved, fears about the Rebecca Vaudin attraction had melted away. Ridding her mind of Leo was just a tad more difficult, but once they'd completed the house sales, the letting go would probably be easier, she told herself.

She and Nick caught up with Celia in the porch and updated her on the house situation.

'I'll keep my fingers crossed for you. The Laurels sounds perfect,' she said, seizing a heaven-sent opportunity. 'So I expect you'll be having a good clear out soon.'

Hattie and Nick nodded. Celia was in full flow by now.

'There's to be a charity event at Quaintly Manor on Easter Monday.'

'Quaintly?' Hattie stiffened. That had to be the event that Zena had mentioned so enthusiastically. So perhaps her modest efforts were not good enough to go on display. Shame really, she thought. It would have been nice to have been asked.

'Well, of course we've been roped in to help. Toby and I are on white elephants, so if you have any bric-a-brac, please do pass it on.'

'I've heard so much about Quaintly,' replied Hattie evenly. 'I believe Marigold Hellaby-Yule and her friend, Zena Gossage, are exhibiting their quilts.'

'And that's not all,' giggled Celia with a faint look of disapproval.

Meanwhile, Nick had just spotted a poster that Celia had pinned to the notice board and was studying it with great interest. Hattie was still wondering why Zena and Marigold hadn't bothered to invite her when her husband enthusiastically accepted the invitation for both of them.

'That sounds just the thing for Easter Monday. We'll definitely be over and I'm sure we can sort out some stuff for the stall.'

Hattie's jaw dropped open in amazement. In the past, he'd regularly grouched his way around dozens of fêtes and fairs when the children were younger and grumbled about paying over the odds for ice-creams and hot dogs. In fact, he'd have willingly cut off an arm rather than put up with dragging around a whining Josh and Laura. Perhaps it was the six-a-side football that had won him over? Whatever had worked its magic spell, it was definitely like having a new husband. As far as Hattie was concerned, he could sit and watch footie highlights all afternoon, if he could bear it, and *she'd* sort through the knick-knacks.

Some three hours later, she was surrounded by piles of old magazines when the phone rang. Nick had fallen asleep on the sofa and was snoring gently, much to Josh's amusement.

'Hattie, um... Zena here. We'd love it if you could join us at Quaintly on Easter Monday. You remember we mentioned there was to be a charity event?'

'Oh, yes, there's a poster about it at church, but my quilt's nowhere near finished,' Hattie explained. 'I've added a border and pinned it to the backing and wadding, but that's all. I haven't even started the hand-quilting yet.'

'Never mind, dear. Just make a start with the centre squares. Remember, the hand-quilting doesn't have to be elaborate. Having a few "works in progress" will be interesting for the visitors.'

'But it's not good enough to go on show, really it isn't!' Hattie protested. 'Those little quilting needles are fiendishly sharp. I'm bound to keep pricking my fingers and end up with blobs of blood all over the place! It'll look more like a battleground than something to put on a bed. I'm sure there are plenty more from the class who have much better ones than mine – Cynthia for instance.'

'Oh yes, Cynthia has already agreed to bring hers and there are at least two other smaller ones promised, but we'd love to have some larger pieces.'

It sounded as if a few from the class had found good reasons to wriggle out of going.

'Marigold and I thought you were jolly plucky to go for such a large quilt at your first attempt.'

'Plucky?' echoed Hattie. 'Actually, I'd describe it as plain stupid. Just carting the thing around is a major operation; that and keeping the cat off it!'

'But it'll be worth all the work once it's finished,' said Zena earnestly. 'You know, we were so taken with your striking colour scheme – such a refreshing change from twee daisy patterns. Oh, do say you'll come! You just have to sit with the others and sew. People *do* love to see traditional crafts and Marigold and I will of course be on hand to help.'

The thought of sitting with some of her old classmates was becoming quite appealing, especially as Cynthia would be one of them.

'Very well, I'll come. It'll take my mind off the house move.' And give me a good excuse for not helping on the white elephants, she realised gleefully.

The Easter holidays! Wonderful, thought Hattie. No more irritating kids and their bothersome parents for two whole glorious weeks. No more staffroom politics and best of all, no playground duty. After despatching Nick early the next morning, full of scrambled eggs and coffee, she shuffled back to bed for a decent lie-in.

'Bliss!' she sighed, pulling the duvet over her head. The school hols almost made up for all the hassle of trying to outwit Jacob Pocock and his merry men, and keeping on top of endless marking and record-keeping. However, it seemed only moments later when she was rudely awoken by the phone.

'Oh, go away,' she yawned, burrowing under the pillows, until she realised that ignoring the rest of the world wasn't an option. 'Yes?' she muttered, stifling another yawn. Jezebel uncurled and stretched from her cosy nest beside her, ready to give her breakfast order.

'Mrs Chesney? It's Ricky Bazalgette here from Jewel and Maidsmith Estate Agents.'

'Ricky? Ah, yes.' The mists in her brain started to clear.

'Good morning, Mrs Chesney. The Elliots have accepted your offer on The Laurels.'

'Really? Oh, that's brilliant!' Hattie was now wide awake. 'I'll arrange a survey report straight away and generally get things moving at this end.'

Perhaps the gods were at last smiling on the Chesney household.

Hattie leapt out of bed, excited, energised and eager to make a few vital phone calls, starting with Nick. She then took out her notebook and made the first of many lists… library, mortgage application, avoid Mia Casa at all costs (underlined twice). Two hours later, she had returned the quilting book and was on her way to the building society. The town was bustling with families, now that the holidays had started and Hattie was greeted with a few calls of 'Hello Mrs Chesney!' by some of her bolder pupils and embarrassed sniggers from her shyer ones. Everywhere, Easter eggs were on special offer, a telling sign of the recession-hit retail trade.

In Chocolate Galore's window a mouth-watering display winked at her seductively as she ambled past, catapulting her into the arms of a passing pedestrian.

'Oops!' she exclaimed, as she nose-dived into a smart charcoal grey jacket.

'Hattie! How lovely to see you!' She felt a firm hand clasp her shoulder to stop her sprawling in the gutter. It was Leo – at the wrong end of town. Best laid plans and all that. As usual, he was looking business-like and almost as good enough to eat as the Easter eggs in the window. Hattie's insides went into melt-down.

'Leo, it's lovely to see you too.'

'You are not at work, cara?'

'Of course not. I broke up on Friday and please don't call me that in public,' she hissed.

'Ah yes, you lucky teachers,' he chuckled. 'So, you are a lady of leisure?'

'Hardly,' she told him crisply. 'Too much to get done and too little time, as usual.'

Here they were, passing the time of day as if they were merely casual acquaintances with no history or guilty secrets. Leo's eyes, however, said otherwise. His intense gaze spoke of passion and longing. Hattie knew she had to make it clear where her priorities now lay. Be firm, be focussed, she told herself.

'On my way to the building society; got a mortgage application to sort out,' she explained brightly, despite the ferment inside her.

Leo took in the information solemnly. 'You really are moving then?'

'We found a house at the weekend, put in an offer and heard this morning that it's been accepted. The couple want to get it all sorted quickly,' she told him matter-of-factly, with a faint smile.

'And so you have a buyer? Which means Samways beat us to it then?'

Hattie nodded.

'I see. Rebecca was rather tight-lipped about an offer that came in too late. That must have been for your house.' Hattie nodded again. Her capacity for sentences seemed to have temporarily dried up.

He paused for a moment and gave a sigh. 'So you have a buyer...' he repeated with a shake of his head.

'Yes, a *cash* buyer. Spanish, I gather,' said Hattie, feeling the need to convince him with a few facts. 'Although I can't understand how Mrs Pil*es* can be attracted to our modest little three-bed semi.'

Leo's expression changed abruptly. 'What did you say?' he asked sharply.

'What? About our modest little three-bed semi?'

'No, the lady's name. What was it?'

Hattie studied Leo's expression. Perhaps Mrs Pil*es* had been a Mia Casa client as well?

'Er, well, we had a bit of a giggle about it to start with, because Brian Samways's secretary told us it was Piles, as in the painful problem in the nether regions. She must have just seen it written down and didn't realise it was pronounced Pil*es*. So it wasn't such an unfortunate name after all.'

Leo visibly relaxed. 'Ah, I see. Pil*es*, you say? Not Pirez?'

'No, but I haven't seen it written down. I'm just going by what the agent told me.'

'This Mrs Pil*es*… What is she like? Her appearance?' he asked frowning.

'Well,' replied Hattie, feeling slightly miffed that Leo was so interested in their buyer and not in her. She might be trying to purge him from her mind, but it didn't stop her enjoying a little of his attention. 'She's sort of Spanish-looking, obviously! But, Leo, why do you need to know? She's not one of Mia Casa's clients is she?'

He was still frowning, but at least the deep and meaningful glances had stopped.

'Er, maybe, but please describe her.'

Hattie was now finding the relentless questioning distinctly irritating.

' Well she's about my age but much slimmer – a sort of supermodel figure – and short, dark hair. She probably *is* a super model if she can afford a second home.' She paused to dredge up a few more useful points. 'And *very* smartly turned out – sort of designer style clothes, although they may have just been clever high-street copies, I suppose.'

Leo's face clouded briefly and Hattie was now convinced that the woman had already paid a visit to Mia Casa and they'd missed out on the sale.

'I see.'

He stood motionless with a troubled expression then looked at his watch. For a moment the suave, sexy Leo had vanished. She had never seen him so distracted.

'You have an appointment?'

'Er… yes.' He reached for her arm and leaned closer. Hattie gulped, imagining dozens of pairs of eyes fixed on them.

'Cara, remember what I told you? Of my plans?' His eyes seemed to bewitch her.

'I remember, Leo, but I'm busy, you're busy and this isn't the time or place.'

'We will speak again though?' he persisted, his voice as silky smooth as a chocolate truffle.

'Very well, Leo.' Before she could stop him, he'd taken one of her hands and had lifted it to his lips. Her stomach and heart lurched in their usual obliging way and she felt a hot flush creep up her neck and cheeks. Nick had rarely had this effect on her. 'I must go.'

She set off for the building society on a wave of embarrassment mixed with a certain amount of resentment over the relentless questioning. If Leo was planning to exchange estate agency for a return to managing the Marcello wine empire, why was he so insistent about the description of their buyer? Surely, the name was enough? How many Spanish women with similar names were there house-hunting in the Aylesbury area, anyway? And if Mia Casa had missed a sale, why should Leo care? It was all so tedious.

Back at home, Hattie had the delightful prospect of Laura paying one of her rare flying visits. She had hinted at holiday plans, but no details. Later that day she arrived in a whirl of excitement and was soon bubbling over with news of her boyfriend Felix.

'Ah, you look happy together,' murmured Hattie, studying the photo that Laura had fished out of her bag.

'Yes, we are,' sighed Laura, obviously smitten. 'There's this amazing chemistry between us. He just has to look at me and my tummy seems to turn somersaults.'

'Ah yes, I know the feeling,' Hattie admitted, remembering how she'd felt that very morning when Leo had taken her hand and kissed it.

'Hmm,' sighed Laura, 'my heart goes flip, little shivers go up and down my spine and I sort of tingle all over.'

'Oh yes,' agreed Hattie nodding, 'I know exactly what you mean.'

'Ah, bless,' giggled Laura. 'Nice to know dear old Dad's a romantic at heart.'

If only you knew, thought Hattie guiltily.

17

Easter Monday dawned overcast and misty, but with a forecast of sun and blue skies later in the morning. Nick, full of rare joie-de-vivre, loaded up the car with boxes of books, ornaments and odd kitchen paraphernalia that would otherwise have ended up in a charity shop. There was a positive glow about him that Hattie hadn't seen for ages. On arrival at Quaintly, he set off in search of Celia, to help organise her stall, while Hattie went to find Zena, Marigold and the quilting room.

'Got to keep Celia sweet,' he commented with a wry grin, 'seeing as she's taking on dear old Josh with his odious undies and sparkling repartee.'

Quaintly Manor boasted many rooms, each spectacular in their own way. One of the grandest ones had been allocated to the quilting display, naturally; whereas many of the stalls and attractions were being housed in a huge marquee on the vast back lawn, as well as in the barns. Zena and Marigold's entire quilting output seemed to be hung around the room and they'd obviously hired specialist display screens and frames for their king-size bed covers. It was a truly stunning sight and made Hattie's half-finished offering seem all the more insignificant. On one of the smaller screens, Cynthia's cot quilt was already in position and of course, she had another project on the go.

'It's just a wee floor cushion,' she told Hattie. Although, by the look of it, there was nothing wee about the piece that comprised six squares on each side. As always, Cynthia was mistress of the understatement. Hattie suspected that her initial lack of confidence at the first class had been a smokescreen and that she wasn't the novice she'd pretended to be. Zena, sporting her daffodil-yellow smock top and bronze velvet, knee-high breeches, was fussing around like a mother hen, but there was no sign of Marigold. She checked her watch and glanced around the group.

'Now girls,' she began, 'we don't expect you to stay here every minute of the day. There's lots to see and enjoy, but maybe we could co-ordinate our comfort breaks and leisure time so there's always two of us here at least.'

Suddenly, the door burst open and Marigold almost fell into the room in a dishevelled state. Her wrinkled navy leggings were covered in straw, an old checked shirt was smeared with dark red smudges, and long loops of her grey hair had escaped from a lop-sided bun. The group started aghast, but it was clear from her triumphant expression that she hadn't just been ravished by a randy retainer in the rhubarb patch.

'Sorry I'm late,' she gasped, 'but Juliet our prize sow went into labour at breakfast time and number seven was breech, so I've been literally up to my elbows in... er... Anyway, all twelve are happily suckling now.'

'Well done, old thing,' said Zena, beaming. She went to give her friend a tentative hug, but then changed her mind and pecked her on the cheek instead. Hattie had never seen Marigold so animated or heard her utter more than a few quiet phrases in the past. This was quite a revelation.

'Goodness! Must get myself to a bathroom,' she murmured, setting off to make herself more presentable.

By ten o'clock, visitors started to trickle in and despite Hattie's suspicion that she was only there to make up the numbers, her work-in-progress drew plenty of enthusiastic comments and admiring glances.

'Oh, there you are, Hat!' Nick ambled in later in the morning, hands in pockets and smiling broadly. Cynthia had gone in search of coffee and husband Donald. Her plan was to take him to the spinning and weaving workshops and twist his arm for a wheel of her own.

'So Celia's let you off the lead has she?' joked Hattie. 'I bet she can hardly believe her luck. Toby's much too single-minded and astute to get drawn into some of her fundraising activities.'

'Hmm, he beetled off straight away when he heard my offer, muttering something about a bowls match. So... all okay here?' he asked, jiggling the change in his pockets and pacing to and fro in front of Zena and Marigold's sale table.

'Fine thanks,' said Hattie, grinning. 'I'll be taking a break later. Probably check out the workshops in the barns.'

'Great idea, Hat. Sounds just your thing and if they're selling any bits and bobs, why don't you treat yourself to something? You certainly deserve it. Well, I must be off. I promised to take Celia some coffee.' He strode off purposefully with a spring in his step.

'Had a good look, have you?' Hattie asked Cynthia when she eventually reappeared.

'Oh, yes the spinning and weaving workshops were fascinating. You could even have a go!'

'So, what did Donald think? Did you manage to persuade him to buy you a spinning wheel?'

'What? At the prices we saw? Afraid not, but he's promised to look on eBay for a good second-hand one, then he went scooting off to watch a falconry display and left me to it!' She raised her eyebrows in exasperation.

'So, what else did you do?'

'Well, I had one of the ploughman's lunches on the back terrace – smoked mackerel pâté, homemade I'm sure, and salad veg grown on the estate.'

'Hmm, my mouth is watering already,' commented Hattie, finishing off yet another section and fastening the thread as neatly as she could.

'And,' added Cynthia, 'apparently, there's local talent in the marquee too – bands and kiddies' choirs and dance groups. You know the sort of thing.'

Hattie draped her quilt artistically over one of the display screens and then picked up her shoulder bag. 'Oh yes, some of the old faithfuls, I expect. Well, I might go and cheer them on if I've got time,' she replied wearily, picturing the geriatric gents with bells strapped to their ankles and hankies flapping in time with a wheezing accordion. 'But loo and lunch are top of my list at the moment.'

'Oh, and don't forget the gardens, Hattie. They're quite spectacular. Although I had a bit of a shock in one of them.'

'Really?' commented Hattie, intrigued. 'Had someone been picking the pansies or trampling the tulips?'

Cynthia shook her head. 'I was looking for Donald, so I went into the dear little walled garden because he's always had a thing about espaliers and there's two rare varieties on the estate – pears, I mean. Anyway, there was I enjoying the blossom and watching a pair of blue tits feeding their young, when I saw… Oh, it was brazen! And he was old enough to be her father! Hands all over the place and goodness knows what might have happened next if I hadn't coughed!'

'Not Donald?' gasped Hattie, finding her memory of Donald impossible to reconcile with Cynthia's shocking scenario.

'No, *not* Donald. Of course not *Donald!*' Cynthia was marginally more amused than shocked. 'I caught up with him eventually and calmed myself down with a nice cup of tea and a ploughman's. Really, I think people shouldn't behave like that in public! Shameless hanky-panky, I call it!'

'Absolutely,' agreed Hattie, feeling the call of the loo a more pressing priority.

As she set off down the corridor, she pondered Nick's metamorphosis and was hopeful of more hanky-panky herself – as Cynthia would call it – now that the air seemed to have cleared.

Leo, on the other hand, who oozed romance from every pore, was taking more of a back seat in her thoughts. It had to be like that if she was to keep her sanity. She hadn't had any more contact with him since that unexpected meeting the week before, other than texting him about their buyer, seeing as he'd been so persistent about discovering her identity. When the letter confirming the offer had arrived, Hattie had been surprised to learn that their buyer's name was in fact Pirez and not Piles after all. Secretary Geraldine had evidently made a muddle of recording the lady's details in the first place, or someone else at Samways was hard of hearing. Leo had simply texted back, *Thank you*, and there was no mention of the half-finished conversation in the kitchen, much to Hattie's relief.

Her stomach was rumbling impatiently once she had queued up and waited an age in the ladies'. Perhaps Nick was ready for a spot of lunch, she wondered, and set off to drag him away from the white elephants. Maybe they'd even take a stroll in the walled garden themselves and soak up the sun that had finally put in an appearance. Eventually, she tracked down Celia's stall, but Nick was nowhere to be seen. Instead, Hilda Makepeace was comfortably established beside her friend, her knitting needles clacking furiously as a khaki-coloured length grew, taking on the appearance of something hairy and masculine. She promptly adopted a long-suffering expression, although clearly she wasn't actually doing anything that demanded much effort.

'Oh, I thought Nick was helping,' began Hattie.

'He *was* dear,' replied Celia with a sigh. 'But when he came back with my coffee he announced that he was needed elsewhere – quite urgently too!'

'Ah, well, it's good to know he's keeping busy,' remarked Hattie amiably. 'Anyway, you've got Hilda here to help now.'

'Only by chance, my dear,' said Hilda stiffly. 'I just happened along to find dear Celia left in the lurch, poor thing.'

'But you're not exactly run off your feet, are you?' retorted Hattie, feeling very defensive of Nick and his willingness to plug a gap elsewhere, especially considering the way Hilda had frequently criticised him.

'Ah, but what if we had a sudden rush?' protested Hilda.

'Then we'd cope very well,' interjected Celia, trying to soothe Hilda's ruffled feathers.

'Of course you would,' agreed Hattie. 'Well, I'm just off to grab some lunch and check out the spinning and weaving workshop.'

'Oh, and don't miss the dancing group,' advised Hilda, suddenly becoming more animated.

'Hmm, I might. Would it be the Markham Morris Men? They seem to pop up everywhere with boring regularity.'

'Er... not exactly,' answered Hilda with a gleam in her eye. 'Someone told me Markham Morris cancelled – one of them fell and broke his hip, silly beggar, but this other group are certainly giving them a run for their money. They've got quite a following.'

'New kids on the block, eh?' Hattie replied, ignoring Hilda's puzzled expression and wandering off in search of sustenance, which silenced the embarrassing rumbles.

From her table at the rear of the house, Hattie was aware of a steady stream of visitors making tracks for the marquee, which was separated from the terrace by a row of stalls and the main ring, where the judging of the 'Pet most like its owner' had just taken place. It had been won by a little girl with auburn pigtails, pulling a sleepy cocker spaniel on a lead. Hattie took her tray back through the French windows into the dining room, which was the hub of the day's food preparation, taken over by Quaintly WI. As she emerged once more, the flow of visitors to the marquee had increased. She'd heard someone in the staffroom mention there was a new Appalachian ladies' dance group in the area. Maybe they were the cause of all the interest?

She set off, giving the white elephants a wide berth, when suddenly some music started, which was not Appalachian by any stretch of the imagination. A pounding drum beat, reedy piping and rhythmic twanging filled the air, shattering the peace and tranquillity of the genteel manor gardens, like a mobile phone at a Prom concert. A small crowd was clustered around the entrance, paying their 50ps when Hattie arrived.

'It's Bombay Mix!' called a young woman to her companion. 'I read about them in *The Herald*!' They pushed past some ditherers and slapped down a handful of coins on the steward's table.

'You're not going in there,' snapped one grey-haired matron, grabbing her mouse-like husband and pulling him away. 'It'll fair turn your head and Lord knows what it'll do to your blood pressure!'

'But Esme, it's art!' he protested feebly.

'Art?' the woman spat. 'And I'm Victoria Beckham!'

He followed dejectedly like a little boy whose ice cream cone had nose-dived into a puddle.

The music inside the marquee had a strong Asian sound, but it was also accompanied by cheers, bursts of applause and the occasional wolf-whistle. With a sinking feeling, Hattie guessed exactly what was happening on the other side of the canvas. A poster pinned to the entrance was advertising Bombay Mix's routine as 'full of Eastern promise'. It had to be Rebecca Vaudin and her dancing troupe. At last the penny dropped and, like joining up the final dot on a puzzle book page, a picture emerged that made sense of several blindingly obvious clues that Hattie had completely missed. Despite the sinking feeling in her stomach, she paid her 50p and eased her way inside the marquee that was crammed full of excited and fascinated spectators. On the stage at the far end was a group of about a dozen females of various ages and figures. Could Madge be one of them? After the Stan Burke incident, would she have the courage to face another audience?

The whole troupe were decked out in bright, silky costumes of pants and skimpy tops, gauzy veils and arms full of jangling bangles. However, resplendent in red and gold and an even skimpier top and taking up centre stage was Rebecca, who was gyrating and moving to the music in an outrageously seductive manner. Hattie moved closer, edging past clusters of bemused onlookers who filled the side aisle. Strategically-placed foliage decorated the stage and a glittering backdrop added to the atmosphere. This routine was several notches up from the improvised table-top display at The Four Seasons and Hattie had to admit there was a precision in the performance that lifted it from the banal. Then she spotted Madge, half-hidden by an urn of greenery, in the back row, with at least two spare tyres that quivered as she moved to and fro. It was not a pretty sight, but at least she was in good company with a few others – Sandra among them – of the same build and vintage.

Hattie stared at the enraptured audience as she edged further along the side aisle. She'd intended to congratulate Madge afterwards and tell her how well she'd done. In fact, it was remarkable that she'd agreed to take part at all. However, all such thoughts vanished when she heard a shout that sounded horribly familiar – Nick! Craning her neck, she at last spotted him in the front row, with his tongue almost hanging out like a dog contemplating a juicy bone. He was not alone. A number of tight-lipped women were sitting beside husbands in much the same state of enchantment. If ever eyes could be described as 'on stalks' this was it.

As the music came to a climax, the sensuous movements followed suit and as the dancers struck their final pose, a huge cheer erupted – mainly from the men in the audience. Nick was on his feet in a flash, whistling and clapping for all he was worth. Hattie experienced a strong sense of déjà vu. She stared at her husband, reviewing his recent form and cursed herself for being so gullible. Perhaps her eyeballs, trained on the back of his head, also burned a hole in his consciousness, because at that moment he turned round and their eyes locked in shock. His expression of adulation was abruptly replaced by a more sheepish one and he shrugged as if to say sorry. Hattie glared back and then turned and pushed her way to the exit, intent on returning to the sanity and peace of the quilting room, all thoughts of spinning and weaving swept from her mind.

As she walked back, her irritation gradually receded as she reflected on Nick's relatively harmless, although hugely embarrassing, public behaviour. With the dancing over, he would have to find something else to hold his attention. After all, wasn't he supposed to be helping out somewhere? Or was that simply a ruse to escape Celia's clutches?

When she arrived, the room was positively buzzing, with streams of visitors circulating around the display boards and eagerly homing in on the stall of quilted tea cosies, cushion covers and wash bags. Zena and Marigold were evidently doing a roaring trade. Hattie carefully removed her quilt and clamped on the frame to the next section that she'd be stitching. She was grateful to have something requiring a degree of concentration that would take her mind off the scenes in the marquee.

'Did you have a good break?' asked Cynthia as they stitched. Hattie decided to keep her remarks to safe, neutral subjects. Food was safe to start with.

'Well, I agree about the mackerel pâté – absolutely yummy! I wouldn't mind the recipe myself.' Animals were also a safe bet. 'I managed to catch some of the pet show too. Some of the owners who looked like their pets – or was it supposed to be the other way round? Well, they must have had a sense of humour!'

'And what about the spinning and weaving?'

'Well, I didn't find it... I was distracted by the crowds who were piling into the marquee, like a lot of lemmings, so I went too.'

'Oh yes? So what was the cause of all the excitement?'

'A troupe of belly dancers. But honestly, Cynthia, some of the flesh on display stretched the boundaries of artistic licence,' she giggled.

'That bad?'

'Well, in some cases, let's say a couple of metres more fabric would have made a world of difference.'

Their conversation drifted onto moving plans and the latest exploits of Cynthia's grandchildren, when she broke off abruptly to exclaim in shocked tones, 'That's the ghastly groper I saw in the walled garden, with his hands all over a young blonde woman!'

Hattie followed Cynthia's gaze, horrified to see she was looking directly at Nick, who had just wandered in and was studying one of Zena or Marigold's most striking pieces.

'Are you sure?' she gasped with a sinking feeling, realising that the garden incident and what she had witnessed in the marquee were inevitably linked.

'Most definitely,' assented Cynthia scornfully. 'I recognise the jumper and I think I recognise his face as well. Although –'

'But…' Hattie floundered, wishing a convenient fainting fit or a rare earthquake would somehow curtail the impending embarrassment. If the ground had opened up and swallowed her that would have been a welcome relief.

Nick had finished his appraisal of the quilt and was on his way, weaving a path between clusters of visitors. Hattie rewound the last few weeks in her mind, trying to recall whether Cynthia and Nick had ever met, but of course, if they *had*, Cynthia would surely never have described the garden incident in *that* way. Noticing the ghastly groper's smiling face directed towards her companion, however, Cynthia became covered in confusion and managed to stab an unguarded finger.

'Hat,' began Nick awkwardly.

'Or I might have been mistaken,' mumbled Cynthia miserably, in between valiant attempts to staunch the flow of blood.

Hattie fixed Nick with her best 'I'm-not-standing-for-any-nonsense' face, frequently used to great effect with class 4R on particularly fraught days. 'Enjoy the display, did you? You were putting on a pretty animated one yourself from what I saw. You could whistle for England!' she remarked as levelly as she could, although under the surface she was fuming.

'Yes, it was quite entertaining. Old Madge was giving it plenty of welly in the back row,' he chuckled.

'Really?' hissed Hattie fiercely, trying to keep her voice down. 'I'm surprised you noticed her. Strangely enough, I didn't get the impression you were there to watch Madge. A little bird told me you had another, more youthful focus of attention.'

At this, Cynthia groaned quietly and went to sit next to Marigold, well out of earshot and on the pretext of discussing the merits of different-shaped embroidery frames.

'Well, er...' Nick, was momentarily lost for words.

'And she's quite a mover, I must admit. Even better than at your leaving do.'

Nick fidgeted, having now spotted Cynthia – the woman who'd walked by at a rather unfortunate moment. 'Hmm, yeah,' was all he managed.

'So, did you know she'd be here today?' Hattie continued. 'You knew, didn't you? That's why you were so keen to help.'

'It was Celia who raised the subject, if you remember. I mean, it's good to support local events, don't you think?' he replied nonchalantly.

'Don't try changing the subject. If I said "walled garden", would that ring any bells?'

'Walled garden?' he asked as innocently as he could, his voice going up an octave.

At this, Cynthia made a hasty retreat to the loo.

'Yes, Nick. You heard! A little bird was flying past and spotted someone wearing exactly the same jumper and looking a lot like you – what was it? Oh, yes – with hands all over the place.' Hattie then paused for dramatic effect. 'Explain!'

Nick froze like a rabbit caught in the glare of car headlights, mouth gaping open and a slick of sweat appearing on his top lip. Hattie jabbed her needle through the fabric with such vehemence that Nick reacted as if he'd been at the receiving end. His frenzied thoughts were slow to come into any sense of order.

'It's not what you think,' he protested. 'In fact, your little bird needs to go to Specsavers or she's got a rather too vivid imagination, based on pure fantasy.'

'So,' Hattie retorted, 'give me *your* version, Nick'

He edged around the furniture until he was beside her then squatted down on the arm of her chair. 'Let me explain, Hat. It's all very innocent – honestly!' he murmured. 'I happened to bump into Becky, who was in a bit of a state. You see, her fiancé, Darren, had refused to come and support her today. So, of course, she was upset. He's gone to some motor-cross meeting over Milton Keynes way.'

'Oh and of course *you* know how putting sport first can upset us girls.'

Nick chose to ignore Hattie's jibe and continued to dig himself out of a rather deep hole. 'They'd been having problems sorting out the wedding arrangements. Apparently, he's being really difficult. Poor Becky's at the end of her tether. She wants traditional white in a church with all the trimmings and he's for a beach in Cuba. Says he'd feel a fraud saying all the religious vows.'

'So she was crying on your shoulder, was she?' replied Hattie with mock sympathy.

'Well, yes, she was, as a matter of fact, and I was simply showing some fatherly concern towards her – poor girl. She's not much older than our Laura.'

'"Hands all over the place," so I was told. That doesn't sound very fatherly.'

'Hold on now! I had a fatherly arm around her and I might have given her shoulder a squeeze, but nothing more than that – I promise!'

Hattie sniffed dismissively and tried to maintain some eye contact, but Nick quickly glanced down at the floor.

'Well, Nick, your fatherly Sir Galahad role certainly did the trick, didn't it? She was going great guns in the marquee. You'd never have believed she'd been falling to pieces an hour or so before.'

'Yes, well, it's a good thing I was around to help her get herself together again then wasn't it, or there would have been a lot of disappointed punters,' he replied, justifying his actions. 'Anyway,

I'm off to run the line for the under-tens six-a-side tournament now – if you approve of course!'

'Oh, stop it, Nick!'

'And tell your little bird to get her eyes tested, right?' He strode off purposefully, almost cannoning into Cynthia who was returning from her loo dash. The two of them locked eyes for a brief moment then continued on their separate ways.

'Oh, Hattie, I'm so sorry,' Cynthia whispered miserably.

'Cynthia, please don't worry. Nick's explained he was acting in a purely fatherly way, giving a bit of support to a poor girl who's having problems with her wedding plans and whose fiancé couldn't be bothered to turn up today. Mind you,' she reflected, 'if she were to chuck her ring back in his face, there'd be plenty queuing up to take his place, judging by her fan club in the marquee.'

'Oh, really?'

'And she's an estate agent too,' added Hattie.

'What's that got to do with it?'

'One of *our* estate agents. That's how we know her.'

'Ah, I see.'

'And a right bossy cow too! You should have heard her pulling my interior décor to shreds.'

There was a pregnant pause in the space where Hattie had imagined some comment from Cynthia. Instead, she stared fixedly ahead, her brows knitted in a frown. Hattie glanced at her, surprised that the conversation seemed to have ground to a halt. Perhaps Cynthia was shocked by her choice of words? Too bad.

'Well, none of us are perfect, are we? Your husband and that girl, I mean. Anyone could find themselves in a similar situation. It's knowing how to handle it that matters.'

'Exactly,' agreed Hattie adamantly, puzzled by Cynthia's observation.

'That chap at the college for instance…' There was a distinct wobble in Cynthia's voice and a sort of 'sorry-to-mention-it' sort of tone.

'What chap?'

Cynthia seemed to have gone off on a new tack and Hattie was at a loss to know who she had in mind. Perhaps she'd had a run in with the caretaker, who really *was* bolshie. Or maybe he'd even tried a bit of inappropriate banter when Donald's back was turned. She was very well-preserved for her age, despite her preference for American tan tights. Cynthia took a deep breath then shook her head. She was obviously struggling with something.

'Whatever do you mean, Cynthia?'

'That dark-haired chap... The one you sometimes met...'

'I don't understand.' Hattie felt a shock surge around her body, sending her heart into a frantic gallop. She'd seen her with Leo? Surely not! She could have sworn Cynthia was well out of the way whenever she'd been with him. She'd been *so* careful.

Cynthia sighed and shook her head again. 'Donald and I went for a coffee after one of the evening classes – just a little treat really. Then, when we went back to the college car park, we saw you Hattie, but you weren't alone.' She glanced up briefly.

'Oh, but... er ...' Hattie floundered.

'You clearly knew him *very* well.'

Ah, thought Hattie, no chance of denying anything, judging by Cynthia's emphasis on 'very'. She gazed, unseeing, at the smiling stream of onlookers who occasionally paused and passed comments.

'Oh, so what you're saying is it's like the pot calling the kettle black.'

She sat there miserably until, mercifully, Zena appeared with a plate of buns, muffins and flapjacks.

'Come on now, girls. Cheer up and have something to nibble.'

Had their faces really been a picture of gloom and despondency? That would not have been a good advertisement for patchwork. They tucked in obediently and Cynthia gave Hattie's hand a brief squeeze.

'I hope it works out for you,' she whispered.

'I hope so too,' agreed Hattie fervently, deciding that the chocolate chip muffin looked particularly inviting. Oh no, she thought with a jolt, was this a sign that her fragile resolve was crumbling? Time for another reality check: Nick was no longer working in Aylesbury, their house was under offer and everything was pointing to a quick move in the next few weeks. Rebecca Vaudin and Leo Marcello would be left behind, so she'd just have to see chocolate muffins in a new light.

Two days later, Nick announced he'd stay with his parents the following night.

'There's a meeting after work about the expansion plans,' he explained, 'so I'm not sure when I'll be at Mum and Dad's, but I'll call you on my mobile, okay?'

'Expansion plans?' remarked Hattie. 'Sounds like you've landed a dream job, considering how so many businesses are struggling.'

'Ah, but the gardening sector is very robust,' he assured her with a chuckle. It sounded just like boardroom spin to Hattie. However, her fertile imagination pictured her own expansion plans for The Laurels: perhaps a real wood conservatory, rather than settling for UPVC. She imagined it, furnished with beautiful rattan sofas and ceramic planters, straight from the pages of the better glossy mags.

Nick's decision came as no surprise. The honeymoon period of long, daily drives had ended more abruptly than she'd secretly predicted, but it suited her perfectly. She and Josh could carry on as normal while Nick's parents would enjoy fussing over their son. One positive result of the Quaintly incident was that she and Nick had now reached a state of truce and nothing more was mentioned. Life was ticking along quietly, with the awkwardness of the past consigned to the recycle bin, from whence it would never emerge. The arrival of an envelope on Thursday afternoon, however, changed things dramatically for Hattie. She had spent most of the afternoon weeding the borders and potting up some of her prized perennials ready for the move, and was gasping for a cup of tea. It was while she was waiting for the kettle to boil that she spotted it. Had someone tried the doorbell? You could seldom hear it from the garden, especially with the kitchen door shut. Her name was printed neatly in capitals, although there was an interesting flourish to the final letter that seemed familiar. Perhaps it was an invitation to a girlfriend's party or one of Daphne's clothes-swap coffee mornings? It was neither.

At the sight of a single, red rose on a simple folded card, her heart lurched excitedly. It was from Leo. It was just like the rose left on her doorstep in Birmingham all those years ago. This one, however, bore a simple message:

Thinking of you, Leo.

Brief though it was, Hattie took pleasure in knowing that she was in his thoughts. But why send a card? Was it his way of putting distance between the two of them, as well as assuring her that she still meant something to him? If so, that was a relief. She hugged the card to her chest then slid it back into its envelope and tucked it into the deep pocket of her gardening apron. This was a message Nick would *not* see.

As Leo drove back to the office, he was not in the best of moods. Why hadn't he texted her just to make sure she'd be at home? He'd stood at the door for over ten minutes, trying the bell, rapping the letter box and then leaving a message on her mobile. It was so frustrating, especially as her car was parked on the drive. She could have been anywhere in the village or simply in the back garden. The tall side gate was securely bolted on the inside, and shouting her name over the fence didn't exactly appeal to him. He would have really had to bellow to make himself heard down the long passage that ran along the house. Leo was not the bellowing type. The old man glowering at him from the neighbouring house didn't help either. What he'd really wanted was to hand over the card in person. He wanted to see her reaction and to see if there was still hope. Time alone would tell.

Back in the office, his frustration level rose even more.

'A woman phoned,' Rebecca told him between sips of coffee and frantic texting.

'A woman? Did she say who she was?'

'No,' replied Rebecca, already sounding bored with the subject.

'A phone number?'

Rebecca shrugged and shook her head. 'Sorry, Leo, she just said she'd phone back, or maybe drop by and see you – something like that.'

Leo stared at the girl, who was clearly busy with something and becoming more irritated by the second.

'Oh no!' she muttered angrily then flounced off to the staffroom at the back of the office.

Missed calls, wasted journeys, thought Leo despondently, pocketing his car keys and dumping his briefcase on the desk. His move back to Montelugia beckoned, but there were too many loose ends and unresolved problems before that could happen.

For the Chesney household, however, everything was steaming along nicely: both surveys were completed and mounds of paperwork arrived regularly, demanding their attention. Then, shortly after lunch on Sunday afternoon, the news that they'd been anticipating came at last. It was Mark who made the call.

'Ma-in-law passed away peacefully earlier this morning.'

It was time to step up to the plate again and Hattie, who had been anticipating this news all week, quickly took charge.

'Drop the boys off as soon as you're ready,' she told Mark.

'Thanks, Hat. You're brilliant as usual. Fliss will be in touch when she feels up to it. She's taken it very hard.'

Later that evening, while Hattie was making a bedtime cuppa and loading the washing machine, Nick came into the kitchen looking slightly frazzled.

'Er, Hat,' he began tentatively, 'I've just had a message from

Clive.' He jabbed the 'off' button on his mobile and started pacing the floor.

'Clive Bennington, I presume?'

'Yeah, he wants to bring the expansion discussions forward and needs to pencil in some more evening sessions. I know it's a pain, but I think I'll have to stay on hand and lodge with Mum and Dad for the week. It won't go down well if I start bleating on about getting back to the wife when we're at a crucial part of the process. You understand, don't you Hat?'

She nodded resignedly. 'I'll call you every night, when I'm finished, just to keep in touch and you can always text me if there's something urgent,' Nick promised.

'But there's so much to do – the sorting, clearing, packing...'

'Ah, but don't forget the removal package includes the packing.'

The thought of removal men fingering some of her belongings filled her with dismay.

'Don't worry, Hat,' Nick soothed, giving her a hug, 'I'll do my share at the weekends. It'll be fine, honestly.' He leaned in and kissed her. 'Okay?'

'Yes, Nick,' she sighed wearily. 'I'll manage. Work comes first.'

18

The summer term had arrived, but not quite the same routine.

'How do you fancy helping out in reception for a few days?' asked Gail when she had phoned late in the Easter holidays.

The prospect of coping with Lorretta the scissor fiend again flashed through Hattie's mind. Some embarrassing remarks had been bandied about after last time.

'What, on top of everything else? Gail, I need time at home or removal day will arrive and we'll end up taking all our rubbish with us.'

'No, Hattie, have you forgotten? Sonia's back full-time now, so no 4R to worry about. I can switch your Year 5 cover too. It's because of the baseline tests you see.'

'Ah yes,' Hattie replied, trying to sound knowledgeable. The poor mites, she reflected; their first week in school and suddenly some strange woman scares the living daylights out of them with a battery of baffling tests.

By the time Hattie was greeting Norma's brood on Friday morning she was feeling in need of a chill-out in a darkened room, rather than a whole day with a bunch of hyperactive rising fives. Damage limitation measures, however, were in place, which meant that the glue and scissors were in a secret location. Whatever else happened, she could rest easy in the knowledge that Lorretta Bailey wouldn't be able to fashion an eye-catching collage out of snippets of school uniform, hair, credit cards or other valuable or sensitive personal effects. Mind you, she mused wickedly, a collage of tampons and panty liners might have raised a few eyebrows at the end of term parents' evening. It had the potential of being quite a talking point, in fact!

Bubbling around in her mind was Josh, who was taking his driving test later that morning. Then there was that little matter of completing outdoor PE with the same number of children she started with – not as simple as it sounded. Young Rooney, who was going through a growth spurt, had the build and disposition for scrambling up conveniently-placed trees and disappearing over the hedge into the adjoining housing estate. Fortunately, though, that amusing little diversion hadn't yet occurred to him.

By the time the class were back in uniform, their PE bags hanging on the right pegs and lined up for hand washing – and generally squirting water over each other – Hattie reckoned Josh would be finishing his test.

'Enough!' she commanded, stepping in and removing Tyler's thumb from under the gushing cold tap. 'You've soaked poor Anneliese! Now go and say sorry and dry your hands. It's *your* fault that your sweatshirt is wet. And you don't need more than *one* paper towel! Mrs Tribbeck, could you lend a hand here?'

Collapsing in relief in the staffroom ten minutes later, Hattie switched on her mobile. 'Oh bless him!' she exclaimed, reading a text that had arrived just minutes earlier.

'What's that Hat?' asked Sally munching on her sandwich.

'Our Josh – he's passed his driving test *first* time! What a clever chap!'

'Uh-oh!' warned Sally wryly. 'Now watch out for your car, unless you buy him one of his own of course.'

'Fat chance of that! I hardly think Nick's salary would stretch to that. Josh will jolly well have to save up his pennies and do a deal with Tarrant's Motors.'

Nick was of the same opinion when he arrived home. What *did* surprise Hattie, however, was the bunch of flowers.

'For my gorgeous, hardworking wife!' he announced, flourishing the ribbon-tied tulips and chrysanthemums.

'How lovely!' Hattie whooped with delight, burying her nose amongst the blooms and sniffing appreciatively.

'Well, you deserve it, old thing, playing host to the Tarrier lads yet again *and* coping with all the moving stuff. And...' he continued, reaching into his briefcase with a broad grin, '...just a little free sample from a business contact. I know you never say no to choccy!'

It was a swanky box of champagne truffles.

'A free sample? For me? Oh, Nick! How scrumptious!' she trilled. 'Thank your business contact from me, won't you? I think I'm going to like you working for Bennnington's.'

All too soon, however, the weekend was over and another school week was starting. Hattie wondered how many more Mondays would find her driving to work to take the bouncy Year 3 classes. It felt an age since she'd spoken to Leo and the arrival of his card was becoming a distant memory. He may have been thinking of her, but that was all. She, in turn, thought of him often, but knew she had to get used to the idea of never seeing him again. His rose card was a sweet thought, but it didn't have quite the impact of Nick's fabulous flowers and tantalising truffles. They expected to be signing contracts before long. In fact, she'd received a message on her mobile that morning and although it was a bit of a bind, she reluctantly made a detour when she'd finished her morning's teaching, to sort out a query that was threatening to slow down the whole process.

After parking in the multi-storey near the library, she set off towards the cobbled back streets of town with their handsome, Victorian properties, much favoured by solicitors and hedge-fund managers. It was the sort of pleasantly sunny day when you could ditch your jacket and start to wonder where you'd last put your sunglasses. Avoid Mia Casa at all costs, she told herself, but the trouble was, it was in the same part of town. She crossed a square and just before turning down a narrow back street, a familiar figure – last seen decked out in gaudy taffeta and an excess of sequins – was observed emerging from a greengrocer's. It was Madge, who was making the most of her lunch hour and popping grapes into her mouth in quick succession.

'Oh, hello, Madge. Hope all's well with you,' she said cheerfully

'Yes, fine thank you, Hattie. Rafiq seems to have settled into his new role *very* well, not that I see much of him. I'm down with Janice and Rhoda now, you know. We get on famously,' she chuckled.

'Excellent!' replied Hattie, choosing to ignore any veiled sideswipes at Nick. 'I was really impressed by Bombay Mix's display at the Quaintly charity do.'

'Well, thank you. I didn't see you there, only your other half cheering us on in the front row. He seemed very keen, I must say.'

'Ah well, I just managed to sneak in for a few minutes. I was one of the exhibitors you see,' she told her proudly.

'Really? Oh, I suppose you were in one of the barns.'

'Oh no, Madge. I was in one of the drawing rooms with Marigold Hellaby-Yule and Zena Gossage, with our quilts. Anyway, I thought your group looked very professional.'

Madge took in Hattie's information with a straight face. She wasn't easily impressed by upper-class females who lived 'alternative' lifestyles, as she coyly referred to them.

'Professional, you say? Thank you, that's very kind of you. It's a shame we haven't had such encouragement direct from the horse's mouth, as it were,' she replied stiffly. This was evidently a sore subject.

'How do you mean? Wasn't Rebecca pleased with you all?' From what Hattie recalled, Rebecca seemed to have been oblivious to the rest of her troupe. They were probably only there as a backing group for her star performance.

'How would we know? We haven't seen her yet this term,' Madge retorted with a sniff. 'The classes *should* have started last week. We all turned up on time, but not Rebecca. Very odd, we all thought. Sandra wasn't at all impressed, I can tell you. She'd put off her village bingo night in aid of blind guide dogs for the deaf, or some such,' she continued angrily. Hattie didn't dare correct her about the dogs in question. 'Rebecca's usually there waiting for us, CD player all set up and ready to go. So there we were, all standing around waiting, until one of the girls from the office came to apologise that they'd forgotten to phone us.' She rolled her eyes and then took a deep breath. 'It turned out,' she complained, jabbing a finger in Hattie's direction, 'that Rebecca had phoned in sick the day before with glandular fever, but nobody had bothered to tell us! I ask you!'

'Oh, what a shame... how unfortunate.'

'Hmm, cutting it very fine, if you ask me. I hope she turns up on Wednesday. We've *all* paid for the term's classes, so we expect our money's-worth!'

'Quite right,' agreed Hattie, nodding. 'Although glandular fever can be quite nasty. It might take her a while to recover.'

'I asked Sandra to find out from Greg if he'd heard any more,' continued Madge irritably. 'But I've not heard a dicky bird.'

'Maybe you could drop into Mia Casa and find out.' A simple phone call was all that was needed, thought Hattie, but stating the obvious probably wouldn't have gone down too well with Madge in her present mood.

'Er, well...' she began, her cheeks colouring, 'I don't suppose you'd come with me, would you, Hattie? Just in case she's there. Rebecca can be a bit sharp at times.'

'Hmm, I *had* noticed. Actually Madge, I happen to know that Rebecca's been going through a bit of a rough patch.'

'Oh really?'

'With her wedding plans.'

'First I heard,' huffed Madge.

'Well, maybe she isn't telling everyone, but she told Nick. Even if she's a bit sharp you've got to feel sorry for her.'

'I see. But I'd still appreciate it if you could come with me.'

Her best intentions to keep well away from Mia Casa started to crumble. 'Alright, Madge,' sighed Hattie, not exactly relishing the prospect of meeting the woman herself, 'I suppose I could come with you. I'm not in a tearing hurry as it happens.'

Regretting her magnanimous offer, Hattie set off with Madge for Mia Casa, like a pair of old friends on a shopping trip. Before long, her heart started pounding at the possibility of seeing Leo – what she'd say and how she'd cope with his range of unspoken, but effective communication. They were barely ten yards away when the door opened and almost as if she'd willed it to happen, out came Leo looking harassed, and most definitely preoccupied. In fact, there was quite an air of Mr Darcy about him on this occasion, making him all the more desirable. Madge and Hattie stopped in their tracks as he turned and strode towards them with glazed eyes. Both women pasted on their brightest smiles, hoping he wouldn't walk straight past. Madge, however, left nothing to chance.

'Hello Signor Marcello!' she called, determined to grab his attention if not his arm.

'Ah, ladies!'

'We've come to see if Rebecca's doing her evening class this week – to see if she's back at work I mean,' announced Madge, business-like but blushing.

Leo shot a puzzled glance in Hattie's direction

'No, she's not back at work yet,' Leo replied. 'We're not sure when she'll be back. We've had to employ a temp…' He paused to check his watch. '…and I'm on my way to cover one of Rebecca's appointments.'

'Oh I see.' Madge was obviously disgruntled but was hardly going to argue with glandular fever. 'Well, I must be off. Janice and Rhoda will wonder where I've got to and I *never* waste the company's time, not like *some* people, who shall remain nameless.'

'Your loyalty is commendable, Madge,' he replied with a smile. She looked up, turning her scowl into a winning smile, then hurried off, realising that a kiss on the hand would not be forth-coming on this occasion.

'Hattie, cara, so good to see you,' Leo murmured warmly once Madge was well out of earshot. Hattie took a deep breath and guiltily let her eyes feast on his fine features – his well-chis-elled cheekbones, his generous mouth and especially his dark, velvety brown eyes. No, no, she thought with alarm. This is too tempting.

'Lovely to see you, Leo.' Wrong reply too, she realised. Should have said 'good to see you' – much less emotional. 'Actually, I'm on the way to see my solicitor – house business, you know.'

'Ah yes.'

As she stood in front of him, wondering what to say next, the delivery of the red rose card seemed like the elephant in the room that neither of them was prepared to acknowledge.

'The tutor at the college is able to take the classes again, so I'm not needed anymore.'

'But what about Mark's course?'

'No problem with that. In fact, that'll run on a different night, so there'll be two courses for the summer term. So, everyone's happy.'

Hattie wondered why he was telling her all this until he added, 'It helps with my plans for the future. But there are a few things to sort out with Greg first. Having Rebecca off work doesn't help though.'

'So, he knows you want to return to Italy then? I expect that came as a bit of a shock.'

'Hmm… well… I'll still have a financial interest in the busi-ness, but I don't think I'm cut out for estate agency, to be truthful.'

This came as no surprise to Hattie. She'd always found it some-what baffling that a wealthy vineyard heir would want to sell houses in England. Given a choice, she would have plumped for Tuscany any day.

'It's a shame our buyer didn't find us through Mia Casa, then you'd have earned some commission,' Hattie said with an air of false brightness. There she was, deliberately taunting him, dangling an innocent remark about Mia Casa's lost opportunity.

'Hmm, Señora... er... Pirez? Well, maybe it's just as well she didn't.'

Leo noted Hattie's astonished expression then continued. 'I'm not sure any of the Mia Casa staff would have possessed the same old-fashioned English charm of Samways and Partners.'

'Brian Samways? Old-fashioned English charm?' she spluttered. 'Well, I suppose if you're from Spain, you might find dear old stodgy Brian quite charming.'

That nailed it, she concluded gleefully. This was definitely his half-baked excuse. Nobody in their right mind would describe Brian Samways as charming: smarmy, creepy and condescending but *never* charming.

'From Spain?'

'Oh yes, but I'm not sure which part. She struck me as a city type though; probably Seville or Barcelona if I had to bet.'

'Ah, well, I must be off, cara,' he said after a pause. 'Work beckons.' He took her hand and pressed it to his lips. 'Ciao!' and set off down the street.

Hattie pressed the kissed hand to her lips and sighed. Forgetting about Leo was going to be more difficult than she thought. However, she galvanised herself for the real world of fixtures and fittings, contracts and searches, and belatedly made her way to Pigeon, Grimes and Co.

She drove home an hour later with the precious contracts in her bag. Now it was simply a matter of posting them to Nick and hoping they'd be back for exchange the following week. She also compiled a mental list of things to do, mainly phone calls. At the very top, of course, was a call to Nick. First she rang his office number, but after several rings it went into a recorded message. Next she tried his mobile, but that immediately diverted to voicemail. Then she tried the main switchboard and managed to speak to someone called Michelle in admin, who left her listening to Vivaldi's 'Four Seasons' for what seemed an age.

'Sorry, Mrs Chesney, he's at on off-site meeting and can't be disturbed,' she finally reported.

Feeling somewhat deflated, Hattie sent a text asking him to call her when he was free.

Next on the list was Fliss. It seemed an age since they'd had a chance to chat. Perhaps she'd drive over and spend some time catching up?

'Oh... hello, Hat.' Fliss sounded distracted, poor thing.

'I've got a free afternoon, Fliss, so I could come over, have a chat and –'

'Sorry, Hat. It's a bit awkward. There's relations due any minute, stuff to sort out, family business, you know.' She sounded very edgy. The bereavement must have hit her harder than Hattie had imagined.

'Okay, I understand, but we'll meet up soon I hope.'

'Of course.'

As the day progressed, Hattie was happily closeted in the kitchen, listening to Vale FM at full blast and constructing one of her famous pasta bakes, when Josh breezed in, wielding an envelope.

'This was on the mat for you, Mum,' he told her then dived into the fridge for a carton of juice.

'Thanks.' She took it from him and tucked it into her apron pocket, knowing at once who had delivered it. Why hadn't he rung the bell? Maybe he had. This second delivery sent a shiver down her spine. She'd wait until Josh was safely out of the way. Grabbing a wooden spoon, she frantically stirred the cheese sauce. A few moments longer and the bottom of the pan would have been a burnt mess.

'Any chance of toast, Mum?' yawned Josh.

'Yes. Just open the bread bin and pop a slice in that natty little electrical gadget that's sitting next to the kettle. It's called a toaster.'

Josh lifted an eyebrow and sucked in his breath. 'Humorous as ever, Mum,' he sighed languidly, pulling out two slices.

'Jam, marmalade, honey, chocolate spread, peanut butter – all on the top shelf of the fridge door. Can you manage that?'

She expertly poured the sauce over the waiting dish of pasta, tuna and vegetables, garnished it with sliced tomatoes and set it to bake. By now Josh was lathering on a thick layer of marge followed by an interesting combination of crunchy peanut butter and lime marmalade. He sandwiched them together, took a huge bite and ambled out of the kitchen with a blissful expression.

Hattie leaned against the kitchen table, closed her eyes and reached for the envelope, her heart pounding fiercely. It had scarcely been five hours since she'd been chatting to Leo, so what was so urgent that he needed to drive over and post this through her door? She took a deep breath and opened the envelope with trembling hands. It was another card bearing a slightly different red-rose design, but the message took her off-guard:

Meant for each other, yours ever, Leo.

She clasped it to her floury apron bib and shut her eyes, recalling their last meeting. 'Oh Leo,' she sighed then shook herself, wiping away a rogue tear from her eye. Why was he doing this? He knew they were moving. It was so unfair! Meant for each other? Was this his roundabout way of suggesting that she should abandon her plans, her marriage and her future in Lydford Cross? Was this his attempt to finish that unfinished conversation and wear her down?

'I'm sorry Leo,' she murmured, 'it's too late.'

Supper was over, coffee was made and Hattie was feeling in control of her future, and for once Nick's timing was perfect.

'Oh, hi, Nick. You read my text?'

'Of course. And what does my gorgeous wife want?' he chuckled, quite the Romeo.

'Flatterer,' she giggled. 'Actually I was just checking where you'd like me to send the contracts.'

'Did you say contracts – as in the plural?'

'I did,' Hattie confirmed brightly. 'I've signed already, but they're keen to get everything tied up as soon as possible. Shall I post them to your parents' address?'

'No, not there. Better post them to work. I'll make sure they're back by return.'

'Excellent! That *does* make sense actually,' Hattie agreed. A sound in the background at Nick's end reminded her that she hadn't spoken to his parents for quite a while. 'How's everything back at the homestead?' giggled Hattie.

'Oh, er just about the same.'

'Well, it would be nice to say hi to your mum if she's around.'

'Er...no, I just heard the front door slam and Dad's out too – round at a friend's, helping to clean out a pond or something. Sorry, Hat, it's just me here, with the TV for company.'

'Ah, well... just tell them I send my love won't you?'

'I'll certainly do that,' he promised then gave a chuckle.

'What's so funny?'

'Oh, nothing. *Men Behaving Badly* on the TV. Those two always make me laugh. Anyway, I'll look forward to getting the contracts. Love to Josh and speak to you soon.'

Later, she wandered down to the village post box. It was a pleasant spring evening and gardeners were busy with mowers, clipper and hedge-trimmers. It wouldn't be long before they'd be settling into a completely new environment, and the thought of living in a Victorian townhouse after years of making do with a mid-sixties semi was quite exciting.

Much later, when she was enjoying a mug of hot chocolate and putting the finishing touches to another square of her quilt, Josh came wandering into the conservatory, munching on a ham and cheese sandwich.

'I tried calling Dad earlier, on his mobile, but it must have been switched off.'

'Hmm?' Hattie had more than half an ear on her Chris de Burgh CD, the next track being 'Lady in Red'.

'So I phoned Gran and Grandpa instead. I asked Grandpa if Dad was there, but he wasn't.'

'Oh, I see,' she murmured, negotiating an awkward corner and managing to jab her thumb instead. 'Oh, sugar lumps!' She quickly sucked at the blob of blood. 'I expect Dad was out with someone from work. He's got a whole new lot of friends now, you know.'

Josh slouched on an arm of the sofa, scattering a shower of crumbs over himself, the cushions and the carpet, and carried on chewing thoughtfully. Hattie gave up on her CD and lowered the volume. There was no chance of enjoying the music with Josh's background chomping.

'It was well weird though,' he commented, after another mouthful. 'Grandpa was a bit, you know, not all there.'

'Really?' muttered Hattie, growing increasingly exasperated with a conversation that was going round in circles. 'Grandpa may appear old and wrinkly to you, and he may not be the fastest fox in the forest...'

'The *what?*'

'Just my half-hearted attempt at humour, Josh,' she replied wearily.

Josh rolled his eyes. 'Don't bother, Mum, if that's your idea of being funny.'

'Anyway,' she continued, 'what I was trying to say was that Grandpa Chesney's still got his marbles.'

Josh looked up sharply. 'Whoa, Mum! Watch your language!'

'What do you mean?' She raised her eyes to heaven. 'I *meant* he's all there, in the head,' she explained.

'Right.' Josh nodded.

'So, did you speak to Gran Chesney?'

'No, she'd already gone to bed.'

'Oh, well, the rest will do her good. Running around after Dad is probably wearing her out. She'll be relieved when moving day comes.' Hattie packed her work and gathered up the dirty mugs and plates.

'I tell you, Mum, it was well weird.'

'Give it a rest, Josh. Has your replay button jammed? Remember Grandpa's nearly eighty, he's a bit hard of hearing and your mumbling doesn't help. I've told you before!'

'Yeah, right,' Josh replied, then stuffed his iPod earpiece in place and wandered out, humming tunelessly to himself.

19

Hattie sat shivering in the coolness of the hallway, wrapped in a bath towel and waiting for Brian Samways to stop his observations on the weather and finally get to the point. Don't say Ms Pirez has changed her mind, she thought nervously.

'So, er, no problems I trust?' she asked, with fingers crossed.

'No, none at all, Mrs Chesney. Everything seems to be going swimmingly, by all accounts,' he assured her with a chuckle. 'Now I have Señora Pirez here in the office. She's flown over to sign her contract and wants to measure up for curtains and such, if that's agreeable with you.'

Señora Pirez, thought Hattie, sounded much better than Mrs Piles.

'How soon does she want to come?' She caught a glimpse of her dripping hair in the hall mirror and calculated how long it would take to make herself and the house presentable enough for visitors. There was a short pause and a muffled conversation, while Hattie pulled her towel tighter and wiped the drips from her face and shoulders.

'Er, well, the señora has a busy schedule, so she'd like to be there in about an hour.'

Hattie gulped, but agreed.

'Excellent, Mrs Chesney. We'll see you soon.'

The memory of the amazingly elegant woman was more than a little disconcerting. But why should she worry? The woman was a cash buyer who was signing on the dotted line any minute. She rushed upstairs, almost squashing Jezebel, who was spread out in booby-trap style on the top step. Flinging off the towel, she pulled on comfy leggings and a baggy sweatshirt, and then performed high-speed smoothing, tidying and Hoovering. Little details such as drying her hair or applying even the slightest smear of make-up were not priorities on this occasion. With seconds to spare, she kicked off her fluffy slippers, exchanged them for loafers and removed the furry step-hazard from the stairs.

Taking a sneaking peep around the curtain in the study, she caught sight of two cars in the process of parking out in the road. Brian was at the wheel of a pale-green Ford Focus, whereas Señora Pirez was crunching the gears of a smart, red Peugeot hire car. The expression on her face was a picture: fiery, flamboyant and very Mediterranean. Hattie ducked out of the way and hovered by the front door, waiting for the bell.

'Good morning and welcome,' she said, smiling warmly as Brian and Señora Pirez entered. All traces of irritation had been wiped from the lady's face as she stood poised and aloof. Hattie noted her tan soft leather blouson, cream linen shift dress and black accessories – so simple and elegant. Not a wisp of hair was out of place, her make-up was flawless and her perfume was exquisite. She must have been up very early that morning to have achieved such perfection. Hattie almost sighed in admiration. Instead, she took a step towards the kitchen.

'Shall I make coffee while you're busy?' she offered. She had a brand new packet of dark-roast filter coffee and her cafetière ready and waiting. 'It's *real* coffee!' she added, making sure her visitors knew she wasn't intending to foist a bland supermarket instant brand on them.

'Ooh thanks, Mrs Chesney. That'll be grand!' replied Brian, beaming and rubbing his hands together. 'Will that suit you, Señora? Mrs Chesney here is *very* hospitable.'

'Thank you, but no. I find English coffee is not to my taste,' Señora Pirez told them dismissively, wrinkling her nose.

Anyone listening carefully would have noted Hattie's quiet but shocked, sharp intake of breath. However, she refused to let such remarks affect her. Instead, she retreated to the kitchen, feeling like a parlour maid at Downton Abbey.

'Mineral water for you, Señora?' she offered, some ten minutes later, feeling awkward that she and Brian were now enjoying coffee and biscuits, while their important guest had refused both.

'So kind. Thank you.' At last there was a suspicion of a smile.

'So, which part of Spain are you from, Señora?' Hattie asked, after enduring several tedious minutes of Brian's mindless chatter about the weather.

'I am not from Spain, Mrs Chesney. I am from Italy,' she declared proudly. The tone she'd used for 'Spain' implied it was a place best avoided.

'Italy? How nice!' replied Hattie brightly. Another piece of misinformation from Samways and Partners! 'And which part of Italy, may I ask?' Rome or Milan were her top guesses.

Signora Pirez took a dainty sip of water and examined the fingers of her left hand, each one finished with beautifully painted nails and not a chip in sight. 'My home is near Firenze... Florence, you say. It is just a little village, small and – how you say in England? – close-knitted community,' she informed her listeners.

Brian spluttered noisily into his mug.

'Close-knit,' corrected Hattie, giving Brian a warning glance and stifling her own giggle.

'Ah yes, as you say, close-knit. It is a very pretty village and in an excellent area for wine.'

The mention of 'Florence' and 'wine' immediately had Hattie's antennae waggling. For her, the words Florence and wine were inextricably linked with Leo. Her interest was aroused and she pressed on, quickly inventing a plausible reason.

'Near Florence, you say?' she remarked innocently. 'Just as a matter of interest, what's the village called? You see one of my girlfriends was on holiday in that area last year. She said how

426

lovely the villages were – some perched on the top of hills with high walls and towers.'

'It's called Montelugia,' Signora Pirez replied, taking another sip and missing the look of shocked surprise on Hattie's face. Brian was engrossed in gingerly dipping a ginger nut in his coffee mug and also missed the reaction.

'Montelugia?' exclaimed Hattie, trying to sound more casual than she felt. 'Oh yes, I believe she mentioned that one. The name made me think of winter sports, for some strange reason.' she giggled and picked up her mug, studying the elegant woman with renewed interest. Just how close-knit was Montelugia, she wondered? Would she know Leo's family? She was bound to if the village was a small community. One wildly amazing thought then occurred to her. She *had* to find out. 'Did you know there's a local estate agent with Italian associations?' she asked casually, after a short pause. 'Small world isn't it!' Why was she saying this? There were Italian themes and associations all over the place these days.

Signora Pirez flashed a wary look in Hattie's direction. 'Yes, indeed,' she replied. 'Especially as one of the partners has family connections. I noticed you also have a Mia Casa board outside.'

'Family connections? Really? What a coincidence! As a matter of fact, it was the Italian partner of Mia Casa who came to take our particulars when we were thinking of putting our house on the market.'

'Ah yes, Signor Marcello,' commented Brian as he swiftly extracted his third biscuit from the tin. 'A relative is he, Signora?'

Hattie held her breath, poised on the edge of her seat. Signora Pirez however, was busy with her diary and appeared not to have heard Brian's question. She checked her watch and remarked that she should be on the way to her next appointment.

The moment had passed, but Hattie had made a shrewd guess about the identity of this lady and her connection with Leo. Then it occurred to her how she could prove it, if only she could somehow engineer the conversation to reveal the vital piece of information. They were at the front door and time was quickly running out.

'So kind of you, Mrs Chesney,' said Signora Pirez, managing a cautious smile.

'Well, it's Hattie actually. And, er... your name, Signora?' she asked. All that had been written on the Samways letter confirming the offer was G Pirez.

'Gina. Gina Pirez.'

'So nice to have met you again, Gina,' replied Hattie warmly, shaking her hand, in the sure knowledge that she must be Leo's ex-wife.

This surprising and totally unexpected discovery had shaken Hattie to the core. After Brian and Gina had driven off, she went and stretched out on the sofa and selected one of the house-makeover programmes on daytime TV. Gina Pirez, she thought incredulously. Gina Pirez decides to buy a second home conveniently near her ex-husband's new business venture! That's some coincidence! She pondered this for several minutes, recalling other coincidences life had thrown her way. There had been those surreal moments when the family in the next chalet on the holiday park in Alicante actually lived only two miles away back at home. Or the couple sitting opposite on the ferry were best friends with someone you'd been with at school thirty years before. It happened all the time.

Hattie gazed at the TV, where a group of jolly plasterers, carpenters and electricians were teasing the token woman in the team, who was agonising over paint shades for the kitchen they were updating.

Pirez, she thought curiously. I wonder if she's remarried or simply reverted to her maiden name? And the remark Pete Ingleheart made about her kids possibly going to college in Oxford? He was wrong about her being Spanish; perhaps he was wrong about Oxford as well. Ah, but did Gina know her ex-husband had plans to move back to Italy? And what about Leo? Her thoughts kept returning to him and the two conversations when

Signora Pirez's name was mentioned. Looking back, it was interesting that the name Pil*es* had obviously struck a chord on the first occasion. It may have been a simple mishearing that reminded him of a name he knew well. That sort of thing happens all the time too.

Then she tried to imagine Gina and Leo as a married couple – what a striking pair! And what do people say about the laws of attraction? Like attracts like. It stands to reason. Women like Gina with their looks, money and sex appeal, only need to beckon and men start a stampede to their door with their tongues hanging out. Women like Gina, who can afford a week's spa treatments or a splurge on new outfits whenever they fancy it, have the pick of all the best blokes. The rest of us, thought Hattie glumly, have to settle for what's left and have to beat off the competition otherwise we get left with the ones with bad breath and two left feet. Still, Nick wasn't bad looking, although there was more than a suspicion of middle-age spread and a receding hairline. How middle-of-the-road Hattie could have attracted someone like Leo was one of the most baffling aspects of the whole situation. Could good old, homespun charm *really* trump dazzlingly good looks, she wondered?

Nick arrived back on Friday, remarkably cheerful and chipper, despite his long drive with the usual rush-hour snarl-ups. Hattie noted, yet again, that the new job, with its added challenges and responsibilities, was certainly reinvigorating him.

'I've a rather cheeky little number here!' he murmured with a wink.

'Another free sample?' ventured Hattie.

'Not exactly,' teased Nick. 'But I've pulled off a very good deal for Bennington's this week, which means a nice fat pay packet, so I thought I'd treat you.'

She wondered what he was about to pull out of a swish carrier bag. Black stockings? Suspender belt? Lacy thong? After her exhausting day with Norma's little darlings, she was hardly in the mood for a frenzied bedroom romp, which included tossing clothes off with abandon. Tossing a salad was probably all she could manage.

'Voilà!' he announced, presenting her with a tissue-wrapped bottle with a wired cork.

'Oh, what a relief! I mean, oh goody – bubbly!'

'Now, why don't I phone for a Chinese takeaway and save you the effort of cooking a meal?' Nick suggested, oblivious to the delicious cooking aroma that was filling the kitchen. He wasn't renowned for spontaneity, so Hattie was somewhat surprised and more than a little annoyed.

'But, Nick, I've already made one of my special shepherd's pies,' she protested, trying not to ruin his homecoming.

'Shepherd's pie? Oh, right.' His expression showed a distinct lack of appreciation.

'Don't you like my shepherd's pies anymore?' she asked irritably

'Of course I like your shepherd's pie, Hat, but I thought you'd like something different.'

You'd like something different, thought Hattie, buttoning her lip but at the same time, considering the options of sweet and sour king prawns over chicken chop suey and fried rice.

'You can always share the shepherd's pie with Josh while I'm away,' he said and unpinned a takeaway menu from the notice board. 'Where is Josh anyway?'

'Out with Tamsin, of course. Didn't you spot an empty space on the drive?' She turned and switched off the oven and then plonked two wine glasses on the worktop.

'Ah, so we're alone are we?' he chuckled, nuzzling her ear.

'Indeed we are,' giggled Hattie. There was no sense getting her knickers in a twist over a stupid shepherd's pie, after all.

Several glasses later and feeling comfortably full, Hattie was relaxed and ready for a snooze, although Nick clearly had other things on his mind.

'And now to bed,' he whispered, pulling her to her feet. 'The dishes can wait.'

Hattie was in the staffroom on Tuesday when she finally received confirmation that the contracts had been exchanged. It was all going ahead.

'Excited?' Sally asked.

'Well…part of me is,' Hattie admitted. 'The house we're buying is gorgeous, just the sort of house I've dreamed of… and living in the middle of town will be quite a novelty…'

'Ah, I sense a "but" lurking there somewhere,' observed Sally gently, as they set off down the corridor towards Early Years.

'I'm not sure. I suppose it's just hitting me about the goodbyes I've got to say, and some of them will be very difficult.' Leo being one of them, she mused.

Sally sighed. 'It'll be sad for me to say goodbye too, but think of all the new exciting things ahead for you. A new house to decorate for one. Oh and have you finished that quilt yet?'

'No, not quite. Oh no, listen to that lot!' she exclaimed, reaching the classroom door. 'We'll catch up later.'

At twelve-fifteen, Hattie shooed the last two slowcoaches out of the cloakroom, picked up a stray plimsoll, hung up an abandoned PE bag and went back to the relative peace of the classroom. Now she had a few minutes to clear her thoughts. The vexed subject of contacting Nick to tell him the news and finalise arrangements surfaced and presented her with a dilemma. Should she try his office number or wait for him to phone her after work? She had begun to accept that his senior role at Bennington's had its minor aggravations. It had been so easy to call him and chat before, but now he seemed so busy.

With a sigh, she picked up a pile of workbooks from the wire basket beside her desk and made a start on the marking, in between mouthfuls of sandwich. After ten minutes, she put her pen down. It was no good; she needed to talk to Nick. She fished out her mobile and texted the most urgent-sounding message she could, but her phone remained irritatingly silent for the rest of the day.

Later, after she and Josh had polished off the rest of Friday's rejected meal, she decided her only course of action was to phone Nick's parents. Sooner or later he'd have to return home and they'd be able to discuss the completion date. Frustrated by his silence, she dialled David and Bryony's number.

'Hello, David. It's Hattie.'

'Oh, hello, Hattie my dear, and how's the move progressing?'

'Oh fine thank you, David. We exchanged contracts today and now I've got to fix a moving day with Nick. I'm suggesting the eighteenth.'

'Hmm, I see, and he's working all the hours God sends as usual!'

Ah, thought Hattie, no need to ask where he is. 'Yes, he's turned into a real workaholic. Still, it won't be long before we're settled at The Laurels.'

'Excellent! It sounds as if you've got a very efficient solicitor. I confess I sometimes found conveyance such a frustrating aspect of my work – broken house chains, depressing survey reports, stroppy estate agents, clients who couldn't make up their minds.'

'It's not as bad as that, is it?'

'Well, not all the time, but the very worst part was when clients would keep phoning up asking if this or that had been done. So… you're moving soon then?'

Oh dear, she thought, maybe his memory isn't so good.

'Well, Hattie, I must say goodbye now. Bryony's making faces at me. She wants me to shift the stepladder before supper.'

'Oh, right… mustn't delay you. I expect Nick will keep you up to date.'

'Yes, yes I'm sure he will. We quite understand the pressure he's under with his company's expansion plans. We don't expect to hear about all the house move details when his priority is his new job.'

Hattie pictured Nick, silent at his parents' supper table, with his head buried in some report or other. 'Oh yes,' she sighed. 'I know exactly what you mean. It's the same when Arsenal are on TV. Well, *all* sport really – can't get a word out of him!'

There was another silence, except for Bryony's voice becoming more agitated.

'Well, goodbye, David, and do give my love to Bryony.'

Mmm, mused Hattie, not quite the talkative son, but Nick *did* have a habit of withdrawing into his own world from time to time. Bryony's endless chatter might easily drive him crazy. Then there was bound to be the daily grilling about his day, his job and the new house. However, the chat with David had left her wondering. Perhaps his memory was failing. Could it be the dreaded senile dementia? As Hattie settled down with her quilting, she realised why Nick was being very protective about his parents.

Eventually, the phone rang. By then it was nearly bedtime and Hattie had hand-quilted one more square, polished off two mugs of hot chocolate, watched three back-to-back episodes of *Escape to the Country* and scoffed four pieces of rum and raisin fudge. Jezebel had added an element of unwanted entertainment by bringing in a worm, and a cold caller had tried to interest her in switching her energy supplier. So, it was just another run-of-the-mill Tuesday evening.

'Hi, Hat. Sorry it's taken me so long. I've had another long meeting after work.'

'Poor you, Nick. They *are* cracking the whip. You must be shattered. But why didn't you reply to my text?'

'I was busy of course and I don't keep the mobile switched on all the time. It sets a bad example, especially in meetings.' For a moment he sounded quite shirty.

Hattie was tempted to point out that setting the mobile to vibrate silently wouldn't disturb any meeting, but he didn't sound in the mood for smart remarks.

'And I told you, Hat,' he continued wearily. '*I'll* call you. Sometimes it's not convenient to call back straight away, like today, but I've called now so...'

'Okay, message received.' The lecture was over, thank goodness. 'So, don't you want to know why I needed to speak to you?' The excitement over the exchange of contracts had now become old news.

'Naturally,' replied Nick equably.

'We exchanged contracts this morning, and they want us to suggest a completion date. I was wondering about the eighteenth.'

'I see. Right… Yes, I guess the eighteenth's as good as any. Now remember, Hat. I'll call you tomorrow and find out how you got on, okay?'

'Yes Nick.' She felt like a misbehaving pupil who'd narrowly avoided detention. After his romantic gestures at the weekend he sounded more like his old self.

There was a giggle in the background. 'Your mum sounds in a good mood! Has your dad just cracked a rare joke? Or was it something on the TV?'

'Oh definitely the TV,' agreed Nick. 'Dad's not really one for jokes is he? He's never been able to remember the punch line. You know my mum. If it's not bridge parties, it's TV sitcoms. The Vicar of Dibley has just hopped across the screen in a bunny costume.'

'Oh, yes I love that episode!', Hattie exclaimed. 'Sounds a bit loud though.'

'Signs of ageing, I guess,' agreed Nick quietly.

'Perhaps I'll catch the rest of the episode myself. Any chance of a quick hello to your mum, Nick? It's ages since I've spoken to her.'

'Er… better not spoil her fun at the moment, perhaps next time. Well, bye for now, Hat, and remember −'

'Yes, Nick, *you'll* call me,' she sighed and switched on the TV. By the time she'd tried out a few channels the show was over. Although it was late she switched over to the news and yawned through story after story about falls in the stock market, job losses and unseasonal weather. The forecast that followed was hardly better.

'While the south coast has been lashed by gales, the rest of the country has been experiencing some drier weather,' chirped the girl with a grin, 'although the temperatures are well under the seasonal average.'

'Thank you and good night,' Hattie muttered crossly. 'Time to bring out my fleecy bed socks and hot water bottle.'

Must call Fliss again, Hattie reminded herself as she cleared the breakfast things on Thursday morning. Time was running out and Fliss seemed to be caught up with family business following the funeral. In fact, she was in danger of becoming elusive and impossible to tie down. Such a shame too, with so little time left before the move.

Surveying the usual kitchen carnage and the rumpled state of the sitting room, she sighed heavily. A quick zoom round with the Hoover was a priority, especially as a removal firm estimator was due later to give a quote. Next, the bedroom and en-suite, thought Hattie. No removal bod would be allowed to catch a glimpse of undies drying on the towel rail or bargain packs of panty liners lined up on the chest of drawers.

Just then the phone rang.

'Good morning, may I speak to Nicholas Chesney?' came a female voice that was Home Counties with a touch of *EastEnders*.

'Er …um he's not here,' replied Hattie, surprised by the Nicholas bit. 'Who is that please?'

'This is the Golden Pheasant Hotel, Lydford Cross,' replied the woman. 'It's about a booking.'

'Oh, I see. But why did you ring this number? He's only here at weekends.'

'I tried the mobile number he gave us but then the call must have been diverted. I'm sorry if I've bothered you.'

'Oh that's all right,' replied Hattie. 'He's probably in a meeting. You'd better try his work number at Bennington's.'

'Ah yes, Bennington's,' said the woman brightly. 'We know Clive Bennington very well. He's a very good customer. In fact his company use our conference facilities quite often.'

'Nick's just started working for them,' said Hattie proudly. 'You'll get him at the work number, as I said.'

'Thank you,' said the woman, and rang off promptly.

Conference facilities, thought Hattie with interest. It all made sense of course. Nick had mentioned late meetings several times. Now she had a shrewd idea where they were being held. It also sounded as if Nick was responsible for organising them.

Whisking the undies and panty liners out of sight, she dashed down to the study and logged onto the Internet. The Golden Pheasant Hotel, she thought with interest, and typed the name into the browser. It was certainly a stylish venue which boasted extensive banqueting and conference facilities. Bennington's must be doing *very* well, Hattie reflected, proudly considering her clever husband's vital role in the planned expansion. The Golden Pheasant had a spa, gym, massage parlour and indoor swimming pool and Hattie started to wonder if Nick's managerial perks might stretch as far as a sauna or session on the hot beds. She noted down the phone number in her diary. Hmm, she thought, a session in the sauna or Jacuzzi sounds just the ticket to soothe away the stress of house moves.

What a clever husband, she thought gleefully, as she punched in Fliss's number. Fliss, however, had very little time to chat.

'You must come round soon,' Hattie urged her. 'I've such a lot to tell you, and we ought to have an evening together before Nick and I disappear off into the sunset.'

'So, how's he settling into the new job then?'

'Er, well... *very* well!' confirmed Hattie.

'You sounded unsure for a moment,' observed Fliss.

'Oh no, it's just that he's so busy. I hardly see or hear much from him.'

'But think of the lovely extra lolly!' chuckled Fliss.

'Well, naturally, and Bennington's use one of the local spa hotels for their conferences,' Hattie boasted. 'I'm wondering if I might have a chance to try out their facilities when we move.'

'Hmm,' yawned Fliss. 'So Nick's probably getting quite blasé about it all. Mark was like that when he had this last promotion, but now he takes it all for granted. Sometimes he's living out of a suitcase and scoffing expense-account dinners for weeks on end. In fact, I sometimes have the feeling he's married to work rather than me.'

'Oh no, Nick's not at all blasé,' protested Hattie. 'He's taking his work very seriously and do you know what?' she chuckled smugly.

'What?' asked Fliss eagerly at the prospect of some juicy disclosure.

'He's been bringing me flowers, posh chocs and bubbly – not just supermarket cava either. In fact, he's quite the old romantic again!' she boasted. Fliss didn't need to know that some of the gifts were only samples.

'Lucky old Hat. Mind you, it could mean a guilty conscience,' Fliss observed cynically.

'What do you mean?' Hattie asked, 'About leaving me to cope with all the last minute house stuff?'

'Well, yes... I suppose so,' agreed Fliss. 'Although it might be his way of making up for all those lunchtimes in Maggie's.'

'Which are all in the past now.'

'Well, I'm pleased for you both and you appear to have your model husband back.'

'Even though he's useless at replying to my texts,' chuckled Hattie, 'which is nothing really, in the big scheme of things.'

'So... have you seen the dishy Signor Marcello recently?'

'Why do you ask? He's not handling our sale so there's no reason for our paths to cross 'Anyway, isn't he meant to be doing some course for Mark's sales teams?' said Hattie, already knowing the answer.

'Ah, well, he *was*,' agreed Fliss, with a sigh, 'but the regular tutor's back now and keen to take on the two courses, so it's bye-bye dreamboat. Shame though, the regular tutor's fat, forty and female.'

'So how about next Wednesday, Fliss?'

'Sounds fine to me. You sort out a DVD and I'll bring some nibbles,' she suggested. 'Or maybe I'll ditch the diet just this once and bring chocolate muffins.'

'Chocolate muffins? Great idea,' agreed Hattie, heaving a sigh as Leo's handsome features lodged in her mind. 'Josh will be out, so we'll have the place to ourselves.'

Once Randall's Removals had paid their visit Hattie felt in need of a bracing walk. Fliss's mention of Leo had unsettled her, just when she was winning the battle of her thoughts too. In fact, a bracing walk and a visit to the recycling bins by the village hall might just rid her mind of unhelpful fantasies which generally included long grass, plenty of wine and Leo doing wonderfully toe-curlingly, unmentionable things to her.

She hauled out a thick jacket, pulled on a woolly hat and stepped out of the front door with two bulging bags of newspapers... and there it was – a red rose pinned to a small carrier bag, just waiting to be trampled by the unwary foot. Her heart lurched.

'Oh no! Not again!' she muttered, surveying the package, which had all the temptation of the 'drink me' bottle from *Alice in Wonderland*. In a heartbeat, she was back in Birmingham again, discovering the ribbon-tied rose on the doorstep of her student digs. Why was Leo doing this? She bent to pick it up and saw at once that the rose was an artificial one, carefully made to look like the real thing. But what was in the little carrier bag? Should she throw the lot in the wheelie bin and text him a 'leave me alone' message? The trouble was, like Alice, there was too much curiosity egging her on to peer inside. Of course, she reasoned, it could simply be a farewell present. A sort of 'I know you are moving away with your husband but here's wishing you well' present. Was that likely? Perhaps not.

Picking it up, she peeped inside to see a plump and tempting chocolate muffin and a white envelope. Ah, she thought, just a little farewell gift after all. What a sweet thought! Then she studied the white envelope. Giving way to her natural curiosity, she gently eased the flap open. The card inside had a similar red rose image to the ones he'd left before, but the message inside was his boldest and most surprising yet:

King's Cross station, Friday 18th May, 12 noon, by the main departure board. I'll be there, will you? Let me know.
Yours ever Leo x

'No, no, no!' she muttered angrily. 'Cruel, cruel man! Why are you doing this?'

Filled with rage, she turned and stomped back into the hall, clutching the bag and note. She had to do something, but what? Hattie leaned against the banister, the thoughts in her brain seemingly all engaged in a long distance obstacle course. However, it didn't take her long to decide.

'Hello, may I speak to Signor Marcello please?'

'Certainly,' answered an unfamiliar girl's voice. 'And who shall I say is calling?'

'Tell him it's Mrs Chesney.' Hattie's temper reached boiling point as she waited for Leo to pick up his phone, trying out a few choice phrases in her mind as she did so.

'Cara,' he murmured in the velvety, dark-brown tone that perfectly matched his eyes.

'How dare you Leo! Just because you know my weakness for chocolate muffins, don't think you can manipulate me *that* easily.' Leo groaned.

'Oh yes, you thought to yourself, I know how to make Hattie come running. Just dangle a muffin in front of her nose and she'll hop into bed without a backward glance.'

'No, no!' he protested.

'And it's all my fault of course. I mentioned muffins, we've eaten muffins together and so you know I'm a pushover for them. And that's so unfair!'

'Dear, sweet Hattie. Please calm down. How can I stop what my heart tells me?'

'*Your* heart, Leo? What about *my* heart?'

'But, cara…' he protested.

'And it's not going to work! Think you can smooth talk me do you? Well, in case you didn't know, I happen to be otherwise occupied on Friday the eighteenth; just a little matter of moving to Hampshire, in fact!' she retorted fiercely.

'I see.' For once Leo was momentarily lost for words. After a pause he began again, realising that Hattie the ditherer had finally made up her mind.

'So, your words were just meaningless trifles after all,' he commented sadly. 'You said they weren't. You said you loved me and when we kissed – oh, when we kissed – Hattie, sweet Hattie, I believed you.' Leo was holding nothing back. On passion and persistence, he was scoring ten out of ten. On convincing Hattie, he was scoring zero.

Hattie considered his reply and braced herself, guiltily remembering the time he'd come to the house and how much she had enjoyed those stolen moments in the hallway. She felt torn in two, but morally she knew, deep down, that her duty was to Nick. Life's not a bed of roses, she thought sadly, nor is it a plate of muffins, tempting though they may be, sitting in their crinkly paper cases and sprinkled with mouth-watering chocolate chunks.

'And I meant it Leo,' she insisted. 'It's possible to love two men, but I *can't* leave Nick. We've talked about how things have been and I really believe he's making an effort to be the model husband, so *I* must make an effort too.'

'You don't sound completely convinced, cara. If your decision is simply from your head and not from your heart, you will never be truly happy. Remember my note? I just wanted you to know my plans.'

'What about your wife – or should I say, your ex-wife?' snapped Hattie. 'I told you our buyer's name but you never said a word about her identity. In fact, I think you were deliberately playing dumb. I know the woman who's buying our house – Gina Pirez

– is your ex-wife. She was here with Brian Samways, measuring up for curtains a couple of weeks ago.'

'Oh.'

'So why didn't you say who she was? What's going on Leo?' she demanded.

'I don't know, cara, believe me! She's nothing to me,' he murmured gently. 'It's *you* I love.'

Hattie considered his reply. Even if she didn't approve of his methods, his motive sounded genuine.

'Very well, Leo, I believe you, but...' She felt the prickle of tears threatening to take over.

'You are not sure? Your head tells you one thing, but your heart tells you another. When you have decided which to follow, perhaps you'll tell me too?'

'I *have* decided, Leo,' she gasped, struggling to keep herself together. 'Just remember this; I'm moving to Lydford Cross, so please stop this... at once!'

'It's your choice.'

There was a click and then silence at the end of the line. Hattie replaced the receiver and the tears that had been threatening, flowed with heart-wrenching sobs. Back in the kitchen, she flopped down, head on her arms and wept away all the pain and regret of the past weeks. After a while, Jezebel came running, her stomach signalling an approaching meal. 'Ah Jezebel,' she murmured, 'dear old pussycat, I know where I am with you: loyal, loving and always thinking of your stomach.' The little animal purred like a miniature pneumatic drill, butting her head into Hattie's hand. 'All right, time for tea,' she sighed and went into the utility room, Jezebel excitedly following behind.

'Good morning, Nicholas!' trilled Madge, struggling with her laden trolley. It was Saturday morning and Hattie and Nick had just arrived at the supermarket to do their weekly shop.

'Oh, hi, Madge! All well?' Nick called back.

'Not too bad, thank you but…' she panted. Nick, however, was in no mood to chat.

'Back to dancing now?' Hattie enquired, remembering Madge's disappointment when they had last met.

'I wish!' she fumed irritably. 'No one's seen hide nor hair of Rebecca for ages.'

'Oh dear,' remarked Hattie, trying to sound convincing.

'Hmm,' huffed Madge. 'I asked Sandra to find out from Greg, but even *she* didn't get a sensible answer. We could have signed up for a term of calligraphy if we'd known. Still, the college is giving us a refund.'

'Come on, Hat,' called Nick impatiently. He stumped off, kicking moodily at one of the trolley wheels.

'Of course Greg hired a temp,' continued Madge. 'They've been trying to get hold of Rebecca to find out when she's coming back to work, but her phone's always switched off, so they have to leave messages on mail voice.'

'Voicemail,' corrected Hattie.

'Whatever!' snapped Madge irritably. 'But she hardly ever returns the calls. Downright rude, I call it!'

'Well I never,' replied Hattie with interest. 'She always struck me as being very professional and efficient. She must be very ill.'

'Maybe,' Madge retorted grimly and then raised her eyebrows, Hilda-style. 'Sandra reckons it's not just glandular fever. Like you said, she's had an upset with her fiancé. She thinks she's staying with her Nan over at Aston Clinton.'

'Hat… come on!' called Nick tetchily, now heading off through the vegetable aisle.

'Sorry, Madge, I think Nick's champing at the bit. There's probably some match on TV. You know what he's like!' Hattie chuckled. 'Like a bear with the proverbial sore head if he misses a minute of it.'

'Oh yes,' agreed Madge, nodding. 'Football mad, like a lot of his gender. His replacement has a more refined interest. He's a keen *Strictly* fan. Hope the move goes smoothly.' She bustled off cheerfully, the dancing disappointment now brushed aside.

'There was no need to be rude, Nick,' muttered Hattie when she had caught up with him. 'She was telling me about the belly dancing, or rather the lack of it.'

'Interfering busybody!' he retorted. 'Always poking her nose in where it's not wanted. She and Hilda Makepeace would make a fine pair. All you need is Evadne Proctor and you've got the three hags from *Macbeth*. Oh yes, I can imagine them crouched around their bubbling cauldron, cackling and throwing dismembered frogs around.'

'Hmm, not a pretty sight,' remarked Hattie, trying to keep a straight face until she recalled Hilda's part in the Nick and Becky saga. 'Anyway, I was only being friendly. It's probably the last time I'll get a chance to chat to Madge.'

'As if you care,' he growled.

They set to with the shopping and Nick brightened up considerably

'Half a mo, Hat, just remembered something,' he said and disappeared briefly, only to reappear flourishing a bunch of yellow rosebuds.

'For my lovely, long-suffering wife!' he said sheepishly, gently kissing her cheek.

Snappy grouch one minute and charming Romeo the next, though Hattie. Guilty conscience, chimed the alarm bells in her head.

'Oh, Nick. What pretty flowers,' she gulped. 'You *do* spoil me!'

'Only what you deserve,' he murmured smoothly. 'Right, let's get this lot through the checkout. The footie starts in − is that the time? After that, what we need is a relaxing evening with our favourite meal and a bottle of wine.'

'But there's so much left to do,' protested Hattie as Nick steered the trolley wildly, missing a pensioner by a whisker and scattering a group of pre-schoolers who were playing hide and seek around the pharmacy shelves.

'Which can wait until tomorrow,' he assured her as they reached the belt and started unloading their shopping. 'And I promise I'll pull my weight.'

'Well, there's enough of it!' Hattie chuckled, patting the beginnings of a beer belly.

20

Sunday night found Nick busy packing his case for another week away, but for Hattie the time to mention the phone call from the hotel was rapidly vanishing. It had been on the tip of her tongue all weekend, but every time she thought she had the perfect moment, her courage took tail and ran. There he was, working his socks off and they still expected him to handle trivial admin. It didn't seem fair and she wanted to get to the bottom of it.

'Another busy week I guess,' she said, bringing five freshly pressed and folded shirts.

'Hmm, busy, busy, busy,' replied Nick wryly. 'All work and no play and all that.'

'Oh, you mean more evening meetings?' she asked, spotting the ideal opening beckoning.

'Still, it keeps you in gin and muffins,' he chuckled.

'Oh, and that reminds me…'

'What, out of gin are we? I could have sworn we bought some yesterday.'

'No, there was a call from a hotel the other day.' She watched to see his reaction, hoping to see him start to boast about the Bennington expansion process and how he was kingpin in it all. Hardly a word on that subject had passed his lips all weekend.

'Hotel?' Nick turned around and suspended his packing.

'Yes, The Golden Pheasant in Lydford Cross, I think,' she told him, then dived into her wardrobe to sort through her summer skirts and tops. 'They asked for you by name. It was about a booking, the woman said.'

'Woman?'

'Well, receptionist then. She said she knew the MD.'

'Sorry Hat, I'm losing you there. She mentioned Clive Bennington?'

'Yes, that's right. She said he was a good customer and she mentioned conferences.'

'And she phoned here?'

'Yes, she said she had your mobile number, but the call must have been diverted when you didn't answer.'

Come on Nick, she thought, sock it to me. Preen, bore me silly, boast as much as you like, I can take it.

'Ah, right, now I know what it must have been about. We've got a division sales conference coming up next month. I had my team there for an evening last week and left my details. God, they're quick off the mark!'

'I told her to phone you at work.' Hattie had reached her accessory boxes by now and was carefully folding scarves.

'Ah, um… yep, I remember now. Someone in reception fielded the call for me.'

This was exactly what Hattie wanted to hear and the niggling worries about his work overload started to drift away. Senior accounts managers like Nick certainly shouldn't be wasting their time making bookings. Perhaps he should remind someone about job descriptions.

'Yes,' continued Nick, now well into his stride. 'We use The Golden Pheasant for conferences from time to time. Tell you what, Hat. I'll take you there for dinner or even an overnight stay in the honeymoon suite when we've moved. They've just won a food award and the breakfasts are excellent, so I hear.'

'Are you sure?' she replied, trying to sound enthusiastic, 'I don't need lots of expensive treats, Nick. I'd rather we saved our money for the new house. Although a swim and sauna would be nice.'

Nick shrugged and smiled. 'Whatever.'

The Year 3s were particularly boisterous the following morning, but even so, Hattie found her mind returning to the same old subjects of Nick, work and guilt offerings. After being a penny-pinching couple for years on end, Nick seemed to be splashing out in an alarming way. Something still niggled in her brain. Moving to the dream house was just days away, but what if Nick's taste for luxury was going to end in huge credit card bills and expensive loans? Perhaps Fliss would have some wisdom on the subject? Possibly not. Fliss knew how to wring every last drop out of Mark's credit card it seemed.

Much later, Nick phoned for a brief chat.

'I was talking to Clive Bennington today.'

'Big boss man?'

'Er, yes, the MD, and he's kindly invited us for supper when we move.'

'On the eighteenth?'

'That's right, so I've accepted. Thought it would save you ferreting around for saucepans and such, or enduring yet another of Mum's steak and kidney puddings.'

'Wonderful,' giggled Hattie. 'Actually, I wasn't planning on ferreting around for saucepans. I was going to suggest a take-away. I don't think I could stomach your mum's steak and kidney either. So, how's things at your end?'

'Busy as usual. Can't call you tomorrow evening; one of the chaps in logistics has invited me round his place, but I'll phone on Wednesday, okay?'

'Make it late then. Fliss is coming round and we're having a girlie night in.'

'Well maybe I'll leave that call till Thursday. Ah-ha, chocolate and a romantic film, eh?' he teased.

'How did you guess?'

'Oh, I can read you like a book, old thing!'

When it came to Wednesday evening, Hattie wasn't sure how much she was prepared to share with Fliss, but her friend's built-in homing device for interesting snippets somehow made it easy. Fliss had brought the promised muffins, while Hattie had taken care of the bubbly and DVD.

'Sorry I've not made much of an effort to come over to you recently,' Hattie apologised, 'but it's easier to relax without teenage company, if you know what I mean.'

'To be honest, I'm glad of an excuse to escape from the testosterone-charged atmosphere myself,' Fliss sighed. 'We've hardly seen Mark recently, so it's good for him to have bonding time with the boys. Exams are horribly close too, and then we'll be walking on eggshells and getting scratchy with each other. He's even taking them off to some extreme sports place the weekend after next to give their poor brain cells a rest – at my suggestion, I hasten to add.'

'I *am* impressed. So, what will *you* be doing?' Hattie poured them both a glass and then took a sip.

'Oh nothing special… potter around the garden maybe or sort out my summer wardrobe. I'm sure it'll be just great being by myself for a change. I can't wait. Lounge around in bed, read a book, watch a film, you know the sort of thing. So how about *you*, Hat? You said you had so much to tell me.'

'It's Nick,' sighed Hattie. 'Something's worrying me. I had a call from a hotel the other day, The Golden Pheasant Hotel in Lydford Cross. It's near Nick's work. The receptionist wanted to speak to Nick about a booking. Bennnington's use the conference facilities there you see.'

'So why are you worried? Did you ask Nick about it?'

'Oh yes, and it was fine. I just thought, with all the long hours he works, surely he shouldn't be dealing with admin stuff, should he? It seems so unfair.'

'Ah, now I see,' agreed Fliss, nodding. 'Has he a PA?'

'I think he does, in fact I'm sure he does. Maybe she's on holiday?'

'Yes, but he still shouldn't be handling that sort of thing, I agree. That's why chaps like Mark and Nick have assistants.'

Hattie beamed. Just hearing Fliss mention Nick and Mark together in the same breath confirmed that Nick had finally made it.

'I think they're taking advantage of him. He seems to have a huge workload.'

'And what does Nick say on the subject? Does he think they're being unreasonable?'

'Well no, he hasn't said anything about it, although he's always saying how busy and tired he is.'

Fliss frowned and took a sip from her glass. 'Unless...'

'Unless what?'

'Unless he's booking the hotel for some out of hours entertainment!' she said pointedly. 'Spa? Gym? Pool? Massage? That sort of thing?'

Hattie wriggled awkwardly in her chair. 'What do you mean Fliss?'

Fliss paused and took another sip. 'Have you checked your bank statement?'

'Whatever for?'

'Well, clues of course, like card payments to hotels for instance, strip clubs or –'

'No, surely not!' exclaimed Hattie. She wouldn't have described herself as a prude, but there *were* some areas of life that she found difficult to talk about, especially if it might be her husband who was indulging in them. Fliss, however, had no such problem.

'Or unusually large cash withdrawals?' suggested Fliss, undeterred by Hattie's open-mouthed horror.

'But what would that tell me?'

'Oh, come on, Hat. Join the real world! Men have urges, needs... You know! They're all the same, basically – brains in their trousers most of them!' She winked knowingly and then picked up her glass.

'What? You mean he might have been...'

'Using an escort agency or using the services of a masseuse?' finished Fliss. 'Could be! He might have seen what the hotel had to offer and thought, why not!'

'I hadn't thought of that,' Hattie gasped. 'In fact I can't believe he'd do that, I really can't!'

'Oh Hat, it's not the end of the world. If *that's* what's going on,' Fliss stated, matter-of-factly, 'then the sooner moving day comes the better and that's only... how long now?'

'Nine days.'

'So, how about checking the bank account? You're online, I guess, unless you're still stuck in the dark ages?'

'Er... I think we've an online account, but Nick takes care of all that.'

'What? So you don't know the password or anything?'

'Um, no. I didn't think I'd need to know.'

Fliss shook her head in disbelief. 'Well, that's *very* convenient for Nick, isn't it? Sounds like he can do whatever he pleases and you wouldn't have a clue!'

'But I trust him,' protested Hattie loyally, 'and he's an accountant after all.'

'Hat, just because he's an accountant doesn't mean he's immune from a bit of deception,' Fliss observed. 'Now what about the bank statements?'

'I don't think we get them posted any longer. I seem to remember that Nick has to log on and then download them or something, but I'm not even sure he gets round to printing them out.' Hattie felt ashamed. It had always seemed so wonderfully convenient to have Nick take care of their finances.

Fliss sighed heavily. 'I'm sure if you go into your branch, someone will be able to help you. Anything else?'

'Well, he was very shirty on Saturday when we met Madge at

the supermarket, especially when the conversation got round to her belly dancing classes.'

'That doesn't mean a thing, Hat,' remarked Fliss dismissively. 'He hated working with the old bat, I gather. I'm not surprised he was shirty. There are some people you really don't want to see again in a hurry, and Madge is probably top of Nick's list.'

'Yes, I expect you're right. Although I couldn't help noticing how his mood changed when Madge started on about Rebecca's glandular fever, and then something to do with a tiff with the fiancé.'

'Hmm, well that's obvious! It's just *guilty memories* about those lunchtimes he spent with her. I wouldn't worry. Guilt does strange things to people and, er...' Suddenly, Fliss's words dried up and all the jollity and worldly-wise self-assurance vanished. For someone who frequented the local solarium, she turned surprisingly pale. Her bottom lip quivered and her eyes took on a haunted appearance. She grabbed her drink and gulped it down, draining every last drop. Hattie stared in alarm.

'What's wrong Fliss?'

'I was remembering... Actually, there's a confession I –' she blurted nervously.

'A confession?' It was almost unheard of for Fliss to sober up so abruptly. It had to be pretty serious. She was gazing down at the glass-topped coffee table, aimlessly tracing figure-of-eight patterns with her right index finger.

'You know there was that rumour circulating a few years back, linking me with a jobbing gardener?' Fliss stopped the finger patterns and started nervously picking at a loose strand on a cushion cover.

'Which you always denied. In fact, I remember you once getting very heated on the subject.'

'Hmm, well... it wasn't actually a jobbing gardener as such... It was Nick.'

Fliss blinked remorsefully in the stunned silence that followed. 'I'm so sorry, Hat.'

'You… and Nick?' gasped Hattie, horrified. 'Fliss, how *could* you? My best friend!'

' It… it wasn't planned… It just sort of happened.'

'My God!' Hattie spat. 'You and *Nick?*'

'Please let me explain.' Fliss implored, draining her glass and then hastily refilling it. 'Remember, we were planning to have a soirée, a charity event in our garden and our petrol mower broke down? Then Nick offered to come over and fix it?'

Hattie gulped and nodded, her eyes wide and staring.

'Well, Mark had taken the kids out to a safari park or somewhere and I was enjoying a bit of midsummer sun on the back lawn.'

It was common knowledge amongst Fliss's close circle of friends and family that she often sunbathed topless or even starkers – the benefit of a secluded garden.

'Well, he turned up, Nick I mean, without any warning.'

'Oh yes?' snapped Hattie suspiciously.

'I honestly didn't know he was coming, believe me! Well, one thing led to another and… Hat, honestly, I didn't know he would suddenly turn up in my back garden at that moment or else I'd have had a bikini on, at the very least.'

Hattie sat gaping at this disclosure. Her mouth kept opening and closing but no sound came out. She was, as her mum would have said, utterly flabbergasted.

'He could have turned around and gone away when he saw I didn't have a stitch on, or sort of coughed loudly to warn me, but no, he tippy-toed across the lawn and caught me completely by surprise. One moment I was fast asleep and the next a bristly chin was nuzzling my boobs and –'

'You could have told him to push off! You could have slapped his face! You could have kicked him in the privates! But no, you colluded with him, behind my back! Behind Mark's back! You, you trollop!' snapped Hattie, reaching for her wine glass and noting it was empty yet again. 'I think this calls for the gin,' she muttered, hurrying into the kitchen, 'and not too much tonic!'

Hattie glugged down her drink in one and sat shaking with fury.

'I didn't mean to… he shouldn't have…' gabbled Fliss imploringly.

'It takes two to tango Mrs Tarrier!'

Fliss hung her head in shame. 'I'm *so* sorry, Hat. Obviously some nasty, evil-minded person knew something – goodness knows who or how – but not the man's identity.'

'And on the back lawn!' Hattie exclaimed in shock, after a few seconds. 'How disgusting!'

'Well, no. We went into the summerhouse…'

'The summerhouse! Oh that's very convenient! So you thought, oh why not? What a lark! Ooh, but better make sure no one sees us!'

But I promise you, it *never* happened again. I made sure of that. I told him it was a ghastly mistake and one I didn't intend repeating.'

'Oh, so you admit some blame? I should think so too! And just to think, all the years we've been friends, you and Nick have had this nasty sordid secret!'

'I'm sorry, I'm sorry,' moaned Fliss, her head in her hands.

In the agonising silence that followed, if the proverbial pin had dropped, it would have sounded loud and clear.

'I think you'd better go, Fliss,' said Hattie coldly.

Fliss put down her glass and stood up to go. 'Is it over between us?' she whispered.

'Just go Fliss and take your poxy muffins with you!' she yelled, hurling the box across the room. The front door slammed and Hattie slumped on the sofa. Inside her head, her brain was engaged in another of those marathon obstacle courses

'Fliss and Nick?' she breathed in disbelief. 'My God.'

Hattie replaced the phone in its cradle and wiped the sweat from her brow. It was the morning after the night before and she was feeling fragile, although not too fragile to withstand a dose of cosy family chat. Now she knew why she only made infrequent calls to her in-laws. Bryony Chesney could talk for England. In fact, if talking was an Olympic sport, Team GB could do no better than enlist her as their ambassador. She had it down to a fine art, and as for stamina, she could go for gold when other less determined souls were having a quick gargle and reaching for the throat sweets. Oh yes, Mrs Chesney senior could out-chatter a chimp, although on details, she was more sketchy.

'Well, it must have been Monday when Nick told us about... now what was he saying?' she droned. 'Because that's when I made one of his favourite steak and kidney puddings...or was that when the rector popped in about the whist drive?' And so it went on ad nauseam. However, Hattie refused to be bored into silence.

'And how do you find him? Don't you think he's rather over doing it?' she asked.

'Well, naturally he must be exhausted,' Bryony agreed, 'all those miles he's clocking up. It's bound to wear him down, poor love, isn't it?' Off she went again, rabbiting on about the state of the roads, the state of the country, the weather and why couldn't it have been like when she was a girl. Getting a word in edge-ways was as unlikely as closing the lid on a solitary strawberry cream.

Next, armed with debit card, cheque book, statement folder and plenty of determination, Hattie set off for the bank. Other women had set up spreadsheets and cash flow projections for their family budgeting and there was she, helpless and dependent. Well, that was going to end.

'I'd like to speak to the manager,' she told a young trainee at the counter who had been giggling with her colleague a moment before. The name on her badge was Ellie Proctor. It had to be Evadne Proctor's granddaughter. There was certainly a passing resemblance, apart from the wrinkles.

'The manager's busy. Can I help?' offered Ellie eagerly.

'No, I'll wait if you don't mind.' If Nick had made payments to a strip club or escort agency, Ellie Proctor was one of the last people on earth she'd want eyeing up their finances. So she waited. Eventually he arrived, listened to her concern over a missing payment and printed out the relevant statement.

'Anything else I can do for you Mrs Chesney?' he asked.

Hattie flicked through the sheets quickly, hardly taking in the columns of figures.

'No, that's all thank you.' She carefully tucked them into her folder and wished him good day. There'd be time to scrutinise them later.

Petrol payments and yet more petrol payments, mused Hattie, as she carefully checked each entry over a mug or two of strong black coffee. It was all very baffling. There were calls she could make, but it was too soon. They must wait until after the weekend. She needed time to think. Then she sat and sewed as if her life depended upon it, while turning around in her mind all that had happened in the past few weeks. It was as if her world had been turned upside down and given a good shake, rather like one of those glass snow scenes. Leo's speech about head and heart choices replayed several times in her mind, as she tried to make sense of it all. As she awaited Nick's return for the final weekend, the feeling in her stomach was rather like a coiled spring.

'Hello, gorgeous!' he called as he breezed through the front door. That was a new endearment, Hattie noted with interest. She took a deep breath then turned to greet him as he strode into the kitchen. She'd become quite the expert at bright, wifely smiles over the past day or so, practising them in the hall mirror every time she passed.

'Another treat for my favourite lady,' Nick chuckled, pushing a gift bag into her hand.

'Favourite?' quizzed Hattie.

'My one and only lady of course,' murmured Nick, closing in for a cuddle.

'Oh no!' she protested. 'You really shouldn't have. We should really be saving our money for –'

'It's just another sample, Hat, don't worry,' he said, putting his hands on her shoulders and kissing her gently on the mouth.

'Thank you, Nick. It's lovely! Wow, Giorgio Armani, my favourite perfume,' she murmured, removing the pretty bottle from its nest of gold tissue paper. 'So many free samples, Nick! You really have landed the dream job!'

Fliss's confession replayed in her head as she gazed at the bottle and remembered the events of the past week, wondering how often Nick might recall that episode in the summerhouse. Did he think about it every time he saw Fliss? Did they exchange little knowing glances because of their well-kept secret?

'What a lucky girl I am,' she remarked brightly.

'Hmm, and I can't wait to get you upstairs so I can have my wicked way with you,' he murmured, pulling her to him and nuzzling her ear.

'Wicked way, Nick? You know about wicked ways, do you?'

'Oh, only a figure of speech, old girl,' he chuckled, squeezing her buttocks playfully. 'Cool beer, a bit of nosh, bottle of vino, Sky Sports round-up … and then bed, I think,' he whispered urgently.

'Oh, I notice I came in fifth place after Sky Sports,' she said tetchily. 'Arsenal 1, Hattie nil, as usual.'

'Hey no, I didn't mean that. You're number one in my life,' he said, lowering his voice in an unusually sexy way. 'You know that, don't you?'

'Now Hat,' Nick reminded her as he was leaving early on Monday morning, 'I've arranged for the packers to come on Thursday to deal with the china and other breakables. You just have to take care of your personal stuff and then drive down on Friday in your own time. I'll meet the van at the other end.' He kissed her briefly then set off on his last long commute. She stood at the door, watching his car until it rounded the bend then sighed at the thought of setting off on her own journey. Meanwhile, there were two days of classes to teach, phone calls to make and a mountain of clearing, sorting and packing to be done.

On Thursday morning, Reg and Jakub from Randalls Removals turned up as promised, with their transistor radio and opinionated remarks about everything they were packing. Back in her bedroom, Hattie surveyed several half-packed cases. The task was worse than she'd realised. Nick had even left a lot of his packing, she noted with irritation. She pulled open his dresser drawers, some still as full as ever and grabbed handfuls to drop into another case, until she remembered that the whole lot could go as it was, clothes and all... except...? Pulling open his underwear drawer, she reached to the back, hoping for a crinkle of paper. But, no, the letter was no longer there.

Checking the other drawers, she drew a blank until she came to the bottom one. There she found a small carrier bag with *Savill and Daughter* printed on it. Oh yes, she thought, the intriguing antique shop from their weekend away. Didn't he say that he'd bought her a birthday present? Curiosity overcame her as she reached inside and pulled out something lumpy that was wrapped in cream tissue paper – two pretty ceramic door knobs. She gasped in delight.

'How sweet,' she sighed wistfully. 'Perfect for my sewing cupboard!' She rewrapped them and stored them carefully in the cupboard in question.

Returning to their room, she pulled out the three red-rose cards from her bedside cabinet. The muffin had already gone the way of all such goodies. In fact, there was not a single muffin left in the house; just a few stale crumbs in the carrier bag and that last message:

King's Cross station, Friday 18th May, 12 noon, by the main depar-ture board. I'll be there, will you? Let me know.
Yours ever Leo x

She read the messages, pausing over each one. Choices, she thought, it's all about choices.

This is it, Hattie realised, waking unusually early the following morning. The house felt eerily empty, without the crash and thump of Josh going about his morning ablutions. Together with the last-minute packing was the crucial administration of Jezebel's calming tablet, which was always a trauma. With this complete, Jezebel was resting in the relative peace of the utility room in her 'Kitty Kage' while Randalls Removals, who arrived well before eight, jostled and heaved around the house. Next a call to Samways.

'Yes, just pop the key in the post, Mrs Chesney, there's no tearing hurry. The signora has asked us to find suitable tenants.' Hmm, thought Hattie on hearing their house was to be Gina's buy-to-let investment – another misunderstanding on the part of Samways.

At nine-fifteen, the last box was being loaded. Five minutes later, as the lorry rumbled its way out of the close, Hattie sensed a rush of adrenalin; time to go at last. Her own bag of belongings was modest compared with those on their way to Lydford Cross. As she loaded it into the boot, drops of rain began to fall. The morning had started dull but now dark clouds were gathering and a cool breeze whipped around her ankles. This was not an auspicious start to the journey. Next came Jezebel's carrier, the creature mewing pathetically and thrusting her nose at the grill. Was the effect of the calming tablet wearing off already? Hattie pulled the front door shut and locked it. End of an era, she thought, gazing back at the home that had seen many changes over the years. The rain was heavier now, slapping against her cheeks and trickling down her neck – the very worst weather for driving to an unfamiliar place, a place that would mark a new chapter in her life.

Epilogue

Right, last check, she thought, rummaging in her shoulder bag yet again: phone, fruit gums, purse, map, make-up bag, extra strong mints, tampons, tissues, cash card, important documents, chocolate; yes, all present and correct. She pushed an Abba compilation into the CD player and pressed play. Imagining what lay ahead, she needed the right accompaniment to lift her spirits and quell her nerves. There was, however, that familiar knotted feeling low in her stomach. Singing along to her favourite tracks would take care of that, she was sure. But as the music started, as she steered off the drive, Jezebel decided that this was *her* chance to join in.

Half an hour or so into the journey, the knotted feeling in her stomach had changed. There was now an odd fluttering sensation, like the swooping and cavorting of a hundred butterflies. Was that her phone, she wondered as she executed yet another roundabout, hoping to follow the correct signs and not find herself zooming into an industrial park or ending up in another gridlocked town centre. Jezebel's yowlings were uncannily like her current ringtone. At last she arrived, listening to the drumming of the rain on the roof and psyching herself up for their meeting. Am I crazy? Am I gullible? Am I a total idiot? She had asked herself these questions endlessly over the past twenty-four hours, but there were still no answers.

'Only one way to find out,' she told Jezebel as she opened the

car door, grabbed the carrier and stepped out into the rain that
fell like stair-rods from a leaden sky. Next she hauled her bag
from the boot, fed the parking meter generously and checked her
watch, pleased to see that she'd made good time, despite the atrocious conditions. If it all worked as she hoped, she'd deal with
the car later. Almost there now, she told herself nervously and
he surely won't let me down. He looked sincere, he sounded
sincere, but can I trust him with my future? The butterflies inside,
however, had now enlisted their friends and relations.

'Black coffee, no sugar,' she heard herself say as she rooted
around for some change. By now her knees were knocking. Was
she a woman or a wimp? If Fliss were here, she'd know exactly
what her answer would be. In the circumstances though, there
was no reason to be wimpish. Bryony Chesney might have been
vague about mealtimes but not about her TV.

'Which *Vicar of Dibley* episode did you say? The Easter Bunny?
Tuesday night? Oh no, I didn't see any TV on Tuesday night
after eight o'clock,' she explained. 'That was the night when we
had a power failure. You must have heard about it on the news.
The whole of our village was down, and a few others as well.
David and I had an early night.'

And as for the bank statements... She'd half expected to see
an entry for The Golden Pheasant, but not for a Premier Inn at
Tring, nor a petrol station at Aston Clinton. Aston Clinton? Who
had mentioned Aston Clinton in the past week or so? Then she
remembered... it was Madge. Hattie's heart had sunk to her
insoles. Quickly logging onto the Premier Inn website she found
the number, then dialled it, her body shaking and a horrible sense
of nausea threatening in her stomach.

'Can I help you?'

'Yes, has Mr Chesney checked out yet?' she asked brightly.
'This is the Golden Pheasant Hotel in Lydford Cross. We need
to confirm a conference booking with him.'

'Ah yes, room 115,' the woman replied. 'I'll try the number
now, shall I, or do you want to leave a message?' The wimp's

reply would have been to leave a message, but having got this far, she had to go on, with the horrible sense of the inevitable building up like a mountainous wave about to crash on a shore.

'Could you try the room first?' she croaked nervously, wondering what she was going to say if anyone answered. But they did.

'Hello?' came a tentative voice; not a voice on the TV this time or the voice of her mother-in-law in another room, but Rebecca Vaudin herself, closeted in a hotel room, just sixteen miles away.

'Oh, sorry. Wrong number,' Hattie had said and then rung off. It was all she needed to know. That accounted for the huge payments for petrol. He must have been driving up to see Rebecca several times a week, possibly driving past the end of the road to his love nest not more than half an hour away. Why hadn't she realised? But the scales had fallen from her eyes and the odd phone calls, the lavish gifts, the syrupy love talk, the exhaustion all pointed to the truth. Nick was having an affair.

Hattie moved away from the counter and found a seat to one side of the concourse. A peep through the Kitty Kage window confirmed that the calming tablet had at last woven its special magic. She sipped her coffee and kept her attention on the arrivals board. It was now seven minutes to midday – *seven minutes*! She gulped a few more mouthfuls, deciding it was time to make a move. Just then, a woman in sunglasses, pulling a suitcase, moved into Hattie's line of vision; a woman bearing an uncanny resemblance to Fliss. However, the more she stared, the more she was convinced it *was* Fliss. What was she doing here? Perhaps she had decided to treat herself to a weekend away after all? It was odd that she hadn't mentioned it on that last evening. Maybe she'd had second thoughts about pottering in the garden and sorting out her wardrobe. Much as Hattie would have loved to have known, she could hardly ask her. After all, *she* was supposed to be in Lydford Cross by now. How did she think she was going to explain her presence at King's Cross Station? Still, she needed to be at Leo's appointed meeting

461

place and the minutes were ticking by. Then, like in those ghastly recurring nightmares, her legs seemed to turn to lead, refusing to go a step further. Instead, she watched Fliss pacing to and fro, checking her watch and glancing, every so often, in the direction of the underground entrance. She was most certainly waiting for someone and growing more agitated by the second.

Keeping out of Fliss's line of vision was becoming increasingly urgent, but the concourse had become irritatingly clear. Filled with panic, Hattie turned and gazed across at the line of shops, praying for a miracle. Then, mercifully, a stream of passengers from the recent arrival straggled across the concourse, giving Hattie the opportunity to dash undetected to a better vantage point. She grabbed her belongings and headed to the opposite side. Perfect! Now she had Fliss *and* the tube entrance in her sight *and* there was a handy pillar behind which she could skulk. But where was Leo? Her watch and the digital display on the arrivals board both now showed eleven fifty-six, and Hattie experienced a sense of déjà vu, although it was a different station to last time. If only Fliss's friend would hurry up and remove her from the scene. The thought of Fliss witnessing Leo scooping her up in his arms was growing increasingly likely. On the other hand, Fliss might applaud her daring and confess her opinion that Nick was a lying toad who didn't deserve her.

See how I care, she thought, wondering how the scene at The Laurels might be unfolding, but preferring not to know. She'd switched off her mobile promptly on arrival. However, if Leo was any later, she'd have to use it. She didn't want a re-run of last time. Fishing out her phone, she turned it on and set it to vibrate. Keep calm! Keep calm! she told herself. His note said he'd definitely be there. But then there was that rhetorical question: *Will you?* Did he *really* need a reply? If she'd decided not to be there, he'd know why.

Two chunky backpackers herding a troupe of giggling guides were the next travellers to emerge from the underground steps.

'No time for that... Anna... Katy!' bellowed one of the leaders as two of the group started off in the direction of Smith's. 'The train leaves any minute.'

'Not *that* way!' yelled the other one, who was desperately rounding up the stragglers like a geriatric sheepdog. Once they had bustled and shrieked past, causing mayhem at the ticket barrier, Hattie had a clear view once more. Her heart was pounding furiously as she scanned the area. Of course Leo might be coming from another direction, although the walkway through from the new concourse was only a few feet from the underground entrance.

She peeped out from behind her pillar and checked to see if Fliss had moved. She hadn't, but even at a distance, Hattie could see a difference in her friend's demeanour. Instead of an irritated frown, there was the suspicion of a smile. At last her companion has turned up, thought Hattie, with relief. There was indeed a surge of travellers from the stairs, none of whom she recognised, except one – Leo!

'Yes! Yes! Yes!' she breathed excitedly, gathering up her belongings and the snoozing Jezebel. I don't care what Fliss thinks, she decided. Nothing was allowed to stand in the way of destiny *this* time. Striding out from her hiding place, she willed Leo to look in her direction, but his attention seemed to be wandering. More travellers streamed from all directions, hiding him from her vision for a few seconds. Because she wasn't standing under the board, perhaps he thought she'd given up on him.

She glanced towards Fliss, whose expression had suddenly changed. Her mouth gaped open and an expression of alarm, or possibly disbelief, had replaced the smile. Had her friend collapsed or skidded on a piece of litter? No, there was no sign of an undignified sprawl, but – far worse – there was now someone who she'd never have expected to see at King's Cross Station that day – Gina Pirez. More to the point, Gina Pirez was standing only inches from Leo, her arms wide open, her body shaking with passion and a torrent of indistinct words pouring from her mouth. What was the woman doing here and why was Leo even listening to her? Hattie stood rooted to the spot. He hadn't sent her a red-rose card as well, had he? Surely not! Now Leo was talking, but at a distance it was difficult to tell if he was telling her to clear off or what…?

'Leo, *please* look this way,' Hattie pleaded under her breath, wondering if she should just carry on walking anyway. Once she was in front of him, he would have to break the news to Gina that his future was with Hattie Chesney. She set off again, more determined than ever. Pausing briefly, a glance to her right revealed that Fliss was still gaping. There was no friend with suitcase in hand beside her, so what was going on? Leo and Gina were the only ones Fliss could be watching, but why? Hattie was just a few yards away now and still the two of them were jabbering away, waving their arms in the air and generally being true to their Italian genes. How dare the bitch hijack my moment of glory, thought Hattie mutinously. Then the unimaginable happened. Leo leaned forward, cradled Gina's cheeks in his hands and kissed her, not briefly as in 'off you go now', but long and lingering, as if he was enjoying every single second.

How could he? How could they? Hattie watched in horror. She simply could not believe her eyes. Eventually, Leo came up for air, a huge smile plastered across his face. Gina looked fairly radiant as well.

'Leo!' Hattie shrieked, but her cry was lost in an announcement about a delayed departure from platform 8. The only person who heard it was Fliss who turned and gaped incredulously then strode across, her bottom lip trembling.

'What are *you* doing here?' she demanded.

'I was about to ask you that myself!'

'I was… er… waiting for someone…'

'I… I… I was meeting Leo,' Hattie burbled, tears pricking her eyes.

'So was I!' gasped Fliss. They both turned and glared in his direction, but all they saw was Leo and Gina, strolling off together arm in arm.

'Oh Leo,' sobbed Hattie, tears streaming down her cheeks.

'The bastard!' breathed Fliss vehemently.

'It was going to be my new life – in Montelugia,' sobbed Hattie.

'It was going to be my dirty weekend in Florence,' snapped Fliss.

'A dirty weekend in Florence!' gasped Hattie incredulously. 'I didn't know you knew him well enough for anything like that!'

Fliss smiled wanly. 'Oh, it's amazing how well you can get to know a man when you spend time together in the sauna at a health and fitness club – especially when the rest of the members have gone home!'

'You didn't… You couldn't… I don't believe it… I mean… Well, after that revelation about Nick I *can* believe it, actually,' she exclaimed. Then she recalled the night she saw her near the Zed Shed. Of course, the man must have been Leo. No wonder he rushed off in a hurry and no wonder Fliss was agitated.

Fliss shook her head regretfully. 'Such a fit man too,' she sighed. 'He never bothered with a towel either and I've never been a prude when it comes to nudity.'

'Oh God!' moaned Hattie. 'I *believed* him! I thought he *truly* loved me!'

'Come on now, Hat,' urged Fliss, putting a sisterly arm around her. 'He's made a fool of both of us.'

'It's my fault. I didn't reply to his message,' mumbled Hattie sadly. 'If I'd replied he would have known I was coming, but I didn't know about Nick's affair till last night. That was the last straw!'

'Nick's *what?*'

'His affair… with Rebecca Vaudin,' murmured Hattie flatly.

'His affair with Miss Bossy-Boots Vaudin!' gasped Fliss. 'How did you uncover that bit of deception?'

'Oh, with a lot of pluck and determination mainly,' admitted Hattie bravely.

Just then, she felt a vibration in her pocket and reached for her mobile. It was a text from Nick.

Hat, where r u?

'Silly fool,' breathed Hattie ruefully.

'Come on, Hat,' urged Fliss, peering over her shoulder at the glowing screen. 'It's not too late. Nick might be a bit of a plonker at times, but he's basically an honest and upright chap who's veered off the rails. I hate to admit it, but this calls for coffee and chocolate muffins all round.'

'Couldn't agree with you more,' agreed Hattie, brushing aside her tears.

On my way, she texted back.

Chocolate Muffin Recipe

Ingredients

250g plain flour
2 level tsp baking powder
2 level tbsp cocoa powder
175g caster sugar
150g dark chocolate, either chips
or small chunks chopped from a bar

250ml milk
90ml vegetable oil
1 large egg
1 tsp vanilla extract

Method

Pre-heat oven to 190°C/Gas mark 5 and place 12 muffin cases in a muffin tray.

Sift the flour, baking powder and cocoa powder into a large bowl. Stir in the chocolate chips or chunks, except for a handful or two.

In a large jug, beat together the milk, vegetable oil, egg and vanilla extract.

Pour the wet mix into the bowl of dry ingredients and stir until just combined. Don't overmix – a slightly lumpy batter is what you need.

Spoon the mixture into the muffin cases and sprinkle with the remaining chocolate. Bake for about 20 minutes, until nicely risen. Cool on a wire rack, then enjoy!

NB: To make even better muffins, why not use Fair Trade sugar, cocoa powder and chocolate!